STAR

With Love & Light   2004.

To My Dearest Friend
Norma.

The STARBROW Series by Tim Ray includes:

Book 1: **STARBROW**

Book 2: **STARWARRIOR**

About the author

Danish-American author Tim Ray is a passionate student of spiritual principles and mental technologies. So far, his *Starbrow* Series consists of Book 1 *Starbrow* and the sequel Book 2 *Starwarrior*.

To spread information about spiritual principles and the mental technologies described in their books, Tim Ray, together with fellow author Barbara Berger, founded *BeamTeam Books*, a publishing company and center in Copenhagen, Denmark. For more information about the center activities and books, see www.beamteam.com

About the editor

American author Barbara Berger has worked closely with Tim Ray for many years and is the editor of The *Starbrow* Series. Barbara Berger has written more than 10 self-empowerment books, including *Mental Technology, Gateway to Grace* and her bestseller *Fast Food for the Soul*. In her books she describes the same spiritual principles and mental technologies that are presented in Tim Ray's novels.

STARBROW
A Spiritual Adventure

TIM RAY
Edited by Barbara Berger

Book 1 in The Starbrow Series

FINDHORN
Press

STARBROW

British Library Cataloguing-in-Publication Data. A catalogue record for this book (2003 revised edition) is available from the British Library.

Original Danish edition first published in 1998 by BeamTeam Books, Copenhagen, Denmark. First English-language, limited edition published in 1999 by BeamTeam Books, Copenhagen, Denmark.

Translated into English by Tim Ray and Barbara Berger.

Cover, book design and maps by BeamTeam Books
Portrait of author by Søren Solkær

Published in 2003 by:
Findhorn Press Ltd
305a The Park, Findhorn
Forres IV36 3TE
Scotland
Tel 01309 690582
Fax 01309 690036
E-mail: info@findhornpress.com
Web site: www.findhornpress.com

Printed in Denmark by Nørhaven Paperback A/S, Viborg

ISBN 1-84409-003-5

A Special Thanks

I would like to thank my editor, Barbara Berger, who accompanied me on the whole adventure, from the first vision to the final manifestation. Without your unshakeable faith, support, guidance, input and expert editing (plus all the fun we had!) Starbrow would not be the book it is today. I couldn't have done it without you Barbara Beamer!

To
Moncler, Telperion
& E.K.
for reminding me of
who I really am

&

To
The BeamTeam:
Barbara Beamer
Mark Ray
Robin Ray
my faithful companions on
The Great Adventure

The Force Is With You!

CONTENTS

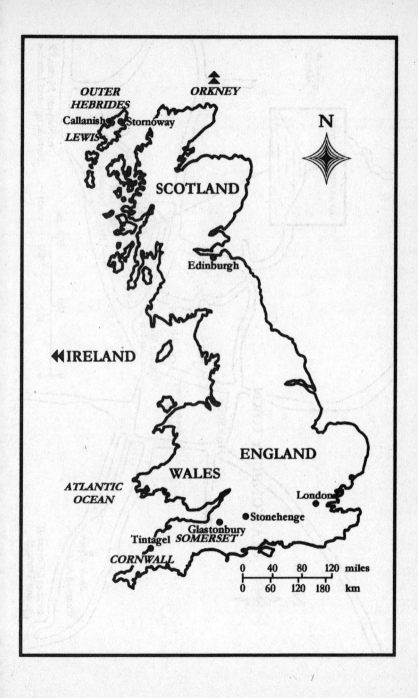

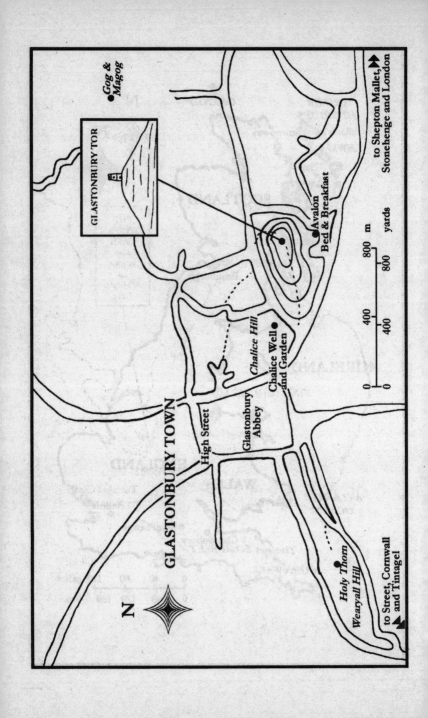

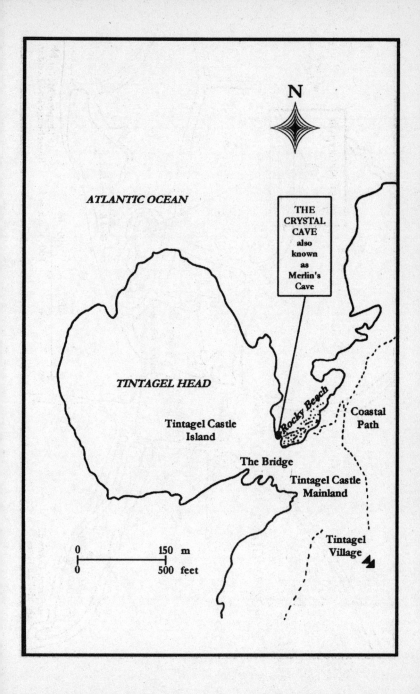

PART ONE

THE CALL

SUNDAY MARCH 22, 23:35:09 GMT EARTH TIME
TO
TUESDAY MARCH 31, 23:04:18 GMT EARTH TIME

1

An Angel on Ocean Drive

"Greetings Starbrow!" said a soft voice inside my head.

I turned around. It was late Sunday night and I was on my way home from my friend Jacob's place when I heard the voice. I'd just reached the bus stop on Ocean Drive.

"Greetings Starbrow…" said the voice again.

"Star who?" I thought to myself and turned toward where I thought the voice was coming from. No one was there. But to my surprise I saw a soft golden light radiating from a cluster of trees and bushes a few yards from the bus stop. It was freezing cold out and Ocean Drive was completely deserted at that time of night.

I gasped.

The voice or the light, I wasn't sure which, was coming from a young woman. I stepped back in amazement.

"Greetings Starbrow," she said once more, "It's good to see you again. I have come to remind you of your mission."

I looked around again to see who she was talking to.

"I'm talking to you, Starbrow," she said as if in answer to my question.

"Starbrow?" I whispered, looking around again.

"Yes, that's your cosmic name… but you seem to have forgotten it…"

That was when I realized that besides being as slim and beautiful as an elven princess, she was barefooted and wearing nothing but a thin, white knee-length dress!

My God I thought. It must be below zero out here on the streets of Copenhagen. It was late March and still winter in Denmark.

She took a step forward and began walking towards me.

For some reason, I panicked and stumbled backwards, right into some garbage cans. The garbage cans and I toppled over and made a loud clanging noise as we hit the sidewalk.

3

"You have nothing to fear, Starbrow," she said kindly, approaching me slowly. "I'm your friend." That was when I realized she talked without moving her lips. But I heard her voice clearly inside my head anyway.

"I'm your friend, Starbrow." She continued to move towards me. "You need not be afraid, I will not harm you. I came to tell you about your mission."

I couldn't think straight; my heart was pounding so.

My mission…? What was she talking about? And me sprawled on the ground like some idiot surrounded by trashcans.

"Yes your mission," she said again inside my head. Now she was almost next to me, positively glowing in the dark. Even in my state of panic and confusion I noticed the way her whole body seemed to radiate this amazing, warm golden light, as if she had a tiny sun inside her.

I struggled to get up.

She kept on talking, "1500 hundred years ago you were given a mission Starbrow—to create peace and harmony on Earth, and now you are being called again to fulfill your ancient oath and complete your mission."

My mission?

"Yes Starbrow, your mission."

It was too crazy. I got up.

"Starbrow…" she said again.

I felt like I couldn't think. Nothing like this had ever happened to me before. Was she a hallucination? Was I losing my mind?

Even before I turned and started running down Ocean Drive, I heard her voice saying gently inside my head. "Wait Starbrow, this is important."

But I ran anyway. In fact I bolted like a terrified horse down the street, without looking back. Past houses, streets, shops, all the way to the next bus stop, which was several blocks away. Then and only then, did I stop running and look back. The glowing woman was nowhere in sight.

I leaned up against the bus stop signpost and tried to catch my breath, all the while scanning the street like a maniac. My legs felt like jelly and my heart was pounding like I'd just run a 100-meter race. Never in all my life had I experienced anything like this. A woman who glowed in the dark and talked without opening her mouth! It just wasn't possible... Maybe things like this happened in the movies or in adventure stories... but adventure stories were just something I believed in when I was a kid... and I wasn't a kid anymore... No I was almost 25 now, a regular

4

guy with a regular job…

I took another deep breath and tried to get a grip.

It was probably just my imagination. Ever since I was a kid, people always said my imagination had a tendency to go into overdrive.

I looked down at my hands. They were trembling like a leaf.

But she seemed so real.

I shook my head and said to no one in particular, "If this is your imagination, bro, it's the most life-like thing you've ever concocted."

I took another look at the other bus stop in the distance. There was no one in sight. All I saw was the night bus approaching fast. I watched it eagerly and wondered if it would stop at the bus stop I'd just run from, but it didn't. I let out a sigh of relief. At least there wouldn't be any passengers on the bus who glowed in the dark!

I took another deep breath trying to get a grip, get a grip...

The night bus stopped right in front of me and the doors opened. I peeked cautiously into the bus. It was empty.

"Are you coming or what, mate?" grumbled the driver.

"Err... yeah," I said and looked up at him. He seemed completely calm and relaxed. Obviously he hadn't seen any glow-in-the-dark supermodels at the last bus stop!

"Well then get a move on it!" he said impatiently. "I haven't got all night."

I climbed on slowly, fumbling around in my pockets until I found my bus card. The driver looked at me as if I'd had one too many of those strong Danish beers. Then he closed the doors and drove on. I went and took a seat at the back of the bus and looked out the window. There was nothing to be seen except the garbage cans I'd knocked over scattered across the sidewalk. I guess my imagination really had played a trick on me... or had it? I stared at the garbage cans as they disappeared from sight. Then I turned and gazed upwards at the dark starry heaven above me. A large golden star caught my attention. It seemed to flicker in the night, far more beautiful than any of the others.

2

The City of Light

A couple of nights after my strange experience on Ocean Drive, I had dinner at my grandfather Elmar's house. Dinner at Elmar's was always a very special event because my grandfather was a real Indiana Jones type of guy. He'd spent most of his life traveling around the world as an explorer, archeologist, mountain climber and art collector. Which was obvious the moment you walked in his door. His house was filled with all kinds of exotic things, even though his style was minimalist. The house was very sparsely furnished, to say the least.

Elmar was now "72 years young", as he used to say, but in fact, it was hard to tell just how old he was. I thought he looked more like a man in his fifties. He was tall and thin—and his tanned body was strong and muscular after his many travels on six continents. According to Elmar, he stayed in such good shape thanks to a special exercise system called "The Five Tibetan Rites", an ancient mix of yoga, breathing exercises and meditation. He told me he learned the system from a Buddhist monk he met on one of his first trips to Tibet. As far back as I could remember, Elmar had always meditated twice a day, morning and evening. "It's my way of recharging my spiritual batteries," he often said as he slipped off into the room where he meditated. The room was totally bare except for the Japanese tatami mats on the floor and a beautiful, old Buddhist mandala on the wall, another keepsake from one of his travels in the Himalayas.

The last couple of years, Elmar had been traveling a little less. Most of the time he lived abroad; but a couple of months each year, he came back to his house in Denmark to do a little "horse trading" as he called it, with the many art dealers and collectors he knew in Scandinavia.

As far as I knew, Elmar had always lived alone. He left my grandmother shortly after my mother Siri was born and since then he

6

never married again.

But Elmar and I had always had a very special relationship. Ever since I was a little kid, I'd loved Elmar and those special occasions when he'd come back from one of his travels, laden with exotic gifts and fantastic tales.

Now we were sitting in his spacious dining room, munching on the sushi and deep-fried tempura he'd prepared for us. He told me he learned Japanese cooking during one of his stays at a Zen monastery in Japan.

"So tell me," he said, "are you working on any exciting projects over there at Fashion Flash?" He looked at me out of the corner of his eye as he poured some more rice wine into my glass. I was a copywriter at a big Danish clothes company.

"Not really," I answered, fiddling with the tempura on the plate before me. I was still in a state of confusion after my strange experience on Ocean Drive. Even though I tried to convince myself it was all a trick of my imagination, I just couldn't get the woman out of my mind.

Who was she? What was it all about?

I wondered what Elmar would say if I told him about her.

"You know, just the usual," I said, trying to sound normal. "Right now I'm working on some press releases for men's underwear. It's pretty boring, but at least my boss promised me that she's going to let me write some real ads pretty soon."

"Well, that's good isn't it?" Elmar asked. "Isn't that what you've been waiting for? An opportunity to use your writing talent?"

"Yeah...well... er... I guess so," I said and stared at my plate.

I knew Elmar was watching me. "I must say, you don't sound very enthusiastic, my boy. Is something wrong?"

"No... well... er...I mean, I just don't know. I've been feeling this strange restlessness all week and... well just kind of weird and spaced out... it's hard to explain."

"I know all about that kind of restlessness," said Elmar with a smile. "What you need is some adventure in your life!"

I took a sip of my rice wine and enjoyed its warmth. "Yeah, maybe..." I mumbled.

"What about that trip around the world you talked about a couple of years ago?" said Elmar. "What ever happened to that idea?"

It was true, a couple of years before, I had planned to take a year off and travel around the world. But after I graduated from the Copenhagen School of Advertising, the sudden job offer from Fashion Flash made me change my mind.

"I can't very well take off now," I said, "and to be truthful, I wouldn't know where to go anyway."

"Well, you could go and see something new. Try something new. You know, just take off—into the unknown," he said. I knew he was trying to be helpful.

"But there isn't anything new to see anymore. Everything's been done and discovered."

Elmar shook his head and laughed.

"What's so funny about that?" I asked.

"Well, that's exactly what I thought when I was your age." He got up and went out to the kitchen to make some more tempura. I leaned back in my chair and drank a little more rice wine as I surveyed the room. There were many rare and exotic things in Elmar's dining room. And every one of his treasures had an exciting story behind it. He'd told me most of them over the years. There was the big handmade drum a shaman from Greenland had given him after he'd trekked across the inland glacier. Next to the drum were the big nets or "dream catchers" which the Hopi Indians over in America had given him after he was initiated in one of their sweat lodge ceremonies. On the opposite wall were several colorful mandalas some monks in Tibet gave him after one of his many stays at a monastery there.

One of the things in the dining room I liked best was the beautiful picture of Glastonbury Tor, which hung over on the wall by the window. Elmar had taken the picture on one of his many visits to the famous Tor, which was located in southwest England. "Tor" was the ancient Celtic word for hill and Glastonbury Tor was in fact a hill. The hill was about 600 feet high and had this very strange pyramid shape. On top of the hill were the remains of an old medieval tower. It all looked very special. I sighed when I looked at the picture of the Tor. Glastonbury was one of the places I planned on visiting on my famous trip around the world.

Next to the picture of Glastonbury Tor was a tiny picture of the Buddha, sitting in the lotus position. His whole body was surrounded by a golden light... I got up and walked over to the little picture to look at it close up. There it was again! That light! Buddha's body was surrounded by the same golden light as the woman I'd seen at the bus stop on Ocean Drive!

Elmar came back with more tempura. I took the picture of the Buddha down and walked over to him.

8

"What is this light that's surrounding the Buddha?" I asked.

"Well my boy, some people call it an aura. The Christians call it a halo," said Elmar. "But whatever you call it, they all agree that one of the most noticeable features of an Enlightened Master is that the life force radiates more strongly from and around him – or her."

"The life force?"

I stared at the picture of the Buddha, fascinated.

"I have more pictures of Enlightened Masters if you're interested. In several of them, you can clearly see their aura or Light Body as some call it, surrounding them," said Elmar. "But eat your dinner first."

I sat down and looked with embarrassment at the sumptuous meal Elmar had prepared for me, but I just wasn't hungry. I had to tell him about meeting the woman who glowed in the dark or I'd explode!

I looked up from my plate. Elmar was watching me with his clear blue eyes. "Alright," he said. "Come on my boy! Tell me what's going on! You've been acting funny all evening. Now out with it!"

"You're probably going to think I'm crazy..." I said slowly.

"It's going to take some doing for me to think you're crazy," said Elmar with a smile. "You ought to know that. I've seen things in my life that even the most open-minded find hard to explain. Come on now my boy! Just relax and tell me what's bothering you!"

"Well Elmar," I said softly, "I think I've met an... er... Enlightened Master—or Mistress."

"Really!?" said Elmar and chuckled in surprise. "Well that sounds interesting. Now where did you have the pleasure of meeting this Enlightened Master, or was it Mistress?"

"By a bus stop on Ocean Drive," I answered slowly, shifting uneasily in my chair. "But I only saw her for a minute or two because I panicked and ran away. But she was glowing with exactly the same kind of light as the Buddha here... and Elmar, when she spoke, she talked without moving her lips." Now that I'd finally started talking, the story just poured out of me like a waterfall. "But I could hear her voice Elmar, really, right inside my head. And she called me Starbrow and said that it was good to see me again..."

I stopped as abruptly as I'd started. It all sounded so crazy. The room was silent. Elmar didn't say a word.

"It sounds completely insane, doesn't it?" I asked after what seemed like an eternity.

"So you finally met her…"

"What?!!" I said and jumped up from my chair in surprise. "Don't tell me you know her…"

Elmar didn't answer me. Instead he leaned back in his chair and eyed me closely.

"What's going on here?" I cried and started pacing the room, acutely aware of my heart pounding furiously in my chest.

Did Elmar know the woman who glowed in the dark?

What was going on?

"Do you know her..?"

"Sit down my boy and relax."

But I just couldn't. I kept pacing the room.

Elmar kept sitting in his chair, all quiet like, waiting I guess for me to calm down. When I finally did, he said very slowly, "There's a lot more between heaven and earth than meets the eye, my boy. I thought you knew that." He had that warm, mischievous look in his eyes that I loved so much.

He got up.

"Look, since you seem to have lost your appetite, I'm going to make us both a cup of good strong espresso. And then I'm going to tell you about a meeting that completely changed my life."

"But the woman… what about the woman?"

"You just take it easy my boy… everything in its own good time…"

Elmar got up and went out into the kitchen. A few minutes later he came out with two small cups of espresso. I found it difficult to contain myself—so curious was I to find out what Elmar knew about the woman. But one look at his face was enough to make me understand he wouldn't tell me anything before he was good and ready.

We moved into the living room and settled into his comfortable sofa. Elmar took the picture of the Buddha I had been examining before and studied it carefully, as if he was trying to remind himself of something he'd seen a very long time ago.

"Let's see…" he began. "It was right after the Second World War. I must have been just about your age. I'd just finished my term as a trainee in my father's firm in Charlottenlund. Back then I was working myself up the ranks so to speak. Actually, I'd reached the point where my father had decided to let me run one of his smaller businesses in town. So things were going very well for me," said Elmar.

"At the time, I was also a member of a semi-secret society. There were six of us in the group and we met every Thursday evening at my tiny flat

10

to talk and read adventure stories... sort of like your... eh... you know, your regular meetings with Jacob and Janus when you... "

"Play Dungeons & Dragons."

"... yes, like your Dungeons & Dragons. Sometimes one of us might read something we'd written for the other members. Other times, we'd read tales about King Arthur and the Knights of the Round Table. In fact we devoured all the adventure stories we possibly could get our hands on. We loved everything that expanded our horizons, from ancient mythology to the latest *scientifiction* as they called it back then. One day, John, who was a bit older than most of us, told us that he'd met this really interesting man that he'd like to introduce to the group. So John brought the fellow around to our meeting the following week. He introduced the man as Stanley Donne, writer and explorer."

Elmar paused for a moment as if trying to remember every detail. "Stanley Donne was probably one of the most extraordinary human beings I've ever met. It's hard to say exactly what it was about him, but he had an energy, a charisma, and a sense of inner peace and wisdom, which only few human beings possess. At first glance, he appeared to be a man in his late 30s. He was tall and thin with wavy, jet black hair and strong, distinctive features. He was immaculately dressed. But there was something decidedly beautiful about him too, an almost oriental feeling about his appearance. And his deep, penetrating eyes were almost hypnotic in their power. From the moment he walked into the room, his presence overwhelmed us. And he held us spellbound for the rest of the evening with his fantastic stories."

"Stories about what?" I asked.

"Well, in the space of just a few short hours, he'd created the most intoxicating cocktail we'd ever experienced... an intricate web of old legends, fantastic tales, biblical history, metaphysics and Einstein's theory of relativity. It was the most amazing experience. We'd never heard or experienced anything quite like it before," smiled Elmar.

"What did he say?" I asked. Now I was getting curious.

"Well, you remember, I've told you that in all spiritual traditions, there's the teaching of the soul's evolution towards higher consciousness."

I nodded. I did remember that Elmar had said something about it several times, but I never really understood what he was talking about.

"Well, Stanley Donne explained to us that all the world's religions, occult brotherhoods, all the mystics and shamans, whether they were

Rosicrucians, Knights of the Round Table, Egyptian high priests, Tibetan Buddhist monks, South American naguals, Indian yogis, Celtic druids or disciples of Jesus, in reality all had the same purpose. And this was to expand and raise the consciousness of the individual to such a degree that in the end, he or she attains cosmic consciousness and ascends into the higher dimensions."

"Ascends into the higher dimensions?"

"Yes. That was what Jesus did. And what Buddha and Moses and many other of the world's greatest spiritual masters did."

"Can human beings really do that?"

"Yes, I believe they can."

"But how?"

"According to Stanley Donne, it's a long and demanding process that takes many lifetimes. The requirements are the most rigorous form of self-mastery, detachment from everything in the material world, and a pure heart. In other words, the will to love all beings equally while working for the welfare of the world order."

"Do you believe in that?"

"Yes I do. And because the requirements are so strict, only very few succeed. Those who do succeed ascend into the higher dimensions and are initiated into the ranks of the Ascended Masters. They become members of an order called the Great White Brotherhood."

"Sounds pretty far out... this Brotherhood," I said, mystified. "Is it only for men?"

"We asked the same question," said Elmar. "Stanley Donne said that the Brotherhood is open to both sexes, and that everyone, regardless of race, color, religion or nationality, can ascend. The word white simply stands for that clear translucent white light which surrounds an Ascended Master."

I looked again at the picture of the Buddha with his shining aura. "Where are the higher dimensions?" I asked.

"According to Stanley Donne, the higher dimensions are right here. The reason why most of us can't see them is because they have a higher vibrational frequency than the physical world which we experience with our five physical senses."

"That really sounds like Dungeons & Dragons stuff!" I grinned and took another sip of espresso. At least Elmar's story was helping me calm down a little—though it hadn't made me forgot that he seemed to know the woman on Ocean Drive. I tried not to think about her for the moment and focused instead on explaining Dungeons & Dragons to him, "In Dungeons & Dragons, a player starts out on the first level. Then, as he gets more experienced, he rises from level to level, gaining more and more power until he or she reaches the 36th level and becomes an Immortal."

"Really?" said Elmar. He never really understood the game that had occupied so much of my time as a boy, even though he always politely said he thought it sounded interesting. "Stanley Donne compared the soul's evolutionary path to climbing up a very high mountain. Usually, it takes hundreds of lifetimes to reach the top of the mountain and attain cosmic consciousness. Some people call this enlightened state the Buddha consciousness or Christ consciousness.

"But Donne also said something else that was very interesting. He said that at this point in the Earth's evolution a shift was taking place. At this time, a soul can go straight from the bottom of the mountain to the top in one lifetime. But such an achievement he said, requires an incredible openness, self-mastery and genuine love of your fellowman."

"Is this what made you start traveling all over the world?"

"Donne told us that the Great White Brotherhood has a sort of headquarters or main base here on Earth. A fantastic city called Shamballa, the City of Light. According to Donne, Shamballa is located in the higher dimensions above the Gobi Sea."

"The Gobi Sea? Don't you mean the Gobi Desert?"

"No. Donne told us that what is now the Gobi Desert once used to be a huge sea in the middle of Mongolia."

"Oh, I see," I said and tried to imagine the Gobi Desert being a huge body of water instead of a desert, right smack in the middle of Mongolia.

"At the end of the evening, Donne told us that there was a Royal Air Force pilot named Gareth Randall who was putting together an expedition to find the City of Light."

"If this here city... Shamballa... is not in the physical world, but in the higher dimensions, how could you find it?"

"The plan was that the expedition was going to go to the Himalayas first, where Gareth Randall intended to find the legendary master Djwal Khul, also known as the Tibetan. Apparently, Djwal Khul knew how to get to Shamballa."

"Sounds more like D&D every minute," I said and laughed, really warming to the subject.

Elmar didn't answer. He got up and walked over to the window and

13

looked out. It was as if he was seeing things far away, from the distant past. Then he continued slowly, "Stanley Donne encouraged us to join the expedition. He said that our love of old legends, adventure and new discoveries was a sure sign that we were ready to begin the ascension process."

"So you said yes?" I asked.

"Well, not at first. We all thought the whole thing sounded a bit farfetched. Just as he was about to leave, I asked him how he knew so much about the old legends. In particular, how he knew so much about King Arthur and the Knights of the Round Table. His answer shocked me. He looked me straight in the eye and said without blinking: 'Because I was King Arthur in one of my past lives.' Everyone else in the group just laughed," said Elmar softly, "but I wasn't so sure. I walked Donne to the door, so we had a moment alone. Then I asked him, 'If you were King Arthur in a past life, then who are you really?' Once again he focused that deep, penetrating gaze of his on me and said 'They call me El Morya.' With that he turned and walked out the door."

"El Morya," I repeated enthralled. What a story! I thought of the picture of Glastonbury Tor hanging in Elmar's dining room. Why that was the very hill which had been at the very heart of so many of the stories and legends about King Arthur and his friend the Wizard Merlin.

"That was the last time I ever saw Stanley Donne," Elmar continued. "A couple of days later, I tried to find him at the address my friend John had given me, but no one named Stanley Donne had ever lived there. In fact, he was nowhere to be found. He disappeared without a trace, just as suddenly as he had appeared."

"Perhaps he just ascended into the higher dimensions?" I said and laughed.

Elmar didn't answer. He had this faraway look on his face.

"So what happened next?" I asked eagerly.

"At first I told myself that Stanley Donne was probably just one of those people who get carried away when it came to the old legends and religious enthusiasm. That was until a couple of days later when I saw a small notice in the London Times about an expedition to the Himalayas that was being organized by a Royal Air Force pilot named Gareth Randall."

Elmar opened the window. "That really got me," he said and looked up at the night sky. The first faint stars could be seen. "I couldn't get the thought of Shamballa and Stanley Donne out of my mind. I dreamt about it at night. I couldn't concentrate on my work. In my heart of hearts, all I wanted to do was drop everything and take the first ship to London and join the expedition."

"Well, why didn't you?" I asked.

"It wasn't quite that simple," said Elmar and turned towards me. "You see I also had a good job, a promising career, status, and quite a bit of responsibility. I was afraid of what people would say if I just suddenly took off into the blue and joined this wild expedition that was searching for a city in the higher dimensions which no one had ever seen..."

"Yeah... okay... I see what you mean," I said. I was so used to Elmar's incredibly independent lifestyle that it hadn't dawned on me that once there might have been a time when he too had been young and unsure of what to do with his life.

"Then one night I woke up in the middle of the night and just lay there wide awake," Elmar continued. "A million thoughts raced through my mind. I felt I stood at a crossroads. If I took the one road, I saw myself working my way up in the family firm and in time becoming the patriarch after my father. I saw myself getting married and having children. We would move into my father's house and carry on the family tradition. It would be a good life, a rich life, far better than most people would ever get the chance to live. Then I saw the other road and I knew if I took it, I would be leaving all security behind me to face an uncertain journey into unknown lands in pursuit of something that I couldn't quite describe, but which I knew was higher and better. Then I knew, with all my heart and soul, that I'd never be satisfied if I chose the safe road. I knew, with this sudden wonderful clarity, that I was destined for adventure. I wanted to experience cosmic consciousness and ascend into the higher dimensions. It was just that simple."

Elmar's words touched me deeply and put the gnawing restlessness I'd been feeling lately into a totally new perspective. I looked out of the window too. The stars were fully visible now. They shone like little cities of light in a desert of jet black sand.

"The next day," Elmar continued, "I packed a few belongings and took off for London. I didn't say goodbye to anyone. I wrote a short note to my parents, but that was all. I knew they wouldn't understand no matter what I said and that trying to explain would just make matters worse. When I got to London, I went straight to see Gareth Randall and told him my story." Elmar smiled at the memory. "I don't think he was looking for any more candidates for his expedition. He already had 16

15

men. And I knew absolutely nothing about mountain climbing or surviving in the Himalayas. But I think he was so touched by my story about meeting El Morya, my longing for Shamballa, my youthful determination and the way I'd just left everything behind to join his expedition that in the end, he took me on."

"For months we traveled in the Himalayas in search of Djwal Khul. We saw the most incredible sights and met the most fascinating people. We stayed with Buddhist monks and masters and learned much from their ancient wisdom. We endured great hardships and had many wonderful adventures."

"But did you find Shamballa?"

"Not in the way I had expected."

"What do you mean?"

For a moment, Elmar was silent, then he said, "Well my boy, that's another long story... so I think we'd better save it for some other time."

I said no more. As soon as Elmar stopped talking, I started feeling restless again. I wanted him to tell me about the woman I'd met on Ocean Drive. But I knew I had to be patient so I went and sat down in the sofa again.

The minutes ticked slowly by. Then softly, ever so softly, Elmar began to sing. He had a good voice, a strong melodious voice, which always touched me deeply and soothed me in the strangest way. He was singing an old English ballad called The Song of the Starseeds. I'd heard him sing it many times before, so I knew it well. It was one of the songs Elmar always sang when he felt the call of adventure. The song's gentle, soothing melody and soft solemn words had always moved me. But this evening they moved me more than ever before.

Who will solve the riddle?
Who will tell the tale?
Who will ride on after us?
After we set sail?

Who will know the magic sign?
Who will find the gate?
Who will wake up to their fate,
Before it is too late?

I knew you when the mystery was still untold
I knew you in your younger days, before you grew old
I knew you in your sunny days, the days of wine and mirth
I knew you in the summertime, way before your birth

Who will solve the riddle?
Who will tell the tale?
Who will ride on after us?
After we set sail?

Who will know the magic sign?
Who will find the gate?
Who will wake up to their fate,
Before it is too late?

I knew you when the world was young and meadows still were fair
I knew you when you hid the secret in your golden hair
I knew you in your younger days, the days of silver song
I knew you, yes I knew you, before the days grew long

Who will solve the riddle?
Who will tell the tale?
Who will ride on after us?
After we set sail?

Who will know the magic sign?
Who will find the gate?
Who will wake up to their fate,
Before it is too late?

Elmar's voice faded softly into the night. I got up and joined him by the open window. I thought about my own life and my strange meeting on Ocean Drive.

Elmar turned towards me. "Stanley Donne told us that once in every person's lifetime, the soul is called to ascend into the higher dimensions, but that only very few heed that call."

There was a long silence.

Then Elmar said, with a strange look in his eye, "Now I hope you understand my boy... you *have* been called."

17

3

Far, Far Away

"Everybody needs a little fast love baby, everybody needs a little fast love..."

George Michael's mega dance hit could be heard all the way down Eastbridge Boulevard. It was Friday night and I stood across the street from one of Copenhagen's trendiest clubs, the Park Café, and watched the eager crowd of people trying to squeeze into this popular nightspot. Once every three minutes or so, one of the huge bouncers would let about five or six more people in. I figured that at this rate, with about 50 people already in the line waiting to get in, it would be about half an hour before it was my turn. Not that it really mattered. Standing in the long line was, after all, a part of the whole ritual. And I'd already spotted at least four or five of my friends in the waiting crowd.

I was looking for Jacob and Janus. Actually, I didn't feel like going out at all, but when Janus called and suggested that the three of us meet outside the Park Café, I said okay. I thought it would be good for me to see some people. Maybe a little dancing and a couple of beers would help me shake off the awful restlessness I was feeling.

But standing there, looking for my friends, a new wave of uneasiness swept over me. What was I doing here? It all seemed so meaningless. Ever since my mysterious meeting with the woman who glowed in the dark on Sunday, I'd been feeling this strange longing. In a way, Elmar's story about the City of Light only made it worse. And when I asked him to tell me about the woman I'd met on Ocean Drive, he would only say, "It is not for me to say, my boy. Everything will be revealed to you in its own good time."

And with that he clammed up completely.

I couldn't get a word more out of him. It was so frustrating.

My thoughts were interrupted by a voice calling... "Master!"

I turned and looked over at the Park Café and saw Jacob come dashing over to me. I could tell by the way he moved that he was drunk.

"Master!" Jacob panted as he caught up with me and bowed in the most uncoordinated manner. "Whither goeth thou, oh Master?"

I smiled to myself. Good ol' Jacob. He very rarely drank, but when he did, he was always very thorough about it. "Actually dude," I said, "I was thinking about going home!"

"Already? But you just got here!" he said and leaned against me. From the smell of his breath, I figured he must have already had six or seven beers.

"Whoa..." I turned my head away.

"We have important matters to discuss, Master. The whole mission could end in disaster, if Telperion and I don't get past that fire-breathing dragon very soon! But he's a crafty weasel, isn't he."

Jacob still took our weekly game of Dungeons & Dragons very seriously. The three of us had been playing the same game since we were boys—and now though we were young men, we somehow couldn't bring ourselves to end our lifelong game. Nerdy Jacob with his thick glasses played Moncler, the mighty Wizard with the magic staff. Good-looking Janus played the powerful Elven King Telperion with the two-handed sword—and I was the Dungeon Master and creator of our fantasy world.

I tried to ease myself away from Jacob's evil-smelling breath. "And where is the good Elven King?"

"He's right over there," said Jacob and pointed towards the other side of the street where Janus was standing near the end of the line, talking to two girls. "And once again I see our mighty Elven King is making good use of the charm person spell I taught him."

I looked at Janus. He was a real looker, tall, slim and well built. His blond shoulder-length hair matched his handsome features perfectly. And yes he had, as Jacob so delicately put it, unprecedented success when it came to babes.

Which wasn't the case with Jacob. Jacob was so shy that he usually just clammed up when he had to talk to anyone he didn't know, especially if it was a beautiful creature of the opposite sex. Of course with his chunky build and nerdy glasses, he didn't exactly look like a movie star.

"Telperion needs our help, Master," said Jacob and began to drag me across the street. I tried in vain to extract my arm from his iron grip. But it was no use. Even when plastered, Jacob was amazingly strong!

"Telperion!" shouted Jacob in Janus' direction. "He's over here!"

Jacob managed to haul me over to the other side of the street where Janus was chatting up these two babes.

"Greetings, Telperion," I said to Janus and gave him our secret D&D handshake.

"Tel-a-what?" said one of the babes, a foxy little number in stilettos and leather trousers. "I thought your name was Janus?"

"His name is Telperion, King of the High Elves," said Jacob loudly and saluted Janus clumsily.

The girl raised her eyebrows and gave her friend one of those "what a nerd" looks. "See you guys inside," she said and kissed Janus on the cheek. She took her girlfriend's hand and walked over to a couple of other babes at the front of the line.

"Telperion!" said Jacob and put his arms around both our shoulders, pulling us together into a tight little circle. Our heads met. "We've simply got to stay together, the three of us!" he bellowed. Janus and I smiled at each other. Usually Jacob was awful shy about showing his feelings, but once he'd had a few drinks it all sort of came gushing out.

"I just love you guys," he was really going on. "I really do. I always have and I always will. Let's never stop playing D&D. Ever!" Then his voice just kind of trailed off and I thought it sounded kind of sad. Maybe he was feeling restless too. I looked over at Janus but he was staring at the ground, deep in his own thoughts.

"Yeah dudes..." murmured Janus. "Let's never stop playing."

Unfortunately, the sad feeling didn't go away. All I wanted to do was get away from it all and go somewhere else, somewhere far, far away... far from the Park Café and the loud music and the drunks and the trendy-looking babes...

But at that very moment, Janus raised his head again. "Look guys!" he said, "We've got to pull ourselves together."

Then he pointed us in the direction of the café entrance and the noisy crowd. The babe he'd talked to earlier waved at him. "Together we can do it!" he said and steered us towards the girls at the front of the line. Jacob didn't say anything, but he had this sad, droopy look on his face...

I looked at the people around me. Most of the noisy crowd had been drinking too much—and everyone seemed totally wired in the weirdest way. After a bit of pushing and shoving, the bouncers finally let us in. Inside people were mashed together like sardines, all trying to make conversation over the blare of the music that was blasting out of the enormous speakers. It was deafening and the air was thick with blue smoke. I scanned the café to see if there was anyone there I knew. I spotted Charlotte, a designer I'd met a few months ago at a Fashion Flash show, standing over by the bar talking to some friends. I squeezed myself through the crowd and walked over to her.

"Hi Charlotte," I half shouted, trying to make myself heard above the bedlam. Charlotte turned towards me and looked at me with those beautiful dark brown eyes of hers.

"Hi," she said and gave me a big smile. She was definitely a babe. Her long black hair highlighted her beautiful pale face and her full red lips. And she was wearing this low-cut silver dress, which did little to hide her sexy body.

"Are you here all by yourself?" she asked. When we'd met at the show we'd flirted a bit, but nothing ever came of it. Maybe now was the time, I thought. She definitely seemed happy to see me.

"No," I'm here with two of my friends," I said and pointed to Jacob and Janus. Janus was standing in a dark corner talking up a storm with his latest target. Jacob was standing right next to them, leaning against a pillar. His head drooping down to his chest as if he was about to fall asleep.

Charlotte took my arm and kissed me on the cheek. "We really didn't get a chance to get to know each other last time we met," she said, snuggling up to me, "now did we?"

"No..." I said, still looking over at Jacob. What's wrong with him?

"Hello! Hello... anybody home?" Charlotte said in my ear. "You had too much to drink?"

"No.... actually I haven't had a drop... not yet anyway," I said, turning towards her again.

"Well, you want to order something?" she asked.

"Eh... well, yeah sure, let's order," I said, trying to forget Jacob and focus on Charlotte.

"You work for Fashion Flash, don't you?" she asked, trying to get the conversation going again.

"Yeah," I said.

"You're one of their Art Directors, aren't you?"

"No... I'm a copywriter."

"A copywriter, oh yeah, that's right. Now I remember."

"And you're a designer, aren't you?" I asked, trying to make a go of it. "You work for Individual, don't you?"

Charlotte nodded. "I'm head of womenswear. Did you see the big John

Galliano show at the Circus Building the other day?"

"Eh... no, I missed it."

"It was totally cool. I mean awesome!"

"I bet..." I said, hoping she wouldn't notice my lack of enthusiasm. Fortunately for me, she didn't. She just blabbered on and on. About her latest collection, about how much John Galliano's latest collection inspired her, about the newest trend which seemed to be wearing non-prescription glasses and about how totally excellent men looked in suits and sneakers... but no matter how hard I tried, I just couldn't seem to focus on what she was saying.

As her mouth continued to wag, I found myself thinking once again about the woman who glowed in the dark I saw last Sunday. And suddenly, it was as if she was standing right in front of me—with her glowing aura, her long golden hair, her enchantingly beautiful face and eyes that sparkled like stars. The thought of her triggered this strange sensation in my chest. I felt like I couldn't breathe. And being stuck inside the Park Café with all these people didn't help.

"Are you okay or what?" said Charlotte, looking hard at me. "Why do I get the feeling that you're not even here?"

I looked at Charlotte and the thought of having to spend another minute with her also suddenly seemed as unbearable as being cooped up in this bedlam. I looked down at my arm resting on the bar and slowly removed her hand. Then I turned and started walking away.

"Hey! Where are you going?" Charlotte's piercing voice reached me through the din that was engulfing me.

"Far away," I said without looking back. "Far, far away."

I pushed my way through the noisy crowd and made for the door. Once outside, I rushed over to the other side of the street and took a deep breath. My heart pounded strangely in my chest. Without looking back I started walking down Eastbridge Boulevard as fast as I could. I had to get away from that place... I had to get away. Far, far away.

22

4

Ticha

The very same night I woke up with a start. My whole bedroom was bathed in a warm golden glow. In fright I thought FIRE! I jumped out of bed with my blanket still wrapped around me. My legs were half asleep so I stumbled and crashed into my night table. The table and I and all my books and alarm clock and everything went crashing to the floor. Lucky for me, my thick down comforter softened the blow as I hit the floor. As I hurried to get up and run out of my bedroom, I realized that my apartment wasn't on fire and that the mysterious glowing woman from the bus stop was standing over by my window. She was surrounded by a golden light and that was what was making my bedroom glow like that!

The realization didn't do much to lessen my panic, on the contrary! I was so stunned, that in my panic I managed to disentangle myself from my down comforter and run out into the hallway where I immediately ran head on into my partly opened bathroom door. I felt an explosion of pain in my nose and fell backwards and landed on the floor. I looked up and saw a bloody spot on the bathroom door where my nose had collided with it. For a moment I felt faint and thought I was going to pass out.

But I didn't. Instead, a new thought entered my mind: What are you doing, you idiot? Why are you running away like this? Isn't this just what you've been hoping for? That you'd get a chance to meet her again?

My head seemed to clear. I sat up gingerly and looked back towards my bedroom, which was still bathed in that beautiful, warm golden light. Then I remembered what Stanley Donne had said to Elmar on that fateful day in Elmar's life so many years ago: *"... once in every person's lifetime, the soul is called to ascend into the higher dimensions, but only very few heed that call..."*

Elmar had said that I had been called.

I stood up. The golden light radiated out towards me. I walked slowly

23

back to my bedroom, stopping in front of the door. I held my nose because it was bleeding a little and it hurt like hell.

"I've lowered my frequency now," I heard her gentle voice say inside me. "Sorry about the sudden wake-up call."

The light in my bedroom seemed less bright. I stepped slowly into the room. She was still glowing and still standing by the window, but now the light coming from her was no more than a faint glow as if she was surrounded by soft moonlight.

"Greetings, Starbrow," she said, without moving her lips. "So we meet again."

"Why do you call me Starbrow?" I said slowly.

"Because Starbrow is your cosmic name—as I told you at our first meeting—before you panicked and ran away."

"Sorry about that, but I'm not used to meeting women who glow in the dark on Ocean Drive. Especially not when they talk without moving their lips and call me strange names like Starbrow."

She smiled and continued. "Starbrow is the name you were known by before you began your mission on Earth."

"What mission?"

"You will learn all about it soon enough..." She answered mysteriously.

I waited for her to continue, but she didn't. Instead she just smiled her dazzling smile at me. I guess it kind of calmed me down because I was surprised when I heard myself change the subject and ask instead, "Well, who are you then?"

"My name is Ticha," she replied. "In your language, I mean in the language of human beings on planet Earth, I am probably what you would call your guardian angel."

"My guardian angel?"

"Yes, that's right. Every human being has a guide or companion to help the soul on its pathway."

I looked at her in amazement. Judging by her appearance, she looked as if she was in her early twenties, but somehow I knew she had to be older than that. A lot older. But I couldn't really focus on that because she was so beautiful... so incredibly beautiful. She truly looked like an angel or a magic fairy princess from some fairy tale.

That was when I realized that I was beginning to feel more normal again, after the shock of waking up and finding her in my room. And I realized there was something familiar about her, as if I really had known her before. But where—and when?

As if in answer to my thoughts, she said, "Yes Starbrow, we've known each other for a long, long time, you and I. But lately you've forgotten me."

"How do you do that? I mean read my thoughts like that?" I exclaimed.

"Oh it's completely natural," she said. "Everyone can do it. But most people on planet Earth have forgotten how."

Neither of us said anything as she allowed me to try to digest this new piece of information. Then I brightened up and asked her, "Ticha, if you really are my guardian angel, where are your wings?"

"I may not have wings," she replied with a mischievous glint in her eye, "but I can fly!"

"You're kidding!" I cried in disbelief. "Show me!"

"Your wish is my command, Master Starbrow." She still had that mischievous glint in her eye as she walked over to the open floor space in the middle of my bedroom. I followed her every move, totally hypnotized by her presence. The soft, golden light that surrounded her was incredibly pleasant to look at.

I didn't have time to speculate anymore because all of a sudden the light around her grew brighter and brighter. I felt the air tingle as if some gentle electrical charge had been added to my room. Then, to my amazement, Ticha slowly began to rise up off the floor!

I stared at her with my mouth wide open. She just seemed to float up from the floor, as easily and effortlessly as if an invisible cord was hauling her up. Pretty soon she was hovering about three feet above my bedroom floor! I couldn't believe my eyes. She was flying! She was really flying! I walked over and gently touched her on her knee. When I did, my hand tingled as if she was emitting some kind of electrical current.

"Well," said Ticha, she was almost touching my ceiling. "Do you believe me now?"

"Yeah..." I said, trying to clear my throat and sound natural when in fact I was totally awe-struck.

Ticha slowly started to descend.

"Hey!" I cried. "Wait a minute..."

"What?" she said softly.

"Er... I mean... " Suddenly I felt all confused. "I just want to know how… how you do it?"

"One day, I'll teach you," she said as she landed on the floor. "But first, I'd better take a look at your nose."

25

"My nose?" I said and touched my nose. Ouch! I looked at my hand, there was blood on it. I'd been so mesmerized by my unexpected guest that I had totally forgotten about my frontal collision with my bathroom door. Now that she reminded me, the pain had returned.

Ticha positioned herself directly in front of me. She looked intently at my nose.

"Perfect health is the one and only reality," she said in a strong, clear voice. "Your nose is now perfect, whole and complete. Your nose is strong and healthy. And so it is." As she said these words I felt a surge of warmth and comfort flow through my entire body. It was as if every cell in my body heard her command and suddenly started vibrating. The pain in my nose disappeared. I touched it tentatively. It didn't hurt anymore. I looked at my hand. The blood was gone. My nose felt perfectly normal... the pain was completely gone!

"Wow! How'd you do that?" I asked, looking up at Ticha in frightened awe. I must have looked pretty terrified because she started to laugh.

"I used the Power of the Word," she replied. "All guardian angels can use the Power of Thought and the Word to heal. So can you humans, but you've just forgotten how."

I touched my nose again. It was completely OK. "But Ticha, this is a miracle!" I cried.

"Not really," she laughed. "In fact, it's only a miracle for those who don't understand the Nature of Reality."

I looked at her in amazement. I didn't understand what she was talking about. All I knew was that my nose was completely OK and that all traces of blood, both on my hand and on the floor, were completely gone. It was as if my collision with my bathroom door had never happened. This is totally groovy, I thought. I decided to ask her if she was an Enlightened Master like Elmar said.

"Ticha if you're my guardian angel, does that mean you're an Enlightened Master?"

"No, I'm afraid not," she laughed, "I've never incarnated on the Earth Plane."

"Well, how come you're glowing all over like that?" I asked.

"What you see is my aura. Everything that's alive has an aura, a vibrational field of light around it. The higher one's vibrational frequency, the brighter the aura."

"Like Buddha you mean?" I asked.

"Exactly."

26

"Well... how come you can speak without moving your lips?"

"Where I come from," she said and laughed again, "we think it's funny that human beings have to use their mouths to communicate. We communicate directly from mind to mind."

"Where do you come from?"

"Here, there and everywhere," she said with that mischievous glint in her eyes again.

I must have looked baffled because she continued.

"From a scientific viewpoint, you'd probably call where I come from, the higher dimensions."

The higher dimensions? Wasn't that where Elmar said Shamballa, the City of Light, was located?

"And the higher dimensions are..." I began.

"Here, there and everywhere. But because they're vibrating on a higher frequency than the physical world which you humans experience with your five senses, most people are not yet aware of the higher dimensions."

"But if what you say is true, how come I can see you now?" I asked, now I was really confused.

"Partly because I've lowered my frequency—and partly because I've helped you raise yours so we could meet halfway, so to speak."

Silence filled the room again as I tried to fathom what she was telling me. A million thoughts raced through my head as I stared at her in awe. Ticha was my guardian angel. Ticha was the woman who glowed in the dark. Ticha was here, now, right in my bedroom. Ticha had just levitated right before my eyes. Ticha had just miraculously healed my bloody nose. Ticha... It all seemed way too far out to be real. But it was real. She was standing right here, right in my own bedroom, smiling at me in the most kind and gentle way.

Finally, I asked her the one question that I'd really been wanting to ask her all along "Why Ticha... why?"

"Because it's time for you to continue your mission," Ticha replied matter-of-factly.

"What do you mean?"

She laughed and said, "Before I can answer your question I have to give you an invitation." She laughed again and spread her arms out. It seemed to me her laughter sounded like stars tinkling.

"What do you mean, an invitation?" I asked.

"An invitation from those whom I work with."

27

"... those whom you work with?" Suddenly I was afraid again. "You mean to tell me there are others like you?" I glanced at the window nervously, half expecting to see a host of shining angels floating above the rooftops of Copenhagen.

"You just take it easy, Starbrow!" she laughed. "I'm the only one who has lowered my frequency at the moment. To meet the others, you're going to have to raise your frequency."

I sighed with relief. At that moment, I felt that coping with one guardian angel was more than enough! I tried to get a grip. My mind was swamped with questions.

Ticha gave me a sympathetic look. "Yes," she said gently. "I understand. You've had more than enough for one night. Now you need some time to think about all this."

Ticha walked over to the window.

"I'll be back tomorrow evening at the same time with your invitation to the higher dimensions." With that, her body started to fade.

"An invitation to the higher dimensions?" I cried out after her, but she was fading fast. "What do you mean? Wait! You can't just leave me like this. Where are you going?"

But it was no use. She was almost gone. It was as if her body was made up of a million tiny shooting stars, which for a brief moment shone and twinkled—and then disappeared.

"Here, there and everywhere." I heard her laughter as she disappeared in a blinding flash of light.

5

About the Dimensions

"Whoa... Just give me a second to wake up," said Elmar sleepily on the other end of the phone. It was three o'clock in the morning. The minute my guardian angel "left", I called him to tell him what had happened.

"I've met her again, Elmar!"

"Hmm... I'm not surprised," Elmar was beginning to wake up. "Where did you meet her this time?"

"Right here in my very own bedroom," I replied. I was so excited I could hardly get the words out.

"Good, good," he said, chuckling at the other end of the line now. "Did you at least speak to her this time?"

"Yes, yes, we really talked a lot. And Elmar, guess what—she flew! Right here in my bedroom!"

"Flew?"

"Yeah, well I guess you'd call it—levitated—you know, she rose right off the floor, right here in the middle of my bedroom! And after that, she healed the bloody nose I got when I crashed into my bathroom door by the Power of the Word..." I kept stumbling over the words I was so excited.

"Sounds like quite a night! Why don't you just slow down and start again from the beginning. And take a couple of deep breaths first, will you."

I followed his advice and then started over again. This time Elmar listened with real delight as I recounted every detail I could remember of my meeting with Ticha.

"So what you do think I should do?" I said after I'd finished my tale.

"What do you mean?"

"I mean about my guardian angel and all the rest of it?"

"Well since she said she was going to give you some kind of invitation

29

or message, the best thing you can do is to prepare yourself."

"Prepare myself? How?"

"Make sure you're very clear," he said, "both in your mind and in your body." I realized he wasn't kidding anymore. "Do some breathing exercises and meditate a little. And try to relax."

"Okay," I said, trying to remember some of the things Elmar had said about meditation. Ever since I was a kid, he'd been trying to teach me to meditate.

Elmar continued, "And try not to have so many preconceived ideas about things my boy. Just relax and let it unfold, you know, like an adventure."

"Okay I'll try," I said. "But I just don't know how I'm ever going to get through the next 24 hours!"

MAAAAAAAA-OOOOOOOOOOMMMMM, MAAAAAAAAAAAAA-OOOOOOOOOOMMMM, MAAAAAAAAAA-OOOOOOMMMMMM I repeated the mantra over and over again, first out loud and then in my head. It was 1:30am in the morning and I was getting ready for my next meeting with my guardian angel. I was sitting, eyes closed, on my bed in the lotus position, trying to meditate on the MA-OM mantra just like it said in one of the meditation books Elmar had given me, which I'd never opened before now. Everywhere in my bedroom, the candles and sticks of incense I'd bought at the local health food shop were burning. All in a valiant attempt to follow Elmar's advice to prepare myself for Ticha by being "clear" in mind and body. Which I had to admit, was proving to be easier said than done. Even though I had meditated now on the MAAAA-OOOOM mantra for several hours, I just couldn't seem to stop the thoughts from whirling around in my head. I kept on asking myself what Ticha meant when she said that Starbrow was my name before I started my mission on Earth? What mission? What was she talking about? And what did she mean by an invitation from the higher dimensions...

I kept trying to stop thinking about her and concentrate on the mantra: MAAAA... I said to myself on the in breath... and OOOOMMM on the out breath. MAAAAAA... it had to be two o'clock soon... OOOOMMMM. MAAAAA... who would have ever thought this lotus position could be so uncomfortable... OOOOOMMMMM. MAAAAA... what if I told Jacob and Janus about Ticha...? OOOMMMMM. No, better wait and see what happens... MAAAAA... those sticks of incense really smell awful... OOOOOM. MAAAAA... I wonder if Ticha will come alone or will she bring some of the beings she works with?... OOOOOOMMMM. MAAAAA... ow ow ow now I've got a cramp in my right leg!

I opened my eyes to untangle my legs and discovered to my surprise that Ticha was standing right in the middle of my bedroom, bathed in that pool of beautiful golden light she always seemed surrounded by. If my legs hadn't been locked in that uncomfortable position, I would probably have jumped up in surprise.

"Good evening, Starbrow," she said and laughed, "this is quite a welcome!"

"Good evening, Ticha," I said, wrenching my legs out of that uncomfortable position and then stumbling onto the floor. I hopped around, trying to get the blood circulating in my legs again.

"Have you decided to become a yogi?" she said teasingly as she carefully surveyed all the candles, incense and colorful mandalas I had placed everywhere.

"It's important to be clear in body and mind," I said, hopping around like an idiot, hoping my legs would soon start to feel normal again.

"True enough," she said, waving away the smoke from all the incense I had burning everywhere. "But then why all these foul-smelling things?"

"If you don't like them, I'll put them out," I said and hurried to put out the incense.

"So, you've been meditating?" she asked.

"Yes," I said, trying to remember everything Elmar had said. "I just thought it was a good idea to be clear in body and mind for our next meeting."

"I can see that it's been good for you to have a day to adjust to the new frequencies," she smiled and seemed pleased with me.

"Ticha," I said seriously, "I have a question..."

"Well... go ahead," she said.

"Last night I had this dream... I dreamt I was in this forest... and I was with you..."

"That wasn't an ordinary dream."

"You know about it?"

"Yes."

31

"Well, what do you mean?"

"You were in your etheric body, in the 4th dimension. And I was working to help you open your heart."

"You were what...? I don't understand."

"Sit down," she said, "and let me explain a little about the dimensions."

I sat down in the only chair in my bedroom—and Ticha sat on the edge of my bed.

"Everything that exists in the physical universe is made up of energy," Ticha said. "Your body, the chair you're sitting on, the air you breathe, this bed—everything is energy, or light. And this energy moves at a certain speed or frequency. Everything that exists in the physical universe, everything that you can see, hear, smell, taste and touch, happens to vibrate at a relatively low frequency. And all this—this physical world—is what we call the 3rd dimension. Do you follow me so far?"

I nodded.

"But there is more to it than that. Besides your physical body, which you see right here in the 3rd dimension, you also have another body, called your etheric body. Your etheric body is made up of your thoughts and emotions—in other words, what you would call your human personality. Your etheric body is slightly larger than your physical body and surrounds and interpenetrates your physical body."

"Really?" I said in surprise.

"Yes, really."

"But if I have another body, Ticha, why can't I see it?"

"Because your etheric body is vibrating at a higher frequency than your physical body. In other words, your etheric body is in the 4th dimension."

"In the 4th dimension? Where's that?"

"Right here."

"But I don't get it," I said.

"Okay," she said, "let me try another explanation. Just imagine, for example, the spokes on the wheel of a bicycle. Now, what happens when the wheel is not turning or turning very slowly? Can you see the spokes?"

"Yes," I said.

"Okay. Now what happens when the wheel of the bike turns very fast? Can you still see the spokes?"

"No, then you can't see them."

"That's right. When the wheel—and the spokes—turn very quickly,

32

they seem to disappear because you can no longer see them. But are they really gone?"

I shook my head. "No."

"Now, it's exactly the same with your etheric body and everything else which is in a higher dimension like the 4th dimension. In the higher dimensions, the energy is moving at such a high speed that you cannot detect it with your physical eyes or your other physical senses. But even though you can't see this energy or hear it, it's still there. And that's what I meant when I talked about your etheric body. It's right here at this very moment, but you can't see it."

I nodded. I was beginning to understand.

"Your physical and your etheric body are connected to each other by an etheric connection called the Silver Cord. When you're asleep at night your etheric body leaves your physical body and flies around in the ether, so to speak. But no matter where it goes, it's always connected to your physical body by this Silver Cord."

"Is that what happens when you dream?"

"Well, yes and no," Ticha replied. "There are different kinds of dreams. Sometimes when you dream, it's just your subconscious mind which is reviewing and processing all the thoughts and emotions you've experienced during the day. That's why this type of dream often doesn't seem to make any sense. Rather these dreams are just a confused, chaotic jumble of images and events. Then there are other kinds of dreams. For example, you might dream at a time when your consciousness is clearer that you've been to some place very wonderful and then you'll wake up feeling very clear and refreshed. Or maybe you'll wake up with the answer to a question that's been puzzling you for a long time. In cases like these, what you've really experienced is that your etheric body has been moving around in the 4th dimension."

"And that was what happened to me when I had that dream the other night?"

"Yes. You, or I should say, your etheric body was with me in the higher dimensions."

We didn't say anything for a few moments. I knew Ticha was trying to give me some time to digest all this. I remembered that Elmar had once told me something similar. He said that when we died, our souls moved on to the higher dimensions.

"Is that what happens when you die?" I asked.

"In principle, yes. The difference between the dream state and death is

33

that when a human being dies, the Silver Cord snaps and the soul is no longer able to return to the physical body. The soul is then in the 4th dimension where it rests, waits, learns and has other experiences before it is time for it to inhabit a new physical body."

"Are you one of those souls who's waiting to find a new physical body?" I asked, looking at Ticha with new eyes.

"No, Starbrow," she said and laughed again, understanding my question. "Not all beings in the higher dimensions incarnate on Earth as human beings. Some have other missions, like we guardian angels. One of our tasks is to help and guide souls on their way... souls just like you who have incarnated on the Earth plane."

"On our way to what?"

"Life is a constant journey of unfoldment and evolution," Ticha said gently. "You see Starbrow, all souls are continually evolving... on their way to greater understanding, greater love, higher consciousness."

"Is there something after the 4th dimension?"

"Yes," she said. "The 5th dimension. In the 5th dimension, energy vibrates at such a rapid speed that a soul must have a very high level of consciousness and a very high frequency to ascend to that dimension. But one day you'll go there too," she said with that mischievous glint in her eyes again. Then she stood up, walked over to the TV, and picked up the remote control. "As a matter of fact, I hope you'll be going there very soon!" With that, she turned on the TV and zapped to channel 75. The screen was black and empty.

"Don't tell me we're going to watch TV?" I said in surprise.

"It is time for you to hear from my superior."

"Your superior? Who's that?"

"Patience, my friend," she said, motioning for me to look at the empty screen, "you're going to meet him right now."

I leaned back in my chair and waited. At least a full minute must have gone by and nothing happened. The screen was still blank. I was just about to ask Ticha what was going on when suddenly I became aware of a faint, high-pitched ringing sound in my ears. It was hard to tell where the sound was coming from. It felt, or sounded, like it was coming from inside my head, but I wasn't sure. All I knew was that the sound was becoming more and more clear. And I was aware that the tones were very high pitched... as if they were beyond the borderline of what I normally could hear. Wherever they were coming from, the high-pitched tones were having a very strange effect on me. Somehow they were making my whole body feel lighter and lighter, until I could barely feel myself sitting in the chair.

Then the blank screen began to flicker.

After a moment or two, patterns slowly began to appear on the screen, forming a shimmering, colorful, mesmerizing panorama of triangles, pyramids, six-pointed stars and other geometric shapes I wasn't familiar with. Then it was as if the high-pitched tones I was hearing and the colors and geometric shapes I was seeing somehow began to merge, forming one harmonious, pulsating rhythm. That was when I thought I could see a face starting to emerge from the strange formation of geometric shapes. Yes, it was a face, a radiant face, a man's face! He had black hair, distinct, almost princely features and deep, penetrating eyes. He was wearing silver clothes that I thought looked like a uniform of some sort because he had this badge or military-style ensign above his breast pocket. A clear white light radiated from him, surrounding his whole body in much the same way as Ticha's body was surrounded. Only his light was much stronger than hers. Much more powerful. The man smiled and looked straight at me.

"Greetings, Brother in the Light!" he said in a clear voice. When he spoke, his lips didn't move, but I heard his voice inside my head, just as I did with Ticha.

"I AM Ashtar," he said, "Commander of Mission Earth Ascension, speaking on behalf of the Intergalactic Council. The purpose of this special transmission is to ask for your help in this critical phase of humanity's evolution. Planet Earth and all its inhabitants are standing on the brink. On the brink of a new era. And you can help determine how this transformation will take place. And whether this transformation will bring chaos or harmony to Planet Earth."

35

6

A Special Dispensation

The high-pitched tones and harmonious colors continued to pulsate in the background of my TV screen, but now the picture of Ashtar was crystal clear. As I sat there, in my chair, I had this strong feeling that somehow the powerful white light he radiated was touching me, right where I sat in my little apartment.

"This transmission has been made possible thanks to a special dispensation from the Intergalactic Council," said Ashtar. "This dispensation may have a profound effect on your role in Planet Earth's ascension into the higher dimensions. But before I go into detail as to your role in these critical events, let me first take a moment to briefly sketch the present situation as I see it.

"For many hundreds of thousands of years, Planet Earth has been a designated test zone for soul evolution. Time and space, birth and rebirth, karma, creativity and free will have all been a part of the curriculum on Planet Earth as souls moved on their way to higher consciousness and the higher dimensions.

"Throughout the ages, only a very few souls have fully mastered the curriculum of the 3rd and 4th dimensions—and ascended into the higher dimensions. This is because the requirements for ascension are very strict and very demanding. And up until now, most of humanity was not even aware that it was possible to ascend to higher dimensions. That is until very recently.

"Now all this is changing rapidly. Here at the dawn of the new Millennium, Planet Earth and all of its inhabitants are faced with the greatest transformation the Planet has ever experienced. A transformation so profound that it makes the events, which took place in Atlantis some 12,000 years ago seem like child's play.

"Planet Earth's time as a test zone is now up and the Planet has begun its ascension into the 5th dimension. And this ascension is affecting every human being on Earth. Suddenly, human beings all over the Planet are waking up and beginning to realize that it is possible for them to ascend into the 5th dimension, together with Planet Earth..."

Ascension? I thought. Ascension into the 5th dimension? Wasn't that exactly what Stanley Donne had said to Elmar many years ago? That now it was possible for humanity to reach the top of the mountain, to attain cosmic consciousness, in just one lifetime?

"... Because of this," Ashtar continued, "the old structures on Planet Earth are falling apart, are collapsing. That is why, on the surface at least, it may look as if everything is deteriorating, that things are falling apart. That everything's going from bad to worse. But the many transformations that the Planet and its inhabitants are undergoing at the moment—both on the inner and the outer planes—are in fact the birthing of Planet Earth into the 5th dimension. And this birthing, and the labor pains that go with it, can be heard in the far corners of the universe.

"Many of the souls who are already in the 5th dimension or in even higher dimensions—soul groups such as the Ascended Masters of the Great White Brotherhood—are now actively working to help each individual human being on Planet Earth and the Planet herself make this transition ... this ascension into the 5th dimension as smoothly and easily as possible. But my friend, this is a very great task. Indeed, a very, very great task.

"This is also why the Intergalactic Council has appointed me to lead a fleet of starships to Planet Earth to assist the Ascended Masters in their efforts to facilitate the ascension process. My fleet, the Intergalactic Fleet, consists of tens of thousands of starships, manned by millions of ascended beings from near and far in the galaxies. They come from Arcturus, from the Pleiades, from Sirius, Andromeda and Orion, just to name a few.

"This fleet, which we call the Ashtar Command, has been patrolling around the Earth now for many years as a part of our mission to help humanity. Most of you human beings cannot as yet see our starships because they are in the 5th dimension. But there are those among you who have been able to raise their frequencies and their consciousness high enough so that they now are able to see the Ascended Masters and the Ashtar Command. In fact, there are a few among you who are in daily contact with us.

"At this very moment, the entire fleet is about to move from quantum level 4 to quantum level 5. This is because the Planet's birthing into the 5th dimension has now really begun in earnest. All our starships are working to capacity in their efforts to stabilize both the Earth's interior and exterior so that all human beings will have the opportunity to ascend into the 5th dimension with Planet Earth.

"In addition to all this, there is another very important reason why the Intergalactic Council and the Ashtar Command are now working so actively with Planet Earth at this moment. You see, up until just a few short decades ago, Test Zone Planet Earth functioned perfectly as a closed loop—or a closed circuit you could say. The souls that incarnated on the Planet could make their choices, reap their karma, and undergo their learning processes without it disturbing or having any great influence on the rest of the solar system—or on any of the neighboring star systems.

"But in 1945, all this changed. This happened when humanity unleashed the Power of the Atom during what you call the Second World War. And all this happened even though humanity had no idea or understanding of what a mighty power it was dealing with. Since then, humanity has continued to use the Power of the Atom without any real understanding of what it is doing. Humanity does not yet realize the immensity of the Power it has unleashed. Human beings have not understood that in the 3rd dimension, the atom is the fundamental building block of the universe. Nor has it understood that by manipulating the atom—with no spiritual understanding of what you are doing and without true love for all your fellow beings—humanity is in grave danger of destroying itself. And not only of destroying itself, but of destroying its own home planet—and of destroying the entire local solar system. And this is something we cannot—and will not—permit!"

I shifted uneasily in my chair. The fact that humanity was in great danger of destroying itself wasn't any big news. Every other story on TV heralded humanity's imminent doom in one way or the other. What I'd never considered before was the bit about how our actions could affect the rest of our solar system.

Ashtar was still looking straight at me. "All this means," he continued in a very serious tone of voice, "that what we call Test Zone Planet Earth is no longer a closed circuit. With the release of atomic energy, humanity's future development and actions are now capable of affecting the entire solar system and the nearby star systems. So this, as I just said, is the other reason why the Ashtar Command is here at this time. Besides assisting humanity in the ascension process, we are here to protect this solar system and the star systems which are your nearest neighbors.

"The Ascended Masters—and we of the Ashtar Command—are not allowed to interfere with the free will of human beings on Planet Earth, except in one instance. And this is in the event of a devastating nuclear war or nuclear catastrophe. If this should happen, then we are empowered to interfere, not so much to save humanity as to protect the actions of humanity from damaging the solar system and your neighboring star systems. We sincerely hope this will not be necessary.

"All of which now brings me to YOU!"

Ashtar paused for a moment as if to make sure that he had my full attention. He then went on. "In order to give Mission Earth Ascension an added boost at this critical juncture, the Intergalactic Council has issued a special dispensation. This dispensation authorizes us to invite a few, specially selected Earthlings to join us aboard the Ashtar Command's Mothership. The purpose of this invitation and proposed visit to the Mothership is to remind these Earthlings of their True Nature. And to offer them an intensive training program which will teach them the fundamentals of living in the 5th dimension. The knowledge we intend to transmit during this training program is absolutely crucial if humanity wants to ascend into the 5th dimension.

"After this short but very intensive training program in the Mothership, the participants will then be sent back to Earth. Once back on Earth, they will find that they are now fully equipped to work closely with the Ascended Masters and the Ashtar Command to help the rest of humanity pass smoothly and easily through the amazing and all-embracing transformations that are going on on Planet Earth at this very moment."

"During the last 14 Earth days," he said and now his eyes had that same twinkle that Ticha's had, "we have been working closely with your guardian angel to monitor you and your level of consciousness. Based on our observations, we have come to the conclusion that you are ready for ascension in this lifetime!" A warm smile suddenly transformed Ashtar's face in the same way the sun transforms the sky when it bursts forth from behind a cloud. "Therefore," he continued, "on behalf of Sananda, the Supreme Commander of the Ascended Masters, also known as the Most Radiant One, I would like to invite you to attend the 5th dimensional training program aboard the Mothership..."

"Me?" I stuttered in surprise and looked at Ticha. She winked at me proudly.

"We in the higher dimensions," Ashtar continued, "sincerely hope you will accept this special invitation. Your personal efforts and your ascension can help bring about a critical mass of enlightened beings that will transform Planet Earth into a new Paradise. So please consider everything I have said very carefully. You have until tomorrow evening at midnight local time to make up your mind.

"This now ends this transmission. In love and peace, I, Ashtar, salute you on behalf of the Ashtar Command and the Great White Brotherhood. Adonai, Brother in the Light! The Force is with you!"

Ashtar's face began to fade and the myriad geometric shapes and colors again danced back and forth across my TV screen. For a few seconds, I heard those high-pitched tones again. Then they too began to fade. Ashtar's face disappeared and the colors and shapes began to fade too until they were gone. My TV screen went blank and I found myself back where I started, sitting in my chair, in my bedroom. My body felt incredibly heavy in comparison to the feeling of lightness I had experienced during Ashtar's transmission. Ticha picked up the remote control again and turned off the TV.

Neither of us said a word. I kept staring at the television set.

After a while I turned and looked at Ticha. She was still standing in the middle of my bedroom. Her eyes were closed and her body was only glowing very faintly. It was almost as if she had retreated into herself to wait for me.

I got up from the chair and started to pace back and forth in my tiny bedroom. My body felt light and heavy at the same time—and I felt like I was both in my body and out of it. My head was spinning. I was just so overwhelmed. Could this be true?

Ticha opened her eyes and said gently, "It's as your grandfather said, Starbrow, there's more between heaven and earth than meets the eye. And besides, you've always liked adventure."

"Yeah... I guess so," I said and continued to pace back and forth like a tiger in a tiny cage. "But I was thinking about something like going on a journey to the Himalayas, like my grandfather Elmar did. You know, to find Shamballa or something like that—BUT THIS!" I cried, no longer able to contain myself, "but this, THIS IS COMPLETELY INSANE! I MEAN THIS IS FURTHER OUT THAN FAR OUT! You are asking me to go on a 5th dimensional training program—in an intergalactic spaceship, hosted by a bunch of space beings called the Ashtar

40

Command... and well... I mean... how do I know that any of this is even real... I mean...!"

"Will you please just try to calm down a little."

I stopped pacing for a moment and tried to breathe deeply.

"That's better. Now tell me exactly what you mean..."

"I mean do you realize what he said—and what you're asking me to do. I mean think about it. Most of the people I know would think I'm totally crazy if I just told them that I was having nightly conversations with you, my guardian angel! Not to mention going on a training program in a spaceship with beings from the Pleiades or wherever it is you're all from!"

"No one's forcing you to do anything, Starbrow," Ticha said very very gently. "So why don't you just calm down. No matter what happens, you will always have your free will. Didn't you hear what he said? All you have to do is decide whether you want to accept this invitation or not. No one is going to force you to do anything...."

"Oh Lord!" I groaned and held my head in my hands. I walked over to the window and opened it wide. The cold March air cooled me off a little. Once again I saw that big golden star I saw the night I first met Ticha, shining brightly above the rooftops of Copenhagen.

"And that golden star up there," I said sarcastically, pointing at it. "I presume it's one of your spaceships."

"Yes," said Ticha. "In fact it is. It just so happens it's the Mothership Ashtar was talking about, orbiting Earth."

That did it.

I just couldn't take any more.

I caved in and fell down on my bed in a heap. Suddenly I felt very, very tired. As I lay there, I felt Ticha's presence reaching out and surrounding me like a warm, comforting embrace. Even from my bed I could still see the big star.

Finally I said, "Well what if I do decide to accept the invitation, how do I get up to your Mothership anyway?"

"You just leave that to me, "she replied. "All you have to do is find out in your own heart what you want to do."

"And what if I decide to say no?"

"The Ashtar Command will respect that decision too—and will go on with the mission without you. But Starbrow," she said very seriously, "try to remember… Planet Earth is in dire need of help... in need like never before."

I thought about what I'd seen on TV just during the past week. The riots in the Middle East, the pollution—not to mention the danger of a devastating nuclear catastrophe. There was no doubt about it—things were a mess. But what could one guy like me do about all this? It just didn't make sense.

"Why have I been chosen, Ticha?" I sat up and asked. "Why me?"

"Because you're Starbrow," she said, "a being with great powers... just like you are when you're playing Dungeons & Dragons with Jacob and Janus... "

"Now wait a minute! Dungeons & Dragons is just a game!" I cried. "It was just our imagination! The whole thing..."

"Are you sure about that?" she replied.

I groaned out loud.

"Well, are you Starbrow? What if your love of Dungeons & Dragons really was your heart whispering to you about your true identity and your true destination?"

"What do you mean?"

"I'm asking you Starbrow. Why do you think all people, no matter who they are or where they come from, love adventure? Be it Dungeons & Dragons or mind-blowing action movies or heart-wrenching romances?"

"How should I know?"

"Well maybe you should think about it. Maybe it's because these stories remind people of who they really are," Ticha said softly. "Maybe it reminds them that they're really heroic souls on a great adventure called Life."

"Oh come on Ticha. Maybe you're right about that but you're wrong about me. I'm no friggin' Dungeon Master. Not in this life anyway! Just look at me, will you! I'm just a restless young Dane..."

Ticha didn't answer. Instead she looked at me as if I was a total moron.

"Oh Lord!" I groaned again and held my head in my hands again.

"Starbrow! Look at me! Look at me!" she said with sudden firmness. In response to her command, I looked straight into her eyes. Their clear blueness reminded me of Elmar. "I have only one thing to say to you. Now listen carefully: *Follow your heart, for your heart alone knows the way.*" She said this very slowly, carefully pronouncing every word while she held me with her gaze. It was as if she was giving me a secret message and it was very important for me to remember it.

"What do you mean?" I asked.

"Just remember what I just said, that's all," she said and released me

42

from her gaze. Then she stepped into the middle of the bedroom.

"You have free will," she said, "and you, and you alone, must decide whether or not to accept the Ashtar Command's invitation. You have one day to think it over. 24 hours. Tomorrow night at midnight, everyone who has accepted the invitation will be transubstantiated to the Ashtar Command's Mothership. I will meet you here tomorrow night at midnight. At exactly 00:00 AM tomorrow you will tell me your decision."

Her body started twinkling as if it was made up of a million tiny shooting stars.

"So until then my friend, be well!"

And then she was gone.

7

Your Heart Alone Knows the Way

I put down the phone again. For the fifth time. It was five o'clock in the afternoon and I had just left my fifth message on Elmar's answering machine. After my second meeting with Ticha, I immediately called him to tell him what had happened, but he wasn't home. When I called him later that morning, he still didn't answer. Nor did he answer when I called him at noon nor again later that afternoon. So far he hadn't returned my call, but I didn't think too much about it because Elmar was in the habit of suddenly disappearing on one of his little expeditions or quick business trips. But today of all days, it was terribly frustrating because he was the only person in the world I could talk to. I sighed and looked out the window. Outside, it was pouring.

I went back to my bedroom and put away all the incense and candles. Then I threw myself on my bed and listened to the sound of the rain and sleet pounding against my windows. Thunder rumbled in the distance.

After last night's meeting with Ticha and Ashtar, I tried to go over everything that happened in the last nine days since I first saw Ticha on Ocean Drive. I tried to remember every detail including Elmar's tale of Stanley Donne and the City of Light, Ticha's first sudden appearance in my bedroom when she levitated and healed my nose, Ticha's second visit and Ashtar's transmission about Earth's ascension into the 5th dimension—and of course his "invitation" to take part in the Intergalactic Fleet's training program.

I sighed and stared up at the ceiling. I felt overwhelmed to say the least. The whole thing was just so far out that I felt that I needed at least a month to digest it. And now all I had was until midnight... I wished Elmar would call.

I turned on the TV and zapped to one of the news channels. I couldn't believe it. Every story was about war and pollution, doom and gloom.

Ashtar and Ticha were sure right about one thing: Planet Earth really needed a helping hand. In fact, a whole army of Divine angels like Ticha was what we needed. But how would people react if something like that happened? Every one I could think of, every one of my friends, even Jacob and Janus my closest buddies, would think that I was crazy if I told them about Ticha. Everyone... everyone except Elmar. Elmar! Where are you?

I turned off the TV and shut my eyes. It was all just too much. I'd barely slept a wink in the last two days and suddenly I just felt so tired, so tired...

The sound of the phone woke me up. I sat up in bed and looked at the clock. It was 10:30 pm. It had to be Elmar! I jumped out of bed and ran over to the phone.

"Hello," I said.

"Hello dear, it's me, Siri." It was my mother, but her voice sounded strange, like she'd been crying or something.

"Hi Mom," I said, disappointed it wasn't Elmar. "What's up?"

"I have some real bad news," she said.

"Really? What's happened?"

"Elmar's had a heart attack."

I froze.

"He's still alive, but the doctors say he may die any moment now."

No, my insides screamed. No! This can't be happening! Elmar can't die!

"We're over at the hospital with him now. He's in the intensive ward. Room 402. Sandra's here too. Come right away..."

I slammed down the phone and ran out of my apartment in a panic.

Ten minutes later I pulled up to the main entrance of the hospital in a cab. I jumped out and ran down the hallway, frantically trying to find the intensive ward where Elmar lay dying. Everything else was forgotten: Guardian angels, nuclear disasters, intergalactic fleets, the ascension of Planet Earth. None of it mattered. All I could think of was Elmar. Elmar! He was my best friend. Without him, I'd have no one to talk to. I loved him more than anyone else in the whole wide world.

Elmar just couldn't die.

45

No!

Elmar must not die!

I found room 402 and stood frozen in the doorway. Elmar was lying in bed with all kinds of wires and gadgets attached to him. A monitoring machine was beeping right next to his bed. My mother and kid sister were sitting by his side. I could see both of them had been crying. A doctor and nurse were looking at his charts on the other side of the bed. Elmar's eyes were closed. He looked as if he was sound asleep.

I entered the room slowly. "Is he...?" My voice was so shaky that I couldn't finish the sentence.

My mother and sister got up and came over and hugged me. They both knew how attached I was to Elmar. They both knew he meant more to me than even my mother. He was like a father and brother and best friend and teacher and hero all rolled into one to me.

"He's still alive," my mother said softly. "But they say there's not much hope." My sister burst into tears when my mother said this.

I walked slowly over to his bed and reached out and touched Elmar's hand. His hand felt very cold. But his face looked peaceful enough, as if he was having the most wonderful dream.

"Elmar..." I whispered, carefully studying every detail of his beloved face. I just couldn't believe this was happening. That he was lying there, about to die. Elmar had always seemed somehow indomitable to me— almost immortal—and far beyond the ordinary ups and downs of everyday life. He had always been there for me. A comfort when I was sad, an inspiration when the world seemed gray and empty, a hero when I needed someone to look up to. What would I do without him?

Elmar couldn't just die.

No!

He couldn't! He mustn't!

I held his hand and thought about all the good times we'd had together. The times when he'd tell me about his many adventures, the times when we'd gone for long walks and looked at the stars and wondered about life and the universe and now... now it was all going to end! The thought was unbearable. I bowed my head in despair and held on desperately to Elmar's cold hand.

The minutes ticked by as the monitor beeped softly by our side. I could hear my sister crying and my mother sniffling behind me. The doctor and nurse had tiptoed out of the room, but I paid them no heed. I just stood there, with my head bowed, at Elmar's side.

Suddenly Elmar's hand clutched mine with unexpected strength. I looked up in surprise. Elmar's eyes were wide open and he was looking me straight in the eye. He clutched my hand harder and pulled me close to him.

"I've been waiting for you, my boy," he said in that clear voice I loved so much. He held my gaze with his blue eyes and for a moment I realized he had the same crystal clear blue eyes as Ticha.

"I have something to tell you before I journey on, my lad," he said. "Remember this: *Follow your heart, for your heart alone knows the way*."

When Elmar said these words, the exact same words that Ticha uttered the night before, a tidal wave was released in my heart.

Then Elmar's whole body seemed to quake. He let go of my hand and went limp. The monitor started to beep wildly. I wobbled woozily and felt my mother and my sister grab hold of me from behind. At that same moment, the doctor and nurse came rushing back into the room. But even before the doctor turned off the machine, I knew that Elmar was gone. That his soul had left his body and was now journeying on to its next adventure. His soul that had longed for so long for the higher dimensions was now on its way. But somehow he had managed to stay with us, just long enough, to remind me of something I already knew, deep within my own heart.

Follow your heart, for your heart alone knows the way.

The doctor closed Elmar's eyes. My mother and sister were crying and holding me tightly. I felt my whole world rock on its foundations.

Follow your heart, for your heart alone knows the way.

Then suddenly I remembered—and looked at my watch. It was 11:40pm. 11:40pm! Just 20 minutes until Ticha was coming back for my answer! I looked at Elmar one last time; then I pulled myself free from my mother and sister's embrace. I turned and started to run out of the room.

"Mom, Sandra," I cried, "I've just gotta go..."

My mother opened her mouth in surprise and started to say something, but there was no time for explanations. I bolted down the hallway like a madman.

I ran out of the hospital's main entrance and down Pale Pond Street, desperately looking for a cab. But it was snowing like mad and there wasn't a cab in sight. I had no time to lose so I started running down Pale Pond Street, oblivious of the snow, sleet and freezing howling wind.

Follow your heart, for your heart alone knows the way.

I was running so fast that I slipped on the icy sidewalk. I got up and ran on. Ticha! Ticha, if you can really read my mind then please hear me! I'm on my way, I'm on my way...

I came to the Triangle Square and turned down Eastbridge Boulevard. The Triangle clock said 10 minutes to midnight. 10 minutes until Ticha was supposed to come! 10 minutes!

I raced on and reached my street at the stroke of 12. I heard a church clock chiming in the distance. I sprinted the last couple of yards to my building, pulled out my keys and hurled myself up the stairs like a maniac. I opened the door to my apartment and ran into my bedroom.

"Ticha, I'm here!" I shouted. "I say yes to the invitation."

But my bedroom was dark and empty. The clock by my bed read 00:03 AM. I was too late! Too late! I collapsed on the floor, completely soaked and exhausted.

"I'm here!" I said in a choked voice. "I say yes!"

Suddenly my bedroom was again filled with a warm golden light.

"Ticha!"

There she was, soaring above me and enveloping me in her radiant, glowing aura. I felt a tingling at the top of my head as if all the hairs on my head were standing on end. Then my whole body started to tingle, as if every single one of my cells were becoming as light as light. I was bathed in light. My body was getting lighter and lighter... I was as light as a feather... and everything was suddenly possible... I was one with the Light... I was one with Ticha... yes, everything and anything was possible... because I had said YES!

PART TWO

WE COME FROM THE STARS

1

Acclimatization

Slowly, slowly I felt myself coming to, as if I was coming out of a long, deep sleep. For a moment I had a hard time remembering who I was ... I opened my eyes and blinked. Where was I?

I looked around and found I was lying on my back in the soft grass in what seemed to be a great forest. Above was a curtain of shimmering green leaves. The trees around me looked like tall, beautiful beech trees and they swayed slightly in the gentle breeze. I felt the warm sun on my face, shining down from a brilliant blue sky. I sighed, the temperature was... well... just perfect. And the air had a sweet fresh smell, like the smell of flowers and green grass. And then I noticed the birds were singing, which surprised me. Was it already summer?

I sat up and looked around, puzzled, it couldn't be summer yet. Then I noticed the bark of the trees around me, which seemed to shine like silver in the bright sunlight. And the leaves... then I noticed the leaves! They were so green! I'd never seen a green like that before. Then I realized that everything—the trees, the bushes, the flowers, the grass—the whole forest was radiating a soft golden light!

I stood up and stretched.

"Where am I?" I said, out loud to no one in particular.

"In the Relaxation Forest," answered a voice inside my head.

I turned around. It was Ticha! She was standing behind me with a big smile on her face. She too was surrounded by a soft golden light, just like the rest of the forest.

"The Relaxation Forest?" I said.

"Yes," she said, "the volunteers are not allowed to enter the inhabited parts of the Mothership before they have been acclimatized—and released all fear and doubt."

"Acclimatized?" I looked at Ticha in surprise. Acclimatized? The

Mothership? What was going on here? Then slowly, it all started coming back to me... The invitation from Ashtar to take part in the Intergalactic Fleet's training program, Elmar's sudden death and his last words, my desperate race to get back to my apartment before midnight, and Ticha who finally appeared after I had collapsed on my bedroom floor in despair.

"So we're in the Mothership now?" I asked.

"Yes. The Relaxation Forest is inside the Mothership."

I looked around in awe.

Ticha laughed. "You can see the inhabited parts if we go over to the plateau at the edge of the meadow... just over there." My guardian angel pointed straight ahead, past the tall trees. About a hundred yards from where we were standing, the forest came to an end and opened up into a lush green meadow. Beyond that, everything seemed to be warm golden light.

As I gazed towards the warm light, it seemed to draw me towards it and make my whole body tingle.

I walked quickly through the trees, towards the meadow and the light. Ticha was by my side. Her movements were so light and graceful that I wondered if she touched the ground at all when she moved. We left the trees behind us. The golden light at the end of the field seemed to light up the whole horizon. When we came to the end of the field, I saw that we were standing on a high plateau, and that below the plateau there was a lush landscape with rolling hills, green woods, crystal clear lakes and meadows full of golden flowers.

Then I discovered the source of the light. I blinked and blinked again. The light was coming from a great city at the edge of the forest! I could see towers and tall buildings, streets and open squares, bridges and landing sites. It was a strange and awesome sight because even though it was a huge city, it was very harmonious to look at. There was something very organic and natural about all the high-tech looking structures, as if the whole city had just sprouted out of the ground.

From where we were standing, the buildings all looked as if they were made of silver or gold, because whatever they were made of, glistened in the sun like smooth silver or gold cones of light. I could also make out small figures walking around in the streets and once in a while, golden vehicles of different sizes took off or landed from one of the city's landing sites. When I focused on these small vehicles, I discovered they were small pyramids! Small golden pyramids, which seemed to fly completely effortlessly through the air. Most of the small pyramids were about the size of a car, but there were also some very very large ones, which seemed to me to be as big as a whole building. On one of the bigger runways, I could see one really enormous pyramid, which must have been at least several hundred yards long. Small pyramids were flying in and out of it!

"Welcome to the Ashtar Command Mothership!" said Ticha with a smile.

As I looked at the city, I realized that it was only inside the Relaxation Forest that the sky was clear blue. The moment we came to the edge of the forest, the sky had turned into deep space, a dark horizon filled with tens of thousands of bright stars. Suddenly a large, blue globe began to rise up over the horizon. It rose so quickly and it was so close that I quickly realized that it must be a planet. A beautiful blue-green planet that was so close that it almost filled the entire night sky. I could see oceans on the planet—and continents and mountains and cloud formations... and that was when I realized, with a shock, that the planet I was looking at was Earth! I was looking at Earth from... from a huge spaceship! It was the first time I'd ever seen the Earth from a perspective like this... and this... more than anything else, really brought home to me where I was.

"I'm really on a spaceship." I was awestruck. "I really am!"

"We call this ship the Mothership, because it is the meeting point for all the starships in the whole Intergalactic Fleet," Ticha explained.

"What are those pyramids I see flying around?" I asked. "Are they spaceships too?"

"You could say so, but we call them Merkabah or Light Bodies," Ticha replied.

"Light Bodies?"

"Yes. You could also call them inter-dimensional transport vehicles. When you're in a Merkabah, you can travel through space and time and through the dimensions. All souls in the 5th dimension have a Light Body or a Merkabah."

"Wow!"

"Yes, it is pretty neat," said Ticha and went on explaining, "Because when groups of individual Light Bodies join together, they form starships. In this way, the fleet is able to cover vast distances and move from galaxy to galaxy, from star system to star system."

Ticha pointed to one of the big runways. A whole squadron of these small pyramids was taking off. When all the pyramids were about a half a mile above the city, they flew straight towards each other. The moment the pyramids meet, there was a blinding flash of light—and then they were joined! Now all the separate pyramids had become one huge, oval-shaped starship! The new starship then turned towards Earth and zoomed off towards my home at lightning speed. It was incredible to watch. I followed the ship until it became a small, glowing spot in the distance... much like the golden star I had seen in the sky over Ocean Drive. That was when I discovered there were literally hundreds of golden glowing spots hovering around the Earth. There were hundreds, no, thousands of starships surrounding Earth!

"Look at all those ships!" I cried in amazement. "What are they are doing, Ticha?"

"They're helping Mother Earth in her ascension process."

"But why can't we humans see them when we're down on Earth?"

"I already told you why," Ticha replied. "Because the starships and the Mothership are in the 5th dimension. It is only when the ships lower their frequency, as I did when I visited you, that you human beings can seem them with your physical eyes."

"Is this the story behind all the UFOs people claim to see?"

"Partly," said Ticha and grinned. I don't know why, but I had the feeling that Ticha was beaming even more now than she did when she was down on Planet Earth.

Three large starships suddenly left the Earth's atmosphere and zoomed back towards the Mothership. As they approached, I could see that they were circular and that their size must have been immense. Of course it was all so new to me that it was hard for me to get a clear idea of how big things really were, but as the three ships sped by us, I had the impression that they were huge... like a mile long or something. As I turned to follow their pathway, I realized that much of what I originally thought were stars were in fact starships. It was totally mind-boggling! The whole night sky was literally alive with starships of every shape and form.

As I studied the star-studded heavens above me and the rest of my surroundings, I noticed that the Relaxation Forest stretched out into the distance behind us. Mile after mile of shimmering green forest. And beyond that... well beyond that, I thought I could faintly make out tall, glinting shapes. Were they...

"Yes, they are mountains," said Ticha inside my head.

"Mountains?"

"Yes. Right now, you can only see a small portion of the Mothership. The Mothership is several hundred miles in diameter. There are entire eco-systems inside the Mothership: Mountains, forests, rivers, lakes and oceans, all teeming with life. The Mothership is designed to transform and program sunlight so that the beings here are able to experience a normal cycle of day and night."

I walked to the edge of the plateau and tried to take it all in: The Mothership, the starships, the Earth floating on the horizon in the distance, the city of light... all of it. It was unbelievable, it really was. Then the thought struck me... it wasn't unbelievable at all. No, it was really true! It really was... In fact, everything that Ticha had told me, right from the beginning, was true! How could I ever apologize to her for not believing her! It was a pretty humbling experience to stand here, after all my doubts and fears. But I knew I'd never be able to explain it to her, so instead I just said, "Well, what happens now?"

"We have a little time before you're going to meet the other members of your group," Ticha said gently. Maybe she'd read my thoughts again.

"The other members of my group? What group?"

"All the volunteers who are attending the 5th dimensional training program have been divided into groups. The Ashtar Command has done this because each group is going to be assigned a different location when you all go back to Earth after the program."

"How many members are there in a group?"

"Well Starbrow, the number varies," she replied. "It depends on several factors like the location you are going to be assigned to and on how many in each group actually said yes to their invitation. Your group has three members."

I looked into Ticha's eyes. I was so happy she was here with me. I smiled at the thought that less than two weeks ago I'd run away from her in panic and now she was like my best friend. The only being I knew and trusted in this strange new world I landed upon.

As if reading my thoughts again, she squeezed my hand. "There's no need to be afraid, Starbrow. Everyone here is your brother and sister—and they're all looking forward to seeing you again."

"Again?" I asked, not understanding what she meant.

"Yes again. Come my friend," said Ticha, "let's go over there and sit down for a moment so I can remind you of something." Ticha led me to some huge rocks that were close by and motioned me to sit down besides her. We sat down with our backs to one of the rocks. From where we sat, we could still see the city in the distance.

Ticha turned to me and said, "Look at me. Look into my eyes." I looked into her clear blue eyes. "Don't you remember me?"

I tried to remember. I looked deep into her eyes and let myself be sucked into their dazzling Blueness. Slowly, I began to see images, pictures, scenes in the clear Blueness of her eyes.

"What do you see?" she asked.

"Well, I see myself with two friends," I said, almost in a trance. "The three of us are very happy. We're having a good time, and we're free. We come from a blue-green planet that is very far away from Earth. We're a team, the three of us. And we travel, the three of us, through the universes. Each one of us has a guardian angel that we're always in contact with. You're my guardian angel..."

"Who are your two friends?" Ticha asked.

I had a vision—in the blue clearness of Ticha's eyes—of my two friends. "The one," I said, "is tall and strong. He has long, golden hair. And he's a real daredevil," I said and chuckled, knowing that we were good friends, even though we were very different.

"And the other one?"

"The other is a very wise soul—with deep insight into the mysteries of the universe. I can see that he loves to create and that he's loyal. A true friend." Again I chuckled because I knew we were also good friends, even though we too were very different.

"When did the three of you decide to come to Earth?"

"A long time ago, a very long time ago," I said slowly because violent images were flashing across the big screen in my head like bolts of lightning in a wild storm. "Atlantis... Atlantis..." I heard myself mumbling, "... humanity unleashed a power that was far too great... far, far too great..." With my inner vision, I saw terrifying scenes... I saw how the heavens and the oceans opened up and swallowed entire continents. I saw gigantic tidal waves sweeping the planet... then chaos ruled.

Slowly the vision of ruin passed and I could continue.

"After that, the Great White Brotherhood requested assistance from the Intergalactic Council," I heard myself saying. "The Council didn't want to send a whole fleet to Earth because at that time there weren't that many people on Earth. But they did send a few starships. We three were on one of those starships."

"Why did the three of you decide to come?" said Ticha, leading me on ever so gently.

"We knew that Planet Earth would ascend into the 5th dimension around the year 2000," I said. "We wanted to help humanity."

"What happened then?"

At this point, I was in a deep trance and the images flowed by like running water. Tall pyramids, knights in shining armor, priestesses and druids passing through islands of mist, American freedom fighters battling English soldiers...

"Many different lives on Earth where we did our best to spread Enlightenment," I slowly said as the visions flowed by, "... but the collective consciousness was strong... slowly, slowly we began to forget who we were..."

"All right," Ticha said and snapped her finger. "That's enough for now."

"Wow!" I said and shook my head. "What was that all about?"

"Call it a brief past life regression," she smiled. "Now you know that you haven't left your home—you've come home!" She laughed and stood up. "Come my friend, it's time for you to meet the other two members of your group. I've just received messages from their guardian angels that they too are ready."

"Really?" I said and stood up. Suddenly I felt nervous. "Where are they?"

"They're in the Relaxation Forest," Ticha said and pointed back towards the tall trees. "And they're looking for you. It's time for you to go and find them."

"But how? How will I find them?"

"Follow your heart," Ticha said and put her hand on my chest, "for your heart alone knows the way."

2

Quantum Leap and Quantum Soup

I stood on top of a hill that was covered with trees and scanned the horizon. There were trees everywhere. There seemed to be no end to the forest!

Then I sat down on the grass with my back against one of the trees. Ever since I'd said farewell to Ticha and entered the forest, I'd been trying to ask my heart where the other two members of my group were. Then I tried, as best I could, to follow the feeling I got. In the beginning, I thought I felt a slight impulse to set out in a northwesterly direction through the trees. That impulse led me past a pond and into a new part of the forest. But now I was stuck. I just didn't feel a thing.

Once again, I scanned the horizon. The forest was so incredibly peaceful and harmonious. I would have been perfectly happy to lie down in the grass and just enjoy the beauty of it all. But I knew in my heart that I couldn't. For some reason, it was important for me to find the two other members of my group as quickly as possible. But where were they?!

I closed my eyes again and tried to focus my attention on my heart. As soon as I did, I had a clear vision of a man dressed in a long, dark blue cloak, wandering through a little valley. I couldn't see his face because of the hood, but I sensed that he too was searching the forest with his bright, clear eyes. Every so often he would stop and close his eyes, as if he too was trying to figure out which way to go. Then I knew with complete certainty that he was searching for me.

I sprang to my feet because now I knew which direction to go. Down the other side of the hill and then to the left. I dashed down the hill and veered left. Then, when I'd walked for almost half a mile, I came to a stream. What next? I closed my eyes. Once again I saw the blue-cloaked man in my mind's eye. He was making his way up a steep hill.

Again I knew which direction to go. Straight ahead, along the stream. I moved as fast as I could. After following the stream for another two hundred yards, it suddenly made a sharp turn to the left. I wondered if I should keep on following it. I closed my eyes. Again I saw the man. Now he was standing with his eyes closed at the end of a large clearing somewhere in the forest. I knew that he too could see me in his mind's eye.

I decided not to follow the stream. Instead I began walking straight ahead. After I'd gone another hundred yards or so, I too came to the clearing. It was the same clearing I'd seen with my inner vision. I looked up and saw the cloaked man standing at the other end of the clearing with his eyes closed. I started to run in his direction, waving my arms wildly.

"Hello there!" I cried. "Hello!"

The man heard me and opened his eyes. He pulled back his hood. I continued to run towards him, trying to see what he looked like. From a distance, he seemed to be about my age, strong and fit. As I got closer, I saw his handsome face surrounded by a thick mane of curly red hair. He had deep penetrating eyes.

He started to walk towards me. His deep blue cloak made him look like some mysterious wanderer who'd just stepped out of an ancient legend. He had a large backpack on his back.

The closer we got to each other, the more I realized there was something very familiar about him. Very familiar. Where had I seen him before...? That shock of curly red hair, the long, determined stride... Then suddenly I knew... yes... I recognized him and my mouth literally tumbled open in surprise. I couldn't believe my eyes!

"Jacob!" I cried in amazement. "Jacob!"

He gave me a confused look.

"Jacob, it's me!" I cried.

Then he too recognized me. "Master!" He cried in astonishment. "But what on earth are you doing here!" His voice was deeper than it had been before, but it was definitely Jacob's.

"Beats me dude..." I said and started to laugh. "I might ask you the same!"

We stood face to face in the middle of the clearing and stared and laughed and stared at each other again. It really was Jacob, my old friend and faithful Dungeons & Dragons buddy—no doubt about that. But not quite the same shy Jacob with the nerdy glasses I'd known before. The Jacob who now stood before me was totally different... transformed. And then I realized what it was. Jacob had become Moncler! Jacob was now the Wizard he'd been playing for the last ten years in our Dungeons & Dragons game!

That was when I realized by the strange way Jacob was looking at me that I obviously didn't exactly look like my old Earth self either. So I looked down and discovered, for the first time, that I was wearing a long, white ankle-length robe. I was almost as surprised at my gear as he was. I must have been so mesmerized by all my adventures that I hadn't noticed I wasn't wearing my trendy Fashion Flash garb anymore. Or that... wow... my short Tom Cruise haircut had turned into a long, golden mane that went all the way down to my shoulders!

We both laughed out loud again—and then gave each other this huge bear hug.

"Of all the most far-out surprises I've had today," I said as I stepped back to look at Jacob again, "this has got to be the most far-out of them all!"

"It really is you, it really is!" said Jacob and laughed again. "But just look at you!"

"You ain't doing too bad yourself!" I chuckled. "I just can't believe it!"

That was when we both became aware that someone else had stepped out of the forest and was approaching us from way off to our left. We turned to look. The man who was coming in our direction was a tall, good-looking guy. He too had long, shoulder-length hair. As he got closer, we could see from his pointy ears that he was some kind of elf. But it was his golden chain mail that gave him away. He was the Elven King!

"Janus!" we both cried and ran to meet him. "Janus!"

Janus stopped and looked perplexed. We knew he didn't recognize us.

"Janus, it's us!" cried Jacob.

It took him a couple of seconds to realize who we were, but when he finally did, he just stood there with his mouth wide open. Jacob and I burst out laughing.

"This is TOO MUCH! THIS IS JUST TOO MUCH!" cried Janus. "I mean... of all the excellent and unprecedented things... I just can't believe it!" And with that he began to dance a little jig. "Do you realize how far out this is!!! After all those years of playing Dungeons & Dragons... and thinking it was all just a game!"

Jacob and I just stood there and gave Janus a moment to try to assimilate it all.

After a minute or two, he stopped dancing around and stared at the two of us. "But how did you two get here? I mean... what's going on?"

"That's what we'd all like to know," I said.

"Well one thing seems to be for sure—we're the three members of our group," said Jacob and laughed again.

"My guardian angel brought me here," I said.

"Mine did too!" cried Janus and Jacob at the same time.

We gave each other our secret D&D handshake and started capering around the clearing again like three madmen. For a while, all we could do was laugh and shout. Then Janus stopped and gave Jacob a friendly pat on the back. "You sure is one looking-good dude," he said. "...now that I think about it, you really do look just like Moncler."

"I think he is Moncler," I said. "Didn't your guardian angel tell you that our Dungeons & Dragons game wasn't just our imagination?"

"Yeah, in fact she did," Janus said. "But if Jacob is Moncler and I'm Telperion, then who are you?"

"My guardian angel says my real name is Starbrow." It was the first time I'd ever said my name out loud, but it felt very natural.

"Wow," cried Jacob, "That must be your true name...!"

"What do you mean?" I said.

"Because well... I saw it right away... from the moment we met... it's as if there's this light, like starlight, coming out of your forehead...from this point right here," he said, touching me right between my eyebrows. "It's so weird, I noticed it the moment I saw you."

Starlight?! Coming from my forehead? I touched the spot on my forehead Jacob had just touched. Right between my eyebrows. I couldn't feel anything with my finger ... yet just for a second, while Jacob was talking about the starlight, I did feel this tingling sensation between my eyebrows. And then in a flash, Jacob and Janus turned into two pulsating rays of light. The vision only lasted for a split second, and then it was gone. I blinked and there they were, standing there right in front of me again... good old Jacob and Janus. Or should I say Moncler and Telperion?

"Well," chuckled Jacob as if he understood, "it looks like the light really is a part of you, Master Starbrow."

All I could do was nod in agreement. It was all so mind-boggling that it was hard to get a grip. Each time we looked at each other and saw how transformed we were, it totally floored us again. First there was Jacob/Moncler—with his curly red hair and noble features, wearing that long, deep blue wizard's cloak of his and carrying his book of secret spells in his backpack. The only thing that seemed to be missing was Moncler's magic staff. Then there was Janus/Telperion—with his long, golden locks and pointy elven ears, wearing that golden chain mail over his super-fit body. The only thing he seemed to be missing to make his transformation complete was that magnificent two-handed sword of his, the one that was set with precious gems. And then there was me, Starbrow, with my long white robe and long, curly hair. Jacob and Janus didn't seem to be in any doubt about my identity. As far as they were concerned, the shining light that radiated from my brow was a clear sign that Starbrow was indeed my real name.

So what could I do? I spread my arms open wide and laughed again. I felt strong and my mind was clear. In fact I felt more alive than I'd ever felt before. Jacob and Janus looked as if they felt the same way.

"If my friends could see me now!" Janus laughed and said.

"We are your friends," laughed Jacob back, "and I tell you, we can see you now—as plain as day!"

"Well friends," I said, "Let the adventure begin!" And we gave each other our secret D&D handshake once more because this was our ritual—the way it had always been. The way we'd always started all our D&D sessions back on Planet Earth. But we knew, in our heart of hearts, that whatever we'd just been through and whatever the future would bring, it couldn't be better than this. This meeting of friends, in this place, at this time, in this way—and the knowing that the three of us would always be together—on a great adventure.

But now it was time to talk, so we sat down on the soft grass.

"Tell me how you got here," Janus asked me.

"Well..." I said, slowly warming to the tale, "it all began last Sunday night..."

"Whoa, that's when it started for me too!" cried Jacob and Janus, almost in one voice.

"After our D&D session, while I was waiting for my bus to come on Ocean Drive, I suddenly heard someone calling my name..." Jacob and Janus were all ears as I recounted in detail all the things that had happened to me during the last 9 days, from my very first meeting with Ticha to Elmar's sudden death. Then I told them about waking up in the Relaxation Forest—and seeing the city of light in the distance and the thousands of starships orbiting around Earth. They nodded as I spoke; they'd both seen the very same things.

As my tale came to an end, we looked up at the clear blue sky.

"It seems like as long as you're inside the Relaxation Forest, it's daylight," I remarked.

"Yes, I think you're right," replied Jacob, gazing at the blue sky. There wasn't a star or starship in sight. "... Amazing technology they have up here... but let's not get side-tracked. Janus, it's your turn to tell..."

"Eh... well, as Starbrow said, it all started last Sunday night, also for me..." Janus mumbled and looked strangely uncomfortable.

"Well...what happened?" Jacob asked.

"I... I—err—I tried to commit suicide!" Janus' face turned bright red when he said this.

"Suicide?!!" Jacob and I cried in surprise. "But why!"

"Because of Cecilia," Janus answered, still looking strangely uncomfortable.

"Cecilia? But I thought you'd broken up with her?" I cried, still shocked by his admission.

"No, that's not what really happened. Cecilia broke up with me," Janus replied. "I know I never told you guys, but I was so totally in love with her..." Then he added, his voice no more than a whisper, "I don't know guys, but well, it was like... like I'd never really been in love with any one before I met Cecilia."

Jacob and I looked at each other. Janus? The no. 1 lady killer? The part-time bartender and full-time party animal. Head over heels in love? It was hard to imagine.

"I just felt I couldn't live without her—and then when she left me..." Janus continued.

"Well... what did you do?" I asked, still finding it hard to believe.

"I decided to jump off the Harbor Bridge and kill myself," Janus replied matter-of-factly.

"But if you wanted to commit suicide, wouldn't Long Bridge have been better," wisecracked Jacob. I knew it was his way of trying to deal with this shocking bit of news.

"Yeah, probably... I guess I wasn't thinking too clearly at that point," said Janus and laughed. "Anyway, there I was in sub-zero temperatures standing on the rail of the Harbor Bridge, determined to drown myself in the freezing water below. Without Cecilia, nothing mattered anyway. I thought of her one last time and then I jumped. A split second before I hit the icy water, a warm golden light seemed to appear out of nowhere and grab me. I felt myself being lifted up and suddenly found myself safe on dry land. The golden light turned out to be Vildis, my guardian angel."

Jacob and I were all ears as Janus continued his tale of his dramatic first encounter with his guardian angel. In many ways, she sounded a lot like Ticha: Beautiful, wise, and caring. But she was completely different too, as different from Ticha as Janus was from me.

"I can't explain it, but somehow Vildis comforted me and gave me new hope," said Janus with a seriousness that was quite out of character for him. "After we'd talked for what seemed to be a very long time there by the Harbor Bridge, she just disappeared into thin air. It was all so bizarre that after my suicide attempt, I really wasn't sure if she was just a figment of my imagination or what... but at least meeting her gave me something to think about besides Cecilia!"

"Did she come back after that?" I asked.

"Yeah, several times in fact. Always at night—and then we'd just sit on my bed and talk. About all kinds of weird stuff. You know, about the dimensions and other worlds. There was much I didn't understand. But somehow it all just felt right. And I felt a whole lot better when I was with her. She's just so... oh I don't know, it's hard to explain. Anyway finally, she showed me Ashtar's transmission on the TV, the same transmission that you saw."

"What made you say yes?" I asked.

"I must admit I wasn't hard to convince," said Janus. "I mean I was going to kill myself anyway, so what did I have to lose? And besides, it sounded like fun!"

After Janus had finished his story, I turned towards Jacob. "And what about you Jacob, what happened to you?"

"Well, I experienced the climactic overthrow of the superstition of materialism in my life," Jacob said, without batting an eyelash.

"The climactic-what?" exclaimed Janus.

"The climactic overthrow of the superstition of materialism! And it all started with a quantum physics experiment at the University that I had been asked to assist in," said Jacob, who was a physics graduate student at Denmark's Niels Bohr Institute. "The experiment was going to be conducted by an Englishman, a quantum physicist by the name of Stanley Donne, who was visiting lecturer at the Institute."

"Stanley who?" I cried.

"Stanley Donne," replied Jacob.

"Stanley Donne! Why that was the name of the fellow my grandfather Elmar met about 50 years ago, who inspired him to go on an expedition in search of Shamballa! What a strange coincidence... But it can't possibly be the same Stanley Donne because if it was, well, he'd have to be at least a hundred years old by now!" I exclaimed.

"No, then it couldn't have been the same man," said Jacob, "because the Stanley Donne I met must have been in his late thirties."

"Describe him," I said anyway. Something about this coincidence made me wonder.

Jacob gave me a quick rundown of what he looked like.

"You're not going to believe me, Jacob, but your description of him is exactly the same as Elmar's description of the Stanley Donne he met 50 years ago," I said. "This is too weird."

"But how can that be?" Jacob asked.

"What a question, Mighty Wizard!" laughed Janus. "Here we are, the three of us, transformed into Moncler, Telperion and Starbrow. On board a mega spaceship which is orbiting the Earth as we speak, hanging out with extra terrestrials, guardian angels and flying pyramids, and you two are wondering if there's a technology that might be able to keep people young for a couple of hundred years or so!"

"Good point!" Jacob and I laughed.

"Okay, so Stanley Donne who was once King Arthur who is really El Morya conducted this quantum physics experiment at your institute... so what happened next?" I asked.

"Well, in order to understand this experiment, I'm going to have to explain a little about the quantum field," Jacob said. "Briefly, it goes like this: Everything that exists in the material world, be it a blade of grass, a tree, the human body, a galaxy, a cell—is made up of atoms. Atoms are made up of even smaller subatomic particles with funny names like quarks and bosons and leptons. These particles are not solid like some people think, but are really just waves of energy. Which means that everything that exists in the entire universe is made up of energy—and that the whole universe is in fact one unified field of energy. We call this field—the quantum field or the quantum soup. Are you with me so far?"

Janus and I nodded. "That's exactly what Ticha told me," I said.

"Now, these subatomic particles that make up the entire material world are so tiny that we are not able to see or measure them. Even with our best measuring instruments, we still can't see them. So how do we even know that they exist? We know they exist by the trails they leave behind them in particle accelerators. That was what Stanley Donne's experiment was all about. We photographed their trails in the Institute's particle accelerator... In other words, by doing this, we were able to verify that these particles really do exist. Do you understand?"

"I think so," I said.

"Okay, so far so good," Jacob continued. "During the experiment Stanley Donne showed us something extraordinary. He actually demonstrated that these particles only come into existence when we observe them. In other words, when we focus our attention on the quantum field, particles actually come into existence. When we remove our attention from the field, the particles disappear."

Janus and I gave him a puzzled look.

"Try to imagine this quantum field as an infinite, eternal, unlimited, invisible mass of living energy. When there's no human being around to look at this field... in other words to observe it, it remains exactly that... a field of pure energy. But when a human being directs his or her attention at the field, the energy just sort of pops out of the field and becomes a physical, space-time event. In other words, something happens. What all this means is that it is the act of putting your attention on something which actually brings that something into existence." Now Jacob was getting excited. "Do you realize what this means!!!"

"Noo..." we replied. "Not really..."

"This means that it is our attention alone which creates the physical world out of the quantum soup! Our attention and nothing else!" cried Jacob, barely able to contain himself any longer. "And this means that we human beings are not victims of some separate, objective, outside world. But that in fact, we are really and truly the creators of our world! And that's why I said Stanley Donne's experiment was the climactic overthrow of the superstition of materialism in my life."

Obviously this was all as plain as pie in the sky to Jacob, but unfortunately it wasn't to us.

Janus asked, really making an effort to understand. "But what is the superstition of materialism?"

"The whole so-called materialistic world view is based on the assumption that there is an independent, objective material world out there which is separate from us. In other words, an objective reality that operates beyond us and which we are powerless to control. But Stanley Donne's experiment proved to me, beyond the slightest doubt, that the materialistic world view is incorrect. We are not separate from the outer world! We, in fact, create what we call the outer world because it is our attention which brings space-time events into existence out of the quantum field!" I'd never seen Jacob so excited about anything before in all the years I'd known him.

"I guess you have to be a scientist to get off on something like that!" said Janus and laughed.

"You only say that because you don't understand what it means!" replied Jacob heatedly. "You guys think all this physics stuff's got nothing to do with your lives. But that's not true. It's got everything to do with your lives and the lives of so-called ordinary people, because your lives and the lives of almost everyone else are based on an assumption that there's a separate world out there, which you have no power to control. And this makes people feel that they are the innocent victims of events, which are beyond their control. But since the basic assumption is not true, the conclusion is not true either!" continued Jacob passionately. "And when you—and the rest of the people down on Planet Earth— understand what this really means, it will completely change your whole life!"

Janus and I looked at each other again. Even though we didn't quite get what was so revolutionary about Jacob's experiment, one thing was obvious, it really had changed Jacob. We'd never seen him like this before.

"I suppose that's what it did to your life!" said Janus.

"That's putting it mildly," said Jacob. "It changed everything for me. Everything! My whole view of the world, everything I'd based my life on up until then... years of study... all of it was in shambles. Nothing, absolutely nothing, was the way I'd thought it was anymore. That very night I decided to burn all my physics books. I collected them all, every single volume, and made this huge bonfire out in the backyard. Then I watched my whole life go up in smoke. It was all very symbolic, you know. Like I was standing there, on the edge of this void... and then suddenly..." Jacob's eyes shone. "well, as I was standing there, staring at my life going up in flames, it suddenly dawned on me that the bonfire was getting bigger. Next thing I knew, I saw this beautiful woman standing inside the fire. For a moment I thought I'd lost my mind. But then she stepped out, and walked slowly over to me. I was too stunned to move." Jacob stopped for a moment as if remembering the sight of her. Then he continued. "As you can guess, she was my guardian angel. Her name is Lia... and well... from then on my story is pretty much like yours. I'd felt I'd lost everything and was ready for anything. Lia taught me all kinds of stuff about the Nature of Reality that I'd always wanted to know.

69

Fortunately for me, I was shook up enough to be open to the information she gave me. Now that I had let go of the superstition of materialism..."

The rest of Jacob's tale was very much like Janus' and mine. When he finally finished his story, none of us said a word. We just sat there, each deep in his own thought, pondering the extraordinary events that had led us to this extraordinary place and our extraordinary transformation. Then I wondered, as I knew my friends were wondering, what the next step in our extraordinary adventure would be.

It didn't take long for us to find out.

3

The Cosmic Library

"Hey Telperion," I called to Janus who had fallen a bit behind Jacob and me, "come and take a look at this baby!" I was surveying a huge tree, which had crashed through the forest and was now blocking the narrow path we'd been following. After we'd finished telling our stories, we decided it was time to go back to the edge of the Relaxation Forest where we'd left our guardian angels. At first, it was easy enough finding our way through the forest, but after a while, we seemed to completely lose our sense of direction. Every time we asked our inner guidance which way to go, we found ourselves being led deeper and deeper into the forest. We ended up following a narrow pathway, which twisted and turned its way through the dense undergrowth. And now our path was completely blocked by this huge fallen tree. And since the undergrowth on both sides was so dense, the only way forward was over the huge trunk.

Janus stood next to me and surveyed the massive block of wood before us. Then he bent down and put one arm under the trunk and lifted it. Jacob and I couldn't believe our eyes. Janus lifted the tree trunk easily with only one arm! It must have weighed at least half a ton!

"I had a feeling I was a pretty strong dude..." Janus mumbled, as surprised as we were at his tremendous strength.

"I guess we forgot that when it comes to strength, Telperion's Dungeons & Dragons score is 19," laughed Jacob as he passed easily underneath the huge trunk, which Janus was still holding up with one arm. I followed after him. Then Janus raised the trunk up over his head and swung his way underneath it. He joined us on the other side and put down the huge trunk as effortlessly as if it was no more than a large branch.

"Whoa!" I exclaimed, "Schwarzenegger go home!"

71

"Now all you need is your magic two-handed sword," laughed Jacob, "then you'd be totally unstoppable!"

At the thought of his sword, Janus began sword-fighting with invisible foes, thrusting and jabbing the air with great vigor. We all laughed. "I feel like I'm as strong as an ox," he cried. "Just give me my sword, and I'll show you some real fightin'!"

Jacob and I continued to laugh while Janus went on daring his invisible foes to face him. Then he came to an abrupt stop right in front of Jacob. "If my strength score is 19, then Jacob's—I mean Moncler's— intelligence score must also be 19," he said.

Jacob shrugged his shoulders. "Well, if that's true then all I need is my magic staff..." The moment he said those words, it was as if a bright light flashed in his hand. For a split second, he was holding a long, exquisitely carved wooden staff, adorned with many strange-looking runes and symbols. But it was only there for a split second, then it disappeared again.

"Whoa again!" cried Janus.

"Now what was that?" I asked.

Jacob looked at his hand in amazement. "I think it was Moncler's magic staff," he said.

"Where did it go?" I asked.

"And where did it come from?" cried Janus.

Jacob shrugged his shoulders again. "I have no idea."

We stood like that for a while and looked at each other; then Jacob and Janus turned towards me.

"What?" I said.

"Well, if I'm an Elven Warrior and Jacob is a Wizard, then what are you?" Janus asked.

"I don't know," I said and raised my shoulders. I thought about the sudden flash of light I had seen earlier when I touched my brow.

"But I'm sure we'll find out soon enough," said Jacob and patted me on the back. "Come on, let's get out of this forest. That much my Wizard's intelligence tells me."

"But which way?" I asked.

"Follow me," Jacob replied and began to walk down the narrow path. We followed.

The further we went, the closer the trees seemed to huddle together. Before long, the trees were so close together that you couldn't see the sky. It was like walking in a long dark tunnel made of branches and leaves.

After walking for about half an hour, the dark tunnel of branches and leaves suddenly opened up. We were still completely surrounded by trees on all sides, but where before there had only been 3-4 meters to our leafy ceiling, now there was at least 15-20 meters to the tree tops that surrounded us. And the pathway broadened so it was as if we had stepped into an enormous hall of trees. Then we realized that up ahead, right in the middle of this huge, huge forest hall, there was a large, four-sided pyramid. The pyramid was as big as a pretty large house. From a distance, it looked like it was made of some kind of shiny silver material, and it appeared to be completely smooth on all sides. As we got closer, it became apparent that we were approaching the front of the "house" because there was a large door facing us, covered with all kinds of runes and symbols. We walked slowly up to the massive door and studied the symbols.

"So what do you make of these symbols, Master Wizard?" Janus asked Jacob.

Jacob closed his eyes and let his hands glide slowly across the symbols. "This is the Pyramid of Time and it contains the Akashic Records of the Starseeds living on Planet Earth," he said slowly.

Both Janus and I looked at him in surprise.

"Well don't look at me like that... That's what it says," Jacob said and shrugged his shoulders.

"You truly are a Wizard, Moncler!" chuckled Janus.

"But how do we get in?" I asked.

"And are we supposed to go in?" asked Janus.

Jacob closed his eyes again and let his hands glide across the symbols once more. "Only the Pure of Heart are granted access to the Akashic Records," he said.

"So what does that mean?" Janus asked.

The moment he said that the door vanished into thin air. We found ourselves looking straight into the pyramid. Inside, the pyramid was illuminated by a faint golden light.

"Looks like we must be Pure of Heart," said Jacob and stepped across the threshold, into the pyramid. Janus and I went in after him.

We found ourselves in a large pyramid-shaped chamber. As far as I could see, the stones in the sides of the pyramid were emitting the golden light we saw. Besides that, the chamber was completely empty except for several weird-looking upholstered chairs with high backs. The chairs kind of looked like open pea pods. There was also a strange sound in the chamber, a high-pitched tone that seemed to vibrate all the time, right at the edge of one's hearing.

"Talk about spacey, man!" said Janus in a low voice.

Jacob walked over to the chairs to take a closer look. Janus and I followed him and as we did, we heard the door behind us reappear and close.

"Trapped!" cried Janus.

"I don't think there's anything to fear here," said Jacob.

"There is nothing to fear here—or any place else in the Ashtar Command's Mothership," I said in a clear strong voice.

Jacob and Janus looked at me in surprise. So incredibly sure had I sounded when I uttered these words. As if I knew exactly what I was talking about. And yes, well, it was true. I did know exactly what I was talking about. In fact, I was absolutely certain that there was nothing to fear in this place. I felt the light on my brow shimmering once again, illuminating Jacob and Janus' faces.

"Well, whoever you are, Master Starbrow, you sure are powerful!" said Janus.

I touched my brow and felt once again that strange tingling, right between my eyebrows. The entire room was illumined by a clear white light and I had a sudden glimpse of rows upon rows of bookcases, filled with books and more books and more books. Then the vision disappeared.

"What is it?" Janus asked.

"I think... " I said slowly, "that this place is some kind of library. I think... this library is filled with an enormous amount of information and many, many records of events gone by."

"Yeah..." said Jacob, also feeling the power of our surroundings, "I feel it too... it's as if this place is just bursting with information... and wisdom... and knowing."

"So what are we supposed to do?" asked Janus.

"Just take it all in," said Jacob and sat down in one of the pea pod-shaped chairs. Janus and I followed suit.

The chair was incredibly comfortable. It seemed to fit my body perfectly. My spine was straight and yet I was completely relaxed at the same time. My feet rested firmly on the ground and the soft armrests provided the perfect support.

"Now this is what I call an armchair!" said Janus with a pleasant sigh.

"Sshhh!" said Jacob, "can't you hear that sound?"

74

The faint ringing sound we'd first heard when we stepped into the pyramid was growing louder. As I focused my attention on it, I found it very pleasant to listen to. It was as if the tone made the chamber and my whole body vibrate with pleasure. I felt myself slowly drifting off into a dream-like state.

"Welcome to the Cosmic Library!" We heard a deep, calm voice say. Then an old man with a long brown beard stood before us. He was tall and wore a long dark purple cloak. In his hand, he held a golden staff. And he stood perfectly still before us, regarding us with eyes that glowed and danced like coals in a crackling fire.

"Please remain seated, my dear friends," he said slowly, as he motioned for us to stay in our seats, "... and please relax. You are on your way into the alpha state right now, but you must descend even further my friends, into theta, in order to read the records stored in the Cosmic Library."

"Who are you?" asked Janus in a sleepy voice.

"I AM the Keeper of the Cosmic Library," said the old man and smiled, "and it is my privilege to be your guide. I am now going to lead you through a simultaneous regression so you can review something of your past lives... this will help prepare you for your 5th dimensional training program."

"A simultaneous what...? gulped Janus.

"I think he said simultaneous regression..." I replied.

"Yes I did," said the old man. "So let me explain. As Starseeds or emissaries of the Intergalactic Council, all three of you have had quite a few lifetimes—or incarnations as we are wont to call them—on Planet Earth where you have diligently worked for the enlightenment of all humankind. Yes, dear friends, this is how it is recorded here in the Akashic records... And even though the Intergalactic Council did not previously focus a great deal of attention on Planet Earth, still, the Great White Brotherhood and the Starseeds have been working ceaselessly for thousands of years to spread Enlightenment on Earth. Ever since the downfall and ruin of Atlantis, Cities of Light have been established on all of the Earth's seven continents. Pyramids in Egypt, Peru and Mexico— and highly advanced civilizations in Greece, Tibet and India, just to name a few. And in all these places and at all times, the Spiritual Hierarchy has been at work. And you, the Starseeds, have been there as well—working actively, even though at the moment, you do not remember. But now the time for remembering has come...!"

4

Total Recall

The pleasant sound of the ringing tone in the chamber grew and grew. I felt as if every cell in my body was beginning to vibrate at the same frequency as the tone and it was very relaxing. In fact, I felt as if I was floating on a soft cloud, wandering somewhere between a beautiful dream and a gentle wake-up call. The Keeper's deep, comforting voice rolled gently through the chamber:

"Close your eyes, my friends—and relax. Breathe deeply and let the air flow gently—gently and deeply—in and out of your lungs. Feel your body becoming heavier and heavier and heavier..."

I closed my eyes and followed his instructions. Soon the sound of the old man's soothing voice, combined with the pleasant high tone, put me into a state of deep relaxation. I felt my body become heavier and heavier, until I couldn't feel it at all. I was nothing but a thought, floating gently in space, a thought, a wisp of consciousness, which was now being gently guided by the old man's voice...

"Imagine yourselves standing in front of an elevator. The doors slide open and you step into the elevator. The doors close. On the wall besides you there is a panel with a button for each floor. Ask your heart, your Inner Wisdom, which floor it is Highest Wisdom for you to visit."

I saw myself stepping into the elevator. Jacob and Janus were at my side. I looked at all the floors we could visit and knew immediately that we were supposed to get off at the 5th floor.

"Push the button for the floor which feels right to you," said the Keeper.

"The 5th floor," said Janus. None of us were in doubt.

I pushed button No. 5 and the elevator began to rise. It was a strange sensation, as if a light breeze was bearing us upward towards white clouds above. After a few seconds, the elevator stopped.

As the doors opened, the Keeper said, "Look out of the elevator and tell me what you see."

We looked out and found we were in fact high up in the clouds. Below us, a beautiful countryside came into view. We could see majestic trees and woods, green fields and crystal clear streams. It all looked incredibly idyllic and untouched. The landscape was level except for a single tall green hill that rose up right in the middle of the picturesque panorama. There was a clear lake surrounding the hill, filled with reeds and water lilies. And the hill rose up in the middle of the lake, like a proud island. As I looked at the green hill in the middle of the lake, I felt the thrill of recognition.

"What do you see?" asked the Keeper.

None of us replied. We were each totally engrossed in the beautiful landscape, which stretched out before us.

"Move closer," instructed the Keeper, "focus on something you find interesting.

I focused all my attention on the hill. The moment I did that, I felt myself float out of the elevator and soar towards the hill. I could feel Jacob and Janus soaring by my side.

We quickly approached the lake and the hill. At the edge of the lake, there was a little village. The houses looked old-fashioned. They were low and thatched and judging from the way people were dressed, we were in the Middle Ages—or even further back in time. In the middle of the village, there was a little church. I could hear bells ringing in the church tower.

"Time for mass," Jacob murmured at my side, "It all seems so familiar..."

We floated over the village all the way to the edge of the lake. I kept staring at the green hill in the middle of the lake. I knew I had seen it before. But where? Then I remembered! But of course! It was Glastonbury Tor, that legendary hill in the South of England—the one Elmar had a picture of hanging in his dining room. No wonder it seemed so familiar.

I remembered that Elmar had told me that "Tor" was the old Celtic word for hill and that Glastonbury Tor was one of the most remarkable hills in all of England. But now, as we soared towards the Tor, there was something very different about it. At first I couldn't put my finger on what it was, but then I realized that in the picture Elmar had taken, Glastonbury Tor was located right in the middle of the rolling

77

countryside of southwesterly England—and that on top of the hill there stood a lone medieval tower. The hill that we were now soaring towards had no tower on top! Instead, there was a large stone circle on top of the hill. And there was something else that was different, too! Yes... the hill was surrounded by water on all sides. As we moved closer to the hill, I felt great power radiating from it. Then I remembered that Elmar also told me that Glastonbury Tor was a spiritual Power Spot or Interdimensional Vortex on Planet Earth. According to Elmar, many people called Glastonbury Tor the Heart Chakra of the World.

"I think the hill is Glastonbury Tor," I heard myself saying, "except that the tower is missing and the hill is surrounded by water."

That was when I remembered that Elmar had told me that many hundreds of years ago, Glastonbury Tor had been surrounded on all sides by water. And that the island or hill in the middle of the lake was then called Avalon. Avalon was the home of the priestesses and druids who worshipped the Goddess. It was first much later in history that the Christians destroyed the stone circle and built a church on the hilltop. Later an earthquake had destroyed most of the church. All that remained after the quake was the square tower, which stands on the hilltop to this very day...

"Yes, I am quite sure it's Glastonbury Tor," I said again, "the only question is when."

"Can you see any people?" said the Keeper's voice inside our heads.

We had now come to the edge of the lake. I could see three people standing underneath some trees. They were apple trees and there were apple blossoms in the trees. It must have been late spring or early summer. I took a deep breath and inhaled the sweet scent of the apple trees. Avalon, Appleland...

"I can see three people standing by the shore of the lake," said Janus. "They all have horses—and it looks like they're wearing clothes from the Middle Ages."

"Move closer," instructed the Keeper, "and take a closer look at them."

We soared all the way down to the ground and stood next to the three of them. We must have been invisible because they didn't seem to notice us at all. We stood looking at them. One of them was a tall young man wearing chain mail. He had a bright sword at his side and a shield. He was sitting on his horse; he looked like a knight. At his side, there was another young man. He was dressed in a brown monk's robe—a large cross hung around his neck. His eyes were deep and clear. The third

78

person was a beautiful young woman with long, golden-red curly hair. She was wearing a long white robe and she had a thin silver belt around her waist. Hanging from her belt were several small leather pouches and a long, sharp silver dagger with many strange symbols carved on it.

"Move closer to them," said the Keeper again. "See if you recognize any of them."

I walked up close to them and looked at them carefully. That's when I discovered that I was the young woman!

"I'm the woman!" I gasped in surprise.

"I'm the monk," said Jacob.

"And I'm the knight," said Janus.

"See if you can step into their bodies," the Keeper said to us. "In order to step into their bodies, you have to stand behind each of them. Then you just move forward into their bodies."

I did as the Keeper said and placed myself behind the young woman. Then I took a step forward and stepped into her body. To my great surprise, I found that I instantly merged with her. I immediately felt right at home in the woman's body, as if it were my own. I found myself looking out of her eyes. I felt how the gentle summer breeze caressed her small, slender shape. Then I looked and saw Jacob in the body of the young monk—and Janus in the body of the young knight.

"Talk about freaky!" cried Janus.

"You're not kidding," I said. "Will you look at me, I'm a woman!" It was kind of a weird feeling.

"I always knew you had it in you!" chuckled Jacob.

"We have all been both men and women in our past lives," said the Keeper sternly, "it's all part of the curriculum of Test Zone Earth."

"So, is this one of our past lives that we're experiencing now?" asked Janus.

"Yes it is," said the Keeper. "Now see if you can learn something more about that life. Who are you, Starbrow?"

I focused my attention on the woman's body I was now inhabiting and immediately felt a stream of information flood my consciousness.

"My name is Dana," I said. "I was named after the Star Elves, after the Tuatha De Danann, because the priestesses and druids on Avalon are still in contact with them."

I looked across the shores of the lake towards the green hill in the middle. I could see small houses and places of worship at the foot of the hill. And there were paths leading up towards the top of the hill and the holy stones where we... The information passed through my consciousness at lightning speed, the experiences of several years, all compressed into just a few seconds.

"I am a priestess of Avalon. Avalon is the island in the middle of the lake and Glastonbury Tor is at its center," I continued. "I've lived here ever since I was a child. This is the only world I know. The only contact I've had with the world beyond Avalon has been when I used the 'Sight'." I touched my forehead and felt a tingling sensation between my eyebrows.

"The 'Sight' is not so well-developed in all of the priestesses on Avalon. All humans have this ability, but only very few of us have learned how to use the 'Sight' and direct it at will. I am one of these few. With the 'Sight', I am able to see what takes place in the outside world... in the world on the other side of the mists of Avalon. But there is also another who gives me information about the outside world..."

"Who is that?" asked the Keeper.

"It's Jacob," I said and looked at the young monk who was standing before me.

"Yes, it's true," said Jacob. "My name is Gaius and I am one of the monks who lives in the monastery at the Christian church in Glastonbury." Jacob pointed towards the little village nestled by the lake. "Glastonbury Church was the first Christian Church in the world. Joseph of Arimethea, one of the disciples of Jesus, came here many centuries ago and founded the church. Over yonder lies Wearyall Hill."

Jacob waved in the direction of another hill, which was a bit smaller than the Tor. It was on the other side of the lake and some distance from Avalon.

"They say that when Joseph and his companions came to the hill after a very long journey," continued Jacob, "Joseph climbed to the top and planted his staff in the ground. Then he said 'We are weary all'. Thus was the hill named. And on that very spot where Joseph planted his staff, there grew a thorn tree. The only thorn tree in the entire world which blooms in wintertime, in memory of Christ and his great gift to mankind."

Janus and I stared at Jacob/Gaius in his monk's robe. Also in this lifetime, Jacob was a man of great learning!

"What is the connection between Dana and Gaius?" asked the Keeper.

I searched my memory bank for the answer. "The Christians condemn the Goddess worshippers and the Goddess worshippers condemn the

Christians." As I spoke, I could feel the sadness in Dana. "All my life I have been unable to understand why it has to be like that... why there should be any conflict between the God of the Christians and the Goddess, our Great Mother..."

"Because in truth," Jacob said, interrupting, "both the Christians and the priestesses are talking about one and the same Universal Creative Force."

"One day as I was sailing on the Lake, I saw Gaius meditating by the shore of the lake," I said.

"I was praying with all my heart and soul, praying to God for understanding and union with the so-called pagans of Avalon," said Jacob.

"By using the "Sight", I recognized who Gaius really was... I saw his prayers and felt his good intentions, so I sailed over to him," I said.

"This was how our friendship began," continued Jacob. "It was an intense spiritual meeting between two kindred souls and between the teachings of Christ and the old druid tradition. Together, we realized that we actually had far more in common than we could ever have imagined. In fact, we discovered that what we had perceived as our differences were basically just our different rituals and terminologies..."

"And if they weren't that, they were just plain, ordinary misunderstandings," I added. "So every day we met in secret and we meditated together. The more I meditated with Gaius, the clearer my "Sight" became. It did not deteriorate—as the other priestesses had often warned. They believed that any contact with Christians affected one's ability to use the 'Sight'".

"For my part, I found that my knowledge and understanding of the Wonders of Creation were greatly enhanced by my meetings with Dana. I did not become bewitched by contact with a priestess as the other monks had warned," said Jacob.

"We both shared a burning desire for peace and harmony in Britain. We longed for peace between all the warring factions, between the Christians and druids, between all the lesser kings, and between the Celts, Romans, Saxons, Scots and all the other peoples who were fighting each other," I said.

"But even though we longed for peace, we did not know how to go about creating lasting peace and harmony in our beloved homeland," said Jacob.

"Yes," I said, "we considered trying to help negotiate peace meetings between the warring factions and fairly dividing the country up into territories... but deep inside, we both knew that efforts like this could not and would not lead to very much. In our heart of hearts, we knew that there had to be a more secure and lasting way to create peace and harmony in the land."

"And what was that way?" interrupted the Keeper.

Jacob and I didn't answer. I focused all my attention on being fully present in Dana's mind, but no answer to the Keeper's question surfaced. It was as if her mind was shrouded in a mist of doubt.

"How does Telperion fit into all this?" the Keeper then asked.

Jacob and I looked at Janus.

"My name is Loran," said Janus. "Sir Loran. I have just been appointed a knight at the court of King Arthur and granted a seat at the Round Table. Camelot is my home. And it is from Camelot that King Arthur sends his knights out into the land to maintain law and order. Arthur has a New Vision. A New Vision of one unified, peaceful Britain. And he is assisted in his work by Merlin the great Wizard..."

"Merlin is from Avalon," I cried. Information from Dana once again welled up in my consciousness. "He also has the 'Sight'!"

"And Merlin is also well-respected by the Christians," said Jacob. "Because he respects their religion and says that all Gods are the One God. Merlin is truly a spiritual bridge-builder."

"Using the 'Sight', Merlin has contacted all who are of like mind, all who share the same desire for one unified, peaceful Britain. And he has done so because he has discovered the Secret!" I cried, now full of excitement.

"What Secret?" asked the Keeper.

"The Secret of how to create lasting peace and harmony in the land!" I continued. "And it is for this reason, and this reason alone, that Merlin is inviting a select group of carefully chosen souls to a secret council at Tintagel Castle in Cornwall. Merlin and King Arthur are calling together this special group to initiate all of the invited parties into the Great Secret. Gaius and I are among those who have been invited."

"And I was sent to escort you," said Janus. "In the deepest secrecy, King Arthur has sent his knights to the four corners of the land to summon and escort the chosen ones to the secret council at Tintagel."

"Why in all secrecy?" asked the Keeper.

"Because there is strong opposition throughout the land towards Arthur and Merlin's plans," said Janus. "The dark forces have been spreading

82

rapidly. King Lot of Orkney, for example, poises a very grave threat to peace because he wants to claim the throne for himself. He will do anything to ruin Arthur and Merlin's plans and unfortunately, many of the Northern kings support him. And then there is the constant threat of invasion by the wild Vikings from the North."

"And besides that," interrupted Jacob, "there is great opposition from my Christian brethren who refuse to cooperate with the Goddess worshippers. That is why the council has to meet in the deepest secrecy."

"If the other priestesses knew that I was collaborating with a Christian monk, I would be banished immediately from Avalon," I said.

"King Arthur and Merlin are aware of all this, which is why they've sent out their knights to escort and protect you," said Janus.

"Good," said the Keeper. "Now move forward to the next important event in that lifetime."

Avalon and the green countryside became unclear and started to fade. The next thing we knew, the three of us were in the midst of a raging thunderstorm. We were standing in front of the gate of a huge castle. The wind raged and howled as we banged on the iron door in the gate.

5

Four Is Company

Dana speaks:

The first two days after our departure from Avalon, the sun shone brightly—and we made good progress on our journey westward to Tintagel Castle on the coast of Cornwall. At night, we slept outdoors under the stars so as not to attract any attention, and the three of us greatly enjoyed the mild summer nights. But then, after those first two days, it began to rain. And as each hour passed, it rained harder and harder. By evening, we found ourselves caught in the middle of a raging storm. It was impossible to continue our journey, and since we didn't want to spend the night outdoors, we decided to seek shelter in a castle we saw on the horizon, not far from the muddy road. So we rode up to the castle as fast as our poor horses could bear us. The huge castle was surrounded by a deep moat. Loran walked over the drawbridge and knocked on the iron door that was built into the massive gate.

"Who goes there?" cried a guard's voice from behind the heavy gate.

"Three travelers seeking shelter from the storm," cried Loran in a loud voice, above the fierce wind.

The guard's ruddy face peered out from one of the hatches in the gate.

"State your names and your purpose!" he called down to us.

Loran said that he and Gaius were tradesmen, and that I was their serving woman. He told the guard we were on our way to Tintagel to offer our services to the King's entourage. The guard considered this for a moment, then told us to wait while he went to ask his superior. When he returned, he opened the hatch again and said we would be permitted to spend the night in the stables. I drew a sigh of relief. After spending the whole day riding in the pouring rain, the thought of sleeping snug and dry sounded good to all of us, even if it was in a stable and we were surrounded by piles of horse dung!

The guards slowly cranked the great gate open and then one of them led us through the courtyard towards the stables. The courtyard was deserted because of the storm, but we could see lights shining brightly in many of the windows high above us. As we made our way across the muddy courtyard, I looked over at the bright lights that shined out from the windows of the main building. We heard loud, boisterous voices coming from what I guessed must have been the main hall where the castle's inhabitants were probably having dinner. That was when I became aware that a richly clad nobleman with a fat face was looking out of one of the windows of the main building. He seemed to be following our progress across the courtyard; I had the distinct feeling he was the lord of the castle. And I knew he was looking at me in particular. In fact, I felt his penetrating gaze follow me all the way to the stable doors.

Once inside, we'd barely finished hanging up our soaking clothes when a soldier entered the stables and told us that his lord and master, Lord Bryn, had asked us to dine with him in the main building. And not only that, the soldier said his master cordially invited us to spend the night in one of his chambers in the main building.

We gave each other a puzzled look. Why this sudden gesture of hospitality? For two lowly tradesmen and their serving maid? It didn't make much sense, but we were too exhausted to give it much thought. So we thanked the soldier for the kind invitation and followed him up to the main building. He led us to a great hall where about fifty people were eating and drinking noisily. We saw the lord of the castle, sitting at the end of the hall at the head of a long, wide table, eating and drinking with several other noblemen. I realized at once he was the man who had stared at me so strangely when we crossed the courtyard earlier. When he saw the three of us enter the hall, he eyed me with the same strange look and then turned to say something to the other noblemen. They all began to roar with laughter. For some reason, their behavior made me feel very uncomfortable. I was about to say something to Loran and Gaius, but they were too far ahead of me and probably only thinking of the prospect of a good hot meal. The soldier led us to his lord and then introduced us. Without paying any attention to Loran and Gaius, Lord Bryn waved his hand and motioned for me to approach.

"Well, well, well... will you look at this one" he said and prodded his elbow into the corpulent man sitting next to him. Then he bared a row of uneven, yellow teeth and said to me. "Sit down besides me little one, and *tell me what brings you here. Your servants may dine with the other servants."*

"But they are not my servants..." I said and looked at Loran and Gaius who were finally waking up to what was going on. Before I could say more, a seat was made for me next to the lord—and Loran and Gaius were being led back to one of the servant's tables.

"This is no kind of weather for a fair maid such as you to be out and about in..." Lord Bryn said. His voice was slurred and his breath stank of ale. As he spoke, he leaned towards me and put his hand on my thigh. In despair, I looked towards Loran and Gaius for help. They were watching us and it was plain that they now had fully grasped the seriousness of the situation. But what could they do? My heart sunk. I knew that if they protested, the lord's guardsmen would immediately set upon them and they'd probably be beaten or thrown out of the castle without so much as a word. And if Loran said that he was a knight at King Arthur's Court, he would reveal our true identity.

I scanned the hall, desperately looking for a way out. That was when I noticed a young man sitting at a table not far from me. He couldn't have been much more than 16 years old. He was watching me intently with his clear blue eyes. I was struck by his sensitive face. Our eyes met for a brief moment and he nodded. There was something about the way he looked at me which made me think that he was different from the other people in this dark and sinister castle. But before I could think more of him, Lord Bryn pulled me even closer to him and started to caress my thigh. I tried to remove his hand without causing a stir while I silently prayed to the Goddess...

It was the most unpleasant dinner of my entire life. I was so mortified by Lord Bryn's uncouth behavior that not a morsel of food passed my lips. He continued to paw at me and I kept trying to avoid him and his vile touch in whatever way I could without invoking his wrath. Finally, he waved to one of his servants to escort us up to our rooms. Three soldiers led us out of the hall. I let out a sigh of relief... perhaps he was finally going to leave me alone! But when the soldiers turned down a new passageway, my heart sank because I knew in my heart of hearts we were being led to the wing of the castle where Lord Bryn's chambers were located.

"Are you alright, Dana?" whispered Gaius, hoping the soldiers wouldn't notice.

"Oh Gaius, my friend, you must have seen what was going on!" I said, *trying to keep my voice from trembling.*

"Let us pray that it's over now," he muttered softly and reached for the cross around his neck.

"I have a really bad feeling about all this," was all I managed to whisper back before two of the soldiers grabbed my arm and led me to one side. The other soldier motioned for Loran and Gaius to go in the other direction.

"What's going on here?" cried Loran and reached for his sword. But before he could draw it, three guards sprang out of nowhere with swords drawn. One of them held his sword point directly to Loran's throat.

"Sorry, my friend," laughed the guard, *"but only pretty maidens are allowed beyond this point!"*

I tried to resist but it was too late. The two soldiers twisted my arm and held it firmly behind my back, pulling me away from Loran and Gaius. Gaius crossed himself. Loran was beside himself, but we knew it was futile to resist at this point.

I was half dragged up another flight of stairs and shoved into a large chamber with rich tapestries hanging from the walls. A fire blazed and crackled in the fireplace. Lord Bryn was already there, seated in a massive wooden chair in front of the fireplace. To his right was a huge bed.

"Come in my pretty one," he said, *"come in."* The two soldiers immediately left the room and closed the door behind them. The loud thud of the door echoed like a death toll in my mind.

"Over here is where I will take you," he said, pointing to the huge bed.

"You have no right to treat me like this," I replied, my voice as cold as ice.

A look of surprise flashed across his face. No doubt, he expected a frightened serving maid, not a woman who would resist. He looked at me for a moment and then smiled. He was going to make me pay for my impudence.

"A poor woman like you, a mere serving maid," he said and leered, *"would do well to show her lord and master how much she appreciates his hospitality! Don't make the mistake of trying my patience!"*

I didn't move, but stood my ground.

He got up and started to walk towards me.

I drew myself up to my full height. *"The Lord Bryn does well to beware! I am a priestess of Avalon,"* I said proudly, *"and I am sworn to the service of the Goddess."* I parted the folds of my cloak so he could see that I was wearing the white robes of a priestess underneath. "If you so much as lay a finger upon me, the Curse of the Ancient Order of Avalon will be placed upon you and your offspring for three generations!" I said in a mighty voice that echoed throughout his chamber.

My words shocked him and he took a step backwards in alarm. I knew that he was both surprised and afraid. Crossing a priestess of Avalon was no laughing matter, not even for a powerful lord. I saw his grim countenance suddenly twist with doubt and rage, and for a brief moment, I thought that he would relent and let me go. Silence hung in the chamber for what seemed an endless moment... but no, it was not to be. His lust and his towering rage won out. He bent over and drew a long dagger from his boot. Then he lunged at me and held it up to my face.

"So you're one of those god-forsaken devil-worshippers, are you!" he said, his lips quivering with rage.

I moved quickly and grabbed a large embossed silver cup from the table next to his chair and smashed it with all my might into his forehead. He dropped his dagger as blood spurted from the gash. He stumbled backwards.

"Guards!" he howled, holding his head with both hands.

The door flew open and the guards came charging back into the room with swords drawn. I looked frantically for something to defend myself with. My little silver dagger, the one I always carried with me, the one from Avalon, had been taken from my pocket on my way to Lord Bryn's chambers.

Next thing I knew, my head exploded with pain—and for a moment I lost consciousness. When I came to, I found myself pinned to the great bed with the two guards holding my arms as Lord Bryn parted my robes and spread my legs. Blood gushed from the wound on his forehead and he panted like a wild animal.

"I'll show you a thing or two... accursed witch!" he roared as he fumbled with his breeches and tried to keep my legs spread apart at the same time. I fought like a wild cat, kicking and biting the guards who were holding my arms. I felt another blow and tasted blood in my mouth. I wasn't sure if it was my own blood or Lord Bryn's. Holy Mother Goddess, I thought, help your poor daughter!

The next moment a dagger whistled through the air and struck Lord Bryn right in the neck. He let out a hideous groan as his face crumpled and blood spurted from his neck. He let go of me and keeled over backwards. The soldiers also let go of me and reached for their swords. I heard Loran bellow as he came flying through the window, "Let go of her, you devils!" He landed right next to the bed, sword in hand. Gaius was right behind him. The poor soldiers were no match for Loran's wrath. Before they could collect their wits, Loran had beheaded the one and run the other through. Gaius ran to my side.

"Dana!" he cried in alarm, "are you hurt?"

"Ahhh Gaius, my head..." I said and held my aching head. "You came just in the nick of time."

But there was no time.

"Gaius!" cried Loran as he ran towards the door, "we haven't a moment to lose... help me block the door. I hear more of them coming this way!"

"But how are we going to get out?" I cried and sat up gingerly in the bed. My head was still throbbing.

"The same way we came in," said Loran as he and Gaius shoved a huge table in front of the door. They had barely moved the table when the door was penetrated by several swords. Someone blew a horn in the hallway outside the door, sounding the alarm!

"The bed!" cried Loran. I tumbled out of the bed and the three of us pushed it in front of the door. Then Gaius and Loran piled the bed with all the chairs and tables that were in the room. A heavy axe began hacking at the door.

"Let's get out of here, before it's too late!" cried Loran and ran to the window. Gaius and I ran after him. Loran put the rope in my hand and pointed to the next window, a few yards away.

"Swing over to that window," he said.

"And after that?" I asked.

"Trust me, I have a plan," he said with an angelic smile.

I grabbed the rope and climbed up on to the window sill. We were on the fourth floor so it was a long way down. It was still pouring outside but I enjoyed the feeling of the rain as it washed the blood from my face and head.

"May the Goddess be with me," I whispered to myself. Then I held the rope tightly and leaped from the window sill, swinging myself towards the window Loran had pointed at. I landed almost perfectly and grabbed the window sill and pulled myself into the room. It seemed I had landed in the guardroom, and fortunately for us the room was empty because all the guards were busy chopping down the door to the next room, trying to capture us. I swung the rope back to Loran. Gaius came swinging over next, and then Loran. Not a moment too soon because just as Loran came flying through the window, we heard the shouts of the guards as they crashed through our barricade and charged into Lord Bryn's room.

"Run for it," cried Loran, "go, go!" We ran out of the guardroom and sped down the hall. A moment or two later, the guards discovered what had happened and came charging out of Lord Bryn's chambers after us. Horns blared and the chase was on. We did not stop to look back. We reached the great staircase we'd originally come up and flew down the stairs. Two soldiers were waiting for us at the bottom. Loran leaped on the one, while Gaius and I charged the other. Gaius drew his mace and I held the dagger I had taken from one of the dead guards. The soldier aimed a savage blow at Gaius who barely had time to duck but I managed to save the situation by somersaulting forward and planting my dagger deep in his thigh. He howled in pain and tried to strike back at me, but before his blow reached me, Gaius had smashed his skull in with his mace.

"Nice work, Dana," Loran said, after he had finished off the other soldier. "Where did you learn that trick?"

"Did you think all they teach the priestesses at Avalon is how to collect herbs?" I said and dried the blood off my dagger. "Where to now?"

"This way," said Loran and pointed to his right. We sped down a long, dark hallway. At the end of the hallway, the passageway suddenly split in two. Loran lunged down the left passageway, it was a dead end. He turned round and we lunged down the right. Another dead end.

"What now?" I shouted.

"Damn!" cried Loran.

"What about your plan?" I yelled.

"This is the plan," groaned Gaius.

"This is the plan?" I cried in despair. "To be trapped like rats with nowhere to run!"

We turned and looked back up the long hallway we'd just come down. In the distance, we could hear the sound of a large party of soldiers coming after us like thunder.

Loran stood up tall.

"Stay behind me," he cried and clenched his teeth, expecting a fight to the death. He raised his sword and readied himself for the final battle. I looked down the two blind alleys in despair. There was no way out. We were trapped!

90

I took a deep breath and readied myself. I thought once more of the Goddess and was just about to turn and face the approaching soldiers when I heard a soft voice calling from the left passageway. "Pst! Milady, milady...this way, milady, if you want to escape. Come! Hurry!"

I blinked and looked back down the dimly lit passageway and realized that one of the great stones in the wall had been moved aside. In the opening stood the young man with the bright blue eyes who'd been watching me so intently in the main hall earlier that evening. He motioned frantically for me to come.

"This way, milady, hurry!" he cried excitedly. "Hurry, I know a way out!"

I grabbed Gaius and Loran and pointed towards the young man who stood beckoning to us from the opening in the passageway. "It looks like the Goddess is with us today!"

We stormed back down the passageway and crawled through the opening. The soldiers were right on our heels. Loran cut off the arm of the foremost soldier with one fell swoop as he tried to stop us from closing the opening. Fortunately for us, our new friend seemed to know the secret mechanism that locked the stone back in place. It could not be opened from the other side. We drew some deep breaths and looked around.

We found ourselves in a dark, narrow passage. We could stand up, but it was so narrow that we had to move sideways. Our new friend had a torch and was already a good way ahead of us down the narrow passage.

"Hurry," he cried, "There's not a moment to spare... Lord Bryn knows this secret passageway and knows where it ends. He uses it often for his nightly excursions. If we do not make haste, we will be greeted by a rain of swords at the other end."

"But Lord Bryn is dead," I said. "Loran killed him... with a dagger right in the neck."

"He did?" Our young friend stopped and gazed approvingly at Loran. "I knew it would happen sooner or later. In the end, justice is always done... in the end." Then he looked at the ground. "That must be a sign that I made the right choice."

"But for heaven's sake," said Gaius, "what if Lord Bryn was not the only one who knows where this passage ends...!"

"He's right," said Loran, "let's get out of here!"

"Follow me," said our friend.

At the end of the passage, there was a wooden ladder that led down to

91

a very narrow, old staircase. At the end of the staircase, there was another staircase, and another. Finally, we seemed to come to the lowest level and our friend led us down another passage, which suddenly came to another dead end.

"Not again!" cried Gaius.

"Do you think I would have led you so far in vain!" cried the young man. At once he began to remove the large stones from the wall. They made loud thudding sounds as they hit the ground. When he had removed enough, we looked out of the opening and saw that we'd reached the outer wall of the castle. Down below us was the churning water of the moat. It was still pouring outside.

"This is the only way!" he cried and motioned for us to jump into the swirling water below. We weren't that high up, no more than 10 feet from the water so I went first. I crawled through the hole and jumped into the swirling black water below. The others quickly followed. I gasped for breath as I fought against the weight of my clothes as they dragged me down towards the bottom. Loran grabbed my hair and pulled me up. I sputtered for air. He held me up for another moment and then we swam towards the other side as fast as we could. When we reached the muddy shore, the sound of horns was already blaring from the castle behind us.

"They've discovered our escape route!" I cried, gasping for breath and struggling with the weight of my wet robes.

We crawled ashore.

"Follow me!" said our friend, once again taking charge. "It will take them a few minutes before they get down to the stables. And when they do, they will discover that their horses are gone. And by that time we will be far, far away."

He ran swiftly into the forest and we followed him as best we could, gray shadows in the gray stormy night.

We sat in a cave and warmed ourselves around a small fire. The raging storm had calmed down a bit, but it was still raining outside. After our young rescuer had led us through the forest for a few minutes, we came to a clearing where four horses stood. Three of them were our own horses. How our young rescuer had managed to get them there, we never

found out. But grateful indeed were we at the sight of them. We sprang up on them and rode deep into the forest as fast as we could. After about an hour's ride, with many detours to the left and right, he led us through some hills and valleys until we at last came to a cave whose opening was well hidden behind a dense patch of thorn bushes. Once inside, we discovered our young friend had a quite a few supplies stacked in yonder corner, a bit of food, some blankets and enough firewood to get us dry. Now he was tending the fire and preparing a meal for us.

Gaius was bathing my wound while I prepared a healing ointment of the herbs I had with me in my little leather pouch.

"How did you manage to get our horses out into the clearing?" Loran asked the young man.

"I am... err... was... in charge of Lord Bryn's stables," he answered.

"Ah," said Gaius, "so that's how you knew the horses wouldn't be where they were supposed to be when the soldiers arrived!"

"Exactly," he said and laughed softly. "It's going to take them some time before they're able to round up all the horses and bridle them again."

"Well done, my lad," said Loran and patted him on the back.

"You've never told us your name," I turned and looked at him.

"Aran is my name, milady," said our rescuer.

"Ah... Aran!" I said, pronouncing it slowly because it was suddenly dear to me.

"We owe you our lives, Aran," said Gaius while he spread the healing ointment over the wound on the back of my head. It stung a bit, but I knew that the wound would be all but gone in a few days.

"How can we ever repay you?" asked Loran.

"It will be easy enough," Aran shot back with a smile.

"What ever do you mean?" said Gaius as we eyed him curiously.

"Take me with you on your journey," he said.

"Take you with us?" laughed Gaius, trying to brush off the matter. "But we're just simple tradesmen on our way south to make our fortune. Why would you ever want to join up with the likes of us?"

"That's a tale you'll have a hard time getting me to believe!" cried Aran in return. The boy definitely had his wits about him. "I've met many a tradesman in my short life, but none who carry magic potions and healing ointments with them—nor any who bear great swords and fight like you do," he said, pointing at Loran's sword, which was set with many precious gems.

I looked into Aran's clear blue eyes as he spoke. Even though it was plain that he came from very humble origins, there was something else about him, too. A slightly different air, a sense of nobility. An unusual purity in his countenance. And when he spoke there was a fine glow in his eyes. As I watched him, I felt the point between my brows begin to tingle.

"It's no use trying to hide anything from him," I said to Gaius and Loran, "I am quite sure he has the 'Sight', quite sure. Even though he's not aware of it yet. Tell me Aran, who do you think we are?"

Aran stood up and collected himself. Then he looked at me. "I don't know what it is... But the first time I saw you, milady..." he bowed his head and mumbled something inaudible. Then he took courage and began again, "... when you entered the great hall... I knew there was something special about you, milady, and about the three of you," he said and lifted his head. "You're not like the others... I don't really know what it is, but something tells me that it has something to do with... King Arthur... and Merlin..."

My eyes met Gaius' and I nodded to him.

"You're right, Aran," said Gaius. "You're so very right. We are indeed on our way to meet King Arthur and Merlin. And our mission is a secret one... to create peace and harmony in Britain."

"Take me with you!" cried Aran eagerly. "Oh please kind sir! It's what I've been dreaming of my whole life, to meet Merlin and King Arthur and to fight for peace and justice."

The three of us looked long and hard at Aran. No one spoke a word as the hidden meaning of our near fatal adventure in the castle began to unfold before my eyes. Then I sighed and said, "Alright, Aran... You're coming with us."

After we had eaten the frugal meal Aran so carefully prepared, Loran, Gaius and I rolled ourselves up in our blankets around the fire to get some sleep. Aran took the first watch. He sat quietly by the fire, tending it and poking at it now and again to keep it from going out. As I lay there, wrapped in the warm blankets, I found myself gazing out of the cave. Outside, the rain had stopped and the dark storm clouds were giving way to patches of clear starry sky. I felt sleep creeping up on me

and I closed my eyes.

As I drifted off, I became aware of a voice, a clear, melodious voice that began to sing, ever so softly. The song was beautiful, yet sad. At first, I was only faintly aware of the song. As if it were waves upon a distant shore, coming from afar... from the Western Sea. And the words... they were fair words, fair indeed. Fair and strange, about the Land on the Other Side. Then the melody waxed stronger and the words rang clear in my heart and mind:

Who will solve the riddle?
Who will tell the tale?
Who will ride on after us?
After we set sail?

Who will know the magic sign?
Who will find the gate?
Who will wake up to their fate,
Before it is too late?

I knew you when the mystery was still untold
I knew you in your younger days, before you grew old
I knew you in your sunny days, the days of wine and mirth
I knew you in the summertime, way before your birth

Who will solve the riddle?
Who will tell the tale?
Who will ride on after us?
After we set sail?

Who will know the magic sign?
Who will find the gate?
Who will wake up to their fate,
Before it is too late?

I knew you when the world was young and meadows still were fair
I knew you when you hid the secret in your golden hair
I knew you in your younger days, the days of silver song
I knew you, yes I knew you, before the days grew long

95

I opened my eyes and looked around. It was Aran who was singing, singing... in that clear, melodious voice of his...

As I witnessed myself lying there as Dana, listening to Aran sing, I realized that I had heard Aran's song many times before. It was the same song that Elmar used to sing for me when he felt the call of adventure. The song had touched me deeply when Elmar sang it, and it touched me now as I in my life as Dana heard Aran sing it in the cave. But how could Aran be singing the very same song that Elmar used to sing for me?

"Look at Aran," said the Keeper of the Cosmic Library. "Look at him carefully. Is he someone that you know in this lifetime?"

I looked at Aran's pure, eager face, his clear blue eyes, the way he smiled... and then I knew! But of course! "Aran is Elmar!" I exclaimed and stared in wonder at the 16-year old lad who was sitting by the fire, singing. It really was him! It really was! Aran was Elmar—or Elmar was Aran! I wanted to jump up and hug him with all my might, but I knew that wasn't possible. This was a past life regression. I was watching a movie that had already been made.

Who will solve the riddle?
Who will tell the tale?
Who will ride on after us?
After we set sail?

Who will know the magic sign?
Who will find the gate?
Who will wake up to their fate,
Before it is too late?

Spellbound, I watched myself lying there as Dana, listening to Aran/Elmar sing about the Land on the Other Side. I couldn't jump up from my blankets and hug him, but this was almost as good. When Aran finished his song, Dana looked out of the cave. The dark storm clouds were completely gone and one could clearly see the stars. Among them was one lone golden star, which shone far more brightly than any of the others.

6

The Secret

I will never forget the first time I saw Tintagel Castle. We had been riding all day through the rolling Cornish countryside with our new companion Aran at our sides, when suddenly we caught our first glimpse of the great ocean in the West. The great Atlantic Ocean, which I had heard tell of, but never before had seen with my own eyes. Suddenly it was there—in the distance before us—a vast, shimmering band of light, twinkling on the horizon. Then we lost sight of it as we passed through several more valleys, and then we emerged again and the whole coastline lay spread out before us like a glittering jewel. As far as the eye could see, we saw the gigantic cliffs facing westward into that vast expanse of ocean. Directly before us, jutting out from the rocky coast, was a huge island of rock, which towered up from the sea like a powerful fortress. We were not in doubt; it was Tintagel Head. We rode forward through the howling wind and saw how the rocky island rose up, hundreds of feet above the Atlantic Ocean crashing mercilessly at its feet. From the top of the craggy isle, its steep sides descended directly into the pounding surf below. And on top was Tintagel Castle or part of it. In truth, the castle was made up of two fortresses. The larger part of the castle was located on Tintagel Head itself, while the smaller part was situated right next to the Head on the mainland. The two parts of the castle were connected by a massive wooden bridge that extended perilously across the raging sea below.

As we approached the castle, we got off our horses to walk the last bit of the way through the tiny village of Tintagel. We were glad to get out of the wind as we walked between the tiny, thatched-roofed houses of the village. Then as we emerged from the village, we caught a glimpse of the magnificent coastline again and saw that there were several ships moored in the bay on the northern side of Tintagel Head.

We came to the castle gate and Loran presented our party to the guards. They bowed and made way for us and Loran led us quickly through the great gate and the castle grounds—and over the long wooden bridge, which led to the rocky island and heart of Tintagel Castle. Waiting for us on the other side of the bridge were two imposing figures. They greeted us solemnly, but with great warmth. The elder of the two was dressed in a dark blue robe. And though his beard was white with many summers, his eyes glinted like simmering coals that at any moment might spring forth into a mighty blaze. Even though many years had passed since he last visited Avalon, I knew him instantly. And the noble manner of the man next to him, left no doubt as to who he was. He was dressed like a warrior and we knew that he had passed the test of many battles.

"My Lord," said Loran and kneeled before his sovereign lord and liege, King Arthur. Aran followed suit while Gaius and I bowed our heads in respect.

"Rise, most noble friend," said Arthur warmly and extended his hand to Loran. "And welcome my friends to Tintagel Castle. I have had news of your journey. So it gives me great joy to see you have arrived unharmed."

"The Goddess has smiled upon us this day," said Merlin, embracing me warmly and kissing my brow. I felt the point between my eyebrows tingle at his touch. "Greetings, sister Dana. And how is your fair head faring this afternoon?"

"Much better, much better," I replied in surprise. We hadn't yet had a chance to tell anyone of our dramatic escape from the clutches of Lord Bryn, but of course Merlin, the wisest and most powerful druid in all of Britain, would know all about it. The Sight was strong in him, stronger than in anyone else in all of this mighty isle.

"Now," said Merlin to Arthur, "Everyone I have summoned to the meeting has at last arrived safely."

"And without, I hope, arousing the suspicion of King Lot," said Arthur. "But let us make haste. Rumor has it that he has entered into a secret alliance with the Northern kings—and also that he is wont to meet with the Vikings. I fear there is not a moment to lose..."

"King Arthur is Stanley Donne!" I heard Jacob cry inside my head.

"What do you mean?" I asked as in my mind's eye I saw myself still standing there—as Dana—conversing with Merlin and King Arthur.

"Stanley Donne, you know the physics professor that I told you guys about. The one who conducted that experiment at the University that totally changed my life. I recognize him now! It really is him!" cried Jacob excitedly.

Stanley Donne? King Arthur? Why of course. "That's right," I said as it all came back to me. "That's exactly what Elmar said too. That Stanley Donne told him that he had been King Arthur in a past life. But Stanley Donne also said that he really was a master called El Morya."

I could hear Janus chuckling inside my head: "King Arthur, Stanley Donne, El Morya, Jacob, Moncler, Gaius, Aran, Elmar... when you travel back in time, it sure is hard to keep track of all the names!"

Our little conversation was interrupted by the Keeper of the Cosmic Library: "Now, my friends, it is time to move forward to the next important event of that lifetime."

The sun was still high on the horizon as Loran, Gaius, Aran and I joined the procession of people who were walking across the rocky beach that the low tide had exposed at the foot of Tintagel Head. All in all, the volunteers Merlin had summoned from the far corners of Britain numbered 24 souls. They were accompanied by the 12 knights of King Arthur who had escorted the different groups to Tintagel. At the head of the procession walked Merlin, King Arthur at his side.

Merlin led us to a cave hidden deep in the side of Tintagel Head, which now towered high above us. Just a few hours ago, both the rocky beach and the cave had been totally inaccessible, completely hidden by the pounding surf at high tide. But now it was low tide and for a few hours, those who knew of it, could safely enter Merlin's secret cave.

Merlin led the procession into the dark cave and ordered the torches to be lit. As the cave filled with light, we could see it was probably at least 50 feet long, 30 feet wide and at least 20 feet high. The walls of the cave, which had been polished over the centuries by the pounding Atlantic surf that roared into the cave every day at high tide, glittered and gleamed in the flickering torchlight. It seemed a magical place, indeed, as if its walls were made of precious gems or polished crystals.

"Welcome to the Crystal Cave," said Merlin. He placed one of the torches between two large rocks and sat down with his legs crossed. He

motioned for the rest of us to sit down too. We all sat down, volunteers and knights side by side, in a half-circle in front of the great wizard. Then Merlin closed his eyes and a deep silence descended upon the Crystal Cave. The only sound we could hear was the sound of the waves crashing on the rocks outside. I took a moment to survey the other volunteers. The other brave souls who like Gaius and I had come at great peril from all parts of Britain to learn Merlin's Secret—the secret of how to establish lasting peace and harmony in our tormented land.

Loran had recounted as we approached Tintagel that the volunteers we would meet would be from all over England—from Avebury, Caerleon, Carmarthen and Stonehenge. He also said there would be some volunteers from Scotland. Two pilgrims from the sacred isle of Iona, a druid from Callanish, and two travelers from Findhorn in northeastern Scotland. Also from Cliffs of Moher in Ireland volunteers had come and I guessed that the tall man and woman with long hair and fair faces were our Irish brethren. Next to each group of volunteers sat one of the 12 Knights of the Round Table. The only one present who was not from Britain, was a dark-skinned man with a noble countenance, dressed in exotic clothes. We had not spoken with him, but we had heard from some of the others, that he had made a long and hazardous journey from his country far away in the Southern Lands to join this secret gathering.

As silence descended, Merlin began to breathe very deeply. We heard him draw his breath in slowly and then exhale again very slowly. We all watched him intently because we had all heard tell of his famous trances. Were we now going to witness one of these trances? The deep, restful sound of his breathing continued, and as we listened, it was easy to get drawn ever so gently into the spell that seemed to be descending upon all of us who sat there in the glittering Crystal Cave.

I felt myself breathing more and more slowly. And as I focused my attention on the point between my eyebrows, I felt my brow begin to tingle. Then I looked at Merlin and found to my great surprise that I could see right through him. It was as if he was a hollow tube, completely empty... nothing more now than an instrument of the Goddess. He continued to breathe. After a few moments of the deepest silence, his whole being was illumined by a brilliant white shaft of light, as if the sun itself had moved down into Merlin's body. I saw him shudder and shake, and as we watched in awe, Merlin breathed even more deeply to integrate into his being the powerful ray of light that had now taken abode in him.

"Greetings, my Brothers and Sisters in the Light!" The words came from the mouth of the Merlin, but I knew that it was not he who spoke. It was the voice of another. The voice of the light that had descended. *"I AM Sananda. And I come here today to speak to you on behalf of the Great White Brotherhood, a secret Order that works from the Higher Realms for the welfare of the Earth and for all of humankind. I thank you for your presence here today because I know that all of you have made difficult and dangerous journeys from the far corners of Britain to take part in this gathering to herald the birth of a New Age. In truth, there would be no gathering and no birthing, were it not for you and the many others on Earth who unceasingly labor for Enlightenment. For you, verily my dear brothers and sisters, you are not alone. And I would have you know that at this very moment, other volunteers much like yourselves are gathered together at other secret gatherings at other points around the Earth to listen to my words, yes, just as you are now doing. In distant lands of which you know not, in lands on the other side of the Western Sea and even beyond that, men and women, sisters and brothers of yours, are sitting together as you are now, with the same burning desire for peace and harmony on Earth."*

Merlin's breathing grew calmer as if he had now integrated the powerful light that had taken abode in him. Sananda continued:

"You all know that there is One Omnipresent and Unlimited Force, which is behind all of Creation. Those of you who are Christians, call this Force—God, the Father—and those of you who are druids and priestesses call this Force—the Goddess, your Divine Mother. But regardless of name, it is one and the same Force, one and the same Presence, which you all honor and worship. This you all now know, and it is this knowing that has brought you here together on this auspicious occasion.

"What you do not know, however, is how this Force creates all of Creation. And when you learn this, when you learn how this Force creates all of Creation, you will possess the Key—the Secret—that you require to create lasting peace and harmony on Earth.

"And this is what I have come to teach you, my friends."

I closed my eyes and concentrated all my attention on Sananda's words. He continued: *"This Omnipresent and Unlimited Force or God is Pure Consciousness. And this Pure Consciousness we call God thinks and thus was this world created. By his thoughts, God created the world. By thinking alone, God has made everything in existence. And God also*

101

made man—in his own image and likeness. This is why man, like God, creates his world by thinking. This then my friends, is the Secret of all creation: First there is the thought, then the word, and then the act of creation. Therefore, man's thoughts and words are Law. Therefore, your thoughts and words are Law. Your thoughts and words form the Universal Life Force into the conditions and circumstances of your life—into your body, your relationships, and everything that you experience. This is the Unbreakable Law.

"In the same way that your thoughts and words create your life, so the collective thoughts and words of mankind create the conditions and circumstances of life on Earth. And it is here that we find the cause of so much misery and suffering. Because the thoughts and words of most of humankind are focused on the lesser, are focused on limitation and separation, on fear and lack, we find humankind is creating and experiencing the very world they wish to avoid, a world filled with fear, war, violence, poverty and great unhappiness.

"The only way that you, my friends, can create lasting peace and harmony in the world, is by changing your own thinking. Instead of seeing death and destruction, darkness and injustice in the world, you must shift your focus to the God Force that is ever present in all people.

"And when you change your focus and your thinking, it affects all of humanity. Because every human being's mind is one with the Force, is part of the Great Universal Mind. So, my dear friends, this is your mission. You are to master and change your own thinking and anchor a New Vision in the collective consciousness of humanity, a New Vision of Peace and Harmony in the world. When you do this, the condition of the world will change.

"And to do this—to anchor this New Vision—we in the Higher Realms have constructed a mighty incantation for you. This incantation contains powerful symbols and codes, which will release new positive images in your minds and help you to anchor the New Vision in the collective consciousness of humankind. Your task is to repeat this incantation and meditate on it many times a day. The more you repeat the incantation and meditate on it, the more powerful will its effect on the collective consciousness be."

Sananda was quiet for a few moments as we tried to understand and assimilate what he said. Then he said: "Now I will ask you to repeat the incantation seven times after me. One time for each day that it took God to create all of Creation:

IN THE BEGINNING: THE FORCE
HERE AND NOW: THE FORCE
AT THE END OF THE END: THE FORCE
HERE, THERE, EVERYWHERE: THE FORCE
FROM ALPHA TO OMEGA: THE FORCE
IN HEAVEN, UPON EARTH: THE FORCE
IN THE GREATEST, IN THE SMALLEST: THE FORCE
IN FIRE, IN WATER, IN EARTH, IN AIR: THE FORCE
IN ME, IN YOU, IN EVERYONE: THE FORCE
ABOVE ME, BELOW ME, AROUND ME: THE FORCE
IN ME, THROUGH ME, FROM ME: THE FORCE
IN MY THOUGHTS, IN MY WORDS,
IN MY ACTIONS: THE FORCE
THE FORCE IS ALL IN ALL
ALL LIFE, ALL INTELLIGENCE, ALL LOVE
THE FORCE IS THE ONE AND ONLY REALITY
AND SO IT IS!"

We repeated the incantation slowly after Sananda. As the sound of our voices echoed back and forth in the Crystal Cave, it was as if the incantation had opened a gateway to the Higher Realms. Now, through that gateway, there flowed a living river of mysterious geometric shapes, pulsating colors and heavenly harmonies. The sound of our chanting grew and grew until I felt that I was completely one with the Force. In that very moment, when I felt that oneness, it was as if something was activated, deep within my consciousness. As if a signal suddenly brought together the stream of myriad shapes and colors and they became living images, which danced as clear as day in my mind's eye.

It was the New Vision!

As clear as day, I saw a mighty wave of Light descend from the Heavens down to Earth... I saw it spread out over the lands... and flow across the oceans and the mountains... moving across Britain, through her towns and villages... passing through the strongest fortresses and the most humble cottages... passing through windows and through doors... entering into every heart... a radiant Light which awakened the slumbering Force in all beings... in princes and in popes, in farmers and in shepherds... in each and every one... and they all arose as one... as the Light touched them, to transform sickness into health... poverty into wealth... darkness into light... and misery into faith, hope and love... all

103

*this I saw in my mind's eye... this New Vision... of peace and harmony
everywhere... and dear Mother Earth, she shone like never before... a
bright shining star in the vast expanse of space... an unspeakable
beauty... a priceless jewel in the Eye of God... and then I knew that what
I longed for was true... Heaven and Earth were now one...*

*And there we lingered... in a place beyond space and time... until the
voice of Merlin brought us back to the Crystal Cave.*

*"Goodbye, Sananda," said Merlin ever so softly, his voice no more than
the merest of whispers. "Truly you too are a priceless jewel in the Eye of
Our Heavenly Father-Mother."*

*Then the old wizard opened his eyes and looked long and lovingly at
the group. Slowly, he let his gaze pass over each of one of us. Then he
said: "Dear children, normally I am not allowed to speak openly of these
things... but today, on this auspicious occasion, I will lift the veils just
slightly and tell you that verily there are no other souls in all of Britain
who are more qualified for this mission than you are. Your noble origins
will not fail you!"*

*Merlin was silent for a moment. Then he stood up and rubbed his
hands together. "But now to the plan!" he said, his eyes shining brightly.
"In order for that which you have now seen with your inner eye to
become real to your physical eyes, the Great White Brotherhood and I
have developed an activation plan to give the New Vision maximum
effect on the collective consciousness. Our plan consists of three vital
elements: The Network of Light or the Light Grid as I am wont to call it,
you the Volunteers, and the New Vision. When we have fused these three
elements together, the New Age of Peace and Harmony on Earth will
become a reality.*

"But how, my dear children, do we go about doing this, practically?

*"Let us begin with the Light Grid. Just as the human body consists of
energy centers and energy lines, so the body of Mother Earth also
consists of Energy Centers and Energy Lines that circulate the Universal*

Life Force in her body. In the human body, these Energy Centers are called Chakras and the Energy Lines are called Meridians. In Mother Earth's body, the Energy Centers are called Power Spots and the Energy Lines are called Ley Lines.

"Many thousands of years ago, our mighty ancestors from Atlantis built huge pyramids, mighty stone circles, great temples and other astronomical measuring instruments on top of these Power Spots and along the Ley Lines. And they created a mighty network by joining together these Power Spots and Ley Lines—and they called this network the Light Grid.

"But why did our ancestors build this Grid? One of the reasons was that the power of any thought or vision which was sent out from the Power Spots along the Light Grid was increased many times over. But, unfortunately, since the downfall of Atlantis, most of these Power Spots have fallen into decay—and the Light Grid has become little less than an old wives tale.

"Our plan—the plan developed by the Great White Brotherhood and myself—is to send you volunteers to these Power Spots to once again re-establish this mighty Light Grid and to send out the New Vision from each of these points.

"Each of you is already closely connected to a specific Power Spot in the realm of Britain. And it is precisely this Power Spot, the one you already feel connected to, that you are going to activate. Now, how is this activation to unfold? This is how... You will meditate without stop on your Power Spot for exactly 24 hours. Each and every hour, you will be called upon to repeat the incantation Sananda has just given us seven times without stopping.

In order to channel enough energy to reactivate the Light Grid, it is absolutely essential—and I repeat this—absolutely essential—that you are all doing this activation meditation at precisely the same time. That is why we will ask you all to begin your meditation during the next full moon at midnight to be exact—and to continue to meditate for 24 hours without stopping, that is precisely from midnight to midnight. If you all do this without fail, then your Power Spot and the Light Grid will be re-activated—and the New Vision will sweep through the collective consciousness of humanity with enormous power, just as you saw a few moments ago."

Merlin stopped his discourse and began walking around the cave, making circular movements with his hand. As if brought forth by his call,

105

the Crystal Cave was suddenly illumined by a blinding flash of light. A moment later, the air all around the old wizard was filled with beautiful and wondrous objects that seemed to float effortlessly around him. There were all sorts of bejeweled swords, and daggers set with bright gems, and long spears, and big bows and bright shields—and many other weapons that glinted and gleamed in the torchlight. There were also belts, necklaces, bracelets, and several staves covered with strange symbols and runes. In the very middle of all the objects, close to where Merlin stood, there was a tiny sun shining brightly and a silver star that shimmered like the moon. At the sight of the little star, the tingling sensation between my eyebrows seemed to explode and I felt an indescribable longing to take the little star in my hand and place it on my brow. It was as if it was an important part of me which I had lost and which I now had found again.

"Where did they all come from?" mumbled Loran at my side. I turned and saw him studying one of the gem-set two-handed swords with great fascination.

"These mighty weapons and sacred artifacts belong to you," said Merlin. "They have been waiting for you—for a very long time—in the Higher Realms. They have been waiting for this auspicious occasion when once again you will take up your rightful places as Guardians of the Earth. When your sacred object has been restored to you, I advise that you take good care of it, for it is very precious indeed. In reality, each one of these objects is a part of you. A part of your being. So guard them carefully and keep them safe, every moment of every day and night, for without your sacred artifact you will not be able to activate your Power Spot."

Merlin walked over to the two Scottish pilgrims from Iona. "Corin, the Great White Brotherhood appoints you to activate the Power Spot on Iona," said Merlin in a clear voice. Corin humbly kneeled before Merlin and bowed her head. Then Merlin placed his hand on Corin's head and said, "Repeat the Oath of the Guardian after me:

> WITH THE FORCE AS MY WITNESS
> I NOW CLAIM
> MY RIGHTFUL PLACE
> AS GUARDIAN OF THE EARTH"

Corin repeated after Merlin. Then Merlin took the gleaming necklace with the great green stone hanging from it and put it around Corin's neck. Then he turned to Corin's brother Darin, who also was appointed to activate the Power Spot on Iona. After Darin had sworn the Oath of the Guardian, Merlin gave him a long spear covered with many strange runes.

Merlin went through each group of volunteers and appointed each of them to activate a specific Power Spot in Britain. After each one had sworn the Oath of the Guardian, each Guardian was given back the mighty weapon or artifact, which belonged to them.

At last, Merlin came to us. Merlin stood in front of me and I kneeled humbly before him. "Dana, the Great White Brotherhood appoints you to activate the Power Spot on Avalon. Repeat after me:

> *WITH THE FORCE AS MY WITNESS*
> *I NOW CLAIM*
> *MY RIGHTFUL PLACE*
> *AS GUARDIAN OF THE EARTH"*

After I had sworn the Oath, Merlin reached out and took the silver star in his hand. Then he placed the shimmering star on my brow. In that very instant, I felt the star melt into my brow and become one with me. It was as if it was a part of my body, which I long had been missing. I sighed a great sigh because now I had been rejoined with that part of me which had been lost so long. And immediately I sensed the great power and clarity that emanated from my star. It was as if the density of the physical world no longer ruled my consciousness... and I could see through the physical to the souls on the Other Side.

Merlin then turned to Gaius. "Gaius, the Great White Brotherhood appoints you to activate the Power Spot on Avalon." Then Gaius too swore the Oath and Merlin gave him back the massive, richly carved oak staff, which rightfully belonged to him.

When Gaius finished repeating the Oath, Merlin walked over to the last volunteer. It was the dark-skinned man who had come from the Southern Lands. The two of them smiled at each other for a long moment. Then the Southerner knelt before the old wizard. "Hatp," said the great wizard in a voice that told us we were witnessing the meeting of old friends, "it is with great honor that I tell you that the Great White Brotherhood appoints you to activate the Power Spot at the Great

Pyramid of Giza. By means of the Power Spot at the Great Pyramid, we in Britain will be connected with all the Power Spots in the Southern Lands, and through them to the whole world." After Hatp had sworn the Oath of the Guardian, Merlin reached out and took the little sun, which he then gave to Hatp. For a brief moment, Hatp held the sun in his right hand and looked at it carefully. Then he opened his great flowing robes and placed the sun on his chest, right over his heart. He closed his eyes and let out a sigh of contentment as the sun seemed to melt into his body. Then he spoke soft words to Merlin in a language we did not understand.

At length, Merlin turned towards King Arthur. The wizard reached forth and took from the air a long, jeweled sword that glinted and radiated immense power. On the hilt of the sword, these letters were engraved:

E-X-C-A-L-I-B-U-R

Arthur kneeled before Merlin and bowed his head. Merlin touched Arthur on each shoulder with the tip of Excalibur's mighty blade. "King Arthur, the Great White Brotherhood appoints you to protect the Guardians of the Power Spots with your Life, your Kingdom and with all the Power given unto you. Now you too must swear the Oath of the Guardian. Repeat after me." Then Arthur too swore the Oath and humbly received his great sword and the Brotherhood's sacred trust.

Loran and the other Knights of the Round Table then stood behind their King and kneeled. Merlin gave each one of the King's knights his weapon and his mission. "Sir Lancelot, the great White Brotherhood appoints you to protect and defend the Guardians of the Power Spot in Avebury, with your life if need be," said Merlin to Lancelot. "Sir Gawain, the Great White Brotherhood appoints you to protect the Guardians of the Power Spot in Caerleon, with your life if need be..." I watched in awe as Merlin appointed each of the 12 knights to protect a group of Guardians. There was Sir Ector, Sir Gareth, Sir Percival, Sir Cai, Sir Accolon, Sir Mordred..."

When Merlin came to Mordred I felt a sudden pang right between my eyebrows, right at the point where my star was. It was a real pain, a physical pain, caused by the sudden contraction of the star on my brow. And for a brief moment, as the pain engulfed me, I saw Mordred's face twist into a horrid mask of rage and anger. I gasped. Aran, who was standing right next to me, heard me and looked at me anxiously. I clutched the spot on my brow and looked away.

As Mordred kneeled and bowed his head, Merlin touched his shoulders with the point of a mace and said, "Sir Mordred, the Great White Brotherhood appoints you to protect the Guardians of the Power Spot on Callanish, with your life if need be." Mordred swore the Oath of the Guardian. By the time he raised his head again, the dreadful vision was gone. The point between my brows seemed to relax and I drew a sigh of relief. I told myself it could not be, that there was nothing to fear in the Crystal Cave. And besides, didn't Merlin have the Sight? The old wizard continued moving down the line of knights as I valiantly tried to forget what I had just seen. At last, Merlin came to Loran. He took the large, gem-set two-handed sword and touched Loran's shoulders with its tip.

"Sir Loran, the Great White Brotherhood appoints you to protect the Guardians of the Power Spot of Avalon, with your life if need be." Loran smiled and winked at Gaius and me.

As soon as everyone had taken their Oath and received their final instructions, we hurriedly left the Crystal Cave. The tide was rapidly coming in again and it wouldn't be long now before the rocky beach and the great Crystal Cave would vanish under the mighty waves again.

On our way back to the castle, Gaius, Loran, Aran and I were walking just a short distance ahead of Merlin and King Arthur when I turned to look up at the castle high above us. As I did so, I gasped in surprise at the sight I saw. High, high above the long, wooden bridge, which connected the land side part of the castle to the rocky island, there, hovered an enormous, four-sided Pyramid of Light! It was huge. Almost as large as the castle itself. And it seemed to hover there, as if suspended in the air. Waves of soft golden, yellow and orange light radiated down from the great Pyramid, engulfing all of Tintagel Castle and the Crystal Cave below. That was when I became aware that a faint, high-pitched tone was also emanating from the great Pyramid. I stood transfixed, as still as a standing stone, looking at the sky in wonder. I knew I was witnessing a great miracle that was far beyond my earthly understanding.

Merlin stopped and stood besides me. No one else seemed to see the Great Pyramid high above the castle. The old wizard reached out and put his arm around my shoulder in a fatherly manner. "I see that since I returned the little star that is rightfully yours Dana, your Sight has grown, grown very great indeed." His smile was as bright as the great Pyramid above us.

"It is so beautiful," I said softly.
"Yes," he said, "we are not alone."

7

Flight from the Sea

After our initiation in the Crystal Cave, the volunteers and the knights who were assigned as their protectors were sent back to their Power Spots, in the deepest secrecy, to reestablish the Light Grid and anchor the New Vision in the collective consciousness of humanity. Gaius and I left with Loran our protector—and we took Aran with us because I wanted to take him to Avalon. Aran was such an open and sensitive soul, that I knew, with his beautiful voice, he was truly a natural-born bard. In Avalon, his gift would flourish and come to fruition.

Special care was taken to ensure our safety because Glastonbury was such an important and sensitive spot in the power struggles that were going on in Britain at that time. So a plan was devised to keep our movements from being discovered by King Lot's spies or any other foes of Arthur. According to Merlin and Arthur's plan, it was decided that Gaius, Loran, Aran and I should leave Tintagel under the cover of darkness by boat. A small ship under the command of Lord Gavin, one of King Arthur's trusty men and a seasoned warrior, was to take us on our journey. Besides Lord Gavin and the ship's hands, a small escort of ten soldiers was also sent on board with us. But we paid them little notice because most of the time, we stayed in our cabin, full of hope, planning our journey or meditating and chanting the mighty incantation Sananda had given us.

Summer was drawing to a close, but the weather was still clear as we set sail from Tintagel and began our voyage back to Avalon. There was a brisk wind as we sailed northward up the coast of Cornwall towards the Mouth of the Severn. For the first several days, our journey was uneventful, until at last we found ourselves sailing along the coast of Somerset. From our tiny ship, we could see the Summer Country where Glastonbury Tor, my beloved Avalon, was waiting.

At long last we were approaching home! We went to our cabin to make ready for the next leg of our journey. To escape the attention of unfriendly eyes, King Arthur had instructed Lord Gavin to set us and our horses ashore on one of the many long stretches of deserted beach on the coast of Somerset. From there, it was only about a half a day's ride to our destination. Not even Lord Gavin knew where we were headed.

We had just finished packing when there was a knock at the door. It was Lord Gavin. He looked worried. "One of King Lot's warships is approaching," he said. "They have signaled that they wish to board and speak with us."

I ran over and opened the hatch. Sure enough, a very large warship was coming up alongside our tiny ship. The standards of Orkney were flying high. The ship was so large, that I knew at a glance there must have been hundreds of men on board. If it came to a fight, we would be outnumbered at least ten to one.

"How can this be?" I cried in surprise.

"There is no reason why they should suspect anything," replied Lord Gavin. "You just stay in the cabin, and I'll take care of them." Lord Gavin left us, closing the door behind him.

Loran loosened his sword from its sheath.

"Do you think there'll be a fight?" cried Gaius.

"How could they have known we were aboard?" I said again, mystified. I could see a gangway had been thrown from the warship over to our little ship. It wouldn't be long before they boarded us. It had all happened so fast.

"I don't understand," I muttered again, the panic rising in me.

"Dana, maybe they don't know anything about us," said Aran. "Maybe their errand is quite different."

I saw Lot's men began to board our ship. They were armed to the teeth. How could this be happening? And happening so fast? One minute, we were packing our bags and the next we were being boarded by emissaries of our enemy King Lot. It didn't make sense. What was Lord Gavin thinking? Something was definitely not right. That was when I felt the point between my eyebrows begin to tingle. It was the Sight. A flood of images flooded my inner eye and I staggered back.

"Dana! What's wrong?" said Aran and caught me as I stumbled. He held me as I sunk down into the nearest chair.

"I don't know," I groaned and held my head. In my mind's eye I saw blood and more blood. Blood everywhere. Blood gushing from a huge

gash in Loran's middle. Blood gushing from the arrows sticking out of Gaius' back. "Blood and death! Blood and death!" I gasped in horror. "Death... Loran and Gaius are dead. Dead... Oh holy Mother..."

My three companions looked at me in alarm. "What do you mean?" cried Gaius. "Speak, for the love of Jesus!"

Then I saw and understood. Lord Gavin! The anxious look on his face hadn't been a worried expression. No! It was nervous agitation!

"Lord Gavin is a traitor!" I cried and jumped from my chair. I felt a sharp pain, like a knife piercing me in the chest. "A traitor!"

"But Gavin is one of Arthur's most trusted men!" protested Loran. "It cannot be!"

"Oh yes it can! "I cried, clutching my breast. "He is a traitor! I see it all very clearly now."

My companions looked at each other in sudden alarm. Loran ran over to the hatch and looked out. "If Gavin really is a traitor, then our situation is rather awkward, to say the least," he said dryly.

"Let's get out of here," said Gaius with sudden firmness. "When you are traveling with a priestess of Avalon and she sees death, you would do well to listen."

"But how?" asked Aran, frantically. "We're trapped like rats in a hole."

Loran looked out of the hatch again. "Luck may be with us still. We're not that far from the shore. Not more than 200-300 yards I venture. We could swim it, I believe, that is if you, Dana, can manage it."

I stood up and tried to shake off the horrible vision. "Yes, of course I can." I said. "If it must be so, the Goddess will protect us."

Loran quickly tied a rope around one of the cabin's bed posts and threw it out the hatch. "Aran first," he commanded.

Aran crawled out through the small opening and lowered himself hurriedly down to the water. I quickly followed him. Now that the vision had left me, my only thought was to escape as fast as possible. Without a sound, I lowered myself into the icy water. Even though it was still summer, the waters of the Atlantic were terribly cold. I started swimming towards the shore, as fast as I could. Fortunately for us, there was almost no wind that day, so the ocean was calm. If it had been windy or stormy, we would have never made it.

Gaius and Loran were right behind us. We were not more than a few yards from the ship when we heard the sound of harsh words and swords clashing. We stopped for a moment and looked back at the ship. There

113

was no doubt about what we saw. King Lot's men were attacking Lord Gavin's men. So I had been right that something terribly wrong was going on. But was I also right about Lord Gavin? Was he really a traitor? Or could I have been wrong about him? But there was no time for further thought. We turned and swam furiously towards the shore. But it was slow going, even though we moved forward with all our might. And with each stroke, we dreaded being discovered and feeling deadly arrows pierce us from behind.

We must have been about 150 yards from the ship when we realized that the sound of fighting had stopped. We were all breathing hard, heaving after air and struggling against the icy sea, but there was still at least 100 yards to go. The waves seemed to grow bigger as we got nearer to the shore and we fought desperately not to be pulled down and out again by the strong undertow. Then we heard a horn braying in the distance and men shouting.

Loran looked back. "They've spotted us!" he cried. But at least we were now out of bow shot range. We swam on madly through the pounding surf. Now there was only 50 yards left until we reached the shoreline. "Come on!" cried Loran fiercely. "We must make it before they put their boats in the water!"

I felt I was fighting a losing battle against the mighty ocean when suddenly there was solid ground underneath my feet! I cried out in relief and thanked the blessed Goddess for watching over us. As soon as we touched the ground, the four of us began running the remaining 20 yards through the crashing surf up onto the waiting beach. Once up on the beach, we turned and looked briefly back at the ships. King Lot's men had already lowered several small boats into the water. They weren't going to be giving up on us that easily.

"There's no time to waste!" cried Loran, urging us forward as we tried to catch our breath after the grueling swim.

We knew he was right. We ran across the warm sand towards the cliffs that surrounded the beach on all sides. Fortunately for us, they were not as high or as steep as the cliffs were in Cornwall. If they had been so, we might never have escaped from that beach. Loran led us toward a wall of rock that looked relatively easy to climb. It seemed to slant rather gently towards us and bright colored wild flowers peeped out from between the rocks, totally unaware of the drama unfolding in their midst. We scrambled up the cliff as fast as we could; half running, half climbing. When we were about half way up, I turned around and looked back.

114

Lot's men had already reached the shore and were jumping out of their boats in hot pursuit.

We climbed faster and reached the top of the cliff, breathing hard. We found ourselves on top of one of the few high spots surrounding the Mouth of Severn. Before us, the countryside was flat and low, stretching out before us like a scroll. I knew the area well. Much of it was marshland and there were many streams and waterways, which wound their way through the green, lush hills and valleys. Straight to the Southeast, we could see a tall hill towering up in the middle of the otherwise flat landscape: Avalon!

"This way," I shouted and began to run across a field of wild flowers with my eyes set on Avalon, rearing up in the distance. This was Somerset now, my blessed Summer Country! The thought seemed to revive me and I set off at a brisk pace, leading my companions in a southeasterly direction, straight towards a vast forest that lay not far from us. After we had run as far as we could without stopping for breath, I threw myself down on the grass, motioning the others to join me. We needed to catch our breaths again.

"Aran," I whispered, gasping for breath. "Tell me what you can see."

Sheltering his eyes from the sun with his long, slender hand, Aran stood up and gazed back towards the coast. "I see Lot's soldiers," he said, "moving very swiftly in our direction, Dana. There must be at least 30 or 40 of them."

We jumped up and looked anxiously back towards the coast. Lot's men were no further than a mile or two away. And they were moving very quickly.

"It's no use trying to outrun them," said Loran grimly, loosening his sword from its sheath. "I know those soldiers, they are some of Lot's best men."

I turned in the direction of the great wood, which I had been leading us towards. It was still about two miles away. "We might just have a chance," I said and pointed towards the forest. "If we trust in the secret ways of the Whispering Forest, we might just escape."

"But no one goes into the Whispering Forest!" cried Gaius with a look of terror on his face. "There is a curse on that forest. It is said that evil spirits wander there. People who go into the Whispering Forest never come out again!"

"Nonsense!" I cried, surprised to hear this from my friend Gaius. "I thought you no longer believed in the wives tales the monks of

115

Glastonbury are wont to tell about the Old Country! The Whispering Forest is not dangerous in itself. Rather it's like a mirror. Whatever you bring with you, the forest reflects back to you. And besides, people do come out of the forest again! Why I've been there several times. The priestesses of Avalon sometimes visit the old forest to gather herbs."

"But even if we passed through unscathed," said Loran, weighing the matter in his mind, "it's still a very long detour. From here there's only 8-10 miles to Glastonbury. But if we pass through the forest, it will be twice as long and much slower going."

"Do you have any better suggestions?" I said, looking back at our pursuers who were fast approaching. "In five minutes time, the chase will be up. Come my friends," I said, making ready to run. "Perhaps this will give you heart. Remember Lot's men don't know that we're on our way to Avalon. And even if Lord Gavin was a traitor, all he was told was to put us ashore on the northern shore of Somerset. If we manage to shake them off in the Whispering Forest, they'll never find us again."

"Dana is right," cried Aran, peering anxiously towards our pursuers. "It's our only chance. And if Dana says it's safe, I trust her."

"But if we are to make it to the forest before they catch us, we must be swift as the wind!" cried Loran as he fastened his sword in its sheath and began to run.

Never before in my life had I run so fast. The soldiers were right behind us. We could hear the sound of their hoarse cries, like the rumble of thunder moving closer and closer. Very soon now, very soon, I knew we would feel their wrath strike us like lightning.

"Faster!" cried Loran, "run for it friends!" Now we were less than 500 yards from the first outcropping of the Whispering Forest. Somehow, the sight of the beautiful old trees gave me new strength and I ran even faster, faster than I ever dreamt possible. And all the while, I prayed silently for the protection of the Goddess as we ran like the wind straight into the heart of the Whispering Forest.

As soon as we entered the old forest, I halted abruptly. Our pursuers were no more than 600-700 yards behind us.

"Why do you stop, Dana?" cried Loran, urging us forward.

I didn't answer. Instead I closed my eyes and focused on the point between my eyebrows. I felt a strong tingling sensation between my brows, now greatly increased by the shining star that was now a part of my physical body. That was when I knew that the Sight would lead me and my companions through the forest. And not the Sight alone. I opened

116

my eyes. A short distance from us, I saw two tall, luminous figures standing in the forest, right between two large oak trees. The figures radiated a golden light. "This way," I said and began to run towards the two luminous beings. "Follow me!"

I sprang forward. My companions leapt after me.

We ran like the wind through the tall trees towards the two huge oaks. When we got there, the luminous beings were gone. I focused my attention on the Sight and looked deeper into the old wood. Then I saw, just a few hundred yards away, their luminous silhouettes beckoning to us from the top of a small tree-lined hill. I began to run swiftly towards them. We could hear our pursuers trampling into the forest behind us. The sound of their panting and hoarse cries echoed through the dense wood. We came to the little hill and began to run up the slope.

"How does she know which way to go?" cried Loran breathlessly behind me.

"I have no idea," cried Aran back, "but I know she's right."

"Jesus Christ, deliver us from evil," I heard Gaius mumbling behind me.

I shivered a little as I heard these words and wondered what the inhabitants of the Whispering Forest would say about a prayer like this. A prayer that came from the very priests who had called this ancient wood an accursed place in the name of Jesus Christ... The Whispering Forest is not dangerous in itself. Rather, the old forest is like a mirror. Whatever you bring with you into the forest, it reflects back to you. And Gaius, my noble friend... why Gaius had no evil intentions. He was here to create peace and harmony on Earth...

When we reached the top of the hill, we stopped for a moment to catch our breath. The luminous beings were nowhere in sight. Nor were our pursuers. But even though we couldn't see them, we could hear the sound of their heavy footsteps trampling through the forest behind us.

All at once the leaves on all the trees began to flutter and tremble at the very same moment. We looked about in surprise for no wind blew. But all the trees and all their branches and all their leaves began to flutter and move as if animated by some unseen yet powerful force. What just a moment before had been a quiet, sleepy forest, was now transformed into an other-worldly realm. The forest was suddenly alive with the sound of a thousand voices, whispering from every tree, leaf and branch.

"Now I know why they call this the Whispering Forest!" cried Aran,

117

regarding the trees with awe. Gaius looked afraid.

I looked down the other side of the hill and caught sight of a stream that seemed to wind its way deep into the forest. The sides of the stream were overgrown with bushes and plants, and after a few yards, the stream seemed to disappear completely from sight into the dense undergrowth. Then I saw our luminous friends again, standing right in the middle of the stream, pointing to where the stream disappeared into the ever deepening forest.

"Who are they?" Aran whispered at my side.

I looked at him in surprise. "They are the Tuatha De Danann," I said and thought that indeed the Sight was strong in him. Without training, only very few could see the Shining Ones of the Old Race. "They are Star Elves," I said softly. "And they live deep in the heart of the Whispering Forest where few mortals have ever tread. And from whence even fewer have returned."

Loran and Gaius looked at the stream blankly. Obviously, they saw nothing. "We have seen the Star Elves," I said to them, pointing towards the stream. "Only very rarely do they appear to mortal men. And usually it is only those who have learned to use the Sight who can see them."

"Are they friendly?" asked Loran. Gaius crossed himself.

"They have great love for the forest and the trees, the plants and the animals. They are the protectors of all living things. They can feel your vibrations from afar. If your intentions are friendly and your mind is at peace, they will usually allow you to pass peacefully. But they say that no one passes through the Whispering Forest without being touched in some way because... here... in this place, the Force is stronger." I looked towards the two figures. Now they were beckoning us once again. "And today of all days, the Goddess is truly with us!" I cried joyfully and began running towards the stream. "The Star Elves are going to help us!"

"Why are they called Star Elves?" asked Aran running by my side, his eyes shining with wonder.

Suddenly I felt as if the grace of the Goddess had descended upon me and I smiled. "Some say the Star Elves come from the Land on the Other Side, the lost continent of Atlantis. But in Avalon, it is said that even before Atlantis, they came from above—from the Stars." As I spoke, I remembered what Morgaine, High Priestess of Avalon, had once told me. She said I too was descended from the Starseeds. That indeed, my mother, who had also been a priestess of Avalon, had come from the

118

union of a mortal and one of the Starseeds... and that that was why the Sight was so strong in me. I looked at Aran. I wondered what his origins were because the Sight also seemed to run so true in him.

We came to the stream and I ran cheerfully into the water. My companions followed suit. The water, which almost reached our knees, was clear and cool. We began to wade in the direction our guides had taken, even though I could no longer see them. But I knew they were somewhere ahead of us. After we had waded on for a few more minutes, the stream suddenly veered to the left. I halted in midstream.

"Which way?" asked Aran. "I can't see the elves anymore."

We climbed up the slippery bank and looked around. The forest around us was thick with many old, gnarled oak trees. It seemed to me as if every leaf on every tree was fluttering and shaking, even though no wind blew. And then I realized that mixed in with the sound of leaves fluttering in a wind that did not exist, I also heard the sound of voices. Voices that were crying and shouting, "This way! Over here! Faster!".

And with a sudden shock of recognition, the four of us realized that the voices we were hearing were our own!

"I told you the forest was bewitched," whispered Gaius, his face now very pale.

I did not reply. Instead I listened even more carefully to the voices. Besides our voices, which seemed to come from all directions at once, I also heard the sound of Lot's soldiers. They were shouting back and forth to each other in the confusion: "They're over here!", "No, they're over here!", "They've split up!", "They've gone this way!" There's a curse over this bloody forest, I'm sure!"

I took a deep breath and smiled. "It sounds to me as if our friends are leading our pursuers in many different directions," I said, "all of which are leading them away from us." My companions' faces relaxed as they slowly grasped the full significance of what was happening. "But how the Star Elves are able to command the wood to speak with our voices from behind every tree and bush is beyond my understanding. But rest assured, my friends, it won't be long before Lot's men have totally lost their way!"

And so we stood there for a while and listened in wonder to the sound of voices as they echoed back and forth from all sides of the forest. It was a strange symphony, indeed, of branches and leaves that fluttered in a forest where no wind blew, accompanied only by the sound of "our voices". Truly, it was far beyond the understanding of mere mortals such

119

as we. And then, to our great delight, the frantic, bewildered voices of our desperate pursuers began to fade into the deafening maelstrom of sound. And we breathed easier, much easier, as the voices of Lot's men became more and more distant... until finally we could hear them no more.

Then we looked at each other, suddenly too tired to speak, but each wondering what would happen to our pursuers. Would they give up the chase and leave the forest? Or would something else befall them, something we were wont to guess? But whatever it was to be, we were not destined to know. All we were to know was that even the sound of our own voices, which had echoed back and forth throughout the forest, was now also gone. All that remained was the gentle sound of green leaves fluttering softly in the forest where no wind blew. Not even a breeze.

I closed my eyes and thanked the Goddess.

"The Star Elves have driven off our pursuit," I said. "At last we can take a rest."

I threw myself down on the soft, green grass and inhaled deeply. The others did likewise. Then I rolled over and lay on my back, looking up at the sky as it changed color from deep blue to dark purple. Somewhere in the West, I knew the sun was setting. We had run for what seemed like many hours and now every fiber of my body was aching for rest. The sound of the rustling leaves spilled over us like a gentle balm, soothing and comforting our tired souls. And it wasn't long before we all fell into a deep, deep sleep.

8

Dance of the Fallen Stars

I awoke suddenly, as if someone had summoned me. I sat up. It was altogether dark in the forest. If it hadn't been for the light of the moon, which was nearly full, I wouldn't have been able to see anything at all. I stood up and surveyed my surroundings. The tall trees towered above us like silent sentinels. A soft wind now rustled gently through the forest, and I could hear the tinkling of the brook that ran swiftly nearby. Somewhere in the forest an owl hooted. A watchful silence lay upon the old wood, and now that it was nighttime, everything seemed much more alive.

I turned around slowly, studying the forest. Yes! Over there! I knew that whoever had summoned me was now watching me. Not very far from where we slept, the two luminous beings were watching us. I knew it was they who had awakened me and were now beckoning us onward.

I awoke the others and said that it was time for us to go.

"What! Right now, Dana? It's the middle of the night," protested Loran sleepily. "We've shaken off our pursuers—and anyway we wouldn't be able to see a thing in this blackness!"

"The Guardians of the Forest are calling us. They say that we must move on," I replied and started to walk towards the two figures that were shimmering ever so softly in the night. The others mumbled sleepily and then followed me.

"Where are they, Dana?" Aran whispered at my side, rubbing the sleep from his eyes.

"Right in front of us," I replied, concentrating on following the two figures.

"I can't see them," said Aran and blinked again.

"That is because you have not yet learned how to activate the Sight at will," I said. "So it only comes to you sporadically. Once we get to

121

Avalon and you begin your training, you will learn how to activate the Sight when you want to."

"How long did it take you to learn to master the Sight?" he asked.

"Learning to use the Sight consciously is only one of many things you will learn in Avalon," I said and turned to the right. The Star Elves were now leading us down a steep slope covered with pine trees. "The length of your training will depend on how quickly you learn," I continued. "There's no fixed length of time. You will continue until you have learned what you need to learn."

"But suppose I am unable to master what I need to learn?" asked Aran, "What then?"

"No one is allowed to begin training as a druid, bard or priestess of Avalon, without first having passed through the preliminary initiations."

"The preliminary initiations? What are they?"

"Oh dearest Aran, all of your young life has been one long initiation," I said and smiled at my young friend. "You see, you can never escape from or hide the level of consciousness you have attained. And this is always quite obvious to those who have eyes to see. And so your teachers will see you as you truly are because you are what you are—and can be no other."

Aran said no more because we had come to the bottom of the long slope. In the light of the moon, we could see that we had now come to an open grove filled with birch trees. Their slender, silver-gray trunks shone in the moonlight. It was a beautiful, other-worldly place.

Gaius stood still and looked around the grove. "What now?" he said.

I could see our two shimmering friends standing at the other end of the grove. Then I became aware of four other luminous beings, perched among the branches of a large oak tree to our left.

"What do you see, Dana?" asked Aran.

"I see Star Elves," I said. Now I could see that there were many more of them. Slender, luminous figures moving gracefully among the trees. They were everywhere. It was as if we had landed in the middle of a cluster of stars. I thanked the Goddess for this rare and wonderful sight.

"I see them, too, Dana! Over there!" exclaimed Aran suddenly. "There are lots of them, in the trees to the left!"

"Beings of light," Gaius said slowly, his voice filled with awe. "I too can see them... they are everywhere."

"Yes..." we heard Loran say, his voice barely a whisper. The entire grove was now filled with Star Elves. They sat perched in the trees or

122

stood around the edges of the grove. Close, yet ever so far. In the faint light, we found it difficult to see them clearly, to see their true forms. As I gazed at them I wondered if perhaps it was because they had no form as we knew it. That perhaps in truth, they were closer to the twinkling golden lights we saw above us in the heavens than to being what we called humans. That was when I had a sudden insight and knew in my heart of hearts that yes, in truth, they were indeed twinkling stars who had descended from the night sky above us to bless us with their presence.

"Truly, my friends, we are blessed this night," I whispered softly. "Truly." I had been in the Whispering Forest four times before in my life, and only once had I dimly perceived one of these luminous beings, as he or she observed me from afar. Thus I knew that this night was truly a precious gift. And as I looked over towards the two elves who had led us through the forest to this place, I felt a great wave of love flow out from them and wash over me. Somehow I knew I had a very deep connection to them. Perhaps what Morgaine had once said was true, that my mother was indeed the daughter of a Star Elf. Had they led us to this sacred place because I was one of them?

The two elves began to walk towards us. As they approached, I saw, for the very first time, how they really looked. They were both very tall and slim. Almost six feet tall, the both of them, and more beautiful than any human being I had ever seen. Both of them had long golden hair, which cascaded down around their fair faces. And their eyes shone like stars. The one was a man, and he wore a long golden robe. The other was a woman, and she wore a long white robe that shimmered with silver threads.

"Greetings!" said the elf man and smiled at us. "I AM Rayek."

"Welcome to the Whispering Forest," said the elf woman in a clear, melodious voice. "I AM Rayel."

"We are deeply honored," I said and looked into the woman's beautiful eyes.

"Only very few mortals have ever been permitted to meet the Star Elves on a night like this. This, you see, is a very special night, the night when we pay homage to the stars we come from," said Rayek.

Aran plucked up his courage and asked, "Then it really is true that you come from the stars?"

"Yes, my friend," smiled Rayel and raised her arms towards a cluster of stars in the sky above us. Among the vast array of stars, I saw one *large golden star that shone more brightly than any of the others. It was the same star I had seen above Aran's cave many days ago.*

"Yes, my friend," said Rayel again. "We come from the stars. From Sirius, from the Pleiades, from Andromeda and Lyra we come. From Arcturus, Orion, Alpha Centaurian and Hydra. Yes indeed, we come from the stars," she said, looking at us with her keen eyes. "And so do you."

"Us?" stammered Aran.

"Yes," said Rayek. "Many thousands of years ago, the Starseeds volunteered freely to incarnate on Earth to help humanity. Some of the Starseeds volunteered to work closely with the nature spirits and devas. That is who we are, we who are called the Tuatha De Danann, the Star Elves. While other souls, souls who were more bold, chose to incarnate as human beings. That is who you are, my friends."

A deep sigh seemed to rustle through the grove as she spoke these words.

"That explains so much," I said, understanding. "Why I have always felt such a great sense of love and such a deep sense of unity with nature. And why I have always felt that there must be more, so much more than just our life on Earth."

"And it also explains why I have always longed for the Land on the Other Side." It was Aran, speaking now in the faintest whisper.

"Yes, my friends," said Rayel. "Even though you have incarnated as human beings on Earth many times, you have never entirely forgotten your true origins. And now it is more important than ever that you remember your origin... now when you are beginning your true mission."

"We know about the Light Grid and the New Vision," said Rayek. "That is one of the reasons why we live here, so close to Avalon. Because we too feel the power that radiates from that place. This too is why we will help you pass safely through the forest to the other side, so that you can fulfill your mission. Because your mission is our mission."

"But first," said Rayel and took my hand, "let us celebrate the stars together on this blessed night! Follow me!" Still holding my hand, Rayel began to dance among the trees. She moved swiftly and with incredible ease and grace. But I found, to my great surprise, that I too was able to move with the same graceful ease. I felt incredibly light, as light as a feather, as I moved along with her. And then I began to laugh, such was the wonder of the swift weaving dance of the luminous Star Elves among

124

the silver trees. Then I heard the soft laughter of my friends, Aran, Loran and Gaius, as they too danced and frolicked through the trees, hand in hand with the elves. It was an intricate dance, a dance of circles and spirals, that wove its way in and out of the trees, until we all flowed together like water or stardust and I became aware that they were singing in their clear, high voices. My mind did not understand the words, but my heart understood everything. They were singing a song of praise to the stars, to the stars we come from, to the stars we long for, to the stars that we are.

9

Avalon of the Mists

Much later that very same night, after sleep had finally overcome us, I dreamt I was standing in the middle of a huge circle of standing stones. I knew that the circle was Stonehenge. A damp, heavy mist swirled around the stones and an icy chill seemed to hold my heart in a cold vice. Standing between two of the huge standing stones at the other end of the circle, I saw someone, wrapped in a heavy cloak. The figure walked across the circle and stood before me. When she pulled back her hood I saw how beautiful she was. She had long golden hair and clear blue eyes. I felt that I knew her. Her whole body seemed to radiate a warm, golden light.

"Starbrow, do not go back to Avalon," she said, gazing deep into my eyes.

Starbrow? The woman took my hands and said again, "Starbrow, you must not go back to Avalon. It is a trap... you must not..." but before I could ask her why and who was Starbrow, the spell was broken and Aran was shaking me gently and saying. "Wake up, Dana, wake up. It's time to move on. The Star Elves have left us some breakfast."

The spell was broken. I sat up and looked around me in confusion. We were still in the birch grove where we had danced the night before with the Star Elves. Now it was morning and there was no sign of the Elves. Gaius and Loran were sitting nearby, munching on the food the Elves had left us.

"Were you far away in the Elven Realms?" smiled Aran.

"I... don't know," I said, trying to understand the powerful emotion the dream awoke in me. I felt I knew the woman who had called me Starbrow... but why had she warned me not to go back to Avalon? The dream had seemed so real. I stood up and stretched. The sun was shining from a clear blue sky and the silver birch trees were swaying gently in

126

the wind. What could there be to fear... here in the Whispering Forest, protected as we were by the Star Elves?

"You'd better hurry before we eat it all," said Gaius, putting another wafer in his mouth.

I walked over and sat down next with my friends. Spread before them on the silvery piece of cloth was food from the Star Elves. Honey wafers, bread, the season's first berries and apples. There was also a clear drink in four small silver flasks. I knew it was our parting gift from the Elves. I smiled at the thought of the night's blessed meeting with them. They were our people and the meeting had been joyous beyond words. All night, we had danced in the grove, paying homage to the stars until everything seemed to dissolve in golden stardust. I found I could not remember exactly when I had actually fallen asleep. I sighed and took a bite of one of the honey wafers. It too tasted of the stars. My strange dream about Stonehenge seemed to fade as I remembered our night of dance with the Elves.

"I must admit," said Gaius, as he munched happily on yet another honey wafer, "that we monks really seemed to have missed out on a great deal when we spoke evilly of the Whispering Forest."

"I told you that only those who brought danger with them into the forest had anything to fear," I replied, glad that my friend was starting to understand.

"Yes," said Gaius and sighed, "but little did I realize that being here would be such a blessed experience. Never before have I felt such a sense of oneness with nature, with the trees and the flowers... and with the stars..." Gaius looked up at the sky as if he could see the starry host behind the blueness.

"Well, they did say that we came from the stars," said Aran, dreamily fingering one of the small silver flasks that the elves had given us. "Andromeda, Sirius, the Pleiades, Arcturus..."

"Yes, and what do you say to that, Dana?" asked Loran.

"It's not the first time that I have heard it," I replied. "In Avalon, it is said that many of the priestesses are descendants of the Star Elves. They also say that the Star Elves come from Atlantis, the Land on the Other Side—and before then, from the stars."

"Yes, but do you believe it's true?" asked Gaius.

"My heart tells me that it's true," I said.

"Mine too," said Aran.

I looked at Gaius. "What does your heart tell you, Gaius?"

Gaius looked uncertain. "I don't know..." he said. "It's not mentioned in the Scriptures."

"Doesn't your Bible say that after his crucifixion, Jesus Christ resurrected himself and then ascended to Heaven? Perhaps he was a Starseed who returned to the stars?"

"That's not exactly what it says in the Bible, Dana!" protested Gaius hotly.

"Easy now!" said Loran. "Let us not waste precious time discussing religion, my friends. Rather let us take thought as to how we are going to get out of this forest. Remember we have taken a solemn oath to fulfill our mission with all due speed."

Gaius and I knew he was right, so we let the matter of the Starseeds rest and finished our breakfast without another word. When we were done, we all rose and surveyed the area. At the other end of the grove, the terrain became hilly again. We walked in that direction and soon left the grove. Then we walked up one of the hills. From the top of the hill, I had a better view.

"Now I know where we are," I said, after studying the area a little. "Actually, we are not that far from the edge of the forest. If we head due east, we should be clear of the forest before noon."

And what then? I thought to myself. Back to Avalon? But what about my dream and the warning I had received not to return? I looked at my companions who were waiting for me to lead them out of the forest. There was no reason to say anything to them yet, I thought. Better wait until we leave the forest. When we were clear of the wood, I would tell them about my dream.

I set my eyes eastward, to where I knew Avalon lay and walked quickly down the hill. The leaves on the trees fluttered, but there was still no wind. As I strode forward, I felt the loving presence of the Star Elves emanating from the forest behind us, but in my heart of hearts, there was dread and apprehension.

"Avalon, Mother Avalon," I sighed and looked longingly at that strange and wonderful hill, towering on the distant horizon. The sun was setting as we began the last leg of our journey. First I had led my companions through the forest and then through the marshlands with its lakes and

streams. After that, we took a short rest and ate the last of the Star Elves' food. Then we left the marshes and entered another forest. Finally, we paused to stand on top of a rocky ledge that commanded a wide view over the tree tops. From where we stood, we could see Avalon on the other side of the forest, not more than 4-5 miles away.

As we stood there, contemplating our destination, I realized I still hadn't told my companions about my dream. Perhaps now was the right moment.

Loran and Gaius turned and began climbing down the rocky ledge, but Aran stayed and waited for me. I think he sensed that I was uneasy about something. As I turned one last time to gaze at the green hill in the distance, I was seized by a sudden fear that I might never see my beloved Avalon again. I shuddered at the thought.

"What is it, Dana?" Aran asked gently.

"There's something I must tell you," I said, and turned to follow Loran and Gaius, who were already halfway down the rocky slope.

"Loran! Gaius!" I cried, as Aran and I followed after them. "Wait for us! There's something I must tell ..." I was cut off by the sharp sound of arrows whizzing through the air around us. One of them drove deep into Gaius' right arm—and he tumbled forward, crying out in sudden pain.

"Get down!" cried Loran. We rushed forward and tumbled down the rocky slope after our friends. More arrows came flying through the air. One pierced my cloak and tore it and then bounced off the rocky ledge as I slid towards the bottom. Aran and I landed on the ground, shaken but still in one piece. We ran towards the trees, and then threw ourselves behind a large, fallen tree trunk where Loran and Gaius lay hid.

"Gaius, are you okay?" I cried.

"Yes," he moaned and held his arm as the blood gushed from his wound. Dana, you fool! I thought. You should have listened to your dream, it was a harbinger! Now look what has happened! I ripped off Gaius' sleeve to examine his arm. The arrow was deeply imbedded in his upper arm.

Loran looked up over the trunk, trying to make out what was going on. We heard the sound of horses approaching. "Those are Lot's men!" he hissed and dropped back down besides us. "And they are on horseback. How could they have found us here?"

I rummaged through my pouch, trying to find something for Gaius' wound, but Gaius pushed me away. "There's no time for that now," he said, clenching his teeth and breaking off the hilt of the arrow.

129

We got up and ran on into the forest. After we had run about a mile, we came to a hill with a ring of mighty oaks at its top. We ran to the top of the hill and looked back. Lot's men were close behind, almost at the foot of the hill. There were at least 20 of them and they were heavily armed.

I leaned against one of the old oaks for a moment and tried to catch my breath. Loran was right. How could Lot's men have known that we would be here? When I had led us through the forest and the marshes I had been absolutely certain that no one was following us—and yet they found us. How could they have known? Unless they knew that we were on our way to Glastonbury Tor. But how could they have known that?

I looked down at our pursuers once again. The man riding the lead horse was wearing the armor and helmet of a man of noble rank. Even from a distance I recognized him immediately. It was Lord Gavin.

"Curse him!" exclaimed Loran, recognizing him at the very same instance.

Thus it was that I came to know that the vision I had seen that day our ship was boarded was true: Lord Gavin was a traitor. Lord Gavin, Arthur's trusted servant, had betrayed his master and us.

But how had he learned that we were on our way to Glastonbury? We were told that Lord Gavin only knew that we were to go ashore somewhere on the coast of Somerset. But if Gavin knew that we were on our way to Glastonbury, and had told King Lot so, then perhaps he also knew where all the other volunteers were going. And had given this information to Lot as well. But how could he have known? How?

Suddenly I knew the answer. Mordred! It had to be him. I remembered the horrid vision I had had of his face in the Crystal Cave. How I had seen a dark cloud of hate distort his face. Now I fully understood the terrible consequences of what I had seen. I felt an icy chill grip my heart. Mordred and Gavin had betrayed us! There could be no doubt about it. King Lot knew Arthur and Merlin's secret plans. I placed my hand on my brow and felt my star pulsate.

"Gaius," I said. Gaius turned towards me and saw me standing with my hand on my brow, trembling all over. "We have been betrayed! I don't know if it's just us, or if this horrible betrayal also includes all the other volunteers. It might well be that we are the only ones who are still alive. We must escape! The New Vision depends on us."

The others stared at me in shock and horror. Lot's men were at the foot of the hill now, with Lord Gavin leading them. In just a few more minutes, they would be upon us.

"We must split up," I cried, frantically. "That's our only hope. Then perhaps one of us will survive. Aran and I will go this way. You two must go that way! Now quickly... run for it!"

Loran opened his mouth to protest. "There is no time to lose," I cried. "A mile from here you'll come to a narrow stream. Cross the stream and continue in a northerly direction until you come to the wide open countryside. From there you will be able to see Avalon. We'll meet you at our secret meeting place, Gaius knows where."

Gaius touched the point of his staff to my brow. "May God be with you, Dana," he said, his face white with pain and fear.

"The Goddess is with you, Gaius," I said and kissed the forehead of my beloved friend.

Loran and Aran clasped hands. "Take good care of her, Aran," said Loran.

"With my life," Aran vowed solemnly.

I turned and started to run; Aran followed me. Loran and Gaius ran in the opposite direction. I didn't look back. Holy Mother Goddess, I prayed silently as I ran. Guide your children safely home.

Aran and I ran in a zigzag fashion through the trees. All the while I ran, I felt the star on my brow pulsating like a beating drum. It was as if I could see Gaius and Loran in my mind's eye. They had reached the stream and waded across it. Now they were running towards the north as I had commanded. I let the vision fade and concentrated on our own route.

We came to another hill, which we ran up as fast as we could, all the while listening anxiously for the sound of horses. Once we reached the top, we stopped and looked around. The sun was already below the horizon and it was growing dark. I could dimly make out Glastonbury Tor in the distance. From the Lake, the mists had already begun to shroud the countryside in an eerie other-worldly haze.

Suddenly I heard the sound of swords and horses neighing. Men screamed. I raised my arms as if someone was about to strike me. Aran grabbed my arm. "What is it, Dana?" he cried. "There's no one here!"

I fell to my knees; the vision was so strong. I touched my brow with my trembling hand. "They are dead, Aran," I whispered hoarsely. "They are dead! Gaius and Loran are dead. Lot's men found them... and killed them."

In my mind's eye I saw Loran lying lifelessly on the ground, while one of Lot's soldiers pulled a great sword out of his belly. Gaius lay dead at

131

his side with two arrows in his back. I felt sick.

"Come on, Dana," said Aran anxiously, pulling me to my feet. Tears were streaming down his face. "Come, we must hurry! Come! We must not let their deaths be in vain."

Our eyes met for a moment, and we both knew what we must do. There was no time to mourn so we ran like the wind down the hill into the waiting mists. We sprang forward and plunged into the strange ghost-like countryside that spread out before us. It was a good thing I knew the way because it was difficult to see clearly. But at last we came again to the open land. The moon was rising and it cast a dull light on the countryside that lay sleeping before us. Avalon was only a mile or two away from us now. Most of the great hill was covered by the mist, but in the moonlight I could still see the top of the hill with its great circle of standing stones.

We were running across the open field when suddenly we heard the sound we had been dreading all along. The sound of horsemen approaching! We turned and saw two soldiers come charging out of the mist towards us. They had spears in their hands and were riding very swiftly. I knew there was no escaping now, so I planted my feet firmly in the ground and pulled out my silver dagger. Aran drew his sword and stood at my side.

The riders came charging with their spears raised. As they bore down upon us, I raised my dagger and threw it with all my might at one of the riders. My aim was true and it plunged deep into his heart. He let out a great cry and tumbled forward in his saddle, dead! His horse raced past us in terror and disappeared into the mist. The other rider charged straight at me and struck me with his spear. I cried out in pain as the spear dug deep into my right thigh. Before he could do more, Aran charged madly at his horse, attacking it with his sword. The horse screamed in terror and fell on its side, throwing its rider. Aran sprang after him as if a great wrath had overtaken him. Before the rider could get up again, Aran felled him with his sword.

I lay on the grass, clutching my thigh. The spear was buried deep. The world seemed to go black around me as Aran ran back to me. "Dana!" he cried out in terror and bent over me, his young face twisted in fright and sorrow.

"I am with you still, Aran..." I gasped. The pain was almost unbearable. "Let me just... get this thing out..." I grabbed the spear and broke it in two. Then I sat up with great effort. We could hear the sound

132

of more horsemen approaching in the distance. Aran looked at me in despair. I tried to get up but it was no use. The wound was too grave. I couldn't move. I lay back as my world spun.

"Aran," I panted, clutching my leg in pain. "There's nothing to be done. You must go on without me."

"But I can't," he cried, sobbing unabashedly. The sound of the horsemen was ever closer.

"Yes you can," I said and held his eyes with my own. "And you must. For the mission!" I put my hand to my brow and for a brief instant, I felt a sharp pain between my eyebrows as I removed my silver star, that special part of me, from my brow. I looked at it for a moment, as it lay quietly in my hand... my very own star, shining softly in the moonlight. And for a brief instant, time seemed to stand still. Then I placed my star in Aran's hand. "Now," I cried, "Run for it! To Avalon, my friend. Fulfill our sacred trust and our mission! For Loran, for Gaius, for Dana! Go now!"

"But how shall I know what to do?" he cried in despair.

I put my hand on his chest and held his eyes with mine again. "**Follow your heart, for your heart alone knows the way**," I said.

Then I turned my gaze from Aran and looked in the direction of our pursuers who would be upon us at any moment. Aran hesitated for one last moment. "We'll meet again, Dana. I know we will. We'll meet again in the Land on the Other Side." Then he got up and ran swiftly into the mist.

I sank back down into the wet grass and used the gift of Sight to pierce the mist around me and above me. And then I saw, high above the mist that covered the land, high above Avalon, how brightly the stars were shining still. Twinkling, and at peace. And among the many, I also saw the large golden star I had seen above Aran's cave when first we met. And I felt the light from that special star flow out to meet me, as if it was caressing and protecting me. A deep, deep sense of peace seemed to fall upon me. And I knew, as I lay there, looking at the beautiful stars far, far above me, that all the strife and all the hatred and all the disharmony on Earth, was nothing more than the mist that surrounded me this night. High above, the stars would go on shining forever.

The next moment I was surrounded by horsemen. Two of them jumped off their horses and strode over to where I lay. They stood on either side of me, spears to my chest. I smiled at them. The deep peace, which had descended upon me, had banished all fear. Nor did I feel any anger

133

towards them. Rather, I felt a deep sense of pity. Pity that they did not understand, pity that they did not see... the beautiful stars twinkling high above the mists...

"She's still alive, my Lord," cried one of the riders. The two men bent over and lifted me to my feet. Lord Gavin got off his horse and walked over to me. He held the point of his sword at my chest. Our eyes met. I knew he was surprised that I was so unmoved.

"Where's Aran?" he said, trying to threaten me.

I didn't answer. Instead I looked deep into his eyes. Now that all fear was gone, I wondered what had led him to betray us. Was it some rich reward? The gift of land? A title? Power? Who was this man really? This nobleman, this human being, who had traveled so far, only to betray us and take our lives?

Lord Gavin trembled slightly and looked away. "After the lad," he cried to his men. "She is just trying to win him time."

Four of Gavin's riders urged their horses to move and galloped off into the mist. The next moment, I felt a sharp pain in my chest as Lord Gavin drove his sword through my heart. But it only lasted an instant, the pain. Then I felt a rushing sensation all around me, as if a strong wind was pulling me upwards. And I felt very light, as light as the wind, as light as my breathing. An instant later, I was hovering above Lord Gavin who was pulling his sword from a woman's body, my body, that lay bleeding on the ground below. Gavin dried his sword on the grass, put it in his sheath and walked back over to his horse. The two soldiers who had held my lifeless body, followed him. I didn't stay to see more. The wonderful rushing sensation around me grew stronger as I turned my attention from the bloody scene below. At my side, I was aware of someone floating close by. The figure was almost like a ray of light... so bright and so crystal clear that I almost could not determine its shape or form, but I knew it was someone... some being. So I tried to focus on the figure and immediately it became clearer. The being of light was the young woman in my dream! The one who had warned me not to return to Avalon! Ah Avalon! For an instant, I longed to return, to go back to Avalon... But somehow, it all seemed like a dream now. Already so far away, and now quite uninteresting... The woman smiled at me and I felt as if I had always known her. And then I knew that indeed I had. We had always been together, she and I. She on the Other Side and I on this side. And then I knew that even though she had been on the Other Side, she always had been with me. Every second of every day. From the moment I

134

was born. She had been there, with me, loving me and protecting me. And now she was here to take me Home. She held out her hand and I took it. And I knew that her name was Ticha—my guardian angel! A great wave of love rushed over and through me. And the next moment we soared together through a long, long tunnel of Light, moving it seemed, at the speed of Light towards the most loving Light I had ever experienced. It was as if we were flying into the Sun itself, only this Sun was alive. This Sun was loving, caring—both a mother and a father at the same time. And I knew I was going Home. As we continued to soar through the tunnel, I sensed other souls were there, also on their way towards the Light. All of them happy, all of them peaceful, all of them like little children who were finally going Home. The Love emanating from the Light was so strong that I felt like I was going to burst. And that was when I saw Him. Far away, on one side of the Light. There he stood, a mighty figure with arms stretched out wide. His heart completely open and unblemished—and from it flowed a Love that was absolutely pure and unconditional for all living things, for all living beings. He was there to welcome us, each and every one of us, back Home. He shone like the Sun itself, like a thousand Suns in a true celebration of Love. And then I knew why they called Him the Most Radiant One...

"Alright, my friend, that's enough," said a kindly voice close by. It was the Keeper of the Cosmic Library. "Return now slowly to the chamber. Back to your body, back to the chair you're sitting in."

But I didn't want to. I didn't want to leave the Light. It was so loving, so blissful. I felt like staying there forever. And the Most Radiant One...

"You can always return to the Light," said the Keeper of the Cosmic Library. "But right now, it is time for you to be here."

I forced myself to turn my attention from the intense Light that I was seeing in my mind's eye and made an effort to return to the chamber. It worked. Immediately I felt my body again—and felt myself sitting in the alpha chair in the Pyramid of Time.

"Now, slowly open your eyes," said the Keeper. "And stretch your arms and legs a little."

I opened my eyes and stretched. The Keeper of the Cosmic Library stood in front of me. He was smiling.

"Excellent work," he said.

135

Now Is Your Time

I turned around in the alpha chair and looked at Jacob and Janus. They both had a blissful, peaceful expression on their faces so I knew that they had also been up in the Light, just like me.

"Gaius and Loran..." I said.

"Dana..." said Jacob and Janus.

The three of us got up and embraced each other. "We've found each other again," I said, moved beyond words.

"Yes," said the Keeper, "you've found each other again. Now you know that you have worked together before... that this is not the first time you have worked with the Great White Brotherhood. You see, my friends, you are Starseeds, voluntary emissaries from a distant galaxy who began incarnating here on Test Zone Earth many lifetimes ago to assist humanity in its ascension to the 5th dimension."

"But our mission failed," I sighed and said to the Keeper of the Cosmic Library. "We failed! And failed—miserably it seems—to anchor the New Vision in the collective consciousness."

"Do not despair, my young friend," said the Keeper. "For even the very Wise cannot see the end of all things. I do believe that now that you have seen one of your past incarnations, you may well be able to understand what I mean."

"But if it's really true that we've had many past lives and come from a distant galaxy, as you say, how come we can't remember any of it?" asked Janus.

"It's all part of the conditions placed on souls incarnating into the 3rd and 4th dimension," replied the Keeper. "In the 4th dimension, which the three of you just briefly experienced after you had left your bodies at that time, the soul rests and recuperates between incarnations. During this time, souls remember some of their previous lifetimes. But when a soul reincarnates again into the 3rd dimension, the veil of forgetfulness falls over your past lives."

"How come?" asked Jacob. "I don't understand."

"At first it might seem discouraging," answered the Keeper. "But once you understand the reason behind it, you will see that it is indeed a wise and merciful arrangement."

We were puzzled. The Keeper smiled, understanding our puzzlement.

"Just think about how much time and energy most people spend being resentful or angry—or feeling hurt over the things that have happened to them in this one life!" the Keeper explained. "There's their dreadful childhood, the husband or wife who left them, there is that special something which someone once said or did... All of these things, which seem to cause people so much pain and suffering. It's difficult enough for most people to cope with what has happened to them in their present lifetime. Can you imagine how they would feel if they were aware of the fact that they'd had many dreadful experiences, childhood traumas, painful divorces, terrible illnesses and all the other so-called tragedies they probably experienced throughout 50 or a 100 or even 200 lifetimes?"

"Yea, I guess it would be pretty traumatic!" said Janus.

"It is only when a soul arrives at the point in its evolution where it can view all the events in this life—and in all of its many lifetimes—as a fleeting, transient dream... without any form of emotional attachment or judgment... that the soul attains full remembrance of its past lives."

"Is such a state of detachment really possible?" I asked.

"It is," answered the Keeper. "There will come a time in your spiritual evolution when you will be able to view your entire life... all the events of your life and the whole external world, your body, your emotions, your thoughts... all of it... as one fleeting, transient, ghost-like dream. Once you reach this stage, you will be free. Then you will become a true Master. And then the way will be clear for you to ascend into the 5th dimension."

"It sounds totally unbelievable that one can ever get to be like that," said Janus.

"It's really not as difficult as you think," the Keeper smiled. "It seems impossible to you because you identify so much with your bodies, your emotions and your thoughts. But once you learn to identify yourselves with the Force, with your True Self, it's really not that hard."

"How does one learn to do that?" asked Jacob.

137

"That's precisely one of the things you are going to learn during your 5th dimensional training program," said the Keeper and started walking towards the door of the pyramid. "Yes, dear friends. Now is the time to prepare yourselves, for a whole new world is about to open." The Keeper touched the door with the point of his staff and it disappeared into thin air. We found ourselves looking out at the Relaxation Forest, which was waiting for us, warm and inviting in the golden sunlight.

"I think some fresh air will do you good after your long regression," said the Keeper with a glint in his eye. "You need a little time to relax and digest all that has happened."

We stepped through the open doorway out into the lush, green forest. The Keeper remained inside the pyramid. "What happens after we've relaxed at bit?" Janus asked the old man.

"You will be transubstantiated to the heart of the Mothership, where you will begin your 5th dimensional training program," said the Keeper.

"And after that?" asked Jacob.

"All will be revealed, my young friends, in its own proper time!" laughed the Keeper. "All you have to do is take one step at a time. Then I promise you, the next step is bound to be revealed!"

No sooner had he spoken than there was a soft whizzing sound and the door to the pyramid suddenly shut tight, right before the old man. He was gone! And we hadn't even thanked him or said goodbye!

We looked at each other in surprise.

"Sweet old fellow, wasn't he!" Jacob said and smiled dreamily.

We nodded in agreement and looked once again at the forest and at each other. There could be no doubt about it, Jacob and Janus were so different... transformed. Jacob (or was he Gaius or Moncler?) now stood tall and proud. His bright, kind eyes gleamed in his unsullied, handsome face as he stood there in his dark blue wizard's cloak, his secret spell book stowed away in his backpack. And Janus (or was he Loran or Telperion?) also stood tall and strong, with his long, golden hair and pointy elven ears, dressed in his massive chain mail. As for myself (or was I Dana or Starbrow?), I knew I looked different too, with my long, wavy hair, dressed as I was, in this long white robe, which went, all the way down to my ankles.

"So how do we do this?" grinned Janus as he patted me on the back, "should I call you Dana or Starbrow!"

"Starbrow's the name," I laughed and placed my hand on my brow.

"Then Starbrow, Moncler and Telperion it is!" cried Janus, "Three

138

Starseeds from—where was it we came from? The Pleiades? Sirius?"

"We never really found out," said Jacob. "Perhaps we should knock on the door and ask the Keeper?"

"Naaah," I said. "I get the feeling we need to digest our life in England before we start cruising around the galaxy and landing on other planets!" Jacob and Janus nodded in agreement. Right now we had more than enough to think about, just contemplating this one past life!

We turned from the Pyramid and walked through the large tree hall that surrounded the Pyramid of Time and then made our way back along the narrow pathway we had followed when we came. After we had walked along the path for a while, we came to a beautiful meadow with bright-colored flowers.

"Where to now?" asked Janus.

"Follow your heart, for your heart alone knows the way!" we all said in unison and laughed. Then we closed our eyes and concentrated on our hearts. Our inner guidance led us easily through the forest. After we had walked in a northerly direction for about half an hour, we turned to the right. Before us was a row of tall, stately beech trees. I sensed that we were drawing near the edge of the forest and I was soon proven right. A little less than a mile further down the path, we could once again see a warm golden light illuminating the whole horizon.

We came to the end of the forest and stepped out on the big, green open space that stretched out before us. A few miles in the distance, we could see the city of light. Pyramids zoomed in and around the buildings and several large, circular starships were taking off. The blue sky of the Relaxation Forest ended here, and the sky over the city was a dark night sky, filled with the light of thousands of starships. Above the Mothership floated Planet Earth, a huge blue-green gem in the night sky.

"Now that's what I call a view," I said.

"Totally awesome!" whistled Janus.

"This must be the ideal spot to follow the Keeper's advice. Why don't we just chill out here for a while," said Jacob, lying down on his back in the soft grass.

"Good idea! I could use a little interdimensional sunbathing myself!" said Janus, taking off his chain mail and joining Jacob. I lay down beside my two friends and looked at the night sky over the city. It was a funny feeling. Since we were lying in the Relaxation Forest where the sun was shining, we could sunbathe, but at the same time, since we were at the edge of the Forest, we could also see the dark night sky over the city in the distance.

"You know what?" said Janus, munching contently on a blade of grass. "Now that I've been up in the Light, I can see there's no reason to be afraid of dying."

"Yeah," said Jacob. "It's just the opposite of what everybody on Earth says. It turns out that death is really a super celebration."

"Yeah, it must be the veil of forgetfulness which lies over our past lives that makes human beings so afraid of death," I said.

"Well, according to the Keeper, we aren't even human beings," said Janus. "We're Starseeds from a galaxy far, far away."

"That's a mind-boggling thought," said Jacob.

"Do you think it's true?" asked Janus.

"Well, you sure don't look like the Janus I used to know!" said Jacob, pulling playfully on one of Janus' pointy elven ears.

"I wonder what ever happened to Aran—I mean Elmar—and the other volunteers," said Janus. "Do you think they were all betrayed and killed like us?"

"Who knows? If Gavin and King Lot knew about us, then maybe they also knew about the other volunteers," I said.

"And remember that no one but us could use the staff, the sword and the star that Merlin gave us," said Janus.

"Which means that the Light Grid was not established," said Jacob.

"And that means that the New Vision was not anchored in the collective consciousness," I concluded sadly.

"Well dudes, I guess we better keep in mind what the Keeper of the Cosmic Library told us," said Janus seriously, "... even the very Wise cannot see the end of all things."

"Yeah," replied Jacob. "What do you think he meant by that?"

I was just about to tell Jacob what I thought the Keeper meant when planet Earth, which was floating on the horizon, was suddenly enveloped in this huge black cloud.

"Will you look at that!" I cried out in alarm as all three of us sat up in surprise.

It looked as if the Earth was suddenly belching out these enormous black clouds. It was really weird. It looked like the clouds were coming right out of the planet itself, enveloping it in a shroud of darkness. And even though most of the clouds seemed to remain close to the Earth, in the Earth's atmosphere, some were being hurled into space at what seemed to be incredible speeds. As we watched in fascination, one of

140

these huge black storm clouds seemed to be heading straight towards us! We jumped up, looking for cover, but before we'd even taken the first step, the black cloud rammed into the Mothership. We all raised our hands as if to avoid the blow. But nothing happened. The cloud was gone. It just disappeared, as if it had passed right through the Mothership!

"Wow!" cried Janus, "Was that weird or what!"

"Totally and completely weird!" said Jacob, as we breathed a sigh of relief and continued to watch planet Earth in fascination. She kept on belching up these huge black clouds. Now the whole planet was so shrouded with black clouds that we could hardly see its surface anymore.

"What on Earth is happening?" cried Janus. The very next instant, the droves of starships that had been hovering peacefully above the Mothership started to move and flew at lightning speed towards the Earth. These were followed by hoards and hoards of starships rapidly taking off from the Mothership. In less than a minute or two, the whole night sky was alive with the light of thousands of starships on their way towards planet Earth.

Planet Earth continued to belch and spew forth enormous black clouds from its interior. The starships passed right through the clouds, as if the clouds (or the starships) had no solid substance. Then another immense black cloud sped towards us, but it too passed right through the Mothership.

We could no longer see the surface of the Earth. It was as if the whole planet was now enveloped in one gigantic black cloud, which was about to strangle the Earth. It wasn't a pleasant sight.

Then suddenly the grassy area where we stood was illuminated by three blinding flashes of light. As we rubbed our eyes in surprise, we found that three beautiful women were standing before us. One of them I recognized: It was Ticha, my guardian angel! She too had a look of alarm on her face.

"Starbrow," she said and ran towards me.

"Moncler," said the second woman and ran over to Jacob and took his hand. She was wearing a wizard's robe, very much like Jacob's. She too was very beautiful. But it was her short brown hair that gave her away. She was just as Jacob had described her so I knew she was Lia, Moncler's guardian angel.

The third woman ran over to Janus. She was as tall and as strong as he was and her hair was long, golden and curly. Her radiant face, emerald-green eyes and pointy elven ears told me at once she was Telperion's guardian angel Vildis.

"What's going on?" we asked in alarm.

"The Earth is entering the 5th dimension," cried Ticha, but she didn't seem all that happy about it.

"I thought that was supposed to be a good thing," said Janus, eyeing the black clouds suspiciously.

"And so it is," said Vildis. Her voice was deep and strong. "But in order to ascend to the 5th dimension, Planet Earth has to release all the negative thoughts of humanity."

"Is that what those black clouds are?" I asked.

"Yes," said Ticha. "The clouds you see are the etheric discharge of all of humanity's negative thoughts."

"When you say etheric, does that mean that the people on Earth can't see the clouds?" asked Jacob.

"Yes," replied Lia. "The reason why you can see them is because you are now residing in the heightened vibrational frequency of the Mothership."

As we spoke, the Intergalactic Fleet's starships were taking up their positions around the Earth. It wasn't long before they had surrounded the whole planet, from North Pole to South Pole. It seemed to me that I could see beams of light shooting out from starship to starship. To my eyes, it looked as if the whole Earth was surrounded by a golden light grid.

"Mother Earth has fever," said Lia. "She is releasing, discharging everything that is not in harmony with the 5th dimension's vibratory frequency of Love and Light."

"A fever...? How can that be..." I asked.

"Humanity's negative thoughts. Fear, disharmony, separation, limitation..." said Lia, "... they affect Mother Earth just like a physical sickness, as you understand it."

"Is it dangerous?" asked Janus.

"If it weren't for the Great White Brotherhood and the Ashtar Command, I would say that humanity's future on Earth looked pretty bleak," said Vildis.

"It looks pretty bleak to me now," grunted Janus.

The Ashtar Command's starships continued sending waves of golden light towards the Earth. At the same time, lots more small ships were taking off from the Mothership and racing towards Earth. They flew right past the starships' light grid and disappeared into the pitch black

142

atmosphere surrounding the planet.

"What are those little starships up to?" cried Janus as they zoomed into the blackness.

"I don't know," said Ticha. She too sounded alarmed. "I've never seen so many ships go so close before..."

Ticha, Vildis and Lia looked at each other for a moment. Then they turned towards us.

"Earth's transition into the 5th dimension has now reached a very critical phase," said Lia seriously. "Every second counts. We have just received a summons from Commander Ashtar. He is calling all the volunteers to join him at once."

Jacob and Janus and I looked at each other nervously.

"Don't be afraid," said Vildis, softly. "Now is your time."

As she spoke, the Relaxation Forest and our guardian angels began to fade. I felt a tingling at the top of my head. Then every single cell and atom in my body started to vibrate. The next moment Jacob and Janus and I were standing in a huge, oval-shaped hall.

11

The Shadow Earth

We looked around in surprise and wonder. The hall or auditorium was a fantastic place. It was enormous, really huge. I guessed it was at least 200 yards long and there must have been at least 30-40 yards to its beautiful vaulted ceiling. The whole place was made of some kind of smooth, silvery material, which was very pleasing to look at. The silvery material was almost transparent and had a fluid, water-like quality. Inside the hall, there were hundreds of the same pea-pod-shaped chairs we had sat in during our visit to the Cosmic Library. Only now, the chairs were arranged in long rows, auditorium style. At the front, there was a massive raised platform with a podium in the middle. Behind the platform was a great archway with a huge door in it. And above the platform, there was this gigantic screen, as big as the screen in a movie theater, which just seemed to float in the air. On the screen, was a big picture of Planet Earth, which was now completely enshrouded by thick black clouds. A bit further out, we could see the whole armada of starships surrounding the Earth.

There were hundreds of people in the hall. Most of them were crowded around the huge screen, following the dramatic events that were taking place. But more groups of people just kept arriving—or popping up as it were, out of thin air. It was funny to watch. Suddenly two, three or four more people would just appear out of nowhere, just as we had done. And then they'd look in surprise, first at themselves and then at their new surroundings, just like we did.

The different groups that kept popping up turned out to be quite a crowd. On closer inspection, the auditorium was filling up with a veritable cornucopia of outlandish looking characters, adventurers, elves and Jedi Knights. It was sort of like mixing Star Wars, the Lord of the Rings and Dungeons & Dragons all into one great hodgepodge. Tall elves and exotic wizards were standing cheek to jowl with weird-looking techies and turbocharged pilots who looked like they came straight from a sequel to Star Wars. Others were so beautiful that I was sure they'd just stepped out of some fairy tale.

"What's going on now?" cried Jacob and pointed at the screen. We looked up and saw how the whole Earth seemed to tremble, as if the planet was desperately trying to shake off the black clouds that were strangling her. I had the feeling that the Earth was about to erupt or have a planetary epileptic fit. The Ashtar Command's starships continued to hold their light grid in place around the Earth. I felt certain they were trying to calm the Earth's violent discharge.

"What do you think the ships are doing?" asked Janus.

"It's hard to tell," I replied. "But I'm sure they're trying to help."

At that moment, one of the very large starships moved away from its position in the light grid and zoomed back towards the Mothership. I had the feeling that now we were finally going to get a chance to meet our intergalactic hosts. The three of us followed the rest of the crowd towards the front of the hall. No more groups were popping out of thin air now and most people were settling into the seats, as close to the front as possible. We followed suit.

As I looked around, I discovered that most of the people present were in their early twenties like us. From the way they looked, I guessed they were probably dedicated D&D, Star Wars and Lord of the Rings freaks, just like we were. But here and there, there were some older people as well, like the group of yogis in loincloths who were sitting on the ground in lotus positions in the front row. The group of sun burnt South American shamans in colorful garb who were talking to a group of bald-headed Shaolin monks in orange robes also looked older. And so did the nuns in their long, white robes—and two men and two women who looked very much like the druids we'd seen in our past life regression in Avalon. There was one group whose age I just couldn't begin to guess—because they looked so strange. As far as I could tell, they must have been Egyptian priests and priestesses because they had these large, elongated heads like the ones I'd seen in books about ancient Egypt.

"Will you check out these weird-looking dudes and dudettes!" chuckled Janus.

"You should talk," kidded Jacob, "You know you don't exactly look like a bank clerk yourself!"

"Howdy folks!" said a young guy with a real Southern drawl as he sat down next to us. There was something about him that made me feel sure he was from Texas. Four more spacey-looking space cadets filed into the seats next to him. They were all wearing the same out-of-sight high-tech gear and the weirdest looking V-shaped sunglasses I'd ever seen. And this guy, well, he was as good looking as Tom Cruise in Top Gun, but dressed more for a new episode of Star Trek.

"Howdy!" I said to him and stuck out my hand.

"The Ashtar Command really seems to know their job, don't they?" he quipped.

"Yeah..." I replied, "though it's kind of hard to say exactly what they're doing."

"Yeah, I know what you mean," he grinned, "but whatever it is, it sure looks like it's helping!"

From what we could tell, it looked like the starships were still maintaining their close formation around the Earth. But I had the weirdest feeling that Planet Earth was kind of like this huge slumbering volcano that would erupt immediately if the Ashtar Command disbanded the network of light it was holding around her.

"Lemme guess," my new friend continued, "you guys have got to be Dungeons & Dragons players!"

"I wonder how you guessed," grinned Janus, joining our conversation.

"What about you all?" asked Jacob.

"Us? Oh, we're United States Air Force," he said and saluted smartly. "King Kevin at your service!"

"Then all the volunteers aren't D&D gamers?" I asked.

"Well quite a few are," Kevin replied as if he was some kind of expert even though he probably hadn't been in the auditorium more than a couple of minutes more than us. "... but some of these dudes do have other backgrounds! You see those Japanese hardbodies over there?" he pointed at four Japanese babes decked out in magnificent samurai-style robes. "The low down on them is that they're all really top-notch business women from one of Japan's most powerful computer corporations!"

"Well what do ya know..." said Janus, "they even had me fooled...!"

Next Kevin pointed to some really far out looking dudes. "Those guys, they're all cyberspace nerds and Star Wars geeks." Which wasn't that hard to tell, considering their Star Wars garb.

"Why they'd even make Luke Skywalker proud," whistled Janus.

"And our curly-haired friends over there in the front row," continued

146

Kevin, "well, the low-down on them is they're Sai Baba disciples. The one with the huge head of hair is supposed to be this famous Indian doctor and the other one is a quantum physicist."

"You must have been here for hours and hours to ferret out all this information," said Janus, awed by Kevin's seemingly encyclopedic knowledge of the people gathered in the hall.

"Oh no," he said, "I arrived just about a minute before you guys. It's these V-shades of mine that do the trick!" He took them off and grinned. "They give me the low-down on everything and everybody. Take a look for yourselves." He handed me his weird-looking glasses. I put them on. It was amazing! No matter where I looked, the glasses gave me a comprehensive read-out of whatever I was looking at.

"Wow!" I said and handed them over to Janus.

"Coolness!" said Janus. "This is better than Terminator 2!"

"Hey Kevin, what about those Shaolin monks over there?" asked Jacob, pointing towards three bald-headed monks. "What's the low-down on them?"

"Well," laughed Kevin as he put on his sunglasses again. "What can I tell you?! Shaolin monks are Shaolin monks! Some folks are just closer to their True Selves than others!"

"Can't those glasses tell you what's happening back on Earth?" I asked, eyeing the big screen nervously.

"Well if they can, I haven't learned how to set them for distant readings yet," he said. "Maybe you should ask one of Baba's disciples over there. They have that knowledgeable vibe!"

At that very moment, the door at the end of the platform slid soundlessly to one side. A bright white light blazed through the doorway and everyone stopped talking. A tall man with a noble bearing emerged and stepped up on the platform. He was wearing a silver spacesuit that shimmered and reflected the light as he moved. His silver suit was tight, like a jumpsuit, and it covered his whole body—only his hands and face were exposed. And on his head, he wore a silver helm that fitted snugly around his head. He strode swiftly across the platform towards the podium, followed by about a 150 men and women dressed in similar silver garb and helms. They all had what looked like military badges or emblems on their left chests. And they all radiated the same bright silvery white light as their leader.

When their leader reached the speaker's podium, he removed his helm. I recognized him immediately. He was Commander Ashtar, the Supreme

147

Commander of the Intergalactic Fleet. The others took up their position behind him, in long rows, and removed their helms.

We watched in fascination as Ashtar and his team of Star People lined up before us. The appearance of the Star People varied greatly. Some were very short, like four feet tall or even less with bluish-green skin and dark, almond-shaped eyes. Others were very tall and thin, like six or seven feet tall—and their skin had a golden hue. But despite the striking differences in their appearance, all of the Star People looked like human beings. And they were beautiful, very very beautiful, In fact, they were the most beautiful, radiant beings I'd ever seen in my entire life. And as they stood there, before us, they smiled at us... radiant, kind smiles, such as I'd never seen before.

"Greetings, my Brothers and Sisters in the Light!" said their leader in a loud, clear voice. "I AM Ashtar." He didn't move his lips when he talked, but I heard his voice inside my head, just as I did when Ticha spoke to me. I wondered for a moment how he could make himself understood to everyone gathered here since everyone spoke different languages, but a quick glance around made it clear that everyone understood what he was saying perfectly.

"I apologize for this abrupt summons," said Ashtar, "but the situation on Planet Earth has suddenly reached a very critical stage, so we need your help right now."

He motioned towards the giant screen above him. The picture of Earth that we had been watching changed. We saw a city and I realized it must be San Francisco because of the Golden Gate Bridge. There were scenes of total chaos. And then we saw the bridge collapsing and cars being thrown into the water and scattered across the highways leading up to the bridge. It seemed as if we were witnessing the aftershocks of a massive earthquake. The scene changed and we saw the ruins of skyscrapers and people everywhere, screaming and fleeing. It was total panic.

"Oh no!" screamed a golden-haired elf-woman, "That's where I come from!"

"For the moment, our starships have stabilized the Earth's violent release process," said Ashtar. "but we cannot keep it up much longer. Mother Earth is ascending rapidly into the 5th dimension. And in order to do so, she must release all the negative thoughts and energies of humanity she has collected throughout the ages and which have polluted her being for so long."

As Ashtar spoke, our eyes were glued to the screen above his head. In quick succession, one terrifying scene after another flashed across the screen. First we saw a violent volcanic eruption and people being evacuated. Then avalanches of snow come crushing down over small villages. Then strange cloud formations and gale force winds—and finally, powerful tidal waves creating havoc in the oceans. It looked like all of Planet Earth was in violent uproar.

"What's happening to Earth?" cried one of the Japanese samurai women in distress.

"Let me explain," said Ashtar and made a circular movement with his hand. Instantly, a huge man-size 3-D hologram of Planet Earth appeared at his side, revolving slowly on its axis. The hologram was about 6 feet in diameter—and it was translucent so we could see through the Earth's blue oceans and brown-green land masses into its interior.

"Planet Earth—Mother Earth—is a living organism," said Ashtar as the blue orb rotated slowly at his side. "A living organism with a consciousness which is evolving—just like you and I are evolving. Now Mother Earth is ascending into the 5th dimension. And in order to do so, she must release all the fear, disharmony, limitation thinking, egotistical behavior patterns and other dense energies she has carried with her for so long. In other words, everything that is not in harmony with the higher levels of consciousness and the higher vibrational frequencies of the 5th dimension must go. If the level of the collective consciousness of the beings residing on Earth was at the same level as that of Mother Earth's, there would be no problem. Then Mother Earth and humanity could— and would—ascend together into the 5th dimension together easily and effortlessly."

As Ashtar told us of this harmonious possibility, the 3-D hologram of Earth began to glow with a bright, golden aura. I saw Planet Earth become a shining star in the heavens...

"Unfortunately this is not the case," said Ashtar, and the hologram went dark again. "The collective consciousness of humanity has fallen woefully behind. This is because as we speak, the focus of the collective consciousness is on limitation, lack, disharmony, fear, war, sickness, separation—and all the other types of negative thinking that have been causing humanity to experience so much pain and anguish."

Ashtar made another circular movement with his hand and another hologram appeared, which surrounded and interpenetrated the first 3-D hologram of Earth. The second hologram was a little bit larger than the first—and it had a dark black-black color. The second hologram

149

appeared like a gray Shadow Earth, surrounding and suffocating the Mother Earth we knew.

"What you now see here," said Ashtar, "is the dark cloud of fear and negativity that is at present enveloping and penetrating Mother Earth. This cloud or shadow is, in fact, nothing more—and nothing less—than all the negative thoughts in the collective consciousness of humanity. And it is this Shadow Earth, which is made up of so many negative thoughts and energies, that is the cause of the violent physical discharges Mother Earth has been experiencing lately. As Mother Earth tries to throw off these energies, the Earth experiences what you call earthquakes, volcanoes, the shifting of the Earth's crust, violent changes in the weather and countless other phenomena you label natural disasters."

We watched as the 3-D hologram of Mother Earth trembled and shook as she tried to shake off the heavy, negative clouds of thought that were strangling her. We saw how the tremors made the earth's crust shift ever so slightly, causing huge disruptions on the Earth's surface. Earth, sky, ocean, all was in uproar.

"Humankind's egotistical separation thinking is so greatly out of sync with Mother Earth's," Ashtar continued, "that wherever human beings tread, they leave behind them huge scars and devastating wounds, the ravages of pollution, greed, war, fear, anger, hatred and cataclysmic violence. But the end has now come. Mother Earth can take no more. She can no longer continue as she did before, so she is sick. She is on fire. She has a fever, because she must release all these dense energies and undergo a total cleansing. All life forms inhabiting her being which are not in harmony with her must now be cast off. And she has no choice but to do this because she is ascending rapidly into the 5th dimension. Nothing can stop her ascension course now because her time as a 3rd and 4th dimensional test zone is finally over. So my friends, you can see why there is no turning back now for Mother Earth. And why humanity today faces the most dramatic choice of its entire history upon Earth. Humankind can either raise its consciousness and vibrational frequencies so they are in sync with Mother Earth—and ascend into the 5th dimension with her. Or humankind can continue on their present destructive pathway—in the lower frequency range—and be wiped out by the cataclysmic Earth changes caused by Mother Earth's cleansing processes. If this take place, all the souls of humanity will depart from the planet and be recycled elsewhere in the Universe to continue their soul evolution."

The whole time Ashtar was speaking, the eyes of his audience were glued to the trembling 3-D hologram of Earth. "Approximately 30 Earth minutes ago, Mother Earth began to discharge unusually large amounts of negative thought energy." The look on Ashtar's face told us how critical the situation was. Again we saw how the 3-D hologram of the dark Shadow Earth threatened to overwhelm and engulf Earth in total darkness. "According to the latest calculations from the Command's Department of Planetary Dimensional Shifts," continued Ashtar, "unless something really drastic is done immediately, Mother Earth will make a total axis shift very soon—an axis shift which will look like this." He pointed to the hologram at his side, which made a sudden shift on its axis. The planet's position changed completely, right before our eyes. In one fell swoop, the North Pole became the South Pole—and the surface of the Earth as we knew it was completely obliterated. At the very same moment, the dark gray Shadow Earth vanished. A collective gasp of horror swept through the auditorium.

"Yes, my friends," Ashtar continued, "such is the critical situation we find ourselves in at this moment. If Mother Earth makes an axis shift such as this, it will completely eradicate all life on Earth as you know it."

A heavy silence descended over the auditorium for what seemed an eternity.

Then Ashtar resolutely raised his arms and broke the heavy silence. "As you have seen, our starships have formed a network of light around the Earth. This network or grid acts to stabilize Mother Earth's process of discharge by balancing the Earth's interior and exterior. This will hold back the axis shift," he said, "at least for a while."

A collective sigh of relief rippled across the room.

"But alas, my friends," he continued slowly, "we cannot hold back the axis shift in this way for very long. No technology can. Our experts estimate that the light grid our starships are holding in place can postpone an axis shift for the next 48 hours. But no longer than that. After that, we will not be able to hold back Mother Earth's releasing processes any longer on our own. That is why we need help. And why we summoned you here, my friends, in Planet Earth's darkest hour."

Ashtar left the podium and walked over to the edge of the platform, as if he felt the need to come closer to us at this critical moment in Earth's history. "The Department of Planetary Dimensional Shifts estimates," he continued, his voice now kind and gentle as a loving father's, "that there

151

is only thing that will be able to stabilize Earth sufficiently to prevent this total axis shift from happening in 48 hours from now. And that is a dramatic shift or raising of the collective consciousness of humankind. In other words, if humanity is able to replace its dark visions of fear and negativity with something more positive and loving—in other words, with a positive New Vision—it should be possible to calm Mother Earth enough so that she can continue her ascension into the 5th dimension in a more peaceful and harmonious way.

"And that, my friends, is why you are here. Now, at this critical juncture in Earth's history, it is crucial that you fulfill the missions each of you failed to complete in your past life." Suddenly I began to understand why we'd been given those past life regressions. "Now, more than ever before, it is crucial that each of you fulfill your mission and anchor the New Vision in the collective consciousness. And now, it is obvious, there is not a moment to lose."

"But... I don't understand," said a tall African dressed in bright-colored tribal garments. "How can a few hundred people change the collective consciousness of a planet with six billion people?"

"Good question," said Ashtar. "The answer is you can do so by creating a critical mass. This will be the key. To create a critical mass. Because only by creating a critical mass will it be possible for you to anchor the New Vision in the collective consciousness and stabilize the condition of Mother Earth."

Jacob took Moncler's spell book out of his backpack and began scribbling in it.

"What are you doing?" I asked in surprise.

"Sshh," he said. "This is really interesting. Critical mass is one of the things I've been wondering about since Stanley Donne's experiment." Janus looked over at me and raised his left eyebrow.

"Some of you may have heard of the 100th Monkey Syndrome," continued Ashtar, "but let me explain briefly. Some years ago, some of your Earth scientists conducted an experiment involving several small Japanese islands. The only inhabitants on these islands were monkeys. And the diet of these monkeys consisted of, among other things, sweet potatoes, which the monkeys dug out of the ground and ate. The scientists conducting the experiment discovered that one of the monkeys on one of the islands had learned how to clean and scrub the potatoes before he ate them. It wasn't long before more and more of the monkeys on that island also learned how to clean and scrub their potatoes before

152

they ate them. But what was really interesting was that a short while after about a 100 monkeys on this first island learned how to do this, the monkeys on all the neighboring islands also started cleaning and scrubbing their potatoes before eating them. And this happened even though these monkeys had no physical contact with any of the monkeys from the first island. Now how could this happen?" asked Ashtar.

"Consciousness," mumbled Jacob as he wrote furiously in his spell book. "Consciousness is non-local in space and time.

"The phenomena can be explained by examining the way consciousness works," Ashtar continued. "On the physical plane, it seems as if we are all separate individuals. But on the inner planes—in the invisible realm of consciousness—we are all one. We are all connected to one and another. This means that when one individual raises and changes his or her consciousness, the entire collective consciousness is raised and changed too, without any form of physical contact. So this explains why the monkeys on the other islands suddenly learned how to wash and scrub their potatoes before they ate them. Because when some of the monkeys—the 100 monkeys on the first island—changed and expanded their consciousness, it had an immediate effect on the entire collective monkey consciousness. Without any kind of physical contact between the monkeys."

"Coolness," whispered Janus, nudging Jacob gently, "now I'm beginning to see why you think this stuff is so interesting..."

But Ashtar wasn't finished. "This is also why, my friends," he continued, "that the Ascended Masters are always saying that the Good of One is the Good of All. Because when you change your consciousness, it affects all of humanity. And mathematically speaking—in other words if we look at the percentages—it doesn't take that many enlightened human beings to effect the entire collective consciousness." Ashtar turned towards one of his team members, "Am I right, Monka?"

Monka bowed slightly and stepped forward. "What you say is correct, Commander. The Department of Planetary Dimensional Shifts has calculated that only 1% of the population on Planet Earth is required to achieve a critical mass on Earth. In other words, if 60 million people—that's 1% of Earthlings—were able to radically change their consciousness, this critical mass would automatically trigger a change in the consciousness of the remaining 99% of the population."

60 million people I thought to myself. That's a whole lot of people. I could only think of very few people in my old circle of acquaintances

back on Earth who'd be interested in drastically changing their consciousness!

"I know what you're all thinking," said Monka. "That 60 million people is a very large number. Very large indeed. And that there are only 600 of you present here today! Please allow me to explain.

"Studies of other planets that have ascended," Monka continued, "demonstrate, beyond a shadow of a doubt, that if a few hundred dedicated and enlightened individuals simultaneously transmit a New Vision along a planet's grid of energy centers and energy lines, the effect of their shift in consciousness will be exponential—or many times increased. This means that, under the right conditions, a relatively few enlightened individuals can actually create a critical mass almost instantaneously. Providing they are working together in a finely tuned and precisely orchestrated effort.

"Wow," said Janus and Jacob in unison.

"And this, my friends, is exactly what we are now going to call upon you to do. And we make this request in full confidence because of your lineage. You are the 600 chosen souls who have the ability to create a critical mass on Planet Earth. We have calculated that when you 600 simultaneously take up your positions on the Earth's most important Power Spots and simultaneously send out the New Vision from these points, the effect of your transmissions will be increased 100,000 times. And if you have followed me so far, you will have guessed my next calculation. That $600 \times 100,000 = 60,000,000$. So we arrive at the figure of the 60 million souls we are looking for. The 1% of the Earth's population, which we must attain in order to create a critical mass which can calm Mother Earth and prevent an axis shift from occurring, in just 48 hours from now."

You could have heard the dropping of a pin, it was so quiet in the hall. Everyone was trying to understand the full implication of what Monka had just said.

Janus whistled slowly and whispered, "It ain't over till it's over!" It was so quiet that everybody heard him. A collective chuckle rumbled though the hall.

"You said it man!" said Kevin and laughed out loud.

Monka stepped back and Ashtar began speaking again. "Now I think it must be clear why we have summoned you at this time, in Planet Earth's darkest hour. And thanks to the past life regressions you have all experienced, I think you can now also fully appreciate why we say that

154

indeed—Now is Your Time! Because now you know that verily you have incarnated on Planet Earth before with this very same purpose—to anchor a New Vision in the collective consciousness of humanity. The only real difference is that never before was the situation so critical as it is now. Today your mission is so crucial that if you do not fulfill it, all life on Earth will be completely annihilated. It's as simple as that."

"Talk about performance anxiety," mumbled Janus, "in our past lives we had thousands of years, now all we've got is 48 hours..!"

"But, my friends, there is another important difference this time," continued Ashtar. "In light of the urgency of the situation and because you have so precious little time, we have decided to send you on the absolute fastest Ascension course in the history of the Universe. And we are doing this my friends, because this time, we do not intend for your mission to fail. But first, I would like to introduce you to the Master Mind behind all of this." It was the first time we had seen Ashtar smile. "Now my friends, it is with great pleasure that I introduce you to the Supreme Commander of Mission Earth Ascension. Here is my dearest friend and brother Sananda, known far and wide throughout the galaxies as the Most Radiant One!"

155

12

The Most Radiant One

Ashtar once again made a circular movement with his hand—and the 3-D hologram of Earth at his side vanished. The door at the end of the platform again opened without a sound and a powerful white light came cascading into the hall like a great wave. Then the light began moving towards the podium and I saw it was coming from the man Ashtar called Sananda!

"Welcome, my motley crew," he said, stretching his arms out wide as he stood before us. "Truly it is a blessing and a wonder to see you all here, shining so brightly once again. Because though I know that your adventures on Earth have at times dimmed your wondrous light a little, I can also see that none of you have suffered any permanent damage from your sojourn on the Earth plane.

"Though you may have forgotten, I still remember that before you descended to Earth, we made a solemn agreement. You promised to do your utmost to assist humanity—and I promised to remind you of your pledge if you forgot," he laughed. "That is why, during this critical time, I asked for a special dispensation for all of you to be allowed to come up into the Mothership. So that I could fulfill my pledge and remind you once again of your true origin, your true mission and your true selves, now that Planet Earth is ascending into the 5th dimension. And as it turns out, we discover that the timing of this event was even more auspicious than even I could have planned!" Here he paused for a moment, as if to consider the synchronicity of events.

"But to sum up the situation for you. Thanks to the tireless and heroic efforts of the Ashtar Command, we have managed to gain a little extra time—48 hours to be exact—until Mother Earth makes a total axis shift. But obviously 48 hours is not enough, so I have devised a plan that we believe—with your help—can succeed. And that plan is, as Monka and

156

Ashtar briefly sketched for you, to create and use a critical mass to anchor the New Vision in the collective consciousness of humanity, thereby calming the etheric body of Mother Earth for a while. Our experts calculate that if we can do this, we can postpone the threatened axis shift for another two to three years.

"And obviously, it is our sincere hope that by gaining these extra two to three years, we will have enough time to help a much larger percentage of the Earth's population raise their consciousness so that humankind will be able to ascend into the 5th dimension with Mother Earth. For even though it may appear at present as if humanity is in a desperate situation, there are in fact, many, many thousands of souls on Earth who are ready for the ascension process. And there are hundreds upon hundreds of thousands who are just about to awaken, even though they are not aware of it yet."

Sananda paused for a moment as if lost in thought. "But now to the plan," he said as if preparing himself and us to take the next step. "In order to activate the Power Spots on Earth, you will need the interdimensional "keys" or weapons which the Great White Brotherhood gave you many hundreds of years ago when you first attempted to establish the Light Grid on Earth. These interdimensional "keys" or weapons are closely connected to your soul emanation and your special Power Spot. Without these weapons, you will not be able to activate your Power Spot.

"When you died and left your bodies, your interdimensional weapons were removed from the Earth plane so that they would not fall into the hands of unscrupulous people who might misuse their mighty powers. And they were taken to a place where they could be kept in safety. This place is called Shamballa, the Great White Brotherhood's headquarters in the 5th dimension. Shamballa is also known as the City of Light. And it is here, in the City of Light, that your weapons have been kept for almost fifteen hundred years now, waiting for you, the Guardians of the Earth, to return and reclaim them.

"So you see, my dear friends, the time has now come when you must go to Shamballa to reclaim your interdimensional weapons, for without them, you cannot fulfill your mission and activate the Power Spots and establish the Light Grid. And without activating the Light Grid, a critical mass cannot be achieved and the New Vision will not have enough impact to prevent the Earth's axis shift, 48 hours from now! So time is of the essence!"

As Sananda talked of our interdimensional weapons, I briefly saw in my mind's eye a vision of the silver star, which I had borne upon my brow for such a brief time in my lifetime as Dana. I also had a glimpse of the magic staff Jacob had carried with him during his days as Gaius, and the mighty jeweled sword Janus had borne as Loran.

"But the Road to Shamballa is not for everyone," I heard Sananda saying. "Only those who have passed their initiations—and understand the Nature of Reality and have learned how to master it—may enter into Shamballa, the City of Light. Therefore my friends, to fulfill your mission, you must first walk the path which all Ascended Masters have walked on their pathway to Ascension. But thanks to the special dispensation that I have called forth, you will be allowed to take the absolute fastest Ascension course in the history of the Universe, as Ashtar called it." said Sananda and winked at the Commander.

"This crash course in Ascension consists of the following initiations. To begin, you will enter the 4th dimension and pass through three etheric Gateways, each of which is governed by the Ascended Masters. In order to advance through each Gateway, you will be given a test, which you will have to pass through. By passing the test, you will prove that you have mastered the Universal Lesson represented by that Gateway. You will only be able to gain access to the 5th dimension and Shamballa by passing through all three Gateways. And this you must do, if you are to reclaim your mighty weapons.

"But as I said before: The Road to Shamballa is not for everyone. The 4th dimension is filled with countless heavens and hells, and you will be faced with great temptations and challenges on your way. If you should succumb to the lure of one of the temptations you meet on your way, there is a real risk you will be stuck in the 4th dimension indefinitely."

Ashtar stepped up next to Sananda again. "I am afraid I must cut this discussion short, my friends. One of my wing commanders has sent me an urgent message. Because of the turmoil being created by the unusual events taking place in this part of our solar system, it behooves us to send you into the 4th dimension immediately. There's not a moment to waste. Now, in order to move into the 4th dimension, you will have to pass through an interdimensional Wormhole," he continued, "... which is an etheric opening between the dimensions. And we will be sending you through immediately. So if you have no further questions, make yourselves ready!"

"I have just one question," cried one of the young Jedi Knights. "Just one question! How can we manage to do all that Sananda described, pass all these tests, find Shamballa, reclaim our weapons—and then return to Earth and anchor the New Vision in less than 48 hours?"

"Fortunately for us, time behaves somewhat differently in the 4th dimension," said Ashtar. "So we must use this to our advantage. Just remember my friends, even though it may seem as if you have been away for days or even weeks, only a few hours will have passed on Earth when you step out on this side again. But still, we must hurry. There's not a moment to lose! With each passing second, your brothers and sisters on Earth are moving ever closer to total annihilation!"

Sparks of lightning flickered and flashed out from the Wormhole as if it were a turbocharged vortex of high-powered electrical current. The vortex—or interdimensional opening—had suddenly appeared at the other end of the hall when seven of Ashtar's Star People stood there for a moment making rapid circular movements with their hands. Now the groups of volunteers stood in hushed silence in a long line in front of the Wormhole, contemplating their strange fate. Jacob and Janus and I were near the front of the line. The first group of volunteers, the four Japanese samurai women, stepped up to the Wormhole. One of the Star People whispered a few quiet words to the four women who then clasped hands and stepped into the Wormhole. The moment they touched the opening, they were immediately sucked into the huge whirling vortex of energy and disappeared. The next group placed itself in front of the Wormhole. As they were preparing to step into the vortex, I looked back at the podium one last time. Sananda and Ashtar stood there still—like two shining pillars of light—watching as we volunteers stepped into the Wormhole.

Sananda placed his hand on his heart—and it went straight to my heart.

When it was our turn, we stepped forward and stood before the interdimensional opening without a word. We felt the mighty force of the vortex sucking us into itself.

"Once you step into the Wormhole, you will pass by different portals, but do not let them tempt you. They are not for you," said one of the Star People. "Your destination is the Crystal Stair! The Crystal Stair leads to the First Gateway that you must pass. So remember, when you come to the Crystal Stair, you must step out of the Wormhole. Now hold each other's hands tightly and don't let go. Keep a firm hold on each other!"

"Sounds like quite a ride!" said Jacob.

"Yeah, just think of the scientific paper you'll be able to write after this... you'll probably win a Noble Prize," said Janus as he grabbed our hands and pulled us into the Wormhole.

The moment we touched the Wormhole, we were sucked into the swirling vortex with enormous force. It felt as if an intense force field immediately surrounded and penetrated us, propelling us through this huge turbocharged tunnel of flashing light and energy. The light was so bright that it hurt my eyes. The vortex pulled at us with ferocious power as we clung to each other and felt ourselves being pressed forward. I heard Jacob and Janus moaning at my side and realized that I too was moaning. When the tunnel turned abruptly upwards, we had to hold onto each other with all our might so as not to be torn apart. We somersaulted around and were sucked forward through more amazing twists and turns.

A moment later, we stopped abruptly and found ourselves being pulled towards one of the portals. As we floated before the portal, we found ourselves gazing through it towards a beautiful azure blue sea, which was stretched out before us on the other side of the portal. We stared in fascination at the scene. In the middle of that fabulously blue sea, there was a beautiful tropical island with tall palm trees swaying in the breeze. It looked just like paradise, surrounded as it was by clear, blue water. And the beach on the island... well the beach looked like it was made of crystals, clear quartz crystals. That was until we looked a little further and found that the beach had changed... now the stones were black obsidian. Then we let our eyes wander a little further down the beach only to find the stones had changed again, to gold-colored citrine.

"What a beach!" I said.

"Yeah," said Janus, "Look, around the bend, the stones change again!"

He was right, a little further around the island, the beach seemed to be made of rose quartz, then the stones changed again, this time into blue lapis lazuli, and then into violet amethyst. Finally, we realized our gaze had circumvented the whole island because we were right back to the beginning of the beach which was made of clear quartz crystals."

"Seven different kinds of stones," said Jacob. "One for each chakra."

Janus and I looked at Jacob in surprise. "How did you know that?" I asked.

"I guess it goes with the Wizard territory," said Jacob, looking as surprised as we were.

"Too bad we only have 48 hours till total destruction," sighed Janus, "'cause I've always dreamed about spending a week or two on a tropical island like this. It looks exactly like the one you see in the TV commercials for Bounty bars..."

The moment he said that, we were sucked on through the swirling vortex again. As the vortex propelled us abruptly downwards, we soared head first down towards a dark opening to the left.

"Yee-haa!" cried Janus, "Now this is what I call a roller coaster ride!"

We stopped abruptly at a dark opening in the side of the Wormhole— another portal. On the other side of the portal, we saw thousands and thousands of people yelling and screaming in front of a large stage. Up on the stage, strobes of blinding, flashing lights were rotating around three half-naked young men who were writhing and shouting into microphones to the rhythm of the loudest, most deafening drumbeat I'd ever heard. Between the strobe lights, the pounding drumbeats, the hysterical moaning and shouting, we were sure we were getting a bird's eye view of the making of some kind of 3-D horror movie.

"This must be what they call hell," I said.

"Yeah," cried Jacob over the deafening noise, "It's hard to tell whether we've landed in the Dark Land of Mordor or a Prodigy concert!"

"This can't be where we're going," I said.

The moment I said that we were sucked into the vortex again with terrifying speed.

"We can't keep on doing this forever!" said Jacob. "It's the Crystal Stair we're after."

The moment he said that, we found ourselves in front of another opening. On the other side of this portal, there was a large rocky cavern. Each side of the cave opened up into a wide passageway. The one on the left led to a long passage with flickering torches hanging on its walls. The one on the right led to a broad stairway, which wound downwards into darkness. The middle opening led to a wide stairway of shining crystals.

"This must be the Crystal Stair," said Janus.

"Let's go," I said. We floated towards the portal and reached our hands out to touch it. The moment we touched it, I felt a powerful jolt as we were sucked through the portal and hurled onto the cold stone floor on the other side.

PART THREE

THE ROAD TO SHAMBALLA

WEDNESDAY APRIL 1, 00:30:16 GMT EARTH TIME
TO
WEDNESDAY APRIL 1, 02:19:11 GMT EARTH TIME

1

The Blue Temple

We got up from the cold stone floor. It felt strange to have solid ground underneath our feet again after our wild ride through the Wormhole. We entered the cave and studied the three openings. A cold wind blew up from the stairway to the right. It had a foul, stuffy smell, which made us shiver. I was glad we weren't going that way.

We walked over to the Crystal Stair. I placed my foot on the first stair and immediately felt a comfortable tingling sensation spread through my body. "This is definitely the way for us," I said. We sprang forward and began climbing the stairs.

It was quite a long staircase, so we climbed for several minutes until we reached the top and stepped out into a long, wide passageway with a high, vaulted ceiling. As we walked down the passageway, we discovered that the walls on both sides of the passageway were decorated with beautiful wall paintings. All the paintings were of men and women who were surrounded by white or golden auras. Many of the people depicted in the paintings I had seen before. There was Buddha sitting in the lotus position, Moses parting the Red Sea, Mother Mary with the Christ Child, Lao Tzu and Confucius, Mohammed, and Daniel in the Lion's Den...

"This must be the Ascended Masters Hall of Fame!" exclaimed Janus.

"Check this one out," said Jacob. He was looking at a picture of a serious looking man with a long beard. "I'm sure this guy is Socrates."

"And there's Merlin!" cried Janus. "Look! Over here!"

One of the paintings, a little further down, was of Merlin, dressed here as if he was an 18th century French nobleman. He was surrounded by the most beautiful violet flames. We stared at the painting in fascination.

"They all have these out-of-sight halos," said Janus.

"Yeah, they're really beautiful, aren't they? "I said. "Elmar once told me that it shows that whoever's got the halo is an Enlightened Master."

"Hey! Isn't that King Arthur over there?" asked Jacob, pointing to the other side of the passageway.

"I think so!" I said and rushed over to the picture he was pointing at. The picture was of a man dressed in the garb of an Oriental prince. He was wearing a white turban with a huge gemstone. It was strange. Even though his skin was golden brown and he had a closely cropped beard, we were completely sure he was King Arthur.

"That must be a picture of King Arthur as El Morya!" I said, remembering what Elmar had said about King Arthur's different incarnations. "You guys remember the story of Stanley Donne, don't you? The one Elmar told?"

"Weird, isn't it?" whistled Janus, "Even if I'd never heard that story, I'd have recognized him. He looks exactly the same as he did in our past life regression, even in these clothes."

We nodded in agreement and continued down the passageway. Some of the pictures were of Masters we didn't know.

"I know who this one is," exclaimed Jacob as he pointed at a young lad from the Orient who was breathing life into a whole galaxy. "It's gotta be Krishna!"

"You mean like Hare Krishna!" quipped Janus, as he walked over to a picture of a man in an orange robe with a huge, bushy head of hair. "Will you check out the afro on this dude!" The guy in the painting was making the same circular movement with his hand as we'd seen Ashtar make.

Then I realized who it was. "Hey, that's Sai Baba," I said. "He's alive—and lives in India today. I know because Elmar told me he'd visited him several times." As a matter of fact, there were paintings of several other Masters that Elmar had visited over the years. Two of them were depicted a little further down the hall. One was Don Juan Matus, a Mexican nagual, and the other was the Dalai Lama.

"Janus must be right," said Jacob. "Just about everyone here must be one of the Masters who have ascended into the higher dimensions."

"Maybe they're all members of the Great White Brotherhood," I said.

"Well if they are," said Janus, "why don't I see Ashtar anywhere?"

"Maybe these paintings are just of Masters who have been on Earth," I said. "I can't tell you why, but I've got the feeling Ashtar's never been an Earthling!"

"You might be right, Starbrow," said Janus. "But let's not forget our mission."

We knew he was right so we hurried towards the end of the passageway, which just seemed to open out into the Blue. Quite literally. Into the bluest of blue skies I'd ever seen. And it started right there at the end of the passageway, this incredible blue sky—and it just seemed to stretch out before us, all the way to Infinity. Everywhere we looked there was blue sky. Above us, below us, all around us. As we emerged from the passageway, we saw that before us, really a part of the Blueness, was a blue stairway leading up to a vast blue temple, which just seemed to float in the middle of the vast blueness that was everywhere. The blue temple gleamed in the sunlight as if it was made of up millions and millions of tiny blue crystals. Even the temple's beautiful pillars were made of enormous blue crystals.

We walked slowly up the broad blue stairway that led up to the blue temple. Out here in the Blue, a fresh wind was blowing. I took a deep breath and found the air clear and incredibly refreshing. We reached the top of the blue stairway and walked between two of the towering blue pillars towards the entrance of the temple. The entrance was a great Blue Gateway—the First Gateway!

"First check!" said Janus.

We stood before the great Blue Gateway and looked at the massive doors. There was a huge golden knocker on one. Jacob stretched out his hand and hammered on the door. A great booming sound echoed all around us.

"Let the adventure begin!" Janus said softly as the great doors opened.

Inside the temple, there was another row of majestic blue crystal pillars. Even the walls were blue, the same clear blue as the sky outside, only the temple floor was white. In the middle there was a circle of strange-looking inscriptions etched into the floor. An old man was standing in the middle of the circle, dressed in a long white robe. He was tall and regal-looking, with a snow-white beard and show-white hair. A clear white light seemed to radiate from within him, making the blue pillars cast long shadows on the floor. He reminded me of Gandalf the White, the wizard from the Lord of the Rings.

"Welcome to the Blue Temple," said the old man in a deep voice that resonated through the great temple.

We walked towards the old man. The Blue Gateway behind us shut without a sound. When we came to the granite circle, the old man motioned for us to enter. "Greetings, Brothers in the Light," he said as we stepped into the circle. "I AM Kuthumi."

167

"Greetings," said Janus and bowed. "I AM Telperion."

"I AM Starbrow," I said and followed Janus' example.

"I AM Moncler," said Jacob and bowed.

"What brings you to the Blue Temple?" said Kuthumi.

"We're here to find Shamballa," I replied.

"Why do you want to find Shamballa?" he asked.

"We must go there," I continued, "to retrieve our interdimensional weapons—our staff, sword and star—so that we can activate our Power Spot and the Light Grid on Earth."

"Why would you want to do that?" the old man asked again. "Why would you want to activate the Light Grid?"

"So that we can anchor a positive New Vision in the collective consciousness," said Jacob, "to calm Mother Earth and prevent her from making a total axis shift which would annihilate all of humankind."

Kuthumi looked at us intently. "Shamballa is in the 5th dimension," he said. "Only initiates on the Ascension Path are permitted to enter Shamballa, the City of Light."

"So we have been told," said Jacob with a sudden fierceness, "But we are prepared to become initiates. We must enter Shamballa to fulfill our mission."

"You speak as one who knows what it means to be initiated," said Kuthumi as he examined Jacob closely. "But do you?!"

"Err... well... not exactly," stammered Jacob.

"Will you not tell us, Master Kuthumi, what it means to become an initiate?" I asked. "We have so little time!"

Kuthumi turned towards me and held me with his penetrating gaze. Then he turned to Janus and then Jacob, and held them both for a long moment with his eyes. Afterwards he said, "Yes, my young friends, I can see the time has come for you three to walk this path. So I will tell you about the Ascension Adventure."

The three of us sighed in relief. For a moment, we feared we were going to be turned back at the very first Gateway.

"For Ascension is an Adventure," Kuthumi continued, "... an Adventure the three of you have been on before."

"We have?" exclaimed Janus in surprise.

"Yes," said Kuthumi with a smile. "When you played Dungeons & Dragons, you had mighty powers, my friends. Do you remember? During the game, it was easy for you to control the wind and weather, travel through time and space, manifest objects out of thin air, heal the sick and

168

raise the dead. You had powers and abilities, which most mortals would consider miraculous. Did you ever stop to think about how you could perform such incredible feats?"

"Well...err ...no," said Janus, obviously trying not to laugh. "I mean, D&D was just a game... it was all just our imagination!"

"So you say. And yet here you are," replied Kuthumi calmly as he pointed to the blue crystal pillars that surrounded us. "I would ask you, my friend, to look around you one more time. Yes! And look at yourself and your two comrades. Do you still think it's all just your imagination?"

I think Janus got the point because he was unusually quiet for Janus.

Kuthumi went on. "The incredible feats that you were able to perform in your Dungeons & Dragons game are the very same feats that all Masters who have ever incarnated on Earth have performed. Jesus Christ, Buddha, Moses, Kuan Yin, Krishna, Mother Mary, White Eagle, Sai Baba and all the others that you saw as you walked through the passageway at the top of the Crystal Stair. All of these souls did exactly what you were doing in your Dungeons & Dragons game. They walked on water, turned water into wine, healed the sick, made the lame walk, and the blind see. They were able to part the sea, move mountains and perform countless other miracles. But how did they do it? How were they able to perform these astonishing feats?"

Kuthumi's question seemed to hover for a moment in the air, right before our eyes. "All the Masters did what they did by using the Force," he said slowly. "And that, my friends, is what the Ascension Path is all about. That, briefly, is what it means to be initiated. To understand, experience, master and use the greatest power in the Universe: The Force."

"Master Kuthumi," I said slowly, bowing once again before him. "The three of us wish to walk this Ascension Path. It is our deepest desire. Will you not teach us about the Force?"

Kuthumi looked at all three of us for a moment and smiled. "Yes, my young friends, I will," he said. "... and for one reason and one reason only. Because you are Pure of Heart. Therefore I, Kuthumi, will initiate you three—Starbrow, Moncler and Telperion—in the ways of the Force." He turned abruptly and started walking across the huge temple hall. "Follow me."

169

2

The Force

Kuthumi led us across the temple to a large blue stone altar at the far end. On the stone altar there was a crystal ball.

"Step forward and look into the Crystal Ball," he commanded.

We placed ourselves in front of the stone altar and looked at the crystal ball. It was totally clear. As clear as glass. I couldn't see anything as I gazed into it.

"The Force is Unlimited and All-Powerful," said Kuthumi. "The Force is stronger than electricity, mightier than an atomic bomb, more powerful than the sun. The Force is Infinite, Eternal and Immortal. The Force is the Source of All Life, the Intelligence back of All the Universes and All the Dimensions and All the Worlds in All their Infinite Diversity and Glory. Nothing is impossible to the Force. The Force is Unconquerable and Invincible."

As Kuthumi spoke I felt myself being drawn deeper and deeper into the crystal ball. I still couldn't see anything, but it was as if I could literally feel and experience every single word Kuthumi was saying about the Force being Infinite, Eternal, Unlimited, Immortal...

"The Force is the mightiest Ally in the Universe. With the Force at your side, you can transform sickness into Perfect Health, poverty into Lavish Abundance, war into Deep Peace, death into Eternal Life, and despair into Faith, Hope and Love. And that is only the beginning..." said Kuthumi.

I felt myself dissolving into the perfect clarity and emptiness of the crystal ball. I was no longer Starbrow, or anyone else... I was the Force itself. Love, Life, Peace, Harmony...

"With the Force at your side, you can do things which—at your present level of consciousness—you cannot even imagine. The Force will give you all the Knowledge and all the Wisdom you will ever need. With the

170

Force at your side, there is no limit to the Good you can do. So vast will your powers be, so mighty will you become, that to those who do not know your Mighty Ally, you will seem a Miracle worker. And to them, indeed you will be."

At that very moment, Kuthumi clapped his hands together and with a jolt, I felt myself land back in my body. I was Starbrow again. I looked around bewildered and saw that Jacob and Janus were just as disoriented as I was.

"Just relax, my friends," said Kuthumi and smiled. "What you just experienced, as you gazed into the Crystal Ball, was but a fleeting glimpse of the Unlimited Nature of the Force."

"Yeah?" mumbled Janus with a spacey look in his eyes.

"I suggest you take a few deep breaths to steady yourselves. Because you see, if you wish to tread the Ascension Path, you must learn how to find and contact the Force—on your own."

I found myself staring at the crystal ball, wanting to leap again into that wild, boundless feeling I just experienced. It was so incredible. But it was not to be. Kuthumi moved in front of the crystal ball, blocking our view.

"Now," he said, "that you know this mighty Force exists, the next step is to learn to contact it yourself."

Kuthumi motioned for us to follow him. He led us back into the circle. There he stopped and turning towards us, said. "Your next question is this... But how? How do I contact this mighty Force? And where, yes where will I find it? Will I find it up in the sky? Or in the distant stars? Will I find it on top of the tallest mountain or hidden at the bottom of the deepest sea? Will I find it in the Ascended Masters? Where indeed can I find this Force? This mighty Ally?"

Since we didn't know the answer, we waited.

"The answer, you see, is so very simple. Divinely simple, you could say. You will find this Mighty Force, hidden within your own consciousness. The last place most people would look for it. But it is so," smiled Kuthumi, "Verily, it is so... you will find the Force right where you least would suspect it— in your own consciousness. Yes, this mighty Force, so near, so very very near, that most people are not even aware of it. Yes, my friends. Thus the Wise say... Closer than breathing, nearer than hands and feet."

"But if the Force is within my own consciousness, how come I'm not aware of it?" asked Janus.

"That is because you have not yet learned to look within," replied

171

Kuthumi. "Throughout your entire life on Earth, in fact up until this very moment, you have been taught to look outside of yourselves, to other people, to the world around you and external phenomena in the hope of finding Happiness. But the true Happiness, the true Power, the Force, is within."

"How does one learn to look within, Master Kuthumi?" I asked, still longing for that wild feeling of Boundless Freedom I'd experienced just a few moments ago.

"Allow me to ask you a question instead," said Kuthumi. "Moncler, you are a mighty Wizard. In Dungeons & Dragons, what did you do when you had used up your magic spells and felt it was time to collect your powers again?"

"I meditated and studied my spell book," said Jacob.

"How did you do that?"

Jacob shrugged his shoulders. "I don't know."

"Oh yes you do!" Kuthumi shot back and chuckled. "You looked within—and experienced the Force. This is what all the Masters of the Great White Brotherhood have taught humanity, since the beginning of time. In the East, the Masters call this art—meditation and yoga. In the West, the Masters call this art—prayer and treatment. And in Dungeons & Dragons..." here Kuthumi stopped to laugh. We didn't know what was so funny, but he seemed to be enjoying himself greatly. "... and in Dungeons & Dragons, you call it studying your spell book! Well my friends, now, as initiates on the Ascension Path, it is this art, you must learn to master."

Kuthumi made a circular movement with his hand and immediately four large high-backed armchairs manifested out of thin air. The armchairs, which seemed to be sculpted out of solid blocks of stone, formed a circle within the circle.

"Please be seated in the Initiation Seats," said Kuthumi. "And prepare yourself for your first lesson in experiencing the Force."

We sat down in the Initiation Seats. Even though they were made of stone, they were very comfortable.

"Make sure that you are sitting comfortably, so that you are able to focus all your attention within," instructed Kuthumi. "To guide you during your first lesson, I will now give the floor to one of our foremost experts in matters of the Force. Enjoy!" Kuthumi walked out of the circle and disappeared between the pillars.

Jacob and Janus and I sat alone in the Initiation Seats and waited. A

172

minute or two went by when suddenly the fourth Initiation Seat in our circle was illumined by a golden-white light. The light was so bright that at first I had difficulty making out the man who was sitting there. He was dressed in a long, white robe and on his head he wore a helmet covered with runes. He looked like he was some kind of a cross between an Egyptian high priest and a Greek god.

"Greetings, Brothers in the Light," I heard him say inside my head. "I AM Serapis Bey."

"Greetings," we three said in unison.

"I am here to serve you and to instruct you in matters of the Force. So to begin, please close your eyes," said Serapis Bey. "Now I will introduce you to a technique which the Ascended Masters have used for thousands of years to contact and experience the Force. This technique is simple, yet incredibly powerful. No matter how high up in the dimensions you go, you will find that you will always be using this technique in one form or another."

Serapis Bey's voice was calm and soothing as it seemed to float through us and the temple. "Focus your attention on your breathing. Just watch how the air flows in and out of your body. Just observe. There is no need whatsoever to control your breathing, just let it follow its own rhythm. If, however, you should feel like taking a few deep breaths, by all means do so."

I focused my attention on my breathing and tried to watch it as it flowed in and out of my body.

"Listen to your breathing," said Serapis Bey. "Feel your breathing. Feel how it moves all the way down into your abdomen. Just relax and observe. If you find your attention starts to wander and you begin to think about other things, then gently—but firmly—bring your attention back to your breathing. Please do this now for a few minutes."

I followed Serapis Bey's instructions and discovered that it was a lot more difficult than it sounded. I found I couldn't keep my attention focused on my breathing for more than two or three breaths. After that my mind would wander and I'd start thinking about something else. About a million other things... the Blue Temple, Elmar, the impending axis shift and then... I would remember that I was supposed to be focusing my attention on my breathing and I'd turn my attention back to my breathing again.

After I had meditated on my breathing for a couple of minutes, I experienced an interval of six or seven breaths in a row where I was completely focused on my breathing. I didn't think of anything else. It was incredible. Somehow during those six or seven breaths, I got a glimpse of the incredible silence and power that was within me. A silence that was Alive, Almighty, Intelligent, Unlimited—exactly like the feeling I had experienced when gazing into the crystal ball a few minutes earlier. It must be the Force, I thought triumphantly, I must be witnessing the Force! And then I realized that I had lost my focus on my breathing once again!

"By focusing on your breathing you keep your mind occupied so that you—the real You—can experience the deeper levels of your own being—the Force," said Serapis Bey. "In the beginning, you will probably find it difficult to focus on your breathing for more than a couple of breaths in a row, but with a little practice you'll be able to keep your focus for longer periods of time."

I continued to focus on my breathing as Serapis Bey spoke... and then suddenly I had this weird feeling that I was no longer confined to my own body anymore. My physical body was sitting in the Initiation Seat and meditating, but I... well I was far above it all, far above the Blue Temple, far above the dimensions, far above Planet Earth and all its events. And I was so big, so huge, so vast that I seemed to stretch out in all directions, all the way to infinity. I was so immense that I could not be contained! Nothing could contain me! I was Infinity itself, Infinite and Free...

"Now slowly allow your consciousness to return to your body," I heard Serapis Bey's voice say. The moment he said that I was back in my body again. It felt strangely small after having expanded into Infinity.

"Now open your eyes," said Serapis Bey, "and stretch a little."

I opened my eyes slowly. Serapis Bey smiled at me. "I believe our friend Starbrow had a glimpse of the Enlightened State," he said.

"Wow!" I said and shook my head.

"And you Telperion," said Serapis Bey to Janus. "I could feel that your experience of the Force was also very powerful."

"It was really weird," said Janus slowly. "But when I meditated on the Force, it felt... it felt exactly like when I was in love with Cecilia."

"Yeah," said Jacob. "I know what you mean. If I were to put a word on the feeling I had... well the only word I can think of would be love."

Serapis Bey smiled. "The Force IS Love. Is that not what all the Masters on Earth have always said? When you experience the Force you experience Love. And when you experience Love you experience the

174

Force. When you are in love you experience the Force. So what you experienced when you were in love Telperion, was the Force. And that is why all human beings seek love, seek that wild, ecstatic experience of being in love. But in truth, what all human beings are really seeking is the experience of the Force, their own True Self, which is Pure Love."

"Does that mean that the feeling of love and happiness that I have been looking for my whole life—in all my relationships—was really just a search for myself, for the Force that was right here, inside me, all the time!" exclaimed Janus.

"Exactly," said Serapis Bey. "I couldn't have said it better myself. But now, my friend, you know that this ecstatic experience is not to be found in the outside world or in other people. It is to be found within yourself because it is your own True Self."

"Do you realize how far out this is!" said Janus.

"Yeah," I said, thinking about all the relationships I'd had and the love I'd always longed for. "It is pretty wild." There could be no doubt about it. The feeling I just experienced when meditating on the Force was exactly that feeling of love, that feeling of being home, of being safe and blissful, that I'd been seeking—yes yearning for—in all my relationships.

"To think of all those babes!" groaned Janus, "... and all the crazy things I've done in my life for love! And all this time, it's been right here! So close that I just couldn't see it."

"Yes," said Serapis Bey, "closer than breathing, nearer than hands and feet."

3

A Critical Mass

After we had stretched a little, we sat back down in our seats and Kuthumi returned. "Congratulations, Brothers in the Light," he said, "you have now taken your first step on the Ascension Path."

"Meditation will be one of your most effective weapons on your mission," said Serapis Bey, "so I strongly recommend that you meditate as much and as often as possible."

"But what has meditation got to do with our mission?" I asked.

"Your mission is to create Peace and Harmony on Earth, is it not?" replied Kuthumi. "But in fact, it is incorrect to say that Peace and Harmony is something you are going to create. Peace and Harmony is your True Nature. Peace and Harmony is the Force, that which always has been and always will be and is Unchanging. As an initiate, all you do is focus your attention on your True Nature, which is Peace and Harmony. And when you do that, Peace and Harmony automatically manifest in the outer world. Because the outer world is merely a reflection of your inner state of mind."

"You mean all we have to do to create world peace is sit on our butts and meditate on the Force!," said Janus, "Sounds like a piece of cake to me!"

"Yes," said Serapis Bey, "you could certainly say it's a pleasant way to create peace. But when you're on the Ascension Path, you will discover that it's crucial to be able to focus on and experience the Force at will. And by this I mean, at any time, in any place, and under ANY circumstance."

"Well, that should be easy enough!" said Janus nonchalantly.

"Even in hell?" asked Kuthumi.

"Well..." replied Janus, "I mean if all you have to do is sit still..."

"We shall see," said Kuthumi, "we shall see. Or should I say, we shall put you to the test. Because in order to pass through the Blue Gateway, you must now prove to us that you are able to focus on the Force at all times, in any place—and as I said before—under ANY circumstance."

Then Kuthumi and Serapis Bey bowed ceremoniously in our direction and clapped their hands together. There was a loud crashing sound and the next moment, Jacob and Janus and I were no longer in the Blue Temple. Instead we were standing in the boiling hot sun in the middle of an open square, surrounded by an angry, screaming mob. All around us, dark-skinned young men with blue and white checked scarves around their heads were throwing Molotov cocktails and stones at the soldiers, police and police dogs that were charging in from every direction. Blood was everywhere and several wounded youths were writhing in pain on the dry sandy ground. The sound of bullets ripped through the air. That was when I realized where we were because I had seen this scene countless times on TV. There could be no doubt about it. We were in Israel, right smack in the middle of one of the hot spots on the West Bank or in the Gaza Strip.

But before my mind could register more, a group of the young Palestinians came charging straight at us and hurled us brutally to the ground. Janus twisted over in pain, after a vicious kick in the stomach. Jacob crawled over to him.

"Are you alright?"

"Yeah..." he groaned, "let's get the hell out of here."

That was easier said than done. Israeli soldiers and Palestinian youths were hammering ferociously into each other, right on top of us. I had to shield my head with my hands to avoid being kicked in the face. Jacob and I grabbed hold of Janus and literally dragged him through the mad, fighting mob. We seemed to move at a snail's pace through the bedlam, all the while being kicked or stomped on alternatively by a mad Israeli or an even madder Palestinian. Near the edge of the fighting, I found myself crawling past a young Palestinian who was lying on the ground moaning as the blood gushed from a deep wound in his head. He was mumbling something in Arabic.

We finally managed to crawl over to a low wall in front of one of the houses. Machine gun fire tore through the wall right above our heads.

"We've got to get out of here!" yelled Jacob, holding one of his hands, the one which had been trampled on. "Or we'll end up dead meat!"

I saw what looked like an alley a few yards away. "Look!" I cried. "Over there, there's an alley!"

177

We started crawling towards the alley, but it was slow going because machine gun shots kept hitting the wall right above us. A few inches lower and they'd have hit us. Finally we came to the corner of the wall and in one frantic burst, we got up and threw ourselves into the alley. Then we ran as fast as we could for about a hundred yards. We came to a juncture, took the right hand turn, rounded a corner and ran down another alley. After about another hundred yards, this alleyway ended and we found ourselves looking out onto another open square.

We stepped out of the alley and looked around. It was more peaceful here, to say the least. No street riots or anything, but we could still feel there was a lot of tension in the air. After all, we couldn't have been more than a block or two from the bloody bedlam we'd just escaped from. You could hear the sound of the battling mob in the distance.

This otherwise peaceful square was lined with small shops, but now I realized that the shoppers, Palestinians and Israelis, were hurriedly leaving the shops and looking anxiously in the direction of the riots we'd just left. In the background, the angry roar of the rioting crowd seemed to be fast approaching and the shopkeepers were scurrying to bring in their wares and close their shops.

Arabs and Israeli shoppers seemed to be dividing up into groups as they departed, eyeing each other warily, as if the slightest remark could set off another bonfire of rage. At the far end of the square, a group of Israeli soldiers were looking nervously in the direction of the street riots. Two of the soldiers were questioning an Arab family—and we could hear angry words being exchanged. Not far from the Israeli soldiers at the end of the square, there was a small sidewalk café. A waiter was hastily stacking up chairs and closing the café.

"I don't believe it!" cried Janus, staring at the café in disbelief.

"What is it?" I said.

"It's Cecilia!" he cried in a hoarse voice.

Jacob and I looked over at the café. Two girls were rushing past the café as they glanced nervously over their shoulders in the direction of the rioting. One of the girls had blond hair, the other had dark auburn hair and looked like an Israeli. The contrast between the two was striking. But there could be no doubt about it. The fair-skinned Scandinavian blond was Cecilia—Janus' ex-girlfriend. The beauty who'd broke his heart just a few weeks ago. The reason he'd almost committed suicide.

"What's she doing here?" I asked.

"Cecilia... has a good friend who lives in Israel. Her name's Natasha.

178

Cecilia meet her when she was Eurailing in Italy last summer," said Janus. "I knew that she was planning to visit her, but I didn't know that she'd be here now..." Janus' face was ashen. It was obvious that he was still madly in love with Cecilia.

"But apart from that, what are we doing he..." It was Jacob, but he never got to finish the sentence because the very next moment a deafening blast came from the café and the whole place exploded. The windows, the entire front facade, everything just seemed to fly through the air as huge flames shot out onto the sidewalk. The blast from the explosion was so powerful that we felt it right where we stood, on the other side of the square. We covered our eyes with our hands to protect ourselves from the rain of glass, stone and fire that flew out over the square.

"Cecilia!" bellowed Janus in horror. Cecilia and Natasha had been walking right in front of the café windows when everything exploded. The two girls, the waiter and a group of shoppers had been flung several meters in the air by the explosion. And now they were scattered along the sidewalk as the flames poured out of the café.

"Cecilia! No!" roared Janus and began running across the square towards the café. Jacob and I ran after him. All around us, people were screaming and running madly in confused panic.

"Cecilia!" bellowed Janus again as he plowed his way through the terrified swarm of people. He charged right through the wreckage and threw himself on the ground next to his ex-girlfriend, who was lying in a bloody heap amid jagged shards of glass. Neither she nor Natasha moved. The heat from the flames was so intense that we had to shield ourselves with our arms. Only Janus seemed oblivious to the flames. He took Cecilia's lifeless body in his arms and bore her away from the flames. Jacob and I looked at each other for a moment and then picked up Natasha and made a run for it. Once we were away from the heat of the flames, we laid Natasha down next to where Janus had laid Cecilia. The sound of sirens droned in the distance.

"Cecilia..." cried Janus in a choked voice as he bent over Cecilia.

Jacob held her wrist, trying to find her pulse. A lone tear rolled down Janus' dirt-covered face. After about a half a minute, Jacob whispered, "I'm not sure, but I think she's still alive."

Janus wiped his face with his blood covered hand and stared at his beloved. Fortunately, Cecilia and her Israeli girlfriend had been walking away from the café so their backs were to the explosion, but they bled from many wounds and they were both severely burned. Neither of them moved.

Two ambulances came roaring to a stop in the middle of the square, followed by a fire engine and two police cars. "Help!" cried Jacob and ran towards the ambulances. All around us, everything was madness. Chaos ruled. The explosion had literally ignited the suppressed hatred in everyone present. Now everyone, Israelis and Arabs, was screaming, pushing, shouting, shoving and hurling curses at each other hatefully.

Jacob came running back with three ambulance men. Janus picked up Cecilia and ran towards them. Jacob and I lifted up Natasha and ran after him.

"Help her!" cried Janus at the top of his lungs. Two of the ambulance attendees took one look at Cecilia, put her on a stretcher and lifted her hurriedly into one of the waiting ambulances. The doctor inside quickly clamped an oxygen mask on her face and began ripping off her bloody blouse. The other two put Natasha on the stretcher right next to her and clamped another mask on her face. Then all three went to work, trying to save the girls.

"Will they live?" cried Jacob to no one in particular.

Janus tried to climb up into the ambulance, his eyes fixed on Cecilia, his lips moving in silent prayer.

"Please," said one of the ambulance people, "please sir, step back. You must let us work." When Janus didn't move, he tried to push him gently back. But Janus was too strong to be pushed away that easily. When he saw what was happening, Jacob moved forward to our friend, took his arm, and gently pulled him back a bit.

"Janus," Jacob whispered softly, "you must let them work. They're doing everything they can." I knew Jacob sounded much calmer than he felt. He too knew how much Janus loved Cecilia.

Janus went limp and let Jacob lead him a few steps away from the ambulance. And there we stood for a moment, as silent as standing stones in a world gone mad, staring at the ambulance men who were fighting desperately to save Cecilia and her friend. Then the ambulance driver slammed the doors shut and ran around to jump into the driver's seat.

Just as the doors slammed shut, I felt a very strong tingling sensation right between my eyebrows. The sensation was so strong that it seemed to continue right through the back of my head, as if some invisible force was trying to draw my attention to something behind me. I turned around to look.

The scene behind us was total bedlam. Firemen were desperately trying to put out the fires, which were spreading rapidly around the square. Ambulance people and police officers were helping the wounded away from the flames. But it was difficult for the rescue parties to do their job because of the angry mob of Israelis and Palestinians who were shouting and screaming and shoving each other.

But it wasn't this scene of hatred and violence that had given me the tingling sensation in the back of my head. It was the two Arabs who were standing at the other end of the square, surveying the damage. For some reason or other, I knew without a shadow of a doubt that they were the ones who had planted the bomb.

I patted Jacob on the back and pointed towards the two Arabs. "They're the ones," I said. "They're the ones who planted the bomb in the café."

Jacob looked at the two Arabs and cried, "Those bastards! We ought to tell the police. Janus...?" He turned towards our friend, but Janus was already gone.

"Janus?" said Jacob again. We looked around and spotted him pushing his way through the screaming horde of people in front of the café. A moment later, he was running like a madman straight towards the two Arab terrorists who had planted the bomb! We saw his golden chain mail glint in the sunlight and knew every muscle in his sinewy body was ready to explode.

"Oh no Jacob!" I cried. "Let's go!"

Jacob and I took off full speed after him, but Janus was already upon the Arabs. He hurled himself at them in a mad fury. As we ran, I saw Janus hammer his fist into the stomach of one of the men and send him crashing to the ground. Then he began pounding the other's face with the most savage blows. Some Arabs who were standing nearby came running over to help their two countrymen defend themselves from the fury of Janus' attack.

At the same time, the fighting between the Israelis and Palestinians on the square was spreading like wildfire, making it impossible for us to reach Janus. We fought desperately to make our way through the crowd, but found ourselves being sucked into the bedlam against our will. I lost sight of Janus as I was shoved to the ground. To my right, a group of Israeli soldiers were trying in vain to separate a furious crowd of the Israelis and Arabs from tearing each other apart. An Arab woman was screaming at the top of her lungs as she tried to drag her wounded

181

husband away from the fighting. She was having difficulty moving him and I could see from her big belly that she was pregnant. In the mayhem, a huge Israeli kicked her husband furiously and when she tried to protect him, he dealt her a savage blow. She toppled over on the ground and screamed, holding her stomach.

"Stop!" I cried in horror and grabbed the Israeli by the arm. Before I knew it, someone struck me viciously in the side. I fell right on top of the pregnant woman. Our eyes met for a brief moment and I saw the terror in her eyes. As I tried to help her up, the man who had hit me in the side, aimed another savage blow at me. I ducked and by accident, he punched the Arab woman right in the face. Blood gushed from her nose as she collapsed on the ground. Without thinking, I pounded my fist into his stomach with all my might. He grabbed his stomach and fell backward, groaning. I turned to help the poor pregnant woman, only to find an Israeli soldier had drawn his pistol and was aiming straight at me. He was just about to pull the trigger when he was knocked over by someone in a blue cape who tackled him from behind. It was Moncler—Jacob!

I knelt down besides the pregnant woman who was lying there with her eyes closed, muttering a prayer in Arabic. Her whole body shook. I touched her on the shoulder and she opened her eyes. She knew I wanted to help so she let me help her up. As I supported the weight of her body, I looked around for help. But it was in vain. Everyone was fighting, screaming, kicking, shouting. It was a madhouse. At the other end of the square, I spotted Janus in his golden chain mail, pounding a whole little army of Arabs into mincemeat. The whole square had turned into one big battlefield.

"Starbrow!" yelled Jacob. After he'd knocked down the Israeli soldier who was about to shoot me, he'd been surrounded by more soldiers who were now beating him from all sides with their batons. The blood gushed from a big gash in his head, but somehow he was managing to hit back quite nicely. He had already downed two of the soldiers. One of the remaining soldiers had pulled out his machine gun and was now aiming it at Jacob.

"No!" I cried and threw myself at the soldier. I crashed into him and we toppled over onto the dry sandy gravel. The soldier pushed me away, then he got up and aimed his machine gun straight at me. Without thinking, I somersaulted forward and hammered my fist into his right knee cap. The soldier howled in pain and tried to shoot me, but before he could pull the trigger, Jacob hit him over the head with an iron baton.

182

Just in the nick of time.

Jacob came over and helped me up. "That was some neat somersault you did there," he said, wiping the sweat off his brow. "Where did you learn that?"

That was when I realized my somersault was exactly the same maneuver I'd used in my lifetime as Dana when we were fleeing from Lord Bryn's soldiers. It was weird. Apparently, the combat tricks I'd learned as a priestess of Avalon were still with me!

"You wouldn't believe me if I told you!" I joked, but before we had time to continue the conversation we were engulfed by the raging mob again.

"These Israelis are really brutal!" cried Jacob.

"These Arabs sure ain't no pussies either!" I cried. "Just look what they're doing to those Israelis over there!"

Everywhere we looked it was mayhem. Israelis pounding Arabs and Arabs pounding Israelis. It was unbelievable. To our left, three Israelis were pounding an older Arab man who had tried to pull his wounded son away from the mob. Jacob ran towards the old man. I was right behind him. Jacob hammered his iron baton into the side of one of the Israelis. I kicked the other one hard in his balls while the third Israeli aimed a savage blow at me. I tried to duck, but it was too late. He hit the side of my head and for a moment, everything went black. The next thing I knew, I was lying on the ground, tasting my own blood. The man kicked me in the stomach and yelled at me in Hebrew.

As I was lying there, battered and bruised, I felt this enormous anger welling up in me. It was as if the wrathful, raging atmosphere of the square had kindled a slumbering rage inside me. The man tried to kick me again, but this time, I rolled away just in time. Like lightening I was up again and charging head first straight into his stomach. As I crashed into his stomach, I let out a furious howl of rage. I didn't stop to see if he got up again, instead I turned towards another one of the Israelis and hit him three times with all my might until he collapsed in a heap. Then I threw myself at two others. My pent-up rage, now suddenly set free, gave me unexpected strength.

"Bastards!" I shouted, as I pounded my fist into the side of another Israeli soldier and kicked another soldier in the gut. Jacob was at my side, dealing out savage blows left and right. We threw ourselves at every Israeli we saw who was beating up Arabs. Finally, Jacob and I had hammered our way all the way down to the other end of the square.

Everywhere we looked, houses were afire. And so were we! I was aflame. The whole world was in flames. I was being devoured—consumed—by anger. The anger that was inside me—and around me—the anger that was everywhere. I looked for a few more Israelis I could finish off. In front of one of the burning houses, I saw some maniac going totally berserk as he pounded the living daylights out of what looked like dozens of Palestinians in one ferocious die hard with a vengeance action scene. I clenched my bloody fists and made my way through the mob, determined to put an end to his bloody deeds. Jacob was at my side. The fighting on the square was now so intense that it was almost impossible to tell the Israelis from the Arabs. I joined a bunch of livid Arabs who were trying to stop the maniac Israeli who was pulverizing their kin. He was standing with his back towards us, dealing out savage blows left and right. I raised my fist, ready to give him the death blow, but he was too fast. Like a flash of lightening he turned and raised his fist, ready to smash it into my head. In that split second, our eyes met. And I saw his clear blue eyes... and pointy elven ears! With a shock of recognition, I realized it was Telperion—Janus!

"Starbrow!" cried Janus in astonishment, his fist not more than two centimeters from my nose.

"Telperion...!" I cried, my fist just grazing his cheek.

Jacob leapt to my side, ready to help me. With a shock, he too realized that our enemy was Janus... "Telperion..." he cried, looking at our clenched fists.

We stood as if turned to stone. Here we were—Moncler, Telperion, Starbrow—three better friends the world had never seen. And yet we had almost killed each other, so consumed had we been by this furious anger.

All of a sudden, the anger in my chest died.

I felt limp as a rag doll.

"Oh My God," I groaned in horror. "What on Earth are we doing?"

"Starbrow... Moncler..." croaked Janus, his voice now just a hoarse whisper.

"Oh God," said Jacob, looking down at his bruised and bleeding hands. "This can't be happening..."

"The Arabs..." whispered Janus, his voice was almost a whimper, "... they've killed my beloved Cecilia." His furious rage had now turned into hopeless despair.

"And the Israelis went amok, killing innocent Arabs left and right..." I moaned.

184

"Yes..." said Jacob sternly. "And we let ourselves be pulled into it... and become a part of it."

The enraged mob continued to battle on around us, threatening to drag us into the fighting again. But now the fire in our innards was completely extinguished. Jacob and I grabbed hold of Janus and dragged him over to the wall by one of the nearby houses. In our wild rage, we had actually fought our way all the way down to the other end of the square. In fact, we weren't far from the alley we originally emerged from.

"The Arabs hate the Israelis and the Israelis hate the Arabs, it's a vicious cycle," I said in disgust.

"Yeah," said Jacob. "This is hell on Earth."

I stared at Jacob, remembering how the enormous rage inside me had erupted like a furious volcano, unleashing huge black clouds of anger, which had completely enveloped my body in darkness. I almost felt as if I had two bodies. My regular physical body and then a shadow body of anger and rage. Just like the Shadow Earth, which surrounded Planet Earth in darkness and threatened to annihilate its entire population...

"We're doing the same thing, Jacob," I moaned and buried my head in my hands in despair. "Right now! Right this minute! We're helping create hell on Earth!"

"An eye for an eye, a tooth for a tooth..." said Jacob, "That's what they say."

"But they've killed Cecilia!" cried Janus. "It's just not fair!"

"And all the senseless killing and violence will continue until the day someone says stop and chooses something else," said Jacob.

"Chooses what?" asked Janus.

"Why do you think Kuthumi and Serapis Bey sent us here?" asked Jacob.

Then I remembered what the two Masters said to us before they clapped their hands and sent us to this hell on Earth. "... when you are on the Ascension Path, you must be able to focus on and experience the Force always, in every situation—under ANY circumstance—no matter what is happening around you..."

Janus looked at us in disbelief. "Do you really think that's the reason?"

"Remember our mission," said Jacob. "We're not supposed to react to violence with more violence."

"Then what are we supposed to do?" exclaimed Janus. "Go out there and politely ask them to stop?"

"Take it easy, Janus," I said and put my hand on his arm. "He's right,

185

you know. The only way we can create peace and harmony on Earth is by radiating peace and love ourselves."

"And how are we supposed to do that?" scoffed Janus. "By sitting here and meditating on our breath?"

I looked back at the enraged mob, still battling on the square and saw how their rage had covered the entire area with an ominous black cloud of aggression and negativity. "Yes," I said slowly, "I think that's exactly what the Masters want us to do."

"But even if we experience peace in our own minds, what good will it do the madmen out there?" cried Janus, pointing at the mob.

"You're forgetting what Ashtar said about creating a critical mass," said Jacob. "The consciousness of each and every human being is interconnected. If only a few individuals change their consciousness radically, it affects everyone else..."

"Okay, okay! You win!" said Janus, raising his arms in a gesture of surrender. "I get the point!"

We just stood there for a while as the thought sunk in. We didn't speak, instead we watched the screaming mob battle on. Janus just couldn't take his eyes off the burnt out café. "The Masters sure do know how to teach you a lesson," he said, slowly.

"Look Janus, I'm sure Cecilia is going to make it, I'm sure," I said, trying to comfort him, but feeling rather lame. Janus just sighed and shrugged his shoulders. I could see what an immense effort it was for him to stop thinking about his beloved Cecilia. But after a few more seconds, he seemed to pull himself together because he said, "Well dudes, if we're supposed to meditate, don't you think we'd better get going!" He motioned towards the alley.

We followed Janus down the alley until we came to the place where the alley branched off in different directions. From where we stood, we could hear the sound of rioting and gunshots coming from all directions. It seemed like the whole world was aflame and we were right in the middle of it. Janus sat down on the ground with his back to the wall of one of the houses. "Okay friends, let's do it," he said.

Jacob and I sat down on either side of him and closed our eyes. I took a few deep breaths and tried to concentrate on my breathing. At first, it was almost impossible because of all the noise, the sound of gunshots, screaming people—and most of all because of the feeling that the air itself was alive with violence and hatred. And also my body was sore and aching all over from all the fighting—and worse yet, inside I could still feel the emotional turmoil I'd set off with my own violent explosion of rage and anger.

I kept telling myself to breathe... to breathe deeply and relax. But the horrible pictures kept flashing across the screen inside my head. I saw the bedlam, the angry Palestinians, the enraged Israelis, Cecilia's burned body, the battered pregnant Arab woman... it was horrible.

I kept trying to force myself to concentrate on my breathing. It took the greatest effort of will to continue because the horrible images just kept returning... but every time they did, I returned my focus to my breathing. It was slow going—and required every ounce of willpower I possessed... but slowly, slowly, ever so slowly, my mind began to obey. Slowly, slowly, I found it easier and easier to return my focus to my breathing. Then, as I kept returning to my breathing, I started to begin to feel calmer. And the more I calmed down, the less I felt distracted by the angry sounds around us or by my aching body. Slowly, slowly, I began to experience the Force. At first it was only in flashes, but then it slowly became more and more real. The Force, that Infinite, Eternal, Immortal Presence which is my True Self. I sighed and dived into the moment. The moment of Perfect Peace which was in me and which surrounded me.

The very next moment it seemed, though I wasn't sure if 10 minutes or an hour had passed, someone touched me on the shoulder. I opened my eyes and blinked in surprise. A young man, a Palestinian, had tapped me on the shoulder and was standing there, regarding the three of us with a puzzled expression on his face.

I smiled at him and blinked again.

He was a young fellow, around 16 or 17 I guessed. His lip was cracked and still bleeding slightly. Obviously he'd been fighting too.

"Hello, my friend," I said, emerging from the Peace.

"I am just wondering," he said in broken English, "what you are doing..."

"We're meditating," I said.

"You're what?" he replied, obviously confused.

"We're meditating," I said again.

"Meditating? What is that?"

"Meditation? Oh, well, meditation is... an ancient technique of focusing your attention on the Peace that is within you," I replied slowly.

He started to laugh. "Why you want to do something like that? In the middle of all this?"

187

"We are meditating to stop the fighting and create peace," I answered.

"But shouldn't one fight against injustice and oppression?" he replied, surprised at my answer.

"Always," said Jacob, who had been listening to our conversation. "But violence only breeds more violence. If you want to experience more love and peace in the world, you have to choose it first for yourself—and find it in yourself. Only thus can the circle of hatred and violence be broken."

"It doesn't help to just sit back and watch!" cried the young man heatedly. "I am willing to die for my cause!"

"So are we," said Jacob. "But we are not willing to kill for our cause."

Jacob's reply made the young man stop and think. "But what good does it do to meditate?" he asked. "I don't understand how it can help."

We explained to him that by meditating we established and experienced peace in our own minds—and that this peace then automatically spread out to our surroundings so that the people around us also became peaceful. He thought about this for a while as he paced back and forth in the alley, looking first at us and then back in the direction of the fighting he'd just left. Finally he stopped pacing and stood before us.

"Can I join you?" he asked solemnly.

"Why of course," I said and smiled in surprise.

Our young friend smiled back, but instead of sitting down with us, he ran out of the alley. We looked at each other in surprise. What was that all about? We were just about to close our eyes again and go on meditating when our young friend came running back with four other young men. From the way they were dressed, we could see that two of them were Palestinians and two were Israelis.

"These are my friends," he said pointing to the others. "We are all sick and tired of all the fighting. We want to try your method instead."

"Great!" said Janus, making room for our guests.

The five young men sat down next to us. I told them to close their eyes and then slowly guided them through the meditation technique we had learned from Serapis Bey. Now and again, I found myself having to raise my voice to make myself heard above the noise of the fighting and the gunshots. But after a while, I was satisfied that I had guided them so well that they were in fact beginning to meditate. So I stopped talking and focused all my attention on my breathing.

I meditated for a while... again I wasn't sure if I had been meditating for a few minutes or a whole hour... but again I was there... at that point where I began to experience the Peace and the Silence within me. The

Living, Pulsating, Intelligent Presence, which is the Force...

That was when I heard a voice next to me saying, "Listen, listen! The fighting has stopped!"

I opened my eyes. Our young friend was standing next to us with a look of wonder on his face. I looked at Jacob and Janus who had also opened their eyes. They both looked very peaceful. We could see his friends standing at the end of the alley, looking out at the square. It was completely quiet in the alley and no sound of gunshots or rioting came from the square.

"The fighting has stopped," cried our friend and started to walk down towards the square. "Come and see for yourselves!"

Jacob and Janus and I got up and followed our friend to the end of the alley. We looked out on the square. It was true. The fighting had stopped. The square was almost completely deserted now, except for a few Israelis and Palestinians who were cleaning up the mess. The fires had all been put out. There were no soldiers, no ambulances, no fire engines. Nothing. The black cloud of anger was also gone. Now there was peace in the air. And there was peace in us...

"Why it's a miracle!" said Janus.

4

Violet Flames

I heard a loud crashing sound inside me—and then Jacob and Janus and I were standing in the Blue Temple with Kuthumi and Serapis Bey again. We stood at the far end of the Temple, in front of a great Blue Gateway, similar to the one we had passed through earlier.

"Well done, my friends!" said Kuthumi. "Congratulations on your first miracle!"

"Did we actually stop the riots?" I asked.

"When two or more like-minded souls gather together and focus their attention on the Force—on Love and Peace—it has an enormous effect on the collective consciousness," said Kuthumi.

"One thing's for sure," said Janus as he tried to wipe the mud, blood and sand off his chain mail, "I'll be a little less cocksure next time!" He was black and blue all over and blood still oozed from the nasty gashes he had on his head and arms. Jacob and I were also hurting all over from our furious street battles.

"There's nothing wrong in believing in yourself," laughed Serapis Bey as he patted Janus on the back in a fatherly manner. "And the three of you did actually manage to focus on the Force—regardless of the circumstances."

"But it was an awfully close shave," said Janus and looked down on his bloody, battered fists. "What about Cecilia? Will she live?"

"This much I will tell you, my friend, if it can be any comfort to you," replied Kuthumi. "In the 4th dimension, time and space behave somewhat differently than what you're used to on the Earth plane. Some of the things you experienced are things that have already happened, while some of the things you experienced are things that just may happen in the future... that is unless human beings choose differently—and more wisely."

"It was incredible to see how just a handful of people meditating on the Force could affect a whole city," I said, trying to change the subject, so Janus wouldn't think about Cecilia.

"Did I not say that the Force is the Mightiest Ally in the Universe?" smiled Kuthumi. "Unlimited and Invincible."

Serapis Bey made a circular movement with his hand and the doors of the Blue Gateway parted without a sound. Outside we saw a beautiful mountain landscape. Now it seemed as if the Blue Temple was situated on top of a tall, snow-capped mountain. An icy wind blew in through the Gateway.

"You have passed the first test and are now free to pass through the Blue Gateway," said Serapis Bey and motioned for us to walk through the Gateway. We walked over to the Gateway and looked out. Outside, the snow-covered landscape had an unusual violet hue that seemed to shimmer in the bright sunshine.

"To pass the second test, you must pass through the Violet Gateway," said Kuthumi.

"Where do we find that?" asked Jacob.

Kuthumi pointed to the mountain top. We followed his gaze and discovered why the mountain landscape had this strange violet hue. A mighty beam of violet flames radiated down from the heavens, covering the mountaintop where we stood.

"Step outside—step out onto the mountain top," commanded Kuthumi.

Jacob and Janus and I looked at each other for a moment, then we stepped through the Gateway. An icy wind was blowing that immediately cut to the bone, even though the sun was shining brightly from a clear blue sky.

We turned back towards our guides. The two Ascended Masters bowed solemnly. "The Force is with you!" declared Kuthumi. "And in you!" proclaimed Serapis Bey.

Before we could say a word, the doors of the Blue Temple slammed shut—and the Blue Temple vanished into thin air! Just like that. Where a moment before, the Temple had stood, there was only a cold, windy mountaintop.

"Well wham-bam-thank-you-mam to you too!" said Janus.

"The Ascended Masters definitely aren't into long goodbyes!" chuckled Jacob.

"And it's bloody freezing out here, too," I said as my teeth began to chatter. All I was wearing was my thin, white robe and sandals.

"Not exactly dressed for the occasion are you Starbrow!" said Janus.

"No," replied Jacob, "but I guess we'll get a chance to get warm very soon!" He pointed to the violet flames.

"Maybe way too soon!" laughed Janus.

We walked over to the flames. They looked like regular flames except instead of being red, they were violet. But as we got closer, we discovered that they didn't give off any heat. I stuck my cold hands cautiously into the flames. The flames didn't burn at all.

Janus stuck his hands in too. "Why they're not even warm!" he cried.

"Do you think we're supposed to walk right through them?" I asked.

"Well, the Masters said that we had to pass through the Violet Gateway to pass the second test," said Jacob. "And besides, it doesn't look like we have a whole lot of other options out here..."

He was right.

We stepped into the violet flames. At first we were just relieved that they didn't burn. Then we realized that the flames had this light and ethereal feeling. They gave you the feeling that there was this nice, fresh breeze just sort of blowing all around your body.

"Groovy!" said Janus, "Will you check this out!" We looked at him and saw that the violet flames had instantly healed every single cut, gash, wound, and bruise he had on his body. And that now even his horribly stained and battered chain mail was completely clean and shiny again, as if he'd never touched a single hair on the head of any Arab living anywhere. It was incredible. Then I looked over at Jacob and it was the same with him too. He was completely clean and healed. Then I looked down at myself and found that my white robe was lily white again, no blood or ripped holes or anything. And my body was back to normal, perfect, whole and complete. Not a bump or a bruise anywhere. It was amazing.

The three of us chuckled in surprise, enjoying the feeling of being whole again. Then we walked further into the flames. With every step we took, I felt as if my whole being was being cleansed more and more thoroughly. But now it had gone beyond just healing my physical body. It was actually as if all the thoughts and experiences I'd ever had throughout my entire life were now being cleansed by the violet flames. Then I even started seeing images of my past life as Dana in England... It was weird. And it was also too much.

In fact, suddenly I felt I just couldn't take anymore. That if this super cleansing continued, there wouldn't be anything left of me. But fortunately, at that very moment, I realized there was a tall Violet Gateway right in front of us, in the midst of the flames. The violet flames flickered and flashed around the Violet Gateway making it shimmer and shine as if it was made of violet crystals.

"Let's go through the gateway!" cried Janus. "I can't take anymore of this!"

I pounded the knocker against the great gateway. The violet doors glided open without a sound. On the other side of the doors, there was a huge chamber. We stepped through the gateway and into the room. The doors shut behind us without a sound. Gone were the violet flames.

"Phew!" cried Janus. "That was intense!"

"Yeah, it was like getting fried—or should I say—purified by the violet flames," said Jacob. "I couldn't have taken a minute more!"

"Me neither!" I said as we looked around at our new stopover. We seemed to be all alone in a lavish chamber that looked like a cross between a sumptuous nobleman's living room, a library, and a museum.

On the left wall, there was a long row of old-fashioned looking portraits. Along the right wall, there were rows of bookcases brimming with ancient-looking books, maps and scrolls. Right smack in the middle of the chamber, there was a huge globe, surrounded by an antique sofa and several comfortable-looking chairs. Besides the antique furniture, there were many other strange and interesting objects in the room. Models of ships, helicopters and airplanes, antique weapons and armor, and two huge chests brimming with jewelry and great gemstones.

At the other end of the chamber, a merry fire—with violet flames of course!—was crackling in a huge fireplace. Next to the fireplace were two large doors. There was something about the place that reminded me of Elmar. One thing was for sure, whoever lived here must be an avid collector. In fact, a lot of the objects reminded me of the kind of exotic stuff that Elmar had collected all his life.

"Take a look at this!" whistled Janus as he beckoned us over to one of the old portraits hanging on the left wall. "It's Merlin!"

Jacob and I joined him. Sure enough, it was Merlin, the old wizard we'd met in Tintagel in our past life. He was standing on the rocky beach just in front of the Crystal Cave where we received our mission so many hundreds of years ago. His long white beard was blowing in the wind. Blowing?

"But look...!" I stammered in surprise, "...the picture is alive! It's moving!" While I was speaking, Merlin began walking across the beach to the stairway that led up the rocks to Tintagel Castle far above. We could hear his heavy boots clanging on the stones and the waves pounding against the cliffs. We could even hear the sea gulls.

"Far out man!" cried Jacob. "Talk about virtual reality!"

We put our faces right up to the painting.

"Wow, it even smells!" said Janus. And he was right, the picture smelled of salt sea air, just like it did in Tintagel! I was sure that if I stuck my hand into the painting I would be transported there. But before I succumbed to the temptation, Jacob beckoned us over to another portrait.

"Look at this one!" he said, pointing to a painting of a man dressed in Renaissance garb, standing at the helm of a ship and peering into the distance through a long telescope. "It's Christopher bleeding Columbus!" cried Jacob. We stared at the picture of Columbus. He had a wonderful, reckless glint in his eyes...

"Hey guys, do you realize it's Merlin again!" I exclaimed. "Christopher Columbus is Merlin! It's the same person in both pictures!"

"Well I'll be darned!" declared Janus, "you're right!"

"And this one's Merlin, too!" cried Jacob, pointing to the next painting. Another living portrait of Merlin, this time dressed as a nobleman, sitting at an ornate writing table, dipping a feathery quill into a bottle of ink while writing on a piece of parchment.

"Now who do you think he is this time?" asked Janus.

"I wonder what he's writing?" I said.

Janus leaned up close to the painting to see what Merlin was writing on the parchment. "To be... or not to be... that is..."

"... the question!" I said. "That's from Hamlet! That must mean..." I spluttered in surprise, "... that Merlin was also Shakespeare!"

"That dude really got around!" dead-panned Janus.

For a moment, we kept on studying Merlin as Shakespeare writing the world's most famous monologue.

"There's just one thing I don't get," said Jacob, ever the brainy one among us, "he really doesn't look anything like all the pictures you see of Shakespeare..."

"You know you're right," I said, now thoroughly confused.

"But it can't be a mistake," cried Janus. "No matter how many lives they've had, I get the impression the Ascended Masters are pretty well organized!"

"Now I know why!" I exclaimed. "He's really Francis Bacon!"

"What does Francis Bacon have to do with anything!" said Janus.

"Well, I remember when I was getting my degree in Communications and we studied world literature," I explained. "... there's long been this theory that in fact it wasn't Shakespeare who wrote Hamlet and all the other famous plays he was supposed to have written, but Francis Bacon! And now we know the theory's true!"

"Good work Sherlock!" smiled Janus. "When we get back, you can publish a paper about this—and if anybody believes you—you might win a Noble Prize right along with Jacob!"

"Talk about believing... take a look at this one!" beckoned Jacob.

Once again, it was of Merlin. This time dressed in 18th century clothing, with a wig and all. He was just about to sign a long document so we again put our noses right up to the picture to see what it said. "... We hold these Truths to be self-evident, that all Men are created equal, that they are endowed by their Creator with certain unalienable Rights, that among these are Life, Liberty and the Pursuit of Happiness..."

"You got to be kidding!" I cried.

"Well, like it or not," said Jacob, "... it's the American Declaration of Independence!"

"He sure did know how to get around," said Janus. "I wonder if there were any great historical events he wasn't a part of!"

We watched Merlin sign the document and then join a group of distinguished-looking gentlemen. "I'm not up on my American history, so I really can't tell you who he was, except that he's definitely not George Washington. That's George over there..." I said, wracking my brain for the answer. "Jacob you ought to know!" But Jacob didn't either. Finally we gave up and moved to the next picture.

The last picture portrayed Merlin in the guise of an 18th century French nobleman, wearing a fine robe made of violet velvet no less. In one hand, he was holding a piece of iron, in the other, a piece of gold.

"Alchemy..." I muttered under my breath.

"Well we knew he was a change artist," said Janus. "I just wonder who he was this time?"

"Le comte de Saint Germain!" said a voice inside our heads. We turned around to find that one of the doors at the end of the chamber had opened. Merlin came walking through the door, dressed just like the French nobleman in the picture. He was surrounded by a white light and there was a faint shimmer of violet flames around his hands. "But since we're old friends," he said and smiled, "just call me Saint Germain! Long-winded titles are such a waste of energy."

"Merlin!" the three of us cried in unison.

"Greetings, Brothers in the Light," he said solemnly and bowed before us. "Welcome my dear Starbrow, Moncler and Telperion! Welcome to the Violet Gateway!"

"But what are you doing here?" I cried, no longer able to contain myself.

"Actually the same as you! I'm also fulfilling my Earth mission!"

"Are all these pictures really you?" questioned Jacob.

"Yes," replied Saint Germain. "You are not the only ones who have incarnated on Earth many times."

"But we haven't all been in the spotlight so many times as you!" laughed Janus.

"Ah my friends..." he said, "... don't be so sure!"

"But now you're an Ascended Master?" I asked.

"Yes, I guess you could say I've graduated!" he replied with a smile. "I ascended into the 5th dimension during my lifetime as Saint Germain."

"But what about King Arthur," asked Janus, "is he also here?"

"But of course," smiled Saint Germain.

"Well where is he?" continued Janus.

"Here, there and everywhere!" laughed the Count.

"I've heard that one before," I smiled.

"Arthur ascended into the 5th dimension some time ago. You would probably consider it quite a long while ago. He ascended during his incarnation as El Morya. Many now know him by this name."

"Or by the name of Stanley Donne," I joked.

"Yes, that's true. But as you will soon discover, an Ascended Master's higher-dimensional lightbody can..."

"... manifest itself as 9 lightbodies, each of which is able to manifest in 21 space/time consciousness zones," said Jacob.

"Exactement!" said Saint Germain. "You're a quick learner, Moncler!"

"A-what-cha-ma-call-it?" exclaimed Janus looking at Jacob in surprise.

"How'd you know that, Jacob?" I asked.

"Well Lia, my guardian angel, told me about it when she was explaining the dimensions to me," replied Jacob.

"Well do sit down, my dear friends," said Saint Germain, beckoning us over to his comfortable-looking armchairs. "The Violet Flames can be rather intense the first time you experience them."

"You're telling me!" smiled Janus as we sat down and sighed in relief. It was nice to get a chance to just sort of hang out for a moment, even if it

196

was with an Ascended Master. Saint Germain seemed to sense our mood and poured each of us a large glass of sparkling wine. "Let us toast to Mission Earth Ascension!" he said and raised his glass up high.

We raised our glasses.

"Cheers!" we toasted and then each of us took a rather large gulp of the sparkling wine. It seemed like a very long time since food or drink had passed our lips. The wine had a very pleasant taste. Very pleasant indeed. In fact, I felt... well if not tipsy... then "high" almost immediately. It was great. After enjoying the sensation for a while, I held my glass up to the light and regarded the delicious liquid. That's when I noticed the red wine also had this wonderful violet glow.

Janus noticed too. "What are the Violet Flames anyway?" he asked.

"You might call them a kind of advanced cleansing tool we offer to all Ascension candidates," replied Saint Germain smiling. "The Violet Flames are one of the most fast, effective ways of getting rid of excess baggage—physically, mentally and emotionally—in the entire Universe!"

"So you know about our mission?" I asked.

"Of course. I am here to initiate you in the next phase of the Ascension Path."

"Which is?"

"Performing miracles," said the Count as he placed his glass on the table.

"I thought we'd just done that!" said Janus.

"Not so hasty my young friend! Remember your vow not to be so cocksure next time around!" replied the Count with a big grin.

"Is there anything you guys don't know about us!" sighed Janus.

"Well, nothing that's worth knowing... at least not as far as I know," the Count said with a twinkle in his eye. He got up. "Now... in order to pass through the Blue Gateway, you had to learn how to contact and experience the Force. You have now demonstrated that you could do this. And I must say, under the most extreme conditions. The next step on your pathway is to learn how to use the Force to create anything you desire. This, I think, would fall into the category of what most human beings would call performing miracles. Am I right?"

"Yes, I guess so," said Janus, not wanting to admit he'd been a little too cocksure again.

Saint Germain went over and stood in front of the last living portrait of himself. The one in which he was a French count sitting behind a table

197

with some bars of iron on it. We watched as the Saint German in the picture chanted an incantation we did not understand. Immediately the pieces of iron turned into shiny bars of gold!

"Now that's what I call a miracle!" exclaimed Janus.

"Yes..." said Saint Germain, without taking his eyes off the animated picture of himself. "They didn't call me the 'Wonderman of Europe' for nothing! Not only could I make gold out of iron and manifest jewelry out of thin air, I managed to stay about 40 years old for more than 200 years...!"

"How did you do that?" asked Janus.

"I did it..." replied Saint Germain slowly, turning towards us, "... by using the mightiest spell in the Universe..." Now he was gazing at us intently as he spoke, "... a spell which you three have used many times before."

"You can't be serious!" said Janus. "As far as I know none of us has made gold out of iron or walked on water recently!"

"Not so fast, my noble Telperion," said Saint Germain. "When you were immersed in Dungeons & Dragons, your life was one long string of miracles. You could, as I recall, travel easily through time and space, or command powerful lightning bolts to shoot from your hands... you even healed the sick and manifested food and drink out of thin air. Was it not so?"

I was just about to say that it was all just our imagination, but this time I decided I'd better kept my mouth shut.

"Yes, we did ..." said Jacob slowly, but I knew he was thinking the same thing as me.

"In order to perform these miracles, first you studied your spell book and then you meditated. And since your visit to the Blue Temple, I do believe that you now more fully grasp the enormous implications of the simple act of meditating. That is why the next step is to learn how to specifically and consciously perform so-called miracles. Tell me, Moncler," continued Saint Germain, "what exactly did you do when you performed one of your many feats of wizardry? Tell me, for example, how you turned stones into bread?"

"You knew I could do that?" said Jacob in surprise. "Well, I chanted a magic spell."

"What exactly did you chant? What words did you use?"

"Oh I don't know," Jacob said.

"Did you say the same thing, use the same magic spell or formula, for

198

every miracle you performed?"

"No. I used different words or spells for different miracles."

"Aha," smiled Saint Germain. "Now we're getting closer! So each miracle had its own magic spell... its own special formula? In other words, certain specific words that brought it about?"

"Yes...?" replied Jacob.

"Now, my friend, why do you think this was so?" asked the Count.

Jacob bowed his head and pondered the question for a long while. Then he literally shot straight up in the air with excitement. "Yes!" he cried. "That's it! That's it! That's exactly what Stanley Donne's—eh, I mean King Arthur's experiment in the particle accelerator proved. It's the observer who forms—by the very act of observation—the quantum soup into the reality the observer experiences. It's incredible! Truly incredible!" Jacob started dancing ecstatically around the room. "I get it, I finally get it!"

Janus gave me that look again. "Now he's going crazy over that experiment again!"

"And wait! Wait! One more thing!" cried Jacob to Saint Germain. "The quantum soup, the quantum field, is the Force! And... the observer is also the Force... and the observer's thoughts are the mighty spell which forms the quantum soup into the observer's reality!"

"Bravo Moncler!" said Saint Germain and clapped his hands. "Bravo! You really do understand it!"

"Yes!" exclaimed Jacob who looked so happy that for a moment I thought our shy friend was going to actually embrace the Count. But no, instead he turned to Janus and me and said, "Do you get it now? Do you get it?" We both shook our heads... no.

The Count patted Jacob gently on the shoulder. "I think, Moncler, we're going to have to explain this to our two friends."

"Oh come on guys! It's so simple!" cried Jacob.

"Patience, my friend," said Saint Germain, "patience! You must remember that your friends have not been trained in la méthode scientifique in the way you have been."

Jacob threw himself into one of the big armchairs and looked at Janus and me as if we were two retards.

"The mighty spell—the magic formula—that Jacob and I are talking about, is the mightiest power in the Universe," explained Saint Germain. "It's the formula which all the Masters, throughout all the ages, have used to perform their miracles. And it's incredibly simple. As a matter of

199

fact, it's so simple, that most human beings have completely overlooked it. The magic formula is simply this: Whatever you wish to manifest, you have to think it first."

"Is that all?" I asked. After all Jacob's jumping up and down, I guess I was expecting something a bit more exotic.

"That is all," said Saint Germain.

"But there's tons of stuff that I want that I don't have," I said.

"That's because deep down inside you don't really believe that it's yours. In order to have something—in order to manifest something— whether it's a new pair of shoes or the ability to walk on water, you have to believe, really and truly believe—believe with all your heart and soul—that whatever it is, it's 100% yours, right here and right now. It's as simple as that. You have to think it, affirm it, visualize it, feel it—in short—you have to know it. There's no other way. This is the basic mechanism of the Universe. This is how it works."

"I still don't get it," I said.

"Let's try to look at it in another way," said Saint Germain. He made a rapid circular movement with his hand—and instantly a slide projector was floating at his side. With another quick movement, he turned on the projector so a strong beam of light was projected upon the wall next to us.

"Try to look at it in this way," Saint Germain continued. "The Force— which Jacob just called the Quantum Field—is the Source of all Creation. Now just imagine that this slide projector is the Force. But the Force is more than just the projector, it's also the beam of light, which is being projected out of the projector. In other words, it's not just the Source, it's also the Substance out of which all of Creation is made. Now we have the projector and the beam of light. The Source and the Substance. Next the beam of light hits the wall. This we will call Creation or Manifestation. This is everything you see and experience in your outer, physical reality. But so far, if you look at the wall, all you see projected there is light. So far there's no picture, no manifestation, it's just a big blank. That is until we decide to put a slide into the slide projector... then what happens..."

Saint Germain made another circular movement and a bunch of slides manifested in his hand. "These slides are like your thoughts and words. You could say these slides are like the mightiest spell in the Universe! Shall we see what happens when we decide to use them... Okay... let's see. Telperion, tell me, what would you like to manifest?"

"Eh... my two-handed sword," said Janus.

"Alright. Here we have a slide of Telperion's sword—in other words—the thought or formula for Telperion's sword. Now what happens when we insert the slide into the projector...!" Saint Germain put in the slide and immediately Telperion's bejeweled two-handed sword appeared on the wall. "You just manifested your sword. Voilà! You performed your first miracle!"

The Count went on, "Now of course, these slides are just a symbol of your thoughts and words. But they show how your thoughts and words take the Universal Substance or Energy—represented here by the beam of light and form it into your reality. That's why your words and thoughts are the mightiest spell in the Universe. Whatever you think and really believe, you create in your life. But remember, it's not enough to just say something or think something, you have to believe with 100% certainty, in other words, with all your heart and soul. You must know it with the same certainty that you have about the sun rising in the East and setting in the West. Otherwise you cannot perform your miracle."

I scratched my head. I was actually beginning to get it. That's when I remembered my favorite Star Wars scene, the one where Yoda, the Jedi Master, lifts Luke's spaceship out of the Dagobah swamp using the Power of Thought. And how Luke says he doesn't believe it... For the first time I actually understood why Master Yoda says to Luke... and 'that is why you fail!'...

"I get it, guys!" I cried. "I really get it! You remember my favorite scene from Star Wars??" Now it was my turn to jump up and down like an idiot. "All I have to do to manifest something is to believe it 100%!"

"Yeah!" laughed Jacob, "I think you really do get it!"

"Hey," said Janus, slowly, "I think I'm beginning to get it too." Suddenly he nodded his head excitedly "... and if I think I'm getting it, well... then I've got it!"

"Ain't nothing but a thing!" I said and the three of us started prancing around the room like maniacs. Saint Germain just laughed and made another circular movement with his hand. The slide projector vanished back into thin air.

"Excellent," he said, "excellent! Now it's time for you to prove to me you really do get it—by manifesting your first miracle!"

"You Masters really are hard task masters," sighed Janus, girding his loins for the next test. "I just hope I get it when push really comes to shove!" I knew he was thinking of the shock of seeing Cecilia during our

201

last test. All I could do was pat him on the back.

The Count motioned for us to follow him and led us through the doors at the end of the chamber into a wide passageway with doors on either side. He pointed to the doors.

"Now my friends, "he said, "you are each going to get your own special chamber. Once you are inside your chamber, you are going to manifest your first miracle. This is what you are going to do. Once you are inside your chamber, you are to choose a thing or a situation that you want to manifest. Next you are going to manifest it. The only tool you have at your disposal is the mighty spell—the mighty formula—we were just talking about. And nothing else. You can take as little or as much time as you like. When you have manifested your miracle, you may come out again."

Saint Germain opened three of the doors and we walked into our rooms. My room was about 20 feet long and 15 feet wide. It was completely empty. There wasn't even a chair to sit on.

Before he closed the doors, Saint Germain gave us the following advice. "There is one very important thing to remember, especially if you're having difficulty manifesting your miracle. And it is this. It is of the utmost importance to remember that it is not you who is creating the miracle. All you have to do is think the thought. And then let the Force do the rest. It is the Force that is creating it, making it, manifesting it. Not you. And another thing. Remember that the Force is Omnipotent and Unlimited. The Force that you are using is the Greatest Power in the Universe. It is the Force that has manifested all of Creation—with effortless ease. If you can remember this and contemplate on this truth, you will see and understand why it's a piece of cake for the Force to manifest your wish. Your only job is to believe in it."

I took a deep breath as Saint Germain shut the doors.

There was an ominous silence.

I looked around and then sat down on the floor. Then I thought to myself... Alright... what do I want to manifest? If I could manifest anything in the world, anything I wanted... what would I manifest...? I scratched my head. Most of the things I used to wish for seemed pretty dull and uninteresting compared to all the things I'd experienced the last few days... but still... there was one thing. One thing I wished I could manifest more than anything in the world. Elmar! If only I could see him again...

I closed my eyes and started thinking about him. I saw Elmar in my mind's eye. His weather-beaten, suntanned face. His clear blue eyes. The way he smiled. I visualized that he was here now, in the room and that we were sitting here on the floor together, talking. I imagined his deep, husky voice. I could almost feel how happy I'd be if he really was here, so I closed my eyes and said. "Elmar is here now. Elmar is here now."

Then I opened my eyes and looked around. No one was there. The room was empty.

"Okay," I said to myself. You've got to try harder. I stood up and said out loud. "Elmar is here now. Elmar is here now." I tried to visualize Elmar wearing his Australian bush hat, striding through the desert with a smile on his lips. Then I pictured him sitting in his favorite rocking chair, singing one of those ballads he loved.

But Elmar was nowhere in sight.

It was just me and this empty room.

Then I remembered how a couple of weeks ago, I tried to lift a potted plant on my windowsill using only the Power of Thought like Luke Skywalker in Star Wars. I failed miserably. Now at least I knew why. It was because deep down in my heart, I never really believed that I could do it... and I realized that this time was no different. I still didn't really believe I could do it. Not really. Not in my heart of hearts. When push came to shove, I just didn't believe that it was possible for Elmar to really appear in this room, out of nowhere. I mean all I knew for sure was that Elmar was dead and gone—or at least gone to another dimension.

I banged my head against the wall in despair.

Maybe trying to manifest Elmar was just a wee bit over my head. Instead of being so ambitious, maybe I should try manifesting something simple like a glass of wine or a new pair of running shoes or... but then again... Saint Germain said that—for the Force—it was just as easy to walk on water as it was to manifest a pair of shoes. For the Force, that is. Come to think of it, I hadn't thought about the Force at all when I was thinking about Elmar.

That was when I remembered Saint Germain's parting advice.

I closed my eyes again and thought about Elmar once more. I saw him in my mind's eye, every detail of his body, the way he walked, the way he talked, how he acted. How it felt to be in his presence. "Elmar is here now," I said firmly, still keeping my eyes closed. Then I started thinking about the Force, about the Infinite, Eternal, Unlimited, All-Powerful Presence which had created All the Universes and All the Dimensions and All the Worlds and All of Creation, from the greatest galaxy to the tiniest grain of sand... with effortless ease. And then I affirmed that that very same Force was now manifesting Elmar. And that it was easy for the Force to manifest Elmar. As easy as manifesting a grain of sand or a galaxy. And that in fact the Force had already manifested Elmar. And that Elmar was here now. Right here. In this room. At this very moment.

I opened my eyes. The room was still empty. I was just about to walk over to the door and acknowledge my defeat when I felt a hand on my shoulder.

"Well done, my boy," said a familiar voice behind me.

I turned around. "Elmar!" I exclaimed. There he was. Elmar, as alive as ever, with a smile on his lips and a mischievous twinkle in his eyes.

"I don't believe it," I gasped.

The instant I said "I don't believe it", Elmar disappeared again into thin air. He was gone! The room was empty again. I ran over to the door and flung it open. Saint Germain was standing in the hallway, talking to Jacob and Janus.

"I did it!" I cried triumphantly. "I did it! I manifested Elmar! It was incredible. But only for a moment, then I doubted and he disappeared again."

"Congratulations!" smiled Saint Germain.

"And what about you guys?" I asked my friends, "Did you manifest your choices?"

Both nodded affirmatively. "But we too could only hold it for a brief moment," said Jacob, "then we doubted and it disappeared."

"Nevertheless, you've done very well," said Saint Germain. "You have demonstrated a greater understanding than most. Next time, you must do more than just believe—you must keep on believing!"

"There's something I've been wondering about," said Janus thoughtfully. "If our thoughts and words really do create our reality, how come they don't manifest instantly?"

"The truth is they do," said Saint Germain. "But in the 3rd dimension, a brake—called time and space—has been placed on the manifestation process."

204

5

The Manifestation Chamber

"Now my friends, let us just briefly review what you learned at the Blue Temple..."

After our first stunning, but short-lived miracle, Saint Germain led us back to his chamber to give us further instructions concerning the Power of Thought—the mightiest power in the Universe.

"... In Truth, everything that exists in the Universe is the Force. The Force is the One and Only Energy and Intelligence in the Universe. Another name for this Energy and Intelligence is Light. And as Einstein discovered, when something moves at the speed of light..."

"Time and space cease to exist," said Jacob.

"Exactement!" said Saint Germain, "and when time and space cease to exist... well then what?"

"Well," said Jacob, "... if there was no time and space, everything would be happening at the same time!"

"Right again... now... can you imagine what it would be like if everything was happening at once?" asked Saint Germain.

"It would be a madhouse," exclaimed Janus.

"It would be total chaos," I said, trying to image this dizzying prospect.

"Your point is well taken," said Saint Germain. "But nevertheless, in Truth, everything really IS Light, which means that in fact, everything really IS happening at the same time. Which obviously makes it rather difficult—at least in earthly terms—to have any kind of coherent and ongoing learning process."

Saint Germain motioned towards the long row of portraits of his past incarnations on Earth. "So in order for a soul to have a coherent learning process—with a past and future, the 3rd dimension was created. In your case, the Ashtar Command calls this phenomenon Test Zone Earth—and it was designed to give you an ongoing evolutionary experience. So now I hope you understand what we mean by the 3rd dimension. It is the dimension of time and space, the dimension where you experience what you call physical reality. And as you have learned in physics, in order for something to be physical..."

"It must exist in both space and time," interjected Jacob. He always loved this type of scientific discussion.

"Exactement!" smiled Saint Germain. "Now the 3rd dimensional phenomena we call time and space tend to act as a braking mechanism so that as far as you are concerned, it makes it seem as if everything is not happening all at once—even though, of course, it is! Thus it seems to you human beings that it takes some time before your thoughts and words manifest. And this, of course, can be an advantage to those of you who have not yet learned about the mightiest spell in the Universe... to those of you who have not yet learned how to control their thoughts and words..."

"I don't understand," interrupted Janus, "what's so great about that..."

"Since I knew you were going to ask that Telperion," laughed the Count, "I have arranged to let you discover the answer for yourself—in the Manifestation Chamber. Voila!" Saint Germain walked over to one of the bookcases and made a circular movement with his hand. The bookcase slid to one side, revealing a massive metallic door, which looked like it was made out of the same shiny silver material that we saw in the Mothership.

"The Manifestation Chamber?" I said slowly, looking at the door, "what is it?"

"I think I can best describe it as a sneak preview of the 5th dimension!" said Saint Germain.

"Wow," said Janus, "you make it sound like going to the movies or something!"

"Your words are truer than you can imagine!" laughed Saint Germain, his eyes twinkling mischievously. "Let me explain. As you know, the 5th dimension is also called the Dimension of Light. Why? Because in the 5th dimension, energy vibrates at the speed of light. In other words, the 5th dimension is beyond space and time, which means ..."

"That everything is happening at once!" cried Jacob, who was getting more and more excited all the time. Especially now that it looked like he was going to be able to participate in some kind of scientific experiment.

"Exactement again!" laughed Saint Germain. "In the 5th dimension, your thoughts and words manifest instantaneously. Since there is no time or space, the braking mechanism you experience in the 3rd dimension is gone."

"Sounds awesome!" laughed Janus.

"And awesome it is indeed," said Saint Germain, "but also quite dangerous for those who have not yet learned to control their thoughts and words."

"What do you mean?" I asked.

"Well just try to imagine—for a moment—how it would be for a human being to be in the 5th dimension if he or she was thinking hateful or destructive thoughts about himself or about others," replied Saint Germain.

Janus whistled, "The person would be like an evil Superman!"

"Yeah," said Jacob, "It would be like instant self-destruction or something!"

"That is putting it mildly," said Saint Germain. "The truth of the matter is that one single human being with a low level of consciousness—for example a person who is consumed by fear or anger—would be able to inflict dreadful havoc upon himself and his surroundings. It would be truly catastrophic."

I shuddered at the thought. Then I remembered the devastating rage we felt when we went berserk on the West Bank. I couldn't imagine what would have happened if we'd been in the 5th dimension...

"No need to worry," said Saint Germain as if reading my thoughts. "The Universe is foolproof—and absolutely safe for all beings. This is because the Universe is so cleverly designed. It is constructed so that only those beings who can control their thoughts and words—and use them for the Good of All—are allowed to ascend into the 5th dimension."

"And that is also why," said Saint Germain, running his hand over the smooth metal door, "that you three must demonstrate that you are able to control your thoughts and words if you want to enter Shamballa. You will not be allowed to pass through the Violet Gateway until you do. So, my friends, in order to find Shamballa and your weapons, you must demonstrate to me that you have mastered your thoughts and words—RIGHT NOW!"

The Count opened the door of the Manifestation Chamber. We peeped in. Inside the chamber, there was a pleasant, golden light. "Inside the Manifestation Chamber, the 3rd dimension's braking mechanism has been removed. In other words, there is no time or space inside the chamber. In there, everything IS happening at once, which is why I said

207

it's like a sneak preview of life in the 5th dimension. And this you must now master. So Telperion, Moncler and Starbrow, please enter. But be careful. Or should I say THINK carefully!"

Suddenly the three of us were overcome by an ominous sense of dread and foreboding.

"What if we can't do it?" Janus said. "What if..."

"If your thoughts become too much for you and all hope leaves you," said Saint Germain, "then remember this one thing. I AM THE FORCE." The whole room seemed to echo with his words.

We repeated his words.

"I AM THE FORCE," we said in unison.

Then Jacob and Janus and I gave each other our secret D&D handshake and stepped into the Manifestation Chamber.

"The Force is with you!" was the last thing I heard Saint Germain say. Then everything turned into light.

As soon as I stepped into the Manifestation Chamber, it was as if my mind went completely blank. I had no thoughts whatsoever—and simply floated around, a weightless being of Light in a sea of Light. The Light stretched out in every direction endlessly... all there was was Light... in front of me, behind me, above me, below me. Everything was Light. There was nothing but Light.

Then I looked down at my body and discovered that it wasn't there. I had no body! I too was nothing but pure Light. I had no solid form, I was one with the golden Light. And I felt this incredible sense of freedom, of being unlimited and infinite. If I had had a mouth to laugh with, I would have laughed out loud, but I couldn't because I had no body...

I don't know how long I floated around like that, at One with the Light... with no physical body, with no thought, with no world, no limits, no boundaries... all I remember is that at some point, I suddenly became aware of myself again. It seemed to happen the moment I started thinking again. Thinking about who I was—and where I was. The moment I did that, I was in my physical body again. Standing in an immense cavern. It was very hot inside the cavern and the whole place trembled with the sound of a hundred bolts of lightening. I held my ears and looked around in shock. Then I saw an enormous red monster was flying straight towards me! It was a huge fire-breathing dragon! Fire spewed out of its nostrils as it flapped its hideous wings. Its mouth was open as it charged straight in my direction.

I just stood there petrified.

"Get out of the way, you fool!" cried a voice somewhere to my left. Out of the corner of my eye, I saw a tall warrior clad in chain mail running towards me. Then, less than a second before the dragon would have roasted me to a crisp, the warrior reached me and knocked me aside. Not a second too soon. The next moment, the spot where I stood was scorched by the dragon's fiery breath.

I rolled behind the nearest rock as the dragon soared over our heads, belching smoke and fire. I was too stunned to move. The hideous beast roared angrily. He obviously didn't like being cheated out of roasting me alive.

"You were awful close to being barbecued spare ribs!" cried my rescuer as he pulled me back up on my feet. I recognized him at once. Of course! It was Telperion—Janus! But before I had time to wonder how we'd gotten here, the hideous dragon had turned around in midair and was making ready for a new attack.

"Moncler!" cried Janus, turning in the other direction. "Are you alright!"

That's when I realized Jacob was on the other side of the cavern, sprawled up against the cave wall. Blood was streaming down his face. He had a deep gash across his forehead.

"We've got to get out of here!" cried Janus as we ran over to Jacob. The dragon spread its wings and was again flying towards us at great speed. The sight of the huge monster made my blood run cold. I felt a sharp pain in my solar plexus and buckled over. What were we doing here? Where were we?

Then suddenly I realized where we were because we'd played this scene before... many times... This was one of our favorite battle scenes from our Dungeons & Dragons game!

The moment that thought entered my head, I found myself sitting at the little table in Jacob's tiny apartment in Copenhagen. Jacob and Janus were sitting across from me. The table was piled high with Dungeons & Dragons books, maps and character sheets. The three of us were dressed in our usual Earth garb. I still had this terrible pain in my stomach.

"What's wrong?" asked Janus, looking over at me.

"I think he's going to throw up," said Jacob matter-of-factly.

My stomach was all twisted in knots. I hunched over in pain. What's going on here? What's wrong with me? Was I seriously ill...

The moment I had that thought, I found myself lying on my back on a stretcher in an ambulance with a tube stuck down my throat. A broad-shouldered ambulance attendant was leaning over me as the ambulance sped down the street, sirens blaring. The pain in my stomach suddenly disappeared. I sat up and spat out the tube.

"Easy, my friend!" said the ambulance attendant.

"What am I doing here?"

"It seems you had some kind of food poisoning."

"Food poisoning? But I haven't eaten anything!"

"I'm glad you're feeling better." Obviously, he was a friendly chap.

"Stop the ambulance," I said. "I want out of here."

"Don't you think it's a good idea we drive you in and let the doctors have a look at you?"

"But there's nothing wrong with me..." I cried. "Stop the ambulance! I want out!"

"Now why don't you just lie down and relax," he said, his voice stern and professional now. He pushed me gently but firmly back down on the stretcher.

"Stop!" I shouted.

The moment I shouted stop, the ambulance came to a screeching halt. There was this loud crashing sound as the ambulance attendant and I were hurled towards the front of the ambulance. Obviously we'd crashed into something hard. There was an explosion of glass and steel. Luckily, I was lying on the stretcher, so nothing much happened to me, but it looked like the ambulance attendant was badly hurt because he was lying on the floor of the ambulance with blood oozing from his head. I crawled over to the door and opened it. We were on Ocean Drive. The ambulance had crashed into a bus stop! The very same bus stop where I first saw Ticha.

I ran out on the street and looked at the wreckage. The front window of the ambulance was totally demolished and the driver was slumped over the wheel. Blood was everywhere. I looked around in panic. Why had Saint Germain sent me back to this place?

I heard a voice inside my head say "Starbrow." I turned and looked around. A few yards away, over by the bushes, I saw Ticha. "Get your act together, Starbrow," she said. "Take control of your thoughts and words."

"Ticha!" I cried and ran wildly in her direction. But before I could get to her, I found myself lying in bed with Sarah, my ex-girlfriend. I was naked. I couldn't understand what I was doing there with Sarah; I'd broken up with her more than a year ago. We were lying with our arms around each other as if we'd just made love.

"I'm so thirsty," she said sweetly. "How about getting me something to drink?"

I felt bewildered and looked into Sarah's dark brown eyes. She was completely naked like me and I felt her breasts against my chest. I wanted to bury myself in her warm body like a little boy and just forget all the confusing things that were happening to me. I rested my head on her breast and closed my eyes.

"There, there, my dear," said a soothing woman's voice, "You'll be fine in a jiffy." I looked up. The woman I was leaning against was no longer Sarah; it was Siri, my mother. And now we were standing in the middle of the playground in Eastbridge Park in downtown Copenhagen. Kids were screaming in the background. Salty tears were running down my cheeks as my mother dried my tears. My hands hurt. I looked down at them and could see I'd scraped them. That's when I discovered that now I was in the small body of a child! I was gripped by panic and started to cry even more. No! I thought in despair. No! This is too much! I've completely lost it! Stop! Stop! Stop! The terrible pain in my stomach came back and I buckled over in pain. I'd rather die, I thought. I'd rather die...

The moment I had that thought, I was surrounded by the thickest, blackest fog I'd ever seen in my life. I could barely make out the dark figures wandering aimlessly in the fog, howling "I'd rather die! I'd rather die!". The sound of their voices was cold as ice and it chilled me right to the bone. They sounded so forlorn and hopeless. In the distance, I heard other voices, high, screechy voices wailing in pain, "I'd rather die! I'd rather die!"

The terrible pain in my stomach started to spread rapidly to my whole body. I clutched my stomach and fell forward into the muddy puddle right before me. The water was cold and foul. I saw faces reflected on the surface of the water. Skulls! Hollow skulls! And the stench... it was the stench of years and years of rancid decay. This must be Hell, I thought...

The moment I thought of Hell, the icy cold around me changed into the most intense heat. My whole body was on fire. My mind was also on fire. Everything was on fire. I was in an inferno. I was in Hell. I tried to move my mouth to call for help, but I was completely paralyzed. Besides, who should I call, who could I call? Would anybody hear me? What about Ticha... Ticha! Ticha, please help me! But Ticha didn't come. The only thing that did come to me was her last words. "Starbrow!" she said.

"Starbrow. Take control of your thoughts and words... Take control of your thoughts and words..."

Boom. Boom. Boom.

I heard heavy footsteps approaching.

Now I was sure I was going to die. This was the end. They were coming to get me. To finish me off. To kill me.

Ticha's last words echoed in my mind. "Take control of your thoughts and words, take control of your thoughts and words..."

I tried to move, but I couldn't. I was completely paralyzed. The only thing I had left was my thoughts. The only thing I could still move was my thoughts. They were all that I had left. I had to take control of them. But the thought that I was going to die was so strong, so powerful that all I could feel now was how all life was ebbing out of my body. I tried to think no, NO, I don't want to die! But it didn't help. The heavy footsteps were getting closer and closer.

The dark figure loomed over me—and my blood turned to ice. Fire and ice. Fire and ice. In me and through me. The dark figure raised a heavy axe and was about to give me the death blow. I tried with all my might to think about something else—but what? What should I think about?

As if in slow motion, the axe began moving down towards me.

I closed my eyes. Think about something else. Think about something else, you fool! But what! Think about Elmar! In a panic, I thought about Elmar, Elmar, I saw his face, his clear blue eyes and his radiant smile...

A split second before the axe reached me, something knocked my foe over and I heard him fall backwards, shrieking like a madman. I opened my eyes.

Elmar was right before my eyes, lying on the bed in the hospital just like he did the day he died. He grabbed my hand firmly and pulled me over to him. "Get a grip, my boy. Get a grip," he said sternly. "Take control of your thoughts and words!"

Elmar's hand released mine and he lay limp and lifeless in the bed. The machine started beeping frantically. The doctor and the nurse came rushing into the room. My mother and sister clutched my hands as the nurse pulled the sheet over Elmar's head. "I am sorry," mumbled the doctor and left the room.

I buried my head in my hands in despair. I knew my thoughts had run amok and I could no longer stop them. I was a helpless victim, watching as each thought led to another new thought which led to another new thought, in an endless chain of... I staggered out of Elmar's room and

212

into the hallway and collapsed in a chair. I closed my eyes. I didn't dare open my eyes again for fear of what would happen next. I heard the sound of horses and clashing swords, men were screaming, there was the sound of a rock concert, electric guitars were screeching, a TV announcer was commenting on the death of Princess Diana, church bells were ringing, no it was an alarm clock ringing, no it was the sound of bus doors closing, no it was my boss at Fashion Flash calling my name... she sounded like Darth Vader with that foul hissing sound he had or was it a washingmachinecashregisterjumbojetpornomoviezootigerroarfiredragon STOP! STOP! STOP! I can't take it any more! God have mercy on me STOP!

With my last ounce of will power, I tried to focus on my breathing. Just breathe. I managed to do it for one inhalation and one exhalation, then my thoughts ran amok again...

ParkCaféGeorgeMichaelcatwalkgirlpartytrendbureau   Stop!   Stop! Again I forced my attention back to my breathing. This time, I managed to keep my attention on my breathing for two inhalations and two exhalations, before I lost my concentration again...

Axisshiftcatastrophejudgmentdayevacuation Stop! Stop!

Again I brought my attention back to my breathing. And again. And again. I knew now that this was no game. This was for real. If I didn't take control of my thoughts and words I would go crazy. I would simply self-destruct. Like a time bomb. No, no, you mustn't think about that! Back to the breathing...

I desperately clung to my breathing, the only safe haven I knew of in all this madness. Finally, I managed to focus my attention on my breathing for 3 or 4 breaths. I felt a surge of Peace inside me. The Force. Ah. Peace at last.

Then I opened my eyes and got the greatest shock of my life. Before me loomed the most horrible, revolting monster I had ever seen. The monster had hundreds of heads, each of which was making the most grotesque, awful and terrifying faces I'd ever seen. The heads were sticking out their tongues, rolling their eyes and coughing and spitting and making weird horrendous grimaces. And each head was on a long, long neck which writhed and squirmed in and out of all the other necks and heads like loathsome tendrils. Hundreds of hateful eyes were gazing evilly in my direction.

I opened my mouth to scream.

But at that very moment, an even worse thing happened. I discovered

213

that each and every one of the monster's heads was exactly the same as the other. And that they were all my head! Each and every one of the monster's hideous heads was my own.

"Oh my God!" I cried looking at the hundreds of heads. And they were all me. All my head... and each one was more distorted and twisted than the one before.

"You cannot pass!" all the heads on the horrific monster bellowed at once. "You cannot pass! I am the Dweller on the Threshold!"

Then all the monster's hundreds of heads—my heads—began hurling epithets at me all at once. A horrible, deafening torrent of maledictions came crashing over me like an evil rain of the sharpest knives and the most deadly daggers.

"You worthless piece of scum!" cried one of the heads.

"You stinking pile of no-good humanity!" cried another head. "You'll never pass!"

"You're not good enough! You were never good enough and you'll never ever be good enough!" bellowed a third.

"You haven't got a chance in hell!" roared another.

"You were born a loser which is why you're a born loser!" cackled yet another with the most evil grin on his (my) face.

"Scum of the Earth, scum of the Earth. You're the lowest of the Low!"

"You'll never make it!"

"The Gateway is closed!"

"Closed to your kind!"

"You good for nothing shit head!"

"Shit for brains!"

"Shit face!"

"Up shit creek without a paddle, you are!"

"Shit ass!"

"Shit head!"

"Shit out of luck you are!"

I covered my ears and tried to shut out their deafening roar, but it didn't help. All their voices were inside my own head.

"You worthless piece of humanity!" one of the heads kept repeating, over and over and over again like a broken record. "Worthless piece of... worthless piece of... worthless, worthless..!"

"Worthless and wretched! You should've never been born! Worthless... You'll never amount to anything!"

"Life sucks! Life sucks! The whole world's going down the drain!"

"You'll never make it!"

"The Gateway is closed!"

"Closed to your kind!"

"You good for nothing shit head!"

"Shit for brains!"

"Shit face!"

"Up shit creek without a paddle, you are!"

"You is shit out of luck!"

"The Gateway is closed!"

As the deluge of maledictions continued to hammer down upon me, it dawned on me that all the voices of all the heads—my heads—also sounded like my voice. Yes, they were me too, my voice... my own voice. And that was when I realized—to my everlasting shame—that yes—and I fell to my knees at the thought of it—at the very magnitude of the thought of it—that yes—all the thoughts and all the words of this hideous Dweller on the Threshold were my very own thoughts... my very own negative thoughts and words!

And the heads just kept on screaming, caught it seemed, in an endless repeat mode. I tried to think of something else, but I couldn't. It was impossible. The deafening noise of the screaming, bellowing heads drowned out everything else. Then I thought... so that's how it is and how it's going to be. I was doomed, no doubt about it. Doomed it seems to suffer the eternal torment of my own negative thoughts. The best I could hope for was a quick death, so my suffering would end...

But even though many of the heads now started bellowing that I was going to die and rot in hell forever and ever, nothing actually happened. I didn't die. I didn't do anything. I was just there, listening to the hideous heads as they bellowed on.

Slowly, ever so slowly, it began to dawn on me that even though the heads—all the heads—all my heads—were screaming all the things I'd been saying to myself all my life, their evil, negative talk was not me. It started to dawn on me that everything the heads were saying—all my negative thoughts, opinions and beliefs about myself and about life— were in fact not me. They were just pictures—and horrible pictures indeed—but still they were just pictures. Pictures that passed before my mind's eye like images on a movie screen. But no matter how evil, they could not touch the real me. The real me—my True Self—was free. The real me—my True Self—was untouchable. Because I was not my thoughts and words. I was not even my beliefs. I just was. The real me

215

was beyond all that. The real me was Pure Consciousness. Pure Presence, Pure Power, Pure Force. THE FORCE. Like an echo from a distant country, far far far away, I remembered at last Saint Germain's words... "If your thoughts become more than you can bear, and all hope leaves you, then remember one thing... I AM THE FORCE."

I lifted my head and said, "I AM THE FORCE." The monster with the hundreds of heads gathered all of the heads together and pressed them right in my face. And there they were, screaming all their hideous curses and epithets, right in my face. But I was not moved. I was no longer afraid of them because I knew that they could not touch me. I was the Force. Untouchable and Invincible. I AM THE FORCE. And not only that. I was the Master of my thoughts and words. I was the choice-maker. I chose where to focus my attention. I stood up and looked around me. The Dweller on the Threshold loomed before me like a mighty shadow of evil, hailing a wild torrent of oaths and threats at me. But I was no longer afraid. I knew who I was. I started to walk forward, straight into the darkness. Where to? I knew that no matter where I wanted to go, I would have to choose to go there first.

"Shamballa," I said. "I am going to Shamballa."

The moment I spoke these words, I saw a Violet Gateway shimmering in the darkness before me. I walked up to the Gateway, without paying any attention to the monster that was right behind me, bellowing all the evil of the world in my ears. I paid the evil creature no heed. Instead I pushed on the doors and they opened easily. On the other side of the Gateway was a rocky precipice. I stepped through the Gateway and turned and looked back. The many-headed monster was right behind me, looming evilly on the other side of the Gateway, all its heads screaming in one voice, "You'll never make it!"

"I AM the Master of My Fate!" I said and with one mighty push, I slammed the doors of the great Gateway shut.

6

On a Pink Cloud

I shook off the nightmare of the Manifestation Chamber and stepped out onto the rocky ledge. It was great to be out in the open again and I took a deep breath, grateful for the warm sunshine on my face. Even though I seemed to be high up in the mountains, I was nicely sheltered from the wind and the temperature was actually quite pleasant. There was soft, white snow on the ground and I kicked it gently as I walked over to the edge of the ledge. Once there, I stood still and surveyed the amazing view that was before me. The mountaintop I was standing on was totally surrounded by pink clouds. I couldn't see the mountain below me at all. Rather it was as if I stood on a tiny island of rock in the middle of a vast pink ocean. Then, as I looked out over the pink clouds, I saw a Pink Gateway out there, floating right in the middle of the pink clouds! Of course! It was the Third Gateway!

When I looked down, I discovered there was another ledge right under me, which jutted a little further out into the clouds than the ledge I was standing on. Janus was sitting cross-legged down there, enjoying the view.

"Janus!" I cried in delight.

"Greetings, Starbrow!" Janus called back, without taking his eyes off the sea of pink clouds before us.

I jumped down next to him. "Have you seen Jacob?"

"No," he replied, "not yet. But sooner or later, he'll show up. Sooner or later."

I sat down next to my friend. For a while, we just sat and watched the pink clouds floating by.

Then Janus said, "You know what? When we were with Kuthumi, Serapis Bey and Saint Germain, and they were explaining to us how Dungeons & Dragons wasn't just our imagination, but was really real...

You know what I kept thinking all the time?"

I looked at Janus in surprise. I don't think I'd ever seen him so thoughtful before. "No, what?"

"Well, I was wondering all the time about the bad guys. I mean if what they were saying was really true, then where were all the bad guys? All our enemies... you know... all those terrible monsters we thought we'd invented. I just kept thinking, what about them..." said Janus, seriously. "And now I finally got my answer because I've met them all. Every one of them, every single monster, beast, dragon, werewolf, beast, bogeyman, zombie, blood-sucking ogre and vampire who ever threatened me... they're all inside of me!"

I laughed softly and gave my friend a pat on the back. Good ol' Janus! "I know what you mean... " I chuckled. "I know what you mean. You know Elmar once told me that a man's enemies shall be those of his own household. But back then I didn't understand what he meant. Now I think I do."

"Yeah, that's for sure! All my life I've been afraid of things that were outside of myself, you know like other people and all the stuff that was happening around me or might happen around me," continued Janus. "And so I did everything I could to protect myself from the outside world and to control it. While all the time, the only thing I had to fear was my own thoughts..."

"But now you know that you're not your thoughts!" said a familiar voice above us. We turned around. It was Jacob!

"Jacob!" we both cried.

Our friend was standing on the ledge above us. Both of us stared at Jacob in awe. He seemed to radiate a strength and self-confidence we hadn't seen in him before. It was as if his experience in the Manifestation Chamber had freed him from some heavy burden.

"Now I know that nothing, absolutely nothing, has any power over me," said Jacob in a voice we'd never heard before. "Not other people, not the outside world, not destiny, not some God up in the sky who is separate from me, not karma, not the signs of the zodiac, not the weather, not my body, not my past, not my future nor any other kind of outer condition or circumstance. Not even my own thoughts and words have any power over me. Because I AM THE FORCE," he laughed and spread his arms open wide.

Janus and I got up too and repeated after Jacob. "I AM THE FORCE!" We spread our arms wide.

218

"I AM THE FORCE!" We cried in unison and the sound of our voices echoed out into Infinity. "I AM THE FORCE! I AM THE FORCE!" we shouted at the top our lungs—to the wind, to the pink clouds, to the sun and to the mountains. "I AM THE FORCE!" we proclaimed to the whole Universe—and the Universe sent our proclamation right back to us... I AM THE FORCE! I AM THE FORCE!

Then, in one perfectly synchronized movement, as if our minds were in total harmony, the three of us stepped out from the rocky ledge onto the pink clouds. Only we didn't think that we were stepping out onto clouds. No! Our one and only thought was "I AM THE FORCE! I AM THE FORCE!". And we kept on and on proclaiming at the top of our lungs that yes I AM THE FORCE! I AM THE FORCE! And lo and behold! We didn't fall through. But rather we continued to walk forward as if our feet were on firm ground. "I AM THE FORCE!" we continued to proclaim loudly as we walked across the pink clouds right up to the Pink Gateway. "I AM THE FORCE!" we hollered fervently as we pounded on the great Gateway before us. And then, without a sound, the great doors opened and we passed through.

Once through the great Gateway, we discovered more pink clouds. In fact, nothing but pink clouds stretched before us as far as the eye could see. Nothing else. Everywhere it was pink. There were no mountains, no sun, not even a bit of blue sky above us.

But there was more. Much more. In fact, our surprise was so great at what we saw, that the three of us went quiet at the very same moment. Everywhere we looked we saw angels! Hundreds and hundreds of angels zooming in and out of the pink clouds at amazing speeds and in breathtaking formations... just like birds of a feather. Then one little flock zoomed right over our heads and we heard their heavenly voices singing inside our heads. It sounded like a combination of tinkling bells, childish laughter and celestial song.

A short distance from where we stood, there was a gap in the clouds. We walked over and looked through. Far far below us, we saw Mother Earth. Her blue-green surface was still surrounded by ugly black clouds. The starships were also still in position, holding their network of light around the planet. Great swarms of angels were shooting at high speeds back and forth between Earth and the pink clouds where we stood. Occasionally, some of the flocks would swoop down and disappear right into the Earth's atmosphere.

"Well I declare," laughed Janus, "that truly must be the Heavenly

219

Hosts!"

"I wonder what they're all doing down there?" said Jacob.

"Every angel you see has the same mission," said a mighty voice far above us, "and that is to help and protect humanity... to guide and comfort..."

We looked up. Far above us we saw a huge mighty being of Light, hundreds and hundreds of feet tall, with enormous, shining silvery wings. His face was like a blazing sun, and on his head he wore a huge crown, which shone like a million diamonds. In one hand, he held a blue sword and from it sprang a mighty flame, which looked like it could cut through everything and everybody.

"Greetings, Brothers in the Light!" he said and his voice made the pink clouds tremble.

We bowed in awe before this mighty being.

"Who are you?" Jacob finally asked.

"I AM Archangel Michael," he replied, "Commander of the Angelic Hosts gathered here to serve in Mission Earth Ascension."

"So you're a guardian angel, too?" I cried.

"Well yes, in a way," replied Archangel Michael, his radiant face softening into a smile. "... You could call me the guardian angel of all humanity because I am the protector of all souls. I am the defender of every human being on Earth and a Champion of Love and Light."

We continued to stare at him, overwhelmed by his breathtaking radiance. One of the swarms of angels whizzed by him and down through the hole at our side. They flew at an incredible speed towards Earth and disappeared in a flash into the Earth's atmosphere.

"Are those angels guardian angels on their way to protect people down on Earth?" I asked.

"No, they were on another mission," said Archangel Michael. "Not all angels are guardian angels. Some work on other projects. For example, there are angels who work closely with Mother Earth and the Nature Forces on Earth. Then there are angels who work with the Ashtar Command and the Great White Brotherhood. And still others are bearers of various Divine Qualities such as Compassion, Inspiration, Beauty and Humor. But basically, no matter what specific mission an angel is on, they're all working on the same project. The Project of Love! For angels are Love. And so are you."

"We are?" said Jacob. "What do you mean?"

"Why did you come through the Pink Gateway?" Archangel Michael

220

asked.

"Well... because we want to find Shamballa so we can retrieve our weapons and establish the Light Grid on Earth," replied Jacob.

"And why would you want to establish a Light Grid on Earth?" continued Archangel Michael.

"So that Mother Earth doesn't make a complete axis shift and wipe out all life on Earth," I said.

"And why don't you want that to happen?"

"Well... because we want... all people to live and be happy..." I stammered.

"Why do you want all people to live and be happy?" the mighty angel asked, gazing at us intently.

"Because... because... I don't know... I just want them to be," I stuttered.

"Whether you consciously know it or not, you want all people to be happy," said Archangel Michael, "because you are Love!

"Well, that might be true of Starbrow," said Janus hotly, "but not all human beings on Earth want other people to be happy. I mean I can think of at least a half a dozen dudes who aren't as nice as Starbrow!"

"And so it may appear to you," said Archangel Michael kindly, "but in fact, if you trace all the things that human beings do—all the way back to their source—you will discover that all human beings are motivated by love."

"Then why do people get involved in violence and pollution and war and all kinds of other negative stuff if they're really love?" I asked.

"It's because they've temporarily forgotten that they're Love," said the mighty angel. "But as soon as they remember that they're Love, they'll start consciously choosing Love again. Then they will choose the Highest Good in every situation, no matter what."

"But how do you do that?" I asked.

"Actually it's very simple. All you have to do is... Follow your heart, for your heart alone knows the way," said Archangel Michael.

"Yeah, that's what Ticha keeps telling me," I said with a smile.

"Well? Does it work?" the Archangel asked me.

"I think so..." I said. "But I don't really know why."

"I'll tell you why. It always works because your heart is the bridge between your own personal, individual consciousness and the Universal Consciousness, the Force—which is Love. When you follow your heart, you follow the Force, which is All Wisdom, All Intelligence, All Knowledge. When you follow your heart you are following the Path of

Love—which is the Highest Good for All. That is why we in the higher dimensions always say... Follow your heart, for your heart alone knows the way."

"But sometimes it's hard for me to figure out what my heart really wants me to do," said Janus. "Sometimes I feel as if there are a million thoughts and conflicting emotions all racing through me at the same time."

"Yeah," said Jacob. "One minute you feel like doing one thing, and the next minute you feel like doing something else."

"I didn't say you should just do what you feel like," said the Archangel. "I said that you should follow your heart. They're not always the same."

"But what's the difference?" asked Janus.

"If you're having difficulty hearing the guidance of your heart, then ask yourself if your choice is for the Highest Good of All Concerned," said Archangel Michael. He placed his hand on his chest over his heart and motioned for us to do the same. "Now focus your attention on your heart and then try to picture yourself doing whatever it is you are considering doing. Then ask yourself the following questions. What are the consequences of this choice I am about to make? Will it make me happy? And will it make the people who are going to be affected by my choice happy? Is this choice for the Highest Good of everyone involved? And then listen to your heart. If you feel discomfort in or around your heart, if you feel your heart is closing—then it's because it is not the right choice. If you feel a sense of peace and comfort in and around your heart, if you feel that your heart is opening, if you feel Love—then you will know it's the right choice."

"Is that the reason why everything is so peaceful and harmonious up here?" asked Jacob.

"Yes," said Archangel Michael. "Everyone in the 5th or higher dimensions always follows their heart, always chooses that which is for the Highest Good of All Concerned."

"You sure do make it sound simple," sighed Janus.

"It is," he said. "And in order to ascend into the 5th dimension, you must learn to always choose that which is for the Highest Good of All Concerned. For great power brings great responsibility with it. When you are an Ascended Master, you will be able to perform incredible feats and miracles. And as you learned in the Manifestation Chamber, your thoughts and words manifest instantaneously in the 5th dimension. So if you are not always choosing thoughts, words and actions, which are for the Highest Good of All Concerned, the consequences can be fatal. That is why all the Masters who have ever walked on Earth have always said that Love is by far the most important thing of all."

"If this is what happens when you always choose Love, then I'm all for it," I said dreamily as a host of laughing angels soared past us.

"In order for you to find Shamballa, you must now pass through the Pink Gateway. This you can only do by proving that you will always follow your heart, no matter what happens," said Archangel Michael. "You must now prove that you are able to listen to and follow the deepest wisdom of your heart, no matter what your passing whims or desires might be, and no matter what the circumstances are or what the people around you might be saying. This is the one hard and fast rule—and there is no exception to it. Even if it means letting go of what seems to be the most important thing in your life, you must prove that you will always choose to follow the wisdom of your heart. Because only by following the wisdom of your heart can you always choose that which is for the Highest Good of All Concerned. And this is because the heart is intuitive and holistic. It sees the Whole. It is truly the highest manifestation of the Force."

"I'd always choose Love, even if they offered me the whole world on a silver platter," I said.

"We shall see," said Archangel Michael, "we shall see!" Then he lifted his enormous flaming blue sword and before I realized what was happening, he drove it straight into my chest. I felt the blue flames penetrate my heart. Then everything went black.

223

7

My Dream Life

A second later, I was zooming down Ocean Drive in my brand new silver blue BMW Roadster—on my way to a press conference in Copenhagen. The sun was shining, the radio was blaring and I was singing at the top of my lungs. Today was a great day. As a matter of fact, today was the best day of my life, the day when all my dreams had come true. Less than an hour ago, my agent called to tell me I'd been nominated for an Oscar for Best Adapted Screenplay. It was the film script I'd written for the movie version of one of my own best-selling books. Which meant that even more people would buy my books and go see the movie. But in fact, it wasn't the prospect of selling even more books or movie tickets that made me so happy on this bright sunny spring afternoon. It was something else. Because I had more than enough money already. My last book was still No. 1 on The New York Times Bestseller List for the 36th week in a row. And the three other books I'd written during my short career had already sold more than 10 million copies and were at present translated into 28 languages—including Swahili. So no, it wasn't the money. It was the sense of satisfaction that getting nominated gave me. I mean an Oscar nomination was the greatest recognition an artist could receive from the Academy, which I regarded as the very heart of the heart of the Hollywood dream machine. So for me, it was like the icing on the cake, because my life already was a piece of cake. In Scandinavia where I lived, everyone loved my books already—and Denmark's European neighbors, the Germans, the French and the English also loved my books. And further afield, the Japanese loved my books, too. As far as I could remember, the most recent award I'd received was when the Czech Republic made me an honorary citizen because they considered me the most influential author of my generation. And now Hollywood was going to honor me too. So yes, it was truly a great day!

I turned up my car radio even louder and kept on singing at the top of my lungs, not caring if anyone saw or heard me. The palatial mansions of the rich and famous who lived along Denmark's Riviera, flashed by on my right hand side. To my left, the blue waters of the Sound stretched out before me. In the distance, I could see the coast of Sweden sparkling in the afternoon sunshine. It was such a nice day, that I considered putting the top down, but no it was still pretty chilly out.

When I stopped at a red light, I checked my tie in the rearview mirror and discovered I had this huge lipstick mark on my neck, right where Helena had given me a gentle love bite just a short while ago. Ah Helena! I was sure she was the sexiest, most beautiful woman in the whole world. She was my muse, my greatest fan—and lucky me—my wife!

Right after my agent had called to tell us about the Oscar nomination, Helena dragged me straight back to our bedroom to celebrate properly. And when my babe decided to celebrate, well, she sure knew how to do it right. Having sex with her was a dream come true. She had this foxy way of being seductive and wild—and sweet and loving all at the same time. And the best part of it all was that she was in no rush to have kids either. I guess because she was just as busy as I was, enjoying her career as one of the world's most famous supermodels. Our friends often said we were the perfect couple, and I was inclined to agree.

I looked in the rearview mirror again and started to wipe the lipstick mark off my neck. But no I thought... why hide it? After all, I was going to a press conference in my honor. So why not give those dudes something to write about!

Suddenly the music on the radio was interrupted by a news flash. "Oh come on, man!" I cried, "that was one of my favorite songs!" I was just about to switch to another channel when the announcement came. San Francisco had been nearly leveled to the ground by a gigantic earthquake. The destruction was so devastating that at the moment, no one had any idea how many people had been killed or wounded. According to first reports, the city was leveled to the ground. As the news commentator was speaking, I suddenly had this very strange feeling in my chest, as if something was happening to my heart. Then I had the weirdest feeling... like I'd forgotten something, something important...

But before I could think more about it, my cell phone rang. I turned off the radio. "Hello," I said.

"Hi, it's me, Casper," said my agent. The line crackled as I sped down

225

Ocean Drive. "Have I got news for you Mr. Superstar," he continued, having a hard time keeping cool. Every time Casper called, he was almost more excited than I was.

"Yeah, well what's up Doc..." I replied slowly. For some reason, the news about the San Francisco earthquake really upset me. Which was kind of strange, considering the fact that disaster seemed to strike someplace in the world every five or ten minutes.

"We're talking Big Time America!" Casper cried.

"Oh yeah," I said. "Well what?"

"The queen of the talk shows, Miss Oprah Winfrey herself, wants you on her show!"

"Oprah Winfrey? You're kidding..."

"No, I'm serious," laughed Casper. "Do you realize what this means! The last time she had a writer on her show, the guy sold 130,000 copies of his book the very next day. When you've been on Oprah, you've reached the very top!"

"Sounds good..." I said slowly.

"Good?" said Casper. "This is more than good, this is out-of-sight excellent!"

When I didn't answer Casper said, "Hey buddy, is something wrong? You have a fight with Helena or something?"

"No, no," I said,. "everything's fine... it's just that..." Just as I was talking, Ocean Drive made a sharp turn to the left and the whole coastline glistened before me in the bright sunshine. Far away, Sweden gleamed like a jewel on the horizon and a few puffy pink clouds drifted by. Pink clouds... they were beautiful I thought... and strange... somehow they reminded of the feeling that I'd forgotten something, something important...

Casper's voice brought me back to reality.

"What did you say?" Casper asked. The connection wasn't too good.

"Tell me, Casper..." I said as I studied the strange pink clouds, "did we forget something important...?

"What do you mean?"

"Did you hear the news... about the earthquake in San Francisco?"

"Yeah, I heard it. Awful, isn't it?" Casper said. "But why do you mention it?"

"Well... shouldn't we... do something about it?" I said, my eyes glued to the pink clouds above Sweden. Maybe it was just my imagination, but it seemed to me they were getting bigger and bigger. They had to be the

226

weirdest clouds I'd ever seen.

"Yeah..." said Casper. "I understand what you're saying... I guess we should send money like we did when those huge fires swept across Indonesia. In fact, you know what you could do? You could donate all the money you make on the Oscar nomination! Now that would be a noble gesture—and the press would really eat it up!"

"I don't just mean money, Casper," I said. "I just have this feeling there's something else, something important that we've forgotten..."

"Sorry, Mr. Superstar," sighed Casper, "but I think I'd better leave the philosophizing to you. After all, you're the gifted one. I'm just your agent. My job is to make sure you remember to mark Tuesday in your calendar. 'Cause that's when you're going to be on the Oprah Winfrey Show!"

"I read some of your new movie script last night," said Helena, her head resting on my shoulder. We were in a cab on our way to Copenhagen Airport to catch a plane to Chicago for my date with Oprah. Helena was going with me because she was going to do a photo shoot in New York afterwards—and then we were off to the Caribbean for a well-earned vacation.

"Really?" I said as I stroked her beautiful black hair. Despite her busy schedule, she was always incredibly interested in my writing. Truly, she was my muse, my inspiration. I leaned over and kissed her.

"You're just so brilliant," she said. "And the story's so exciting, especially when your hero meets that woman who glows in the dark at the bus stop on Ocean Drive. Where do you get all your inspiration from?"

"From you, darling," I replied playfully. "How many times do I have to tell you—you're my muse!" Helena looked up at me with those big blue eyes of hers. Our lips met again and we kissed passionately.

As we approached the airport, I watched the planes circling above us, waiting for permission to land. One just disappeared into the big pink clouds... clouds like the ones I'd seen the other day on Ocean Drive...

"So this woman who glows in the dark," Helena was saying, "who is she going to turn out to be?"

I didn't answer because I was far, far away... lost in thought and

227

wondering about the strange sensation I was feeling again in my chest.

"Sweetheart, are you there?" asked Helena.

"Err, yeah... what were you saying?" I couldn't take my eyes off the pink clouds.

"Who is the glowing woman at the bus stop going to turn out to be?"

"Well... as a matter of fact, I think she's going to turn out to be an angel," I said slowly.

"An angel? Now that's one I haven't heard before," laughed Helena. "Why does she contact him?"

"I think she wants to remind him of something important. Something he's forgotten," I said, "You see he's on an important mission, but he's forgotten it."

"Really? What kind of mission?"

I didn't answer because our cab pulled up in front of the Departure Hall and we were in a rush. We didn't want to miss our plane. We both jumped out and I ran over to get a baggage cart. As I pulled a cart out of the row of baggage carts, I noticed this tall, gangly guy standing by the entrance to the Departure Hall. He was wearing thick glasses and his hair was kind of tousled. There was something about him that reminded me of the Dungeons & Dragons freaks I used to hang out with when I was younger. He had the same nerdy look that lots of my old friends had. He was staring at me as if he knew me, but I didn't recognize him.

I walked back over to the cab and stacked our luggage on the cart. As we pushed our cart towards the entrance, Helena put her hand on my arm. "Sweetheart... you can't just leave me hanging like that... you've got to tell me about the mission the hero in your new film script has forgotten..."

I was just about to tell her when I felt a hand on my shoulder. I turned around. It was the tall, nerdy guy I'd noticed before. Up close I could see that he was really nervous about something. But before I could say anything, he threw his arms around me and started to hug me. "Starbrow!" he cried fervently, "I'm so glad I've found you at last!"

I wrenched myself free and pushed him away. He didn't seem to mind because his face was still beaming with happiness...he really seemed to believe that I was his long-lost friend... someone by the name of Starbrow!

"It's you! It really is you!" he cried triumphantly. "I can see the star on your brow, Starbrow!" The young man threw himself at me again. I struggled to free myself from him. For some reason, when he said the

228

word "Starbrow", I felt a strange tingling between my eyebrows. Helena cried out in alarm and ran through the doors of the Departure Hall.

"Will you please let me go!" I cried, starting to get pissed at the guy. I tried to extricate myself from his grip, but he was awfully strong, despite his thin, gangly frame. And he just wouldn't let go!

"Starbrow! Starbrow!" he cried, holding onto me for dear life, "... you've got to follow your heart!" As I tried to free myself, we both tumbled backwards onto my luggage. In the struggle, we both ended up on the sidewalk. He still didn't release me. "The New Vision depends on you," he cried.

Helena came running out the Departure Hall with two security guards. The guards grabbed the man and pulled him away from me. I staggered to my feet.

"Oh baby," cried Helena, "are you OK?"

"Yeah..." I said, brushing myself off, "I'm fine..." I could still feel that strange tingling sensation between my eyebrows.

"Starbrow!" he screamed as the security guards dragged him away. "You've got to follow your heart!"

I kept on watching the strange young man. "Starbrow!" he cried as he feverishly tried to turn in my direction. "Remember... Once in every person's lifetime, the soul is called to ascend into the higher dimensions, but only very few heed that call..."

I stared at him in amazement. How could he be saying exactly the same thing that Elmar had said to me so many years ago? Elmar...

"Sweetheart, are you sure you're okay?" said Helena, with a worried look on her face.

"I don't know, Helena," I said. "I just don't know."

Helena was in a talkative mood. "Now that you know Random House is going to give you such a huge advance on your new book, couldn't we go ahead with our plans for the guest wing?" she asked me sweetly. We were sitting in the green room right next to the main studio, waiting for the call for me to be the guest of honor on the Oprah Winfrey Show. We were following the show from the monitors they'd thoughtfully placed in the room. Oprah was talking about one of her many amazing projects, oozing charm like she always did, warming the audience up for me. A

229

studio assistant peeked into the room, "Three minutes," she said.

Helena repeated her question about the guest wing again.

"Why do we need it?" I said, without taking my eyes from Oprah. The woman was a walking, talking angel.

"Well, for one thing, the next time my sister visits, she won't have to sleep in the room right next to ours. And besides, we'll need the extra space when we decide to have a family," Helena explained sensibly.

"Actually," I said, "I've already decided to give the money to the emergency fund Oprah's set up for the victims of the earthquake in San Francisco," I said and looked down at my new Tag Heuer watch. Two minutes.

"All of the money?" asked Helena in surprise. She was used to us giving lots of money to good causes, but I'd never given so much money before. "Why so much?"

"Why? Because I think it's the right thing to do!"

"But you'll be getting more than a million dollars? Don't you think you're going a bit overboard?" She sounded upset.

I didn't reply. We usually agreed on everything.

"It's just that it's so much money, sweetheart... I don't get it..." I could tell by the tone of her voice that she didn't want to upset me. "... but why does it have to be so much?"

"Because... I want all human beings to be happy," I replied slowly.

"You do?" she said. "But why do you want all human beings to be happy?" There was something strangely familiar about that question.

"Because... well," I stammered, "because... I am... Love."

Helena's mouth dropped open. "Whatever do you mean?"

The moment I said the word *Love* several things happened. First, the producer poked her head in the door and said, "30 seconds and you're on!". At the same instant, a Pink Gateway suddenly manifested in the middle of the room. The Gateway sparkled as if it was made of a thousand pink crystals.

That was when it all came back to me. Starbrow, my true name and identity. Mission Earth Ascension, the imminent danger of an axis shift, the urgent need to anchor the New Vision in the collective consciousness, Moncler and Telperion... I stood up.

My heart opened.

And I knew that the wisdom of my heart wanted me to step through the Gateway.

"Now is your time!" the producer cried as she swung open the main

230

door leading into the studio. I turned and looked in. Oprah was standing there with my books in her hand, showing them to the audience. The audience started clapping and Oprah turned towards me.

Helena kissed me proudly on the cheek. "Now is your time," she said and looked at me with her beautiful blue eyes. Instead of walking over to Oprah, I stood riveted to the spot, staring first at Helena, then at Oprah and finally at the Pink Gateway. Helena, my beloved... you don't understand...

In my mind, I heard the frantic cry of the man at the airport, "Remember... Once in every person's lifetime, the soul is called to ascend into the higher dimensions, but only very few heed that call..."

When I didn't move, Helena panicked, "Darling, what's wrong?"

The producer ran over to me and grabbed my arm. "We are broadcasting live!" she cried. Oprah was looking in my direction now, a big smile on her face, my books in her hand. The books I'd always dreamed of writing... The audience was clapping and cheering wildly.

Helena kissed me on the cheek again. "Enjoy it, honey," she said. "This is the moment you've been waiting for, for so long."

Yes, I thought. This is the moment I've been waiting for. This is the moment I've dreamt of my whole life. To be a successful writer, to reach so many people with my words. I would never be given such an opportunity again. The Ashtar Command could easily manage without me. Jacob and Janus were strong enough to complete the mission on their own, to activate our Power Spot and anchor the New Vision...

I started walking towards Oprah. With every step I took, I felt more and more strange. Sweat was pouring down my back. I stopped again. Was this really what I had been waiting for my whole life? No! my heart cried. No! This wasn't it. Your mission Starbrow is to help humanity, that is what you came to Earth for. *Love* Starbrow! You're Love! And you came to help humanity ascend into the 5th dimension, to create a critical mass. Now is your time...! I turned towards the Gateway. The pink doors glistened in the blazing studio lights. I began to walk towards the Gateway.

"You can't do this!" cried the producer, pulling me in the other direction. "We're broadcasting live!"

"Sweetheart, this isn't funny anymore!" cried Helena in despair. "Please darling, won't you go in?"

I closed my eyes. I felt that I stood at a crossroads. On the one road was everything that I had dreamed of all my life. Life as a successful,

231

respected author. With a beautiful, wonderful wife who supported me in every way. With more than enough money to do everything I ever dreamed of... On the other road was great danger and huge risks—and everything I knew in my heart of hearts I must do. Because on that road, my task was to fulfill my mission on Earth and help humanity in its darkest hour.

I turned back towards Oprah. The TV studio was completely quiet now. No one was clapping anymore. The cameras were rolling but no one said a word. Helena and the producer were staring at me with eyes opened wide.

But I was looking at Oprah. Our eyes met. For some reason, I wanted to tell her I was sorry I couldn't be on her show. But there was no time... no, there wasn't a moment to lose... Any second now, the Pink Gateway would disappear... and the chance to help would be gone forever...

Oprah put her hand on her heart and smiled. Then she nodded at me. She understood! I put my hand on my heart and smiled back at her gratefully. Then I yanked myself from the clutches of Oprah's angry producer and sprang through the Pink Gateway.

232

8

In the Desert

I soared through the Pink Gateway and landed right smack in the middle of a desert. I stood still for a moment, trying to get my bearings, and then I looked around. I found that I was surrounded on all sides by huge sand dunes. Right behind me, the massive doors of the Pink Gateway closed without a sound and the Gateway vanished into thin air.

But I didn't care. From the second I landed in the desert, I felt strangely at ease and free again. As if I was back, back to being who I was supposed to be. In my dream life, even though everything seemed so wonderful on the surface, I had the feeling the whole time that I was drowning in murky water that made me forget who I really was and why I was alive. But as soon as I leaped through the Gateway, it was all crystal clear again. Who I was and where I was going.

And my heart sang.

That was how I knew I'd made the right choice, the choice of the heart.

The desert around me seemed endless. As far as the eye could see, there was nothing but one gigantic sand dune after another. But at least I wasn't alone in this desolate place. On top of the great dune to my right, I saw Janus. He was standing high above me, surveying the view. And about 50 yards from him, on the next dune, Jacob was shading his eyes from the sun and studying the awesome landscape.

They both saw me at the same time and we started running towards each other. As I ran towards my friends, I saw how their shining auras surrounded them—and I thought how calm and determined they both looked. Jacob had obviously conquered his demons and followed his heart. He'd faced the temptation, whatever it was, and had chosen wisely to follow his true self, Moncler the Wizard. It was the same with Janus. I don't think I'd ever seen him looking so powerful or peaceful before. It was as if the old kick-ass Janus, with all his petty vanities and frustrations, had just evaporated. And before me stood the true Janus, Telperion the Elven King.

"Greetings, friends!" cried Janus as we met and gave each other our secret D&D handshake. "For a while there, I thought I was the only one who hadn't given in to temptation!"

I shook my head and laughed. "You gotta be kiddin' dude! You think Moncler and I'd let you have all the fun without us!"

After we'd patted each other on the back a few times, we started studying our surroundings again. The desert seemed endless and empty.

"Gotta hand it to those Ascended Masters," muttered Janus, "they sure know how to pick exotic travel destinations."

But Jacob was puzzled. "To be honest," he said, "I just don't get it. I mean after all those tests and Gateways, I thought we were going to be admitted into the 5th dimension and allowed to go to Shamballa."

"Yeah, it is kinda weird," said Janus and scratched his head.

"Well, Elmar once told me that according to legend, Shamballa is located in the higher dimensions above the Gobi Desert," I said, trying to be helpful.

"So you're saying that this must be the Gobi Desert?" said Jacob.

"Well, that's comforting!" laughed Janus, "But if it is, then where's Shamballa? I don't see a thing out here."

"Me neither," I said as I scanned the vast desert landscape. There wasn't a sign of life anywhere. Not so much as a cactus or a bird. Then I looked up at the sky. There was nothing there either, not even one white cloud. "Seems like we're really out in the Great Wide Open!" I said, but nobody laughed.

"Still I think you're right, Starbrow," said Jacob, "Shamballa's got to be here somewhere!" Jacob began trudging up the next dune. Janus and I scrambled after him, sweating like pigs. The sun was right above us and it was as hot as a furnace. I wondered how long we could survive out here in this intense heat.

"I sure hope Shamballa ain't too far away," moaned Janus and started undoing the breastplate of his armor. "... and that the place is air-conditioned when we get there. This heat is killing me!"

We'd reached the top of the next dune and stood there, looking around. As far as the eye could see in every direction, there was nothing but desert. Desert, desert and more desert. There wasn't the slightest sign of life anywhere. Absolutely nothing to make us think that we were anywhere near Shamballa.

"Without water, guys, we'll soon be done for it out here," said Janus matter-of-factly.

"Yeah," said Jacob, "at the rate we're sweating, we'll soon all be totally dehydrated—and you know mental confusion is one of the first signs of dehydration..."

"Thanks for the info, dude," Janus remarked dryly.

"Well maybe we'd better stop wasting time and start asking our hearts for guidance," I said. "You'd think we'd have learned our lesson by now."

"Finally somebody's talking some sense around here!" said Janus, immediately closing his eyes.

I closed my eyes too—and focused my attention on my heart. First I imagined us going straight ahead—and then concentrated on my heart to see how it felt. There was no reaction. So it wasn't that way. Then I tried going to the left. No reaction there either. So I tried focusing on the right, but there was no reaction there either. Then behind me. Nope, no good there either. Since none of the directions on the ground seemed to be the right one, I imagined us going straight up into the air. But again I drew a blank. Finally I focused straight down into the ground, but again I didn't feel anything.

"It's weird," I said, "no matter what direction I focus on, I get no reaction. My heart doesn't seem to go for any of them."

"Same here," said Janus. "It's a total blank."

We both looked at Jacob. He didn't say anything, but he had this thoughtful look on his face, like he was just about to solve a great mystery.

Suddenly Janus' newfound peace of mind seemed to desert him. "I just can't believe it," he cried. "Do you mean to tell me we've come all this way, passed through all those far-out initiations, just to die of thirst in this stupid desert!" He kicked the sand in desperation. "It can't be right, Shamballa's got to be here somewhere!"

"Easy action," I said. "Easy... we'll never find the answer if you ... " but Jacob cut me short.

"Maybe..." he was saying in that special nerdy way of his that sometimes could really infuriate Janus and me, "just maybe, we're in Shamballa right now!"

"Oh come on!" cried Janus, "You must be joking!"

"Just hold on a second," said Jacob and turned to me. "Didn't you just say that Elmar said Shamballa was in the higher dimensions above the

235

Gobi Desert?"

"Yeah."

"Well if we just consider for a moment, everything our guardian angels and the Ascended Masters have told us about the dimensions," Jacob continued slowly, "then just where are the higher dimensions?"

"Well," I said, trying to remember what they said, "they're here, there and everywhere!"

"Oh that's a real big help," said Janus in disgust.

"Well actually it is," continued Jacob, "because if what Starbrow says is true, then it must also be true that we are in fact in Shamballa right now. And the only reason we're not experiencing Shamballa is because the city is in the higher dimensions?"

"Whoa," said Janus, the sweat streaming down his face.

We looked around again. Time was running out fast.

A slight breeze fluttered through the sand, whirling up little clouds of sand. For a moment, I could have sworn I saw shining towers and glittering spires right behind the whirling sand clouds. But when the sand settled again, there was nothing but endless desert...

"Well," said Janus, "if Shamballa really is here right now, but in the higher dimensions, then how are we supposed to get there? You think we're supposed to look for another Wormhole?"

Jacob pondered the question for a while. "No, I don't think a Wormhole's the answer," he said finally. "Even if we found one, I don't think it could get us to Shamballa."

"Well what will get us there?" cried Janus. "We haven't got forever you know." The heat was really getting to him.

Jacob didn't answer. Instead he got down on his knees and let the sand run through his fingers.

"I don't believe it!" cried Janus. "I mean, this is worse than not being able to find Shamballa at all! Einstein over here says we're in Shamballa, only problem is, since it's in another dimension we can't see it, feel it— or ask any of its good citizens to give us a drink of water before we die of thirst!"

"I didn't say that we couldn't get to it," said Jacob slowly.

"All this is way beyond me," cried Janus and threw himself down on the hot sand.

Jacob still didn't say a word.

I frantically searched my mental computer files for everything Elmar ever told me about Shamballa. He said Shamballa was in the higher dimensions, right above the Gobi Desert. He said that Shamballa was the headquarters of the Great White Brotherhood on Earth... When I asked him if he found Shamballa... what did he say... He said... not in the way he'd expected to find it... now what did he mean by that? If only I could understand what he'd meant by that, I was sure I'd be able to solve the mystery.

"The one thing my heart tells me is that the Ascended Masters wouldn't have let us come this far without there being a way." I sat down too.

We sat with bowed heads, as the sun beat mercilessly down upon us. It was obvious that without water, we would soon die. I felt myself struggling to keep calm.

Finally Jacob said, "Now why do you suppose we couldn't just go directly from the Mothership to Shamballa—and get our weapons?"

When we didn't answer, Jacob went on.

"Why did we have to pass through the Three Gateways before we could go to the higher dimensions and enter Shamballa?"

"Well," said Janus, "because... we had to prove that we were worthy first."

"Yeah, well maybe there was more to it than that," said Jacob slowly. "Maybe we had to pass through the Three Gateways first because the Ascended Masters wanted to give us something we needed in order to get to Shamballa."

"Well what could that be," said Janus. "They never gave us anything. All we've done so far is learn how to meditate, how to use the power of thought—and how to expand our consciousness."

"That's it, Janus!" cried Jacob and jumped to his feet.

"That's what?" said Janus, looking up in surprise.

"That's it!" cried Jacob again and danced around like he'd struck water." But of course! It's so obvious. So absurdly simple when you see it! Now I know why we had to pass through the Three Gateways before we could get to Shamballa."

"OK Einstein," I said, trying not to laugh at his exaltation, "would you please share your little insight with the rest of us before we die of thirst!"

"OK, OK, "he said and sat down next to us again. "It's like this... Shamballa is in the higher dimensions, right?"

"Right," I nodded.

"And the higher dimensions are right here... right?"

"Right," I said again.

237

"So why can't we see them and experience them?" asked Jacob.

I thought about what Ticha had told me about the higher dimensions. "Because the higher dimensions are on a higher—and faster—vibrational frequency than the one we are on now," I said, suddenly seeing the light at the end of the tunnel.

"So all we have to do to get to Shamballa and the higher dimensions is raise our vibrational frequency," cried Jacob. "And we raise our vibrational frequency..."

"By raising our consciousness!" I cried. "Brilliant Jacob, brilliant!"

"Exactly. Because the higher your consciousness is, the higher your vibrational frequency must be," said Jacob. "So now you can see Janus, that when you said all we learned by passing through the Three Gateways was how to expand and raise our consciousness, you were spot on. The Masters had to teach us that or we'd never get to Shamballa!"

"So what do we do now?" asked Janus.

"We raise our consciousness!" cried Jacob. "It's simple. All we have to do is do what we've learned by passing through the Gateways. First we contact and experience the Force. Then we use the Power of Thought to envision and create the reality we desire. And finally listen to our Hearts and choose the Highest Good for All Concerned. Because all of these activities are consciousness-raising activities."

"You really are a wizard, Moncler!" laughed Janus.

"Yeah man, Einstein can go home!" I said.

"So let's get to it," said Jacob.

"Where should we sit?" I asked.

"One place is as good as the next out here in this frying pan," said Janus, "so I guess this will do. Everybody ready for a trip to the higher dimensions? I got a feeling we'd better make it quick, before we all get fried!"

We closed our eyes and Jacob began to speak. "The Force is the One and Only Reality." Janus and I repeated after Jacob. "The Force is Infinite. The Force is Eternal."

The three of us tried to relax and breathe deeply.

"The Force is Unlimited," continued Jacob. "The Force is All-Powerful. To the Force, nothing is impossible because the Force is the One and Only Power and is therefore Immortal, Invincible and Unconquerable. I AM One with the Force.

"The Force is Life. Life Itself. The Force is Substance. Divine Substance. The Force is Love. Unconditional Love. The Force is

238

Intelligence. Infinite Intelligence. And Wisdom. And Perfect Harmony, Health and Wealth. The Force is the One and Only Reality. The Force is in Everything—and Everything is the Force. One Power, One Intelligence, One Presence, One Element, One Law, One Life. And I AM THE FORCE."

After Jacob had described some of the attributes of the Force, the three of us were silent for a while, while we each meditated on our breathing. It didn't take long before I began to experience the deep silence within me and that Living, Pulsating Presence that I knew was the FORCE.

Then Janus began to speak. "We now use the Power of Our Thought, the Mightiest Spell in the Universe, to envision and create the reality we desire." Jacob and I repeated after him. "We are now in Shamballa, the City of Light. We now see Shamballa all around us. We now experience Shamballa. We are now in the 5th dimension, the dimension of Light, for we are Light. And we easily and effortlessly find our interdimensional weapons."

And I added, "And all this takes place with effortless ease because it is the Force that does all this."

Then I went on. "We now focus all our attention on our hearts. On the Love in our hearts, which is the Force in our hearts. We affirm that our desire only manifests if it is for the Highest Good of All Concerned. Our desire only manifests if it will bring more Love, more Harmony and more Happiness to ourselves and to all our fellow human beings. In other words, we affirm that our desire is truly our heart's desire."

Jacob and Janus repeated after me. As we said these words, I knew in my heart that only the Highest Good would manifest. Then I opened my eyes.

Nothing had changed.

Absolutely nothing!

We were still sitting in the middle of this desert inferno. Nothing had changed... that is...except for one thing. One tiny little thing. Right before us in the burning sand, there was an itsy bitsy tiny weeny little green plant. It couldn't have been more than four or five centimeters high. It was so tiny that we didn't notice it at first. But yes, it was there alright, right there, right before us in this barren, lifeless place. We stared at it in wonder and surprise... because it seemed like a miracle, a true miracle. And indeed, it was... this tiny tiny living thing...

And then, I realized that the little plant was growing! It was growing, right there, right before our eyes! In two seconds flat, it was twice as big as when we first spotted it. Then the tiny thing started sending out these tiny little shoots—and then the tiny shoots suddenly had these itsy bitsy tiny weeny small leaves on them. And it kept on growing. It was almost a foot tall now and buds were starting to appear and one of them sprang open into the most beautiful red rose I'd ever seen in my whole life.

We laughed out loud.

Then all around us, green plants started sprouting up. Growing with lightning speed, as if a split second was a whole summer and before we knew it, we were surrounded by hordes of beautiful bushes and the whole place smelled of roses and lilacs. Then right behind the bushes, a tree shot up from the sand—and another—and another—and they all grew and sprouted branches and green leaves... and the three of us just sat there, chuckling and breathing in the sweetness of the air because now the air was cooler, as if a whole forest had suddenly materialized out of nowhere.

And indeed it had. And it was a miracle. And it all happened in the twinkling of an eye.

Then Jacob turned to Janus and I and said, "Do you hear that?" And he pointed towards the trees. We listened as he sprang to his feet. He was right. It was the sound of water! Running water! We ran after him.

On the other side of the trees, there was a beautiful green park that looked as if it belonged to an old Oriental palace—and in the middle of the park grounds, there was a great white marble fountain, built in the shape of two huge swans. We ran over to the fountain and dipped our hands in the bubbling water. It was cool and lovely beyond words, so we splashed our faces. And then we bent over and gratefully drank our fill.

When we were satisfied, we splashed around a bit more until Janus cried, "Look, over there!" and he pointed at the tall tower that loomed high above the treetops.

Funny we hadn't noticed it before. But it was there now. And it glinted in the sunlight as if it was made of white gold or some other precious metal. Two golden pyramids whizzed past the tower right over our heads. At the other end of the grounds, we realized there were more towers ... and mansions and palaces and other tall buildings.

"This must be Shamballa," cried Janus.

"Yes," I laughed, "Let's check it out."

Then we noticed there was a narrow marble pathway leading down from the fountain and we followed it until we came to a white gate. We walked through the gate and found it led to a great open piazza that was filled with people. For some reason, I knew we were right in the middle of Shamballa. On all sides of the great piazza, Shamballa's dazzling buildings and palaces towered around us. All were amazingly beautiful and resembled the beauty we'd seen inside the Mothership. And like inside the Mothership, there were hundreds of pyramids soaring through the air here too. Obviously the preferred means of transportation in the higher dimensions! But there was one thing about Shamballa that didn't remind me of the Mothership... the feeling here was more earthly than it was in the Mothership...

Then I noticed that all the people we saw walking around the great piazza were surrounded by radiant auras. Everyone smiled kindly at us as they passed by, folding their hands in a gesture of greeting. That was when I realized they didn't actually speak out loud as we do on Planet Earth. But as I looked into their shining faces, I understood why. In Shamballa, no words were necessary. Here everyone communicated directly from heart to heart.

After we watched the inhabitants of Shamballa for a while, we left the piazza and began walking down one of the wide boulevards that led away from the great piazza. The boulevard was lined with great trees and after we had walked a bit we discovered that at the end of the boulevard, there was a great hill. Without knowing how I knew, I knew the hill was special, the very heart of Shamballa. And on top of the hill, a white tower stood. I recognized it immediately.

9

The White Tower

The White Tower shone in the sunlight, like the crown jewel on top of the green hill.

"Avalon," I said, "Mother Avalon."

"Yes," said Jacob, "It's Glastonbury Tor."

And he was right. The green hill and the White Tower we saw before us was Glastonbury Tor as it really was. A brilliant beacon of light, a transmitter, a power station, a tower of love. Without all the fear and negativity that had cast its dark shadow over Glastonbury Tor on the Earth plane in England. This was the real Avalon. Here we had found the White Tower, in the heart of Shamballa, City of Light.

We followed the winding path from the foot of the hill and hurried as fast as we could to the top. It took a while because the path wound its way back and forth. But finally we were at the summit, high above the City of Light below us. On the way up, I saw two white eagles soaring high above the tower. They reminded me of something, but I couldn't remember what.

The top of the hill was flat and in the middle stood the White Tower. The tower was square, about 50 feet high and about 15 feet wide. The tower had large arched portals on each side, which were open so you could see straight through the tower. And there was no roof either, so when we stepped into the tower, we could still see the sky straight above us. One of the massive stonewalls opened into a powerful Wormhole, which emitted a strong electric charge. There was an ancient stone bench up against the other wall. On the bench, there was an exquisitely carved oak staff covered with runes and symbols and a mighty two-handed sword set with many precious gems.

"My staff!" cried Jacob.

"My sword!" cried Janus.

242

Janus stood silently before his two-handed sword and regarded it with great reverence. Then, with both hands, he took his sword and lifted it high into the air. The sword flashed as if it had been struck by lightning. And waves of light burst from the sword and flickered through Janus' hands and body. He closed his eyes in ecstasy. Then Jacob took the great oak staff in his hands. The staff flared like a burning bush, illuminating the inside of the tower. Jacob smiled blissfully and closed his eyes.

I looked everywhere for the little silver star that I had worn on my brow as Dana, but it was nowhere to be found. I looked around again, in dismay.

Then a voice behind me said, "Is this what you're looking for, my boy?"

I turned around. Just outside the doorway to the tower, a man stood smiling at me. He had shoulder-length blond hair and bright blue eyes. His whole body was surrounded by a warm golden light; in his right hand, he held the silver star. But I took no notice of the star, so great was my amazement at our unexpected visitor.

"Elmar!" I cried and leapt forward. "Elmar!" I couldn't believe my eyes! It really was Elmar, standing there with the star in his hand! Elmar! It didn't make sense—and to top it all, he looked absolutely fantastic, like he was 30-40 years younger than when I'd seen him last. His face was literally beaming with health and vigor. I couldn't believe it, but it was true. There could be no doubt about it. It was Elmar! No one else in the whole wide world had his smile or bright blue eyes!

"Good to see you again, my boy," he said with a mischievous grin on his face.

"Elmar!" I cried as I threw myself into his arms. "Is it really you!" I squeezed him with all my might to make sure he was real. "You mean you're not an illusion or a test or anything like that!"

"No," laughed Elmar, "I'm not an illusion and the tests are over, my boy! You're here, so you must have passed!"

I was so happy I couldn't speak. I forgot all about Shamballa and Avalon and our weapons—and just stood there smiling like a bumbling idiot. Of all the strange and wonderful things I'd experienced in the last few days, meeting Elmar here in Shamballa was the strangest and most wonderful of them all.

"But, but..." I stammered, "... what are you doing here? I thought..."

"You didn't think I was dead, did you!" he laughed again. "After all you've been through, you should know better by now!"

243

"But, you disappeared so suddenly..."

"Of course! I mean I had to do something drastic—or you'd never have gotten your act together! It was really touch and go for a while..."

I just stood there with my mouth open.

Elmar opened his right hand again. The silver star sparked in his palm. "This belongs to you," he said. "You gave it to me, many long years ago, when my name was Aran. Do you remember?"

I looked at the star and smiled.

"And now," Elmar continued, "the time has come for me to return it to you, because it belongs to you, Dana! Starbrow!"

Elmar placed the silver star on my brow and for an instant, I felt a sharp pain between my eyebrows as the star once again became a part of me. Then everything turned into light, the point on my brow, my head, my body, Elmar, the tower. In my mind's eye, a whirlwind of images raced by in such swift progression that I could barely register them. Images of other times, other places, other lifetimes. The whole cavalcade lasted a split second or two, then as suddenly as it began, it was over. I felt light-headed and lighter than ever before. Then I realized that a pulsating light really was shining from my forehead because it lit up Elmar's beloved face. He smiled and patted me on the back.

"I'm proud of you, my boy," he said. "It's no small achievement to have come as far as you have in such a short time."

"So you know what's happened since..."

"But of course," laughed Elmar. "Just because I left my physical body doesn't mean that I haven't been keeping an eye on you. I've been with you every step of the way."

"Then how come I didn't know it?" I asked. "I mean I wasn't aware of your presence."

"Well, you could have been—and you should have been!" Elmar scolded me, that mischievous glint in his eye again, "and if only you'd used that brain of yours a little more, my boy, you would have been!"

I tried to think back to all the times I'd wished Elmar was around.

"But you know, in the end, everything worked out just fine and anyway, the Ascended Masters seemed to think it was best for you not to know anything. You had to pass through your initiation on your own, those are the rules you know."

"Was it you who saved me in the Manifestation Chamber when that hideous dark figure came to kill me?" I asked.

"No, it was your own thoughts that saved you," said Elmar. "And just in the nick of time, if I may say so myself. Half a second more and you might have been stranded in some ghastly Hell for a rather extended period of time."

"It's hard to explain... but being in the Manifestation Chamber was..." I trembled again at the thought of the Dweller on the Threshold. "... was worse than being in a runaway car going 150 miles an hour and discovering the brakes were gone."

At that moment, Janus and Jacob came barging out of the tower. "Greetings, Elmar!" they both cried at the same moment. My friends were surrounded by the most beautiful auras.

"Greetings, Loran! Greetings, Gaius!" cried Elmar and warmly embraced first Janus and then Jacob. "Or should I call you Telperion and Moncler!"

"Then you remember our past lives in England?" asked Janus.

"But of course," said Elmar. "After I left my physical body, many things came back to me."

"And many things left you too, by the look of it!" cried Jacob in wonder at this younger version of my grandfather. "You look like you've lost about 40 years since I saw you last!"

"Yeah, well, I guess you could say I left my wrinkles behind when I left my physical body!" grinned Elmar.

"Where did you get the silver star?" asked Janus.

"Right before her death—Dana—Starbrow—gave it to me," Elmar explained. "As Aran, I guarded it until my death. And when I passed on, it was removed from the Earth plane and brought here to Shamballa for safe keeping. After my recent death, I was re-united with it again... here in Shamballa. But I figured it wouldn't be long before Starbrow came back for it."

"So Lord Gavin's men didn't catch you and kill you?" I asked in surprise.

"No, I managed to escape and after hiding in the woods for many days I made my way to Avalon where I was initiated as a bard."

"Have you heard that the Ashtar Command is planning to send us back to Earth to complete the mission?" asked Jacob.

"Yes, I know all about your mission. We've been very busy here in Shamballa the last couple of hours," said Elmar. "The Great White Brotherhood is in Beacon Alert Mode 1, the Brotherhood's highest alert mode, because of Mother Earth's violent etheric discharges and the imminent threat of an axis shift. But now that you and the other volunteers are retrieving your interdimensional weapons, there's hope that the New Vision will at last be anchored in the collective consciousness. The Masters have put out the call far and wide in the galaxy to win a little more time for Mother Earth so together we can trigger a critical mass of enlightened beings on Earth."

"Is that what you're working on here in Shamballa?" asked Janus.

"It's the only thing anyone in this part of the galaxy is working on at the moment!" cried Elmar. "Beacon Alert Mode 1 means everyone... You, me, the Ascended Masters, the Ashtar Command, the Guardian Angels. Everyone's rolled up their sleeves so to speak to bring about an era of Peace and Enlightenment on Earth."

It was an amazing thought. So we stood for a while, looking out over Shamballa—and contemplating our role in these great, earthshaking events. The sun was setting and the city was bathed in the warm evening light. For a moment, I felt an overwhelming desire to stay here in Shamballa with Elmar. But I knew that this was not the way for me... at least not yet anyway...

Jacob broke the silence. "To get back, do we have to go through the Wormhole again?"

"Yes," said Elmar. "Go back into the tower and step into the Wormhole. It will take you directly back to the Mothership."

Jacob and Janus left me alone with Elmar for a moment—and went back into the tower. I struggled to keep the tears back. I couldn't bear the thought of leaving him again; I'd only just found him!

He knew what I was feeling. "You and I have been together for many lifetimes before this lifetime, my boy," he said and put his hand on my shoulder. "We come from the stars and nothing can separate us. Not death nor the dimensions... or anything else between heaven and earth."

"But why can't you go back with us and help us anchor the New Vision?" I stammered, trying to hold back the tears.

"My time on Earth is over," Elmar said slowly. "And... Now is your time."

"But how am I going to make it without you?" I cried.

"Starbrow!" he said in a stern voice. "Look at me, lad! Look at me."

I wiped away my tears and looked at him.

"You no longer need my help. You know who you are now. You know what to do. This is what you have been trained for."

Then Elmar smiled gently and said, all the sternness now gone from his voice. "And besides, you're forgetting everything you've learned about the dimensions, my boy! You should know that they are here, there and everywhere. I will be with you and Moncler and Telperion, every step of the way. Just call upon me, and I'll be there!"

Then he kissed my brow and embraced me.

"Now go and complete your mission, Starbrow! And remember what you said to me when you were called Dana... Follow your heart, for your heart alone knows the way!"

I hugged Elmar one last time and then turned and stepped into the tower. Janus and Jacob were standing before the Wormhole waiting for me. They patted me on the back. Both knew how much Elmar meant to me.

I looked back at Elmar one last time. He gave us the Victory sign and said, "Call upon me as soon as you've activated the Power Spot at Glastonbury Tor. I'll be here—in the White Tower—on this side of the interdimensional Light Grid!"

And then as we stepped into the Wormhole, I heard him cry in a loud voice, "And remember lads, the Force is with you!"

10

Final Instructions

Jacob and Janus and I shot through the Wormhole at a speed we could not comprehend. We zoomed past one interdimensional opening after another and caught glimpses of beautiful rainbow bridges and glittering crystal towers, dark dungeons and haunted castles rushing by. We passed heavens and hells and every other conceivable circumstance in between as we were propelled through the Wormhole. But this time nothing could stop us, not even for a moment, because our focus was crystal clear. We knew exactly where we wanted to go and wasted no time getting there. We had only one goal and one goal only and that was the Mothership, the very heart of the Intergalactic Fleet!

Then just as suddenly as we'd started, we found ourselves being sucked through the interdimensional doorway and tumbling out into the great hall of the Mothership. All around us, Star People were talking to other volunteers who were also arriving.

"Welcome back!" exclaimed the same Starman who had instructed us when we first left the Mothership and stepped into the Wormhole. "It is good to see you again with your auras shining so bright! And I can see you have found your weapons! So hail and well met Brothers in the Light!"

Just then another group of volunteers tumbled out of the Wormhole right behind us. We made way for them. One of them was a young woman who looked like she could have been a member of the Ashtar Command, except that her space-garments were deep blue. On her brow shone a beautiful blue star. The tall Starman greeted her by name, calling her "Blue Star". Her companion, a Nordic goddess with long fiery hair had an orange shield in one hand. On the shield, there was a golden lion. In her other hand, she carried a flaming blue sword. I smiled at her and felt I knew her from somewhere. The two women were accompanied by a young man with shoulder-length blond hair and gentle blue eyes. In his right hand, he held a white staff that twinkled in the light of the great hall.

But there was no time for talk. The Starman signaled for us to move back into the hall because most of the other volunteers were already assembled in front of the speaker's podium. Commander Ashtar was conferring with some of his officers and above him, the screen showed that Planet Earth was still completely enveloped by black clouds. All around the planet, the Ashtar Command's starships still maintained their grid of light. Sananda stood alone with his eyes closed as if he was far away in some other realm.

"How long have we been gone?" Janus asked the Starman who was accompanying us.

"In Earth Time? "he replied, pressing some buttons on the strange-looking calculator he had on his wrist, "... you were gone exactly 1 hour and 53 minutes."

"Wow!" whistled Jacob. "Is that all? All these different dimensions sure do make time act weird!"

"What about Mother Earth?" I asked, motioning up towards the screen.

"As you can see, the situation is unchanged," he replied. "Ashtar and Sananda have asked for all the volunteers to be seated at once for your final instructions. The situation now is so critical that we are all now on Beacon Alert Mode 1... every second that goes by is bringing Planet Earth rapidly close to the axis shift."

"Then let us sit down at once!" said Jacob.

We hurried towards the front of the auditorium. It looked as if almost all the volunteers were back. And I could see that each member of each group now had his or her own special weapon, hallmark or token with them. Janus stared in awe at the Shaolin monks. A bright light seemed to follow them as they walked down the aisle—and each of them was now carrying an awesome-looking weapon in their belt. One had a long spear, one had a double-sword, one a staff and one a scythe. I heard Janus mutter 'excellent' more than once under his breath. I, for one, couldn't take my eyes off our friends, the Air Force pilots. Those guys were always in such high spirits and now they were all wearing these far-out looking silver belts with a special octagonal insignia engraved in them. Jacob nudged me and pointed over to the yogis, who now seemed to hover a few centimeters above the ground. Each one of them had a little transparent pouch of crystals around his or her neck. And the young Star

Wars freaks were now in the most excellent spirits having been reunited with their light sabers and blasters. Even the nuns seemed more blissful—with pulsating golden crosses around their necks. It was most amazing. No matter where we looked, our new friends seemed somehow to be complete now that they were reunited with their lost weapons or objects of power.

We found some seats right near the front and sat down. Sananda opened his eyes and looked out at the assembly. "Hail and well met, my initiates," he said.

Ashtar joined Sananda. "And congratulations on your initiation!" he said. "I see that you all have regained your interdimensional weapons."

"And much more," smiled Sananda. "For I can see that your True Selves are shining more brightly than ever before."

Ashtar took out a platinum gold logbook. "If I may recount, for a moment," he said and flipped open the book. "The Mission Status is as follows. Out of the 144 groups we sent through the Wormhole two hours ago, 139 have successfully completed their initiation and returned with their weapons," said Ashtar. "The remaining five groups from Helsinki, Sydney, Buenos Aires, Delhi and Tokyo have not returned. I just conferred with our experts from the Department of Planetary Dimensional Shifts and they assure me that an activation of 139 Power Spots—instead of the 144 as originally planned—will be enough to activate the Light Grid and anchor the New Vision."

"This kind of interdimensional mathematics is way beyond me, dude," Janus mumbled to Jacob.

"I wonder what happened to the missing five groups?" I whispered to my buddies. "Do you think they're stuck in some interdimensional hell...?"

"No way!" Janus shot back. "I bet some lucky dude just scored the winning goal in the final minute of the Superbowl!"

"Ha," grinned Jacob, "I bet I can guess what your dream life was all about...!"

"As far as the missing groups are concerned," continued Ashtar, "there is no reason for undue worry on your part. We've already dispatched two of our best rescue teams into the Wormhole to find them. Right now, I would ask all of you to focus all your attention on your mission.

"In exactly seven minutes from now, you will all be transubstantiated back to Earth—to exactly the same spot where you were transubstantiated up to the Mothership. From there, it will be your solemn duty to proceed as quickly as possible to your Power Spot and begin the activation of the Light Grid.

"Now to the activation process. To activate the Light Grid, it is of the utmost importance that all groups and all members of each group begin the activation meditation at precisely the same moment. Since you are all going to be in different time zones, we have designed a special watch for each of you so all of you are perfectly synchronized with each other."

Several crews of Star People began immediately walking up and down among the volunteers, putting watches on everyone's left wrist.

"OK design if I must say so," murmured Janus under his breath. And he was right. The watches were incredibly light and beautiful, and seemed to be made of the same shimmering, silvery, etheric material that the rest of the Mothership was made of. On the face of each watch were two small digital displays. The bottom display flashed **21:42:11 TO ACTIVATION MEDITATION**. The top display flashed **45:42:11 TO AXIS SHIFT**.

"The bottom display shows you exactly how many hours you have until it is time to begin the Activation Meditation at your Power Spot," said Ashtar. "In other words, everyone is to begin in exactly 21 hours, 42 minutes and 8 seconds—no matter where on Earth you may find yourself. This time corresponds exactly to 00:00:00 Greenwich Mean Time on Planet Earth. We have calculated that 21 hours and 42 minutes should be sufficient time for all of the groups to proceed from your homes to your Power Spots.

"But I must repeat my friends, it is *vitally* important that all of you begin the activation meditation at precisely the exact same time. If you have been following our discussions, you will understand why this is crucial. Without this exact synchronization, not enough energy will be generated to activate the Grid. Therefore—and I cannot stress this enough—when you arrive back on Earth, go to your Power Spots *immediately*. And I repeat, *immediately*. Unfortunately, due to the massive Earth changes that are going on at the moment, I must prepare you all for unexpected changes when you get back... Expect to find things quite changed when you return home... And these changes may cause unexpected delays as you proceed to your Power Spots."

I shivered when he said this and looked up at the pictures of Earth on the screen over his head... and wondered what else might have happened while we'd been away...

"Now to the actual activation procedure," said Ashtar. "To activate your Power Spots, you must meditate continually on your Power Spots for one whole day. In other words, 24 hours non-stop. Once every hour on the hour, you are to repeat the formula that was given to you by the Great White Brotherhood in your past lives. This is one of the reasons why we sent you back to your past incarnations. We wanted you all to regain full memory of your experience and of the power of the formula so it would be completely clear in your mental and emotional bodies.

"Now, during the activation, we request that you repeat the formula every hour on the hour—seven times in a row. When you have done this for 24 hours consecutively, your Power Spot and the Light Grid will be fully activated. Then the New Vision will wash over and saturate the collective consciousness with great force. This will take place in exactly 45 hours and 42 minutes—and coincide exactly with the precise instant in time when the impending axis shift is predicted to occur. In other words, the number on the upper display of your watch shows you how many hours there are until the impending axis shift.

"As you now know, our experts tell us that by saturating the collective consciousness with the New Vision, you will cleanse and calm the Energy Centers and Energy Lines of Mother Earth's etheric body to such a degree that it will stabilize her interior for a while. As a result, the axis shift will be postponed for two or three years."

"Not bad," said Janus.

"But what happens after that?" an Egyptian priest stood up and asked.

"Anchoring the New Vision is only the first step, and a stop-gap emergency measure at that," said Ashtar. "It is only the beginning. After that, it will be your mission to change the collective consciousness by helping people replace their negative thoughts and images with a positive and loving New Vision so that all of humanity can ascend into the 5th dimension with Mother Earth."

"But what will happen in two or three years?" asked another volunteer. "Will there be an axis shift?"

"Yes," said Sananda. "If humanity continues on its current course of negativity and destruction, Mother Earth will have no choice but to rid herself of negativity by means of an axis shift which will destroy all of humanity. So you see my friends, you're going to be busy!"

"They're really riding us here in the higher dimensions!" muttered Janus.

"But let us not think too far ahead, my friends," said Sananda. "Instead, let us concentrate on the task at hand. Before you go back, let us

252

repeat the Great White Brotherhood's formula together."

"All rise!" commanded Sananda in a great voice, motioning us to rise. The whole assembly stood up.

"Now repeat after me:

IN THE BEGINNING: THE FORCE
HERE AND NOW: THE FORCE
AT THE END OF THE END: THE FORCE
HERE, THERE, EVERYWHERE: THE FORCE
FROM ALPHA TO OMEGA: THE FORCE
IN HEAVEN, UPON EARTH: THE FORCE
IN THE GREATEST, IN THE SMALLEST: THE FORCE
IN FIRE, IN WATER, IN EARTH, IN AIR: THE FORCE
IN ME, IN YOU, IN EVERYONE: THE FORCE
ABOVE ME, BELOW ME, AROUND ME: THE FORCE
IN ME, THROUGH ME, FROM ME: THE FORCE
IN MY THOUGHTS, IN MY WORDS,
IN MY ACTIONS: THE FORCE
THE FORCE IS ALL IN ALL
ALL LIFE, ALL INTELLIGENCE, ALL LOVE
THE FORCE IS THE ONE AND ONLY REALITY
AND SO IT IS!"

As soon as we started chanting, it was exactly like being in the Crystal Cave during our past lives in England. The sound of our voices immediately opened a magnificent gateway to the Higher Realms and beautiful, mysterious geometric shapes, pulsating colors and heavenly harmonies began flowing through the gateway. But before the shapes and colors had time to coalesce and become images, Sananda clapped his hands and said. "It is not yet time, my children. First you must return to Earth and proceed to your Power Spots. And there's not a moment to lose!"

Ashtar made a swift circular movement with his right hand and I felt that tingling sensation at the top of my head again. "Remember what you have learned during your initiation," he said. "Let the Force be your ally, let your Thoughts be your weapons—and let the Love in your Hearts be your guiding star!"

"Adonai, Guardians of the Earth," said Sananda. "The Force is with you!"

I looked up as a bright beam of light enveloped me. In the light I saw a familiar face smiling at me. It was Ticha, my guardian angel! She was still by my side. And I knew she would be by my side on all my Earth adventures, just like she had always been. The tingling sensation exploded in my head and everything turned into light. Then I remembered no more.

PART FOUR

MOTHER EARTH
IS BURNING

1

The Night the Earth Quaked

I found myself lying on my bedroom floor. The room was completely dark. An icy rain pounded furiously against the windows. I sat up. I still felt that strong tingling sensation at the top of my head. How long had I been gone? I looked at my alarm clock. The display read 03:57. And the day? Wednesday, April 1st. So I'd only been gone for... four hours. Four hours! It seemed like weeks... weeks... but only four hours had gone by on Planet Earth since my midnight rendezvous with Ticha.

I got up and turned on the light by my bed. The footprints I'd made when I came charging in from the freezing sleet and snow four hours earlier were still there. Apart from that, everything looked normal. My bed, my night table stacked with books... it all looked so bleak and dreary after the radiant beauty of the Mothership...

I wondered for a moment if it was all just a dream...

I went over to the window and looked out. It was still stormy outside. Dark clouds raged across the turbulent night sky as the wind rattled against my window.

I went into my living room and discovered there was a message on my answering machine. I turned it on. It was my mother. "Hello, dear," I could tell by the sound of her voice she'd been crying. "I'm just checking to make sure you're alright. You scared Sandra and me when you ran out of the hospital like that... So I just want you to know we're here if you need us."

I picked up the phone, but not to call my mother. She'd have to wait. There were two other people I had to call first...

I stared at the phone in my hand for a long minute before I punched in Jacob's number. While I was waiting for him to answer, my eyes came to rest on my bookcase piled high with all my adventure stuff. Our Dungeons & Dragons games, my Lord of the Rings books and my

259

precious Star Wars movies... When Jacob didn't answer the phone, I was overwhelmed by sudden doubt. What if he was asleep? What if I woke him up and he didn't know what I was talking about? What if the whole thing was just my imagination... something I dreamt after falling asleep on my bedroom floor? What if...

Jacob picked up the phone. "Hello," he said. He didn't sound sleepy at all.

I strained to read the hidden message in his voice. Was it the ordinary guy I'd always known... or did he sound different... more like a mighty wizard might sound...

"Hello, hello?" he said, "Who's there?"

My train of thought was broken when I noticed the stack of papers by my phone. A plane ticket, an Avis rent-a-car voucher and a map of England. I picked up the ticket. It was a British Airways ticket from Copenhagen Airport to London Heathrow for Wednesday April 1st at 07:00 AM. That was in less than three hours!

"Moncler," I laughed. "It's me, Starbrow."

"Greetings, Brother in the Light," Jacob laughed back. "Are you ready for a trip to Glastonbury?"

I stood in front of my bathroom mirror, studying my face. After I'd spoken to both Jacob and Janus about our interdimensional adventures, it was time to get ready for our trip to England. I saw myself in the mirror for the first time when I went out to my bathroom to pack a few things. The change stopped me cold. My transformation was awesome, to put it mildly. Instead of short, dark brown hair, I now had long golden locks. And my face looked different too, as if I was this fierce warrior or something. I couldn't help saying "Way to go, dude" to the guy I saw in the mirror. Plus my aura was dazzling to say the least.

The other thing that surprised me was my outfit. Of course when I saw it, I remembered it. The long white robe that went all the way down to my ankles—and my weird space sandals that must have been designed in another galaxy. I had to laugh, thinking of what my friends would say if they saw me in this get up. Not to mention the fashion-conscious crowd I worked with at Fashion Flash!

On my left wrist I was wearing the silver Ashtar Command watch. The top display read 44:11:03 TO AXIS SHIFT; the bottom display read 20:11:03 TO ACTIVATION MEDITATION. 20 hours till the three of us were to begin the activation meditation on Glastonbury Tor. It was all pretty overwhelming. But the greatest change of all was the shimmering silver star on my brow. I had to admit, it made me look like a prince out of some fairy tale. I chuckled and realized how truly excellent it made me feel. It was almost as if the light from the star flowed out into my whole body, filling me with newfound power.

I went back to my bedroom to throw the bare necessities into my backpack. The three of us had agreed it was important to travel light. Finally I pulled out the long trench coat Fashion Flash had given me— and everybody else in the Marketing Department—after our last big show. Little did I realize how handy it would come in. It was perfect. It was long enough to cover my white robe completely. Then I traded my space sandals for my sturdiest running shoes.

Right before I left, I flicked on the TV for the latest update on the situation on Planet Earth. Ashtar had really been right in his predictions. Channel 2 was right in the middle of a special report about the strange earthquake that rocked southern Denmark. And most shocking of all— Denmark's new pride and joy—the Great Belt Bridge had collapsed during the earthquake and completely disappeared into the sea! I had to sit down. A reporter with his back to the Great Belt was describing the chaotic scene. Hoards of people were running around, and rescue boats and helicopters were everywhere. The wind was howling and it was still pouring rain. All that was left of the huge bridge were a few stray pillars that stuck up in the raging sea.

"The earthquake that caused this massive damage," the reporter was saying, "struck here at exactly 01:00 local Danish time. First reports say that fortunately there were few cars on the bridge at this hour of the night, but at present we still do not have any precise figures as to the number of casualties. Eyewitnesses do however report that all the cars on the bridge went down with the bridge which apparently crumpled like a deck of cards into the sea."

The camera zoomed in on the raging sea right behind the reporter where rescue workers were searching heroically for survivors. Then the scene switched back to the studio where a newsman was saying, "Denmark is not the only country in the world that has suffered a massive earthquake," he said. "In Germany, there were violent tremors in Schleswig-Holstein." The scene switched to pictures of a German city in ruins. Everywhere houses and buildings had crumpled. "The greatest danger of all arose at the nuclear power plant near Brokdorf. One of the main reactors was so seriously damaged by the quake that the threat of massive radioactive pollution was alarmingly grave. Fortunately, prompt emergency action by the plant's security forces saved the day. All the systems were shut down in time—and a major environmental disaster here in Northern Europe was averted."

"Italy, China and Russia were also hit by violent earthquakes during the night. But worst hit of all was California." The camera began to show pictures of San Francisco—taken from a helicopter. The city was in ruins; and everything was in total chaos. Huge sections of the city were simply wiped off the face of the earth. It was hard to imagine how many people must have been killed.

The newscaster continued speaking, "Everywhere in the world, the earthquakes hit at exactly the same time: 00:00 Greenwich Mean Time. 15 minutes later the earthquakes stopped, as suddenly as they had began."

I remembered the Ashtar Command's rapid emergency action—their network of light around the planet.

"So far, experts have no explanation for this sudden global shaking and quaking," said the newsman, "but already this night is being called... The Night the Earth Quaked."

I switched off the TV and walked over to the window. It was still pouring outside and the wind was howling. Even though it was almost dawn, it was pitch black outside because of the heavy storm clouds. I thought about the night less than two weeks ago when I had stood before this very window, wishing I was a Jedi Knight on a heroic mission to save Planet Earth. Now my wish had come true.

2

Look Mommy, the Man's
Got a Star on His Brow!

The taxi pulled up in front of the Departure Hall at Copenhagen Airport. I grabbed my backpack, paid the fare and jumped out of the taxi. Rain and wind lashed against my face. I rushed into the Departure Hall. It was already a quarter past six, just 45 short minutes until departure time.

I spotted Jacob and Janus standing by the monitors with flight information, studying the screens. They were both wearing the long Fashion Flash trench coats I'd given them over their exotic garb. On his back, Jacob's backpack was bulging a bit because of the large square object he had inside. I guessed it was his secret spell book. In his hand he had his long staff. Janus was carrying a king-size ski bag on his back; the perfect way to hide his two-handed sword. Without discussing it, we'd all obviously reached the same conclusion. Attract as little attention as possible, so we could carry out our mission without arousing any unwanted attention.

But neither trench coats nor ski bags could hide the radiance and power of my friends' faces. They were completely transformed. In the fantastic surroundings of the Mothership, it all seemed quite natural. But here in Copenhagen Airport at 6:15 on a dismal Wednesday morning, they were like two shooting stars blazing through a gray and dreary world.

"Moncler! Telperion! Greetings, friends!" I exclaimed. We embraced each other warmly.

"Greetings, Starbrow!" laughed Janus. "What a bright shining star you are dude!"

"You're pretty excellent, too!" I said, pulling Janus' pointy elven ears.

"I can see the star on your brow, Starbrow!" said Jacob.

"Can you? You know I thought about wearing a headband, but it just seemed too uncool."

263

"If anybody asks, just say you're a pop star. They're always wearing the most atypical attire!" chuckled Janus.

"Did you guys see the news?" I asked.

"You can say that again!" said Jacob.

"Did you notice on your way out here that all the flags are already flying half-mast because of all the people who went down with the bridge?" said Janus. "The Danes are really gonna be blown away when they wake up to the morning news."

"And it might not be over yet," said Jacob. "Did you catch the bit about the volcanic eruptions?"

"Volcanic eruptions?" I said. "No... tell.."

"I heard it on the radio on the way out here," continued Jacob. "An hour ago, several of the world's dormant volcanoes suddenly started erupting."

"You're kidding.. where?"

"All kinds of places. Iceland, Montserrat, the Philippines..."

I looked down at my silver wristwatch. The bottom display read **18:40:21 TO ACTIVATION MEDITATION**. "Then I guess we'd better get a move on," I said. "Let's check in."

There was already a line in front of the British Airways counter. Mostly business people going to meetings in England, but there was also a mother and her little girl in the line next to ours. As we stood there waiting, the little girl kept staring at us.

"Look Mommy!" the little girl exclaimed and pointed up at me. "The man's got a star on his brow!"

Jacob and Janus and I looked at each other. The girl was the first one who'd said anything about the star on my brow. Neither the taxi driver nor anyone else at the airport had seemed to notice until now.

The little girl kept pulling her mother's coat. "Look Mommy, look!"

"Ssshhh Emma," said her mother and turned towards us. "Don't pay her any notice," the woman apologized. "My daughter's got such a lively imagination, she's always seeing angels and stars everywhere."

"It's quite OK," I said to the woman and winked at the little girl.

"She's probably a Starseed," whispered Janus in my ear. Then he went over and started talking to the little girl. "Have you ever been in an airplane?" he asked her, "because you know there are lots of angels up there in the sky. So maybe you'll be lucky and get to see some."

"Mommy! Mommy!" the girl started hopping around excitedly as Janus talked to her. "Can't you see, the man's got magic ears! Look at

264

how long and pointy his ears are... I bet he's an Elf Lord!"

The mother tugged her back to her side. "I want you to stop talking nonsense, Emma!"

But even though Emma stopped talking to us, she kept on staring at the three of us, totally spellbound. And we realized that the little girl saw everything. Including all the things nobody else seemed to see like Moncler's magic staff and Telperion's chain mail under his coat... When she started staring at Janus' ski bag, I was positive she could see right through it and knew he had his magic two-handed sword inside.

The check-in line seemed to come to a standstill. Then we heard the BA woman behind the counter telling the people in front of us that the night's outbreak of natural disasters had seriously messed up flight schedules all over the world. Right now our flight to Heathrow was delayed more than an hour. Expected departure time was now 08:15.

Finally it was our turn to check in. Emma's mother in the next line had just finished checking in and was now trying to haul Emma away. But the little girl didn't want to leave .us. She ran over to me and clung desperately to me as if we, and not her mother, were her real parents. Her mother tugged at her angrily, not understanding what had gotten into her little girl. Sensing the bad vibes, I squatted down and looked Emma straight in the eye. I concentrated on the Force within her. "Emma, listen to me," I whispered in her ear. "I know that you are a mighty angel princess. I can see your great white wings and I know that you can see my star. But right now you and I are on a secret mission here on Earth. Not everyone can see who we really are and that's part of our mission. We must keep it secret. But soon, all will be revealed. But right now, you mustn't tell anyone what you know because they won't understand you yet. So let's keep it secret. Your mother needs you to go along with her because you're going to go up and fly around with a lot of other angels... and well, your mother is a little frightened. But having you along will make her feel better because she knows you know how to talk to angels. Now isn't that right, Emma?"

"Yes, I guess so," said the little girl, thinking over what I'd said.

"OK Emma," I said, patting her on the head, "Now you just remember you are an angel princess and go take care of your mother," I said slowly. "It's your job to look after her—and that's the most important thing you can do right now. Do you understand?"

Emma nodded—and then slowly turned and reluctantly took her mother's hand. As they walked away, she kept turning back and staring at us.

"Poor kid," said Janus, "Think about having the Sight and not having anyone around who understands you. You said the right thing to her."

"Yeah," said Jacob, "and your words were probably a lot truer than you'll ever know."

We showed the woman behind the check-in counter our tickets. She told us the expected time of departure for our flight was now 08:25. Almost an hour and a half behind schedule! Fortunately, the Ashtar Command had given us Business Class tickets. With so many flights delayed, they were combining flights and Business Class passengers had first priority.

"Do you have any baggage you'd like to check in?" she asked us.

"No," we replied in unison.

"I'm sorry Sir," she said looking at Janus. "but you cannot carry a ski bag with you on board. You are going to have to check it."

Janus looked at Jacob and me, obviously not relishing the thought of parting from his precious sword. But on the other hand, how would he get through security with it? Then I thought of Emma. Suddenly I had an idea.

"Janus," I said, "are you sure you really packed your skis?" I eased the bag off his shoulder. Even though I could feel his sword inside, I said to the check-in woman, "He's always forgetting things!" I winked at Janus and opened the bag right in front of her nose. Telperion's two-handed sword was snugly packed in its beautifully engraved scabbard, but the BA woman couldn't see a thing.

"See I told you!" I laughed. "My friend would probably forget his head if it wasn't screwed on properly."

She smiled politely, obviously thinking we were really a bunch of nerds.

"Well Sir," she said to Janus, "I guess there's no reason to check the bag after all. You can just roll it up and take it with you!"

"Good thinking dude," said Janus and winked to me.

It was 8:25. We were still sitting in the Departure Hall, listening to one announcement after the other about delayed flights. As far as we could make out, all flights to and from London Heathrow seemed to be delayed indefinitely. The terminal was filling up with people, all waiting nervously to go somewhere important. But it was not to be. It seemed that the whole world's airport traffic was in chaos because of all the earthquakes and volcanoes.

We were starting to have serious doubts as to whether we would be able to get on a plane to London at all. But we had to. We couldn't wait till tomorrow. I forced myself to think positively.

"I've done a little calculating of my own," I said to Jacob and Janus. "If we're lucky and the plane leaves here at nine, we'll land in London at about 10:50. That's 9:50 English time. Then it will take us about an hour to get out of the airport and to the rent-a-car place, so we should be ready to actually leave the airport by about 11 o'clock." I took out the map of England and showed my friends the route I had drawn in from London to Glastonbury. Glastonbury was to the west of London, in Somerset.

"It's about 175 miles from London to Glastonbury," I continued. "There's a big motorway the first third of the way, but after that the roads get smaller and smaller. The last stretch is basically small country roads so I figure we won't be able to drive so fast. Still, as far as I can see, I guess if we drive without stopping, we should still be able to make it to Glastonbury in about four hours. So I peg our arrival time at around four or five in the afternoon. Which will still leave us six or seven hours to get to the top of Glastonbury Tor and start the activation meditation at midnight."

"That is if our plane ever leaves the ground," muttered Jacob.

"Whoa dude," said Janus as he nudged Jacob. "Have you forgotten everything we learned about the power of positive thinking?"

"You're right," said Jacob, straightening up. "The Force is with us. I see our plane taking off any minute now."

I decided it might be a good idea to buy a newspaper, so I told my buddies I'd be back in a minute. Just as I was about to walk into the newsstand, two airport security guards came walking by with a ferocious-looking German Shepherd. The dog came to a full stop and looked at me intently, first turning its head one way and then the other. The guards stopped too—and watched the dog watching me. By the way the dog turned its head, I realized it was mesmerized by the star on my brow, but I knew the guards couldn't see it. Suddenly the dog began wagging its tail excitedly and rubbing itself up against my leg.

The guards looked on in surprise. "Well, I'll be darned..." said the one. "Wolf here is usually ready to tear everyone's head off... Say, you're not carrying anything illegal on you... are you?"

"Eh... no," I said, feeling my face turn red, "I... I just seem to get along really well with dogs." I bent over and patted Wolf on the head. "Niiice doggy," I said. Wolf was overjoyed and began licking my hand. His tail wagged even faster as if he was completely besotted with me. It was getting embarrassing.

"Wolf!" commanded the guard. "Heel boy! Heel!" But the dog didn't pay any attention. Instead, Wolf began barking at me playfully. People started looking at us and I began to panic. What if the guards decided to take me in and search me because I was making their dog so happy! I squatted before Wolf and looked him straight in the eye. Then I focused on the Force within him. Intelligent, Alive, Loving, All-Knowing. I whispered in Wolf's ear—and told him exactly the same thing I'd told little Emma. That I knew he'd had recognized me, but that now was not the time to reveal my true identity because I was on a secret mission. Finally, I told Wolf there was a heavenly bone waiting for him if he just went peacefully with his master.

But it didn't help. The dog wouldn't budge.

The other guard said, "There's something awful fishy about all this..."

For a moment, I feared the worst.

In desperation, I stood up and focused all my attention on Wolf. Then I spoke the Word of Command. "Wolf, obey your master!"

To my great surprise, Wolf immediately went back and sat down docilely, right next to his master.

"Good dog," I said and ducked into the newsstand as fast as I could.

When I got back, Jacob and Janus were both sitting straight-backed in their seats with their eyes closed. "Are you guys meditating?" I whispered as I sat down next to them.

"Yeah," said Janus. "We're visualizing getting to Glastonbury easily and effortlessly—and very fast!"

I decided to join them. I closed my eyes and tried to shut out our noisy surroundings. I focused all my attention on my breathing. It didn't take long before I began to feel the Force within me. Infinite, Eternal, Unlimited, Omnipresent. Pure Life, Pure Power, Pure Love, Pure Intelligence. I AM THE FORCE.

Then I visualized us standing on top of Glastonbury Tor. In my mind's eye I saw us inside the tower, chanting the Great White Brotherhood's mighty formula.

Next I focused my attention on my heart and affirmed that the Force now manifested this vision, if it was for the Highest Good of All Concerned. After a few moments, I released my vision and plunged into the deep peace that had settled over me. Somehow I knew that our vision really was for the Highest Good of All, and that the Force, the Light that is Unlimited, now would manifest it.

I breathed deeply.

The voice on the loudspeaker said, "All passengers on British Airways flight 830 to London Heathrow, please proceed to gate B7 for immediate boarding. Departure time is 09:00..."

"That's us!" cried Janus jubilantly.

"Way to go!" said Jacob. "That's exactly what you said Starbrow! That the plane would leave at 9 o'clock!"

"The Force is with us!" I smiled and threw my backpack over my shoulder.

Our First Miracle

Finally! At 9 o'clock, our plane took off from Copenhagen and headed out towards London Heathrow, exactly as we had visualized in our meditation. We leaned back in our seats and looked out the windows as the plane flew up towards the dark storm clouds above. Soon we could no longer see the earth underneath us but after a couple of minutes, we emerged above the thick clouds. On the other side, the sun was shining brilliantly from a clear blue sky and everything seemed peaceful and harmonious.

I had the window seat so I scanned the skies around us looking for signs of our new friends, but saw nothing. I poked Jacob and whispered to my two pals, "Oh most noble friends, I see neither starships nor angelic hosts... How doth thou explain this phenomena, O Venerable Wizard Moncler?" Jacob leaned back in his seat and unfastened his seat belt. His magic staff was propped against the seat in front of him—and Janus' two-handed sword was right next to it. So far, no one seemed to notice the staff, the sword or the star, but the other passengers and the flight attendants did eye us curiously as we stepped onto the plane. Of course it was probably just that we looked so different from all the business people on their way to their high-powered meetings in England.

The three of us had kept our unusual outfits well-hidden under our long trench coats, but what we couldn't hide was our auras. I wasn't sure if people could actually see the bright white light that emanated from us; but on the other hand, the bright white light could have been the reason that people were eyeing us so curiously. I settled back in my seat. Or maybe the explanation was less exotic and they just thought we were three young pop stars on our way to a gig at Wembley Stadium. Oh well, at least there were no little kids or dogs around to reveal our true identity!

"If I've understood everything we've learned during the last few days correctly," said Jacob in reply to my question, "then the sky around us is actually teeming with starships and angels. But since they're all in the 5th dimension, only those whose consciousness and vibrational frequency are high enough are able to see them."

"So you means ours isn't any longer?" I asked, scanning the horizon in the hope of seeing a silver starship or a glorious host of angels. In the distance, a brilliant ray of shining light shot through the clouds. I wondered... Was it sunlight... or indeed a swarm of angels on their way down to Earth to shower humankind with their love and encouragement?

"I don't know..." said Jacob as he leaned over me and looked out the window. "Do you see anything?"

"See over there..." I said as the ray of light reappeared and then disappeared again, "... what d'ya think Moncler!"

Jacob smiled blissfully and was about to say something when we were interrupted by a stewardess who asked if we'd like breakfast. Breakfast! We looked at each other and laughed. Not a bad idea! We shook our heads and said, "Yes thank you!" in unison. Until that very moment, neither food nor drink had passed our lips during all our inter-dimensional travels! So it was about time. We gratefully accepted our trays and prepared to dig into the BA chow.

"I can't remember when I last thought of food," chuckled Janus, who was carefully inspecting every morsel on his tray. "Aren't you guys famished?"

"I don't know..." I said slowly, inspecting my tray. "Do you think initiates ever eat anything?"

"I don't suppose two excellent dudes like Sananda and Ashtar would mind if we grabbed a quick bite," said Jacob, already munching away on his breakfast. Jacob was a true Dane and always partial to his victuals.

After we'd eaten breakfast and had a nice cup of tea, we leaned back in our seats and sighed contentedly.

Jacob looked down at his Ashtar Command watch. The bottom display showed **15:23:09 TO ACTIVATION MEDITATION**. "Since we really did take off at 9, I think your calculations are going to be right on, Starbrow," said Jacob. "We should land at Heathrow at 10:50—which is 9:50 English time. From then, we'll have 14 hours until we're supposed to be in place on top of Glastonbury Tor and start the Activation Meditation. 00:00:00 Greenwich Mean Time is the same as midnight on Glastonbury Tor."

"Maybe we should be using our time constructively and meditate?" I

271

suggested. "You guys remember what Kuthumi and Serapis Bey said? That it was important that we meditated as much as possible when we were on our mission."

"Yeah," yawned Janus and rubbed his eyes, "... you got a point there..."

"Hey, hey, no falling asleep Telperion!" said Jacob, elbowing Janus. "He said we were supposed to be spending our time constructively, remember!"

We folded up our tables and closed our eyes. It didn't take long before we were wandering blissfully in that relaxed state of no thought.

I don't know how long I was in this state of no thought, but suddenly I felt someone tugging at my sleeve. I felt the plane drop and opened my eyes. A stewardess was leaning our way, pointing to the Fasten Seat Belt sign, which was now on.

"I am sorry to disturb you, Sirs," she said, "but we must ask all passengers to fasten their seat belts immediately."

The plane dropped again and I felt a sinking sensation in my stomach.

The Captain's voice came on and he was saying something about the sudden turbulence. We fastened our seat belts and looked out the window as the plane bobbed up and down. Outside, all we could see were dark storm clouds.

"Welcome back to Planet Earth," mumbled Jacob.

"What a way to come out of your meditation," said Janus. "I was right in the middle of the most pleasant..."

The plane shook and everyone's portable computers and bags went sailing through the compartment. The flight attendants were holding on for dear life and smiling cheerfully.

"How long have we been gone?" asked Jacob.

Janus looked at his watch—his ordinary Earth watch—which said 10:40. He set it to English time. "It's 9:40 English time," he said. "So we were meditating for almost an hour. According to my calculations, we should be landing in about ten minutes..."

He was interrupted by more violent turbulence. It was kind of weird, but I didn't even feel nauseous like I usually did if the weather got rough. Maybe it was the calming effect of meditating, but anyway I thanked my lucky stars because the man across the aisle from us sure looked like he

272

was about to puke. He was completely white and was holding onto the armrests for dear life.

The Captain's voice came on again. "This is your Captain again," he said calmly. "I'm sorry for the unusual turbulence we've been experiencing, but it seems that last night's earthquakes and volcanic eruptions have had a strange effect on weather conditions—even here in England which has been relatively quiet up until now. Unfortunately, the situation has deteriorated over here and an unexpected storm seems to be suddenly crossing our approach path. This means our arrival at London Heathrow is going to be delayed somewhat. At the moment, I am unable to give you any exact information about how long we will be delayed because it will depend on how Control decides to organize all the incoming flights. As soon as I know more, I will let you know. I apologize for this unexpected delay and can assure you we will do everything we can to get you down on the ground at Heathrow as soon as possible. Please keep your seat belts fastened until we have landed."

The tension in the airplane mounted as we continued to circle around Heathrow. We'd been in this holding pattern for at least a half an hour—and still there was no news from the Captain. The only one we'd gotten any news out of was one of the stewardesses. She told us that if we had important business in England we were really lucky to be on this plane at all because apparently, right after we had taken off from Copenhagen Airport, all flights to and from England had been cancelled because of the violent storm that was now approaching.

The Captain's voice came on again. "Ladies and gentlemen, this is your Captain again. I am sorry for the very long delay, but as I said we are now, unfortunately, beginning to feel the combined effect on the weather of last night's unexpected events. At the moment, we are one of many planes that Control has been keeping in this holding pattern above Heathrow. Because of the fuel situation, we have been instructed to wait another 15 minutes. If we are still unable to land, I am afraid we'll have to fly on and land in Manchester instead. Once again I sincerely apologize and hope that you will understand that Ground Personnel is doing everything possible to bring in as many of the waiting planes as possible before the storm closes in and shuts down Heathrow completely..."

"Manchester!" cried Janus. "Now where's that?"

"Isn't it somewhere up north?" I said.

"Get out the map, Starbrow," said Jacob.

I pulled the AA Road Atlas of Britain out of my backpack. We opened the atlas and tried to find Manchester.

"There it is!" I said, pointing at the map. It was pretty far North.

"How far is it from Manchester to Glastonbury?" asked Jacob.

I used my fingers to approximate the distance from London to Glastonbury—and then from Manchester to Glastonbury. "About twice as far as from London to Glastonbury I guess."

"Twice as far!" cried Jacob. "You already said it would take us four or five hours to get from London to Glastonbury. That means it will take about ten hours to get from Manchester to Glastonbury!"

"And it's already 10:30 English time as it is," said Janus, looking at his watch. "And who knows when they'll let us land in Manchester? With this storm, it could take several more hours!"

"You're right," I said, studying the map, "and even if we landed in Manchester Airport soon, we'd still have a hard time getting all the way to Glastonbury before midnight. It's not like we know our way around or anything!"

"There's only one thing to do," interrupted Jacob.

"What's that?" said Janus.

"We'll just have to make sure that we land in London!" he replied and leaned back in his seat.

"And just how do you propose we do that?" asked Janus.

"We need a little miracle," smiled Jacob. "We need to part the clouds over Heathrow so that we can land right away."

"Good thinking, Moncler," I said, smiling back. "Just like Moses parted the Red Sea!"

"Exactement," said Jacob, sounding almost exactly like Saint Germain. "We have to contact the same Force that Moses and all the other Masters contacted when they performed their miracles."

"For the Highest Good of All..." I added, "... naturally!"

"Naturally!" said Jacob, pointing to the mass of angry storm clouds outside our window. "But our mission *is* for the Highest Good... is it not?"

"Alrighty," said Janus, leaning back in his seat and closing his eyes. "Let's get to it before the Captain sets course for Manchester."

We closed our eyes and focused our attention within. I tried to remember what Master Kuthumi had said about the Force when he was instructing us in the Blue Temple...

"The Force... is Unlimited and All-Powerful... The Force is stronger than electricity... mightier than an atomic bomb... more powerful than the sun... The Force is Infinite, Eternal and Immortal... The Force is the Source of All Life... The Intelligence back of All the Universes and All the Dimensions and All the Worlds in All their Infinite Diversity and Glory... The Force is the mightiest Ally in the Universe... With the Force at your side, there is no limit to the Good you can do... People will call you a Miracle worker...

"... and where do you find this Mighty Force? You find this Mighty Force hidden within your own consciousness... right there, in the Secret Chamber of your own consciousness it lies waiting for you to discover it... closer than breathing... nearer than hands and feet..."

Then I remembered what Master Saint Germain had told us about the Mightiest Spell in the Universe:

"Whatever you wish to manifest, you have to think it first... In order for something to become a reality... you have to believe 100% that it is real... that it is here now... you have to think it... affirm it... visualize it... feel it... in short, you have to know it... Then once you know it... you can leave the rest to the Force... for the Force is All-Powerful and Unlimited..."

In my mind's eye, I visualized our plane landing easily and effortlessly at Heathrow Airport. The clouds parted and the other planes were held back... all so that we could land and complete our mission. Because our mission was for the Highest Good of All Concerned. In my mind's eye, I saw Archangel Michael's crystal clear gaze piercing my heart:

"... focus your attention on your heart... and ask yourself... is this choice for the Highest Good of All Concerned... and then listen to your heart... if you feel a sense of comfort in and around your heart as you think of your choice... if you feel your heart is opening... if you feel Love... then it is because this is the right choice..."

I focused my attention on my heart. Instantly I knew that what I wished to manifest was for the Highest Good of All.

The next moment, the Captain's voice came on again. "This is your Captain speaking. It looks as if the Lord is on our side today. Suddenly the clouds opened up over Heathrow and we have been granted permission to land."

"Yeehaa!" I opened my eyes and cried triumphantly.

"Our first miracle!" laughed Jacob.

"Thank you, Lord!" said Janus.

"Look!" Jacob pointed out the window. Right below us, we could see the opening in the storm clouds and the runway lights blinking on the ground.

We gave each other our secret D&D handshake; then we smiled and sank back in our seats. Janus patted the scabbard of his trusty sword. "Soon it will be your turn, my friend," he said.

Even though the clouds had parted so we could land, it was far from smooth going. In fact there was so much turbulence that we got quite a shaking. The businessman across the aisle really looked sick. He was holding his head in his hands, his eyes shut tight. I visualized him strong and calm. I saw him breathing peacefully so that his whole body became calm and relaxed. I was convinced my visualization was working because even though the plane kept bobbing up and down like we were on a wild roller coaster ride, he didn't throw up.

Then, as we approached the ground, everyone held their breath. As our wheels touched ground, the plane lurched dangerously from side to side in the violent gusts of wind, until finally it stabilized itself on the runway. We were safe on the ground! Everyone in the plane breathed a sigh of relief, and then all at once, started to clap.

Once on the ground, we still had to wait a long time before our plane was allowed to taxi over to the gate. In fact, a whole hour passed before we pulled up to our gate and were allowed to debark. It was almost 12 noon English time.

As we rushed to get off the plane, I noticed that the business man who I'd visualized well again was staring at my brow. I wondered if he could see my star. Well one thing was for sure, he looked fine again.

As we filed out, he was right behind me. He tapped me on the shoulder and said, "Thanks for the help!"

"My pleasure!" I replied.

Once inside the airport, Janus asked me what that was all about.

"Oh... I was just testing one of the Masters' ideas. You know the one about there only being One Consciousness, One Mind that we all use and live in," I said. "Well, I figured if there was only One Mind and I could convince myself that that guy was not going to puke, he wouldn't... And it worked!"

"Way to go, Starbro'!" exclaimed Janus. "Slip me five!"

Heathrow Airport was in total chaos. It looked like a lot of people were waiting for baggage that never came so we were glad we only had our carry-on stuff. Once through customs, we found the terminal bursting with people. Thousands of passengers were now stranded at the airport because of all the cancelled flights. People were milling about everywhere, sitting, standing, squeezed into every corner, seat and bit of floor space available. A small army of British Airways personnel was trying to calm people down and help all the stranded and confused passengers. The lines by the airline counters and telephones were endless, and the atmosphere in the terminal was tense, to say the least.

One of the groups we passed was a group of little kids about kindergarten age who were all wailing and crying as their teachers desperately tried to calm them. Then a strange thing happened. The moment we walked by, all the kids looked at us and stopped crying at the very same moment. And their teachers stared at us in wonder, thinking some miracle must have befallen them.

"The man's got a star on his brow!" cried one little girl, who looked very much like little Emma back at Copenhagen airport. "Yeah," piped in a couple of other kids, all beaming at us in approval. So we stopped in our tracks and smiled back at them. Then a little red-headed boy darted over to Jacob like a jack rabbit—and shyly touched Jacob's magic staff. Jacob patted him kindly on the head.

"You be good children!" said Janus, sternly, like the great Elf warrior he was. And for some reason, we knew that they would.

At the Avis counter, the woman told us to take the airport bus over to the Avis lot, so we walked out of the terminal and joined the line of people by the bus stop. Everywhere we looked there were lines of cars and busses, stretching out in all directions—moving at a snail's pace through the pouring rain.

"Mother Earth's definitely in a change mode," I said, surveying the scene and pointing at the dark clouds above us.

"It sure was a good thing we landed when we did," said Jacob as he checked his Ashtar Command watch. The bottom display read **10:32:27 TO ACTIVATION MEDITATION**. The top display read **34:32:27 TO AXIS SHIFT**.

"I just hope we'll be able to get through this traffic," said Janus.

"Yeah," said Jacob, "or we just might have to perform another miracle!"

Ten minutes later the Avis bus appeared and fortunately, we didn't need another miracle to part the sea of cars. But it was slow going so we studied our maps as the bus crawled along, trying to determine the fastest route to Glastonbury. It seemed there was more than one way to get there. As we studied the map, we discovered that Stonehenge was about halfway to Glastonbury—and that we were going to pass right by it!

"Stonehenge, dudes!" said Janus, putting his finger right on it. "I always wanted to see it."

"Yeah," said Jacob, "and it's also a Power Spot."

"You suppose anyone's been appointed to activate Stonehenge?" asked Janus.

"I doubt it," said Jacob. "I mean with only 139 groups of volunteers, the Masters could only pick a few Power Spots in each country for activation. So I guess they probably picked the most important ones."

"Good thinking dude," I said, "but I thought Stonehenge was one of the most important Power Spots on Earth."

"Well, if anyone's there," said Jacob, "I guess we'll find out when we get there!"

We'd made up our minds about our route and decided we'd only stop to change drivers. Janus and I were going to take turns driving because Jacob didn't have a driver's license. But we appointed him navigator of our Quest since he was a wizard.

Just then Janus whistled.

"Get a load of the way these dudes drive over here!" he cried, pointing out the window. "It's all backwards!"

We'd been so occupied with planning our route that we never thought about the fact that they drive on the left side of the road in England.

"Bet this'll take some getting used to," I said, whistling. "I never drove on the left side before."

"Hope it won't slow us down none," groaned Janus. "It's not like we've got a whole lot of time."

"Get a grip guys," interjected Jacob, "if the Brits can do it, then it should be a piece of cake for two excellent dudes like you."

"Easy for you to say," said Janus, "considering you're not driving!"

"Now everybody just calm down," said Jacob, trying to smooth the matter over. "Let's just affirm that driving on the left side is a piece of cake. And besides, may I remind you who's the real driver!"

"Well it sure ain't you!"

"That's right," continued Jacob, trying to get us back on track. "The real driver is the Force, just remember that. And as you know the Force is

Unlimited and All-Powerful. So it's just as easy for the Force to drive on the left side of the road as it is to drive on the right!"

"Right again, dude!" I said.

Janus seemed to be giving the matter some serious thought. Probably because he was looking forward to driving fast, like he usually did, and he was afraid driving on the left side would slow him down.

"You know," he said seriously, "if we rent a car with automatic transmission, it'll make things a lot easier. You know getting used to shifting with the opposite hand might take some getting used to."

"I wonder," I said, "what kind of car our voucher is for."

Janus rummaged through his backpack and pulled out the Avis voucher. "Let's see, "he said, studying it. "It says a Ford Escort. 4 doors. Air-conditioned. Automatic transmission!"

"Way to go!" I grinned. "The Ashtar Command seems to have thought of everything!"

4

Black April

At Avis, we joined the long line of people waiting to rent cars. Everyone in line was staring at the TV monitor hanging from the ceiling. We could see why. CNN had become a veritable cavalcade of horrors, transmitting non-stop pictures of what had been going on on Planet Earth since midnight. It was amazing. On top of the violent earthquakes, it seemed that many volcanoes had become active during the course of the morning. I had the definite feeling that Mother Earth was having fever convulsions just as Ashtar had predicted.

And the experts were without a clue. No one could explain why during the course of one morning almost every volcano on earth had suddenly become active. And why now? Why today? It seemed the experts were at a loss to explain.

It wasn't a pretty sight, but it was fascinating to watch the pictures of the huge eruptions as they spewed out lava and huge clouds of gas... on Iceland, around the Mediterranean, on Montserrat... in the Philippines. It was hard to keep track.

And as if this wasn't enough, the weather all around the globe was reacting violently to these massive earth changes. Fierce storms seemed to appear out of nowhere. As we stood and watched, the commentator told of a freak storm, one with characteristics never seen before, that was coming down from the northwest and heading towards continental Europe. Already, the monster storm was wreaking havoc in large parts of Ireland, Scotland and Northern England. In the Caribbean, a killer hurricane was making its way towards the coast of Florida and Georgia. And in many places in Asia, tornadoes and violent storms had also suddenly appeared out of nowhere during the morning. Again experts were at a loss to explain this global storm.

"Looks like the Night the Earth Quaked ain't over yet," muttered

Janus.

As if in reply to his statement, we saw that CNN had fittingly baptized the day "Black April".

I looked around at the other people waiting in line and wondered how all these Earth changes were affecting them. Were they just upset over the fact that their plans had been messed up—or did they have a sense that something was seriously wrong, that Mother Earth was having fever convulsions which might well be humanity's last warning...

Then I remembered what Sananda had said to the volunteers in the great hall of the Mothership. "... even though it may appear at present as if humanity is in a desperate situation, there are in fact, many, many thousands of souls on Earth who are ready for the ascension process. And there are hundreds upon hundreds of thousands who are just about to awaken, even though they are not aware of it yet."

Slowly I let my eyes pass over each of the travelers waiting in the line. Most of them looked tired and worried. Was it just because of the day's long delays? Or was I in reality seeing a deeper dissatisfaction and longing in each of these tired faces? The same dissatisfaction and longing for something higher and better which I myself had felt only a few short days ago in Copenhagen when I ran like a maniac from the Park Café?

Suddenly I felt a wave of compassion wash over me as I looked at all these people... and I knew that this was how Sananda felt when he looked at us. When he looked at us, he saw us all, each and everyone of us, as Divine and Mighty Incarnations of the Force who had forgotten who we were, who had forgotten our true nature... just as I ... not so very long ago... had forgotten that I was Starbrow. Sananda knew that each and every being longed to remember who they really were and to experience their own True, Unlimited Divine Nature.

Then I realized that probably Mother Earth's ascension into the 5th dimension was Her gift to humanity. The heightened vibrational frequency on Earth was giving every person that extra impetus to ascend to new and as yet unimaginable heights of Love and Freedom. And it could all happen now. Right now, in this lifetime. "Now is your time" Sananda had said. And I understood that it was not only the volunteers' time, the Guardians of the Earth's time, but that it was all of humanity's time. We weren't that far from the critical mass. The critical mass of enlightened beings who would raise humanity into the 5th dimension, into a new era of Love, Harmony and Enlightenment on Earth. We were so close now. All we needed was a little more time, just a little more time...

I looked at my Ashtar Command watch. The bottom display read 09:27:08 TO ACTIVATION MEDITATION, the top display read 33:27:08 TO AXIS SHIFT. There was still time enough. Time enough for us to get to Glastonbury Tor and give humanity a little more time, that little bit of time humankind needed to take the next step.

Finally, it was our turn and we stepped up to the desk and gave the woman our voucher. Everything was in order and even paid for (there seemed to be no limits to the Ashtar Command's travel arrangements!) and before long we had the keys to our car.

Out in the parking lot, the wind was blowing so fiercely that it nearly knocked us over. So we rushed over to our blue Ford Escort and settled in as quick as we could. Janus behind the wheel and Jacob at his side with the map—and me in the back seat. Janus checked the mirrors and all the dials on the dashboard—and was ready to roll.

"Hit the road, Telperion!" I leaned forward, surveying the dashboard, "We haven't a minute to lose!"

Janus started the engine, turned on the windshield wipers and backed out of the parking lot. An Avis man in yellow rain gear was directing the cars out onto the rain-swept road.

"Don't forget the left side, my good Elf," said Jacob. "If you make a heinous mistake, we'll never make it to Glastonbury in time."

"The Force is with us!" said Janus and drove out of the parking lot.

The road from the Avis lot to the big main road that circled Heathrow Airport was packed with cars so we crawled along at a snail's pace until we reached the main road. A friendly driver signaled us to pull in front of him, so we did—and the view opened up before us.

Janus whistled in surprise. "Will you look at this!"

We came to a full stop.

In front of us, behind us, to the left and to the right of us, were literally hundreds and hundreds of cars. In fact, all we could see were cars, stretching out in every direction as far as the eye could see... and all of them were practically standing still.

"Well most noble friends," I said and leaned forward, "I do believe we need another miracle."

282

"Just keep focusing on the Force, Starbrow," said Janus. "It's helping, it's helping... I can feel it."

We'd started moving again, but very, very slowly. But at least we were moving. Janus and Jacob had given me the job of focusing on the Force and visualizing us moving swiftly, easily and effortlessly on the road to Glastonbury. And in fact, my focus on the Mighty Power of the Universe did seem to be helping. Even though the cars hadn't parted like the Red Sea before Moses, we were actually beginning to move.

"The Force is the one and only Reality," I said slowly while focusing on the Presence within me. Janus and Jacob repeated after me. "I AM one with the Force..." I went on, "I AM THE FORCE..."

"I AM THE FORCE!" repeated Janus and Jacob after me. Just the thought that we were Pure Consciousness—and independent of outer circumstances—filled us with a feeling of Power and Freedom. "I AM THE FORCE!" I said again and then placed my hands on each of my buddies' shoulders. "You know dudes," I continued, "it just struck me that if we can get just as strong a realization of the Force—that I AM THE FORCE—as we did when we walked over the pink clouds together... well then I know the Force will bring us through this traffic in a most atypical way!"

"Let's tell it like it is!" cried Janus.

"I AM THE FORCE!" the three of us cried in unison. "I AM THE FORCE!"

We weren't in doubt any longer. The line of cars in front of us was picking up speed.

"I AM THE FORCE! I AM THE FORCE!" we shouted over and over again, until we were totally focused on the Mighty, Free Presence, the Unlimited Consciousness that we really were.

And then we were rolling.

Janus drove like he'd been driving on the left side all his life. And neither rain nor storm could deter us. We three had become one unit, moving forward, totally focused on THE FORCE.

"I AM THE FORCE!" we cried and now it was no longer Janus who was driving the car. Rather it was the Force in Janus, the Force in Jacob, the Force in me...

"I AM THE FORCE! I AM THE FORCE!" we proclaimed at the top of our lungs. We came to a confusing roundabout with a million cars and a million exits, but Jacob knew the way. Or should I say, the Force in Jacob knew the way. And the Force in Janus and the Force in me...

283

We picked up speed as we turned into a three-lane motorway, but the highway was still packed. Fortunately for us, everyone was driving faster and faster. It seemed as if it was the Force in everyone, in all the cars, in all the trucks, in all the busses that was driving faster and faster. It was the Force, which was making this whole long procession of vehicles move like a huge school of fish... all driven forward by one and the same Intelligence... The Force... I AM THE FORCE...

Jacob signaled to Janus to turn onto the M3, the big motorway leading west. West to Glastonbury, west to Avalon... It was a five-lane motorway so the cars started to spread out as soon as we were on the M3. Now there was a little space in between the cars and we felt the sweet rush of freedom!

"I AM THE FORCE!" we cried again triumphantly.

"Yeeha," cried Janus.

"Step on it, Telperion!"

Janus stepped on the accelerator and began weaving in and out of traffic as if he'd been driving on the left side his whole life. In fact, Janus drove as easily and effortlessly through the pouring rain as if he was Telperion galloping over the fields on his white elven horse. Telperion... King of the High Elves. The Force was truly with him!

After we'd sort of settled into the driving mode, Jacob turned on the radio and began searching for the news. When he found a news channel, he turned up the radio. The speaker was talking about Black April and about how the Night the Earth Quaked had now become the worst weather and environmental disaster in the history of man. And still, scientists and experts all over the world had no explanation for what was going on.

According to the speaker, the military, the reserves, the national guards and all the world's rescue teams were still struggling with the aftermath of the night's global earthquakes. And now the civilian population was being evacuated on a large scale in the many areas affected by the various volcano eruptions. Huge amounts of gas and lava were being spewed out into the atmosphere. In some cities, people were beginning to wear gas masks. And on top of all this, a huge global storm was brewing and now beginning to wreak havoc around the globe. The hurricane called "Black April" was causing great destruction in the southeastern United States, and in Southeast Asia, there were reports of more than one typhoon running wild. Flooding was also being reported from numerous spots and in Germany, the Rhine was beginning to spill over its banks.

"Do you think the other volunteers are having just as hard a time as we are getting to their Power Spots? I asked.

"Well, if only half of what we just heard is true, I'd say there's a very good chance that they are," said Jacob as he tried to find another news channel. "Unless of course, they happen to live right next door to their Power Spot."

"The Force is with them, too!" cried Janus as he passed a huge truck. I couldn't believe how positive Janus had become since we returned from the higher dimensions!

Jacob found another news channel and turned it up. This time it was a local radio station, so the news was also more local. The great storm from northwest had now reached London and all flights to and from Heathrow and Gatwick had been cancelled indefinitely. According to the report, all of London and the Greater London area was now one gigantic traffic jam. Apparently, we had gotten out just in time.

Then the news broadcaster began warning the local population of a new, unexpected weather phenomenon that had arisen without warning: Tornadoes! All of a sudden, people were reporting tornadoes from different locations in and around Ireland, Scotland and England— something that was totally unheard of in Great Britain. And these violent weather phenomena were destroying everything in their pathway. Roads and houses, bridges and cars, trees and forests. It seemed that these freak storms were totally leveling everything to the ground. Then the speaker began listing the names of different places where tornadoes had been seen and started advising people in these areas to seek cover below ground and listen to their radios for tornado warnings.

"Tornadoes!" whistled Janus, "Now that's really news!"

"Shh!" said Jacob, "I want to hear where all these tornadoes are." He opened up the map and I leaned forward to join him as we listened to the speaker report on tornado sightings... the Cliffs of Moher in Ireland, the Aran Isles in Ireland, Callanish in Scotland, Findhorn in Scotland, Iona in Scotland, Carmarthen in Wales, Tintagel in England, Avebury in England...

"All those places..." I said, "they sound so familiar. Where have I heard those names before..."

"They're all Power Spots!" cried Jacob. "Those are all the Power Spots that the volunteers in England were asked to activate!"

"You're right, man!" said Janus. "I remember it from the Crystal Cave—in our past life."

285

Jacob motioned for us to be quiet. The speaker was reporting on other areas that had been struck by tornadoes: Stratford, Glastonbury...

"Glastonbury!" cried Jacob. "I wonder how that's going to affect us..."

I looked at my Ashtar Command watch. The bottom display read **06:58:32 TO ACTIVATION MEDITATION**. Less than seven hours until midnight. Then it dawned on me that maybe it wouldn't be enough time.

5

Stonehenge

"I wonder why the tornadoes all seem to be happening around the Power Spots?" Jacob said thoughtfully as he pored over the map of Great Britain in his lap. We'd left the motorway and were now zooming down a road with two-way traffic, heading west towards Somerset where Glastonbury was. We were just about halfway to Glastonbury and were closing in on Stonehenge where we planned to stop and change drivers. According to the map, Stonehenge was right next to the road we were on.

"In a way, it makes perfect sense," said Janus, concentrating on the wet, slippery road. "I figure that since the Power Spots are the Light Grid's Energy Centers and since they've been blocked by all the negative thoughts of humanity... well, it makes perfect sense... because the tornadoes are probably Mother Earth's way of cleansing and opening the Power Spots."

"But how are we going to carry out our activation meditation, if Glastonbury Tor gets struck by a tornado?" I asked. I'd never seen a tornado before but I imagined them to be these enormous giants that just sort of chewed up everything on their pathway.

"Tornadoes don't stand still," said Jacob. "In fact, I think they move rather quickly. And as far as I know, they usually don't last for more than an hour."

"I just had another thought," said Janus. "If the tornadoes are Mother Earth's way of cleansing her Energy Centers or Power Spots, then maybe the tornadoes also move along her Ley Lines, you know Mother Earth's Energy Lines, to open them up too."

"You might be onto something," said Jacob. "If I follow you rightly, you're saying that if one knew where the Ley Lines were, one could predict the pathway of these tornadoes?"

"Exactement," said Janus.

"For once your insight surpasses your courage, my good Telperion!" I cried in amazement. "But how do you think one goes about finding out where these Ley Lines actually are?"

Janus didn't answer. We had come to another roundabout and Jacob was directing Janus towards the exit we were supposed to take. A sign said 1½ miles to Stonehenge. I surveyed the landscape eagerly. Stonehenge was located on Salisbury Plain, a flat, wide open space with fields and hills and woodlands. There were flocks of white sheep grazing on both sides of the road, and many farms. We were definitely out in the country now. And yet there was something different about this place. As we approached Stonehenge, it felt as if a mighty Force was beginning to pulsate in and around us.

"There it is!" cried Jacob pointing straight ahead. We'd just come over a hill and there, as the view opened up before us, we saw Stonehenge. It was less than a quarter of a mile away. I stared in fascination at the ancient circle of enormous standing stones, which suddenly rose up, right in the middle of the English countryside.

Right before Stonehenge, the road divided into two, passing the huge stone circle on both sides. Janus turned up the road to the right. As we approached the stone circle, we realized that the narrow tract of land between the two roads where Stonehenge stood was all fenced in. Janus slowed to a halt right next to Stonehenge, and we gazed at the stone circle on our left. Many of the 15-20 foot high stones had toppled over or been removed throughout the course of history, but there was no doubt that Stonehenge must have once been a formidable place. It was almost dusk and Stonehenge looked dark and ominous in the late afternoon light, like the gathering of ancient giants guarding a deep secret.

To our right, there was a visitor's center and parking lot. Janus pulled into the lot, which was almost completely empty, probably because of the bad weather and everything else that had been going on in the world.

"Your turn, Starbrow!" said Janus as he got out of the car and stretched.

I opened the door and stepped out into the pouring rain. The moment I got out of the car, I felt a strong tingling sensation between my brows. All of Stonehenge was transformed, right before my eyes, into gigantic rays of light.

"What is it?" asked Janus when he saw me staring at the stone circle.

"Did you see that light?" I asked. The strong tingling sensation between my eyebrows continued. Jacob got out of the car, staff in hand.

288

Immediately, his staff began to glow. When Janus saw Jacob's staff, he drew his sword from its scabbard. It too began to glow. I felt irresistibly drawn towards Stonehenge. We began walking towards the stone circle. I felt an enormous power welling up in me, a power that was in the Earth and which flowed up through my whole body. It was as if Stonehenge was a magic magnet, which drew everything to it. We ran across the road and stood in front of the high wire fence.

"We can't get in!" said Janus, tugging at the high fence.

"No. Not unless we go back over to the visitor's center and buy tickets," said Jacob who'd obviously surveyed the whole scene while we were in the parking lot. "The only way to get in is through the visitor's center."

Jacob was right. There was a tunnel from the visitor's center, which ran underneath the road. From where we stood by the fence, we could see that even once you were in, you still couldn't get close to the standing stones. Visitors had to walk along the pathway that circled around the stone circle.

Today the place was deserted.

So we just leaned up against the wire fence and gazed at the standing stones. That's when we discovered that there were two men on the pathway at the far side of the stone circle. They were fumbling with some kind of equipment. From the look of them, they didn't seem like guards.

I studied the fence. It was quite high and there was barbed wire along the top so obviously climbing over wasn't a serious option.

As if reading my thoughts, Jacob said, "Our mission is to activate the Power Spot at Glastonbury Tor. Not the one here at Stonehenge."

"Yeah," said Janus, turning to walk back to the car, "Let's get a move on." At that very moment, a powerful bright light began to shine on the other side of the road, illuminating a field about a hundred yards behind the parking lot. I couldn't tell if the light was coming from the sky above the field or from the field itself, but I felt an enormous wave of energy emanating from the field. Then it appeared as if all the plants on the field were suddenly standing up perfectly straight, almost as if they were being sucked upwards by some invisible force. Then, in one harmonious movement, all the plants seemed to be whirled down flat on the ground, almost as if they were one long row of dominos tumbling over into intricate patterns. A moment later, the light disappeared as suddenly as it appeared. But the mysterious twirls of plants remained, forming an intricate pattern almost one hundred yards long, right across the field. The pattern had a beautiful spiral shape.

"It's a DNA-molecule!" cried Jacob.

"Whoa, dudes, this is most unprecedented!" laughed Janus looking upwards. "I wonder what made it happen? Do you think it could have been one of the starships?"

I scanned the sky, but all I could see was dark storm clouds.

"It's a crop circle! A crop circle!" cried a voice behind us. "Quick, Jean-Paul! Get out the camera!"

We turned around. The two men who had been fumbling with their equipment over by the standing stones were now standing by the fence, staring at the fantastic pattern on the other side of the road. One of them had pulled out a camera and began taking pictures as fast as he could.

"Mon Dieu! This is the fifth crop circle we've seen today! And we saw it happen!" exclaimed the photographer, a thin, dark-haired, thirty-somethingish man who was wearing the most super functional rain gear I'd ever seen. He spoke English with a French accent.

"Has this happened before?" Janus asked the man.

"Crop circles? But of course... They happen all the time, all over the world," said the other man as he carefully checked the dials on the device he had in his hand. He was a big, stocky fellow with gray hair and bushy eyebrows. He was obviously an Englishman.

"Do you know what causes these crop circles?" asked Jacob.

"We're not quite sure..." replied the stocky Englishman.

"I'll bet you anything it was an UFO, I'm absolutely sure it was an UFO!" cried the Frenchman ecstatically as he kept on taking pictures of the field across the road. I stared at the perfect pattern on the other side of the road and wondered why the Ashtar Command would make a pattern like that? What was the point?

"So what's this triangle thing?" asked Jacob, pointing at the strange-looking contraption in the Englishman's hands.

"It's an instrument I've designed," said the Englishman, "to measure the movement and fluctuation of magnetic energy along the surface of the earth."

"And why would you want to do something like that?" asked Janus.

The Englishman looked at us for a moment as if he was trying to ascertain whether or not we'd be capable of understanding him. "With my little contraption here, I can measure the fluctuation of energy around the Earth's Power Spots and along the Ley Lines," he said.

"Wow!" said Janus, "that sounds interesting!"

"So you've heard about Ley Lines?" said the Englishman, seeming relieved that we didn't laugh at him.

"You bet," said Janus. "And what's your little contraption telling you right now?"

"Since the earthquakes began at midnight, Jean-Paul and I have been measuring the energy levels at the Power Spots here at Stonehenge, in Avebury, and in Glastonbury."

"Glastonbury!" cried Janus excitedly. "And what do your readings say?"

"For the last four years," said the Englishman, clearing his throat as if for a long dissertation, "Jean-Paul and I have been studying the energy fields around all the Power Spots in Great Britain—and I can now tell you most definitely that during the past 18 hours, the total surge of energy has been far greater than all the energy increases we've measured during the last four years—combined! And what's more, reports are coming in of increased UFO activity and crop circles near every one of the Power Spots in Britain!"

"Do you really think these UFOs are behind the crop circles?" I inquired, scanning the sky with its turbulent storm clouds in the hope of seeing a starship or a flying pyramid.

"Tell him your theory, John," said the Frenchman, who was changing to another one of his powerful zoom lenses.

"Alright," said John, seeming delighted to have some listeners who seemed to know what he was talking about, "No, I don't think that the UFOs are behind the crop circles. What I do think is that the Earth is a living being and that the crop circles are coming from Her. Because you see, when you study the Power Spots on Earth, you will discover that they form exact geometric patterns, which are in perfect harmony with the stars out in space. I believe the crop circles are a kind of signal, which the Earth is sending out into the Universe. Perhaps some kind of distress signal, who knows. And I believe that the many UFO sightings near Power Spots and crop circles are, in fact, beings from other places in the universe who are coming here in response to the Earth's call."

We were all silent for a moment, looking up at the sky.

"And who do you think these beings from other places in the universe are?" I asked.

"Don't ask me kid," he replied. "All I know is that someone out there is communicating with the Earth Herself."

"Tell him the good news, John, tell him what we discovered today!" cried Jean-Paul, who was rummaging in his bag for more film.

"I suppose you've heard about the tornadoes which have suddenly been occurring in the last few hours?" said John.

We nodded.

"Well, we've discovered that all these tornadoes are occurring in the vicinity of the Power Spots," John continued. "And what's more," he said, leaning against the fence as if he was about to tell us some deep secret. "We've discovered that the tornadoes are all moving along the Ley Lines!"

"What did I tell you, dudes!" cried Janus. "That's exactly what I've been saying!"

The Englishman and Frenchman stared at Janus with their mouths wide open.

"Mon Dieu!" cried the Frenchman, "but they know!"

"Yes, we know," said Jacob, matter-of-factly, "but what we don't know is where exactly these Ley Lines are located. Do you?"

"But of course," replied John. "We've been studying the Ley Lines for years."

"That means that you should be able to warn the civilian population about the movements of the tornadoes," I said, moving closer to the fence.

"Yes, we should. And I've tried to contact the authorities," said John, "but no one will listen to what I have to say. Unfortunately."

"They never listen to us!" cried Jean-Paul heatedly.

"Well, maybe it's because last year you were foolish enough to contact the local Civil Guard and tell them that a flying saucer was going to land on top of Stonehenge on Midsummer's eve!" replied John just as heatedly to his friend. "I don't think it helped our credibility much!"

Jean-Paul shrugged his shoulders.

"But at least you can help us," I said. "We simply must get to Glastonbury Tor as fast as possible. Your knowledge of the Ley Lines could prove invaluable."

"Getting to Glastonbury is going to be difficult," said John. "The whole countryside around Glastonbury Tor has been devastated by tornadoes. According to the latest report, most of the roads are blocked."

The three of us looked anxiously westward towards Glastonbury. Black storm clouds had formed huge clusters on the horizon, which were hastily moving in our direction. Thunder rumbled uneasily in the distance. There could be no doubt about it—a great storm was on its way. And in order to stop it, we would have to enter into the very heart of it.

6

The Old Road

"The Force in me drives just as easily on the left side of the road as on the right," I mumbled to myself while trying to get the hang of driving on the 'wrong' side of the road. The rain pounded against the car as the Ford's windshield wipers worked frantically to clear the windows. To our left was the wide open countryside, which was lit up at regular intervals by huge jagged flashes of lightning, followed by deep resounding rolls of thunder. On the right side of the road, a column of mighty old trees was pitching back and forth in the wind. I drove as fast as I dared in such stormy weather, but the road was slippery and I had to take care. It was almost seven o'clock and occasionally we caught glimpses of the sun going down between the dark storm clouds on the horizon. We were still more than 30 miles from Glastonbury.

"According to Jean-Paul's map, this road should soon pass right over a Ley Line," said Jacob as he studied the hand-made map of Britain's Power Spots and Ley Lines our two friends had given us. "But it's pretty hard to read his notations, so it's difficult..." mumbled Jacob, his nose almost touching the map, "to make out exactly where this Ley Line is... but I think it looks like it's somewhere between Warminster and Frome." Jacob looked up and stared out the window trying to figure out where we were.

We were driving through a tiny old village and the road was so narrow that two cars couldn't pass each other so I had to slow down. There wasn't a soul in sight, but there was light in most of the windows. It seemed that everyone—both man and beast—had sought shelter from the storm and the tornado warnings. Right outside the village, we saw the remains of what looked like a recent car accident. The demolished truck had apparently skidded into a giant oak and crumpled like a match box when it hit the mighty old tree. But it must have been a while ago, because there were no people around. I slowed down even more at the sight of the wreckage.

"Now, you just take it nice and easy, Starbrow," said Jacob and patted me on the shoulder. "It won't do us no good if we end up in a ditch."

Once outside the village, the countryside opened up again. There wasn't a car on the road besides us so I started driving faster. That was one of the good things about the storm,; at least there was very little traffic on the roads. In fact, it must have been more than fifteen minutes since we'd last passed another car.

"What was it you were saying about the Ley Lines, Moncler?" I said as we came over a hill.

Jacob didn't answer but was staring straight ahead as if he'd just seen a ghost. "Drive slowly, Starbrow," he said, slowly. "I think we've just come to a Ley Line."

I slowed down and then realized what Jacob was staring at. The countryside we'd been driving through was pretty hilly, with patches of woods and a lonely house here and there. Now, less than 500 yards ahead, there was this unbelievable belt of destruction a couple of hundred yards wide stretching as far as the eye could see. The belt seemed to run from north to south, crossing right over the road we were driving on. And everything, absolutely everything in that belt had been completely razed to the ground. Trees, bushes, fields, rocks, boulders, telephone poles, everything. The debris was all spread out helter-skelter, as if a giant vacuum cleaner had sucked up the entire countryside and then spit it out again. We even saw the remains of what must have been a house, just scattered like match sticks across the field. A tractor was laying upside down right smack in the middle of a jumble of devastated trees, telephone poles and power cables. To our left, right in the middle of an empty field, there was a squashed car. Apparently it had been thrown several hundred yards from the road. I stepped on the brake and came to a full stop.

"Whoa dudes, this is most heinous indeed!" whistled Janus.

"Wow..." I was dumbstruck. I'd never seen a tornado before so I never realized they could do so much damage. Obviously nothing could withstand an onslaught like this. There was no doubt that Mother Earth was in uproar.

"May the Force be with us," said Janus solemnly.

"And may it be with those who were caught by the tornado," said Jacob.

We looked around uneasily. The storm had in no way abated and it was still thundering and lightening all around us, but there was no sign of any tornadoes in the vicinity. All we could see as we gazed westward in the direction of Glastonbury, were black storm clouds in the waning light as the sun was slowly setting.

We started driving again, but very slowly, because even though the tornado hadn't crossed the road just where we were, there was still all kinds of debris and branches and rocks everywhere. So we just sort of plowed our way through the flotsam and jetsam until we came to a stretch of road that for sure had been hit by the tornado. Before us was a wide belt of total devastation maybe two hundred yards wide. The road directly in front of us was all ripped up and big pieces of asphalt were scattered all over the place. What was left of the road was dotted with gaping holes and craters. Other than that, the place was completely deserted. There wasn't a person in sight, dead or alive. And though it was still raining hard and thundering, an ominous silence seemed to lie upon the land. I drove as far as I could and then pulled to a complete stop right before a huge twisted tangle of trees and bushes that was strewn across the road.

"First check," said Janus. He opened the door and got out to investigate the roadblock before us. Seeing there was no way around it, he started lifting the branches and other debris and dragging it away from the road. Jacob got out and joined him. Janus worked with amazing speed, moving the huge branches and rocks away as if they were light as a feather.

"Not bad Telperion!" I cried, sticking my head out the window. "I knew your D&D strength score of 19 would come in handy sooner or later!" I began driving forward slowly since my buddies had now cleared the first part of the road. The next obstacle was the crumpled remains of a big telephone pole that somehow had gotten completely entangled in a small tree. For a moment, Janus and Jacob both tugged at the heavy telephone pole, but nothing happened. Then Janus pulled out his big two-handed sword from his scabbard and began to cut the tree free from the telephone pole. With great skill, Janus guided his sword through both the branches and telephone pole as if they were made of butter. Then my friends lifted the remains of the tree and the pole and lugged them far enough so our car could pass. Next they pushed aside the rocks so I could start driving again. Jacob walked in front and directed me around the largest potholes in the road. Finally, we were halfway through the belt of destruction—to the point where the center of the tornado must have

295

passed. I knew because I felt a clear increase in energy as we passed over this spot. I realized it was the power of the Ley Line.

Janus and Jacob kept clearing the road of obstacles. We still hadn't seen any signs of life and I prayed that whoever lived in the demolished house on the right side of the road had managed to get away in time. When we were about three quarters of the way out of the tornado belt, the car suddenly sunk down in a pothole we hadn't noticed. I stepped on the gas, but nothing happened. We were stuck! I stepped on the gas again, but the wheels just spun.

I honked on the horn and signaled to Janus and Jacob to give me a hand. They went around behind the car and started to push.

"Be excellent now," I said to the car and stepped on the gas. I knew my friends were pushing with all their might, but all I could hear was the wheels spinning. I looked back at my buddies through the rearview mirror and saw them straining so hard that their faces had turned red.

"Come on baby," I said softly to the car, "be a most excellent car now!" I looked back at Janus whose muscular body was strained to the bursting point. Then, with a sudden jolt, the car moved forward. It all happened so quickly that my buddies almost landed on their noses in the mud! I stepped on the brake and gave them the thumbs up sign. Jacob wiped the sweat from his brow and patted Janus on the shoulder.

"Not bad, guys!" I said as they went round in front of the car again to remove the last couple of branches from the road. Now the coast was clear again.

Janus and Jacob hopped into the car again and we gave each other our secret D&D handshake.

"That was most excellent!" I said.

"We can thank Telperion for it," said Jacob, looking down at his grimy hands. "Without his strength score of 19, we'd never have gotten through."

I looked at Janus in the back seat. He was leaning back with his eyes closed, soaked and exhausted, but otherwise fine.

"We'd better get going," said Jacob. "Who knows when another tornado just might decide to mosey down this Ley Line again... not that any of us are in the mood to stay and find out."

I stepped on the gas and we were moving again. After a few minutes, the road left the open countryside and entered a dense old forest. Once again there were branches strewn all over the place and around one curve, a tree had split in two and fallen into the other lane, leaving just

296

room enough for me to drive by. But all the debris was slowing us down.

We emerged from the forest and a few miles of hedges and then found ourselves out in open countryside again. A huge flash of lightening illumined the open plain to our left and for a brief moment, we could clearly see an old medieval castle looming up on top of a hill in the distance. I had the distinct feeling that we'd entered an old, forgotten corner of England, a musty place where the old forests, roads and castles hadn't yet been touched by the modern age. Then suddenly we came to a crossing and I stopped so Jacob could consult the map.

"Straight ahead," said Jacob. "... towards Frome—and from there to Shepton Mallet."

"Check out the size of this road, will ya..." I said. It was so narrow that in some places there was only room for one car. "Good thing it ain't rush hour!"

Fortunately, there were no other cars. In fact, it felt like we were all alone in the world, but Jacob said we were somewhere between Warminster and Frome, not that that meant much to us. First we passed another stretch of open countryside and then we entered another old forest. On our left, we suddenly passed an old Celtic-looking stone cross. It kind of made me shiver, like we were really driving on a very old road, in a very ancient part of England.

"What does the Ley Line map say now, Moncler?" asked Janus, who seemed to have revived a bit.

"I'm looking, I'm looking," mumbled Jacob. "It's just so hard to understand this guy's scribbles... but as far as I can make out, these Ley Lines seems to run under the old roads or along ridges and rivers." He turned the map around again. "Or maybe it's the other way around... that the old roads were built on top of the Ley Lines."

"We're definitely driving on one of those old roads now," I said as we drove down a long alley way, which suddenly curved sharply to the right. The moment we rounded the curve, I felt a strong tingling sensation between my eyebrows. I knew there was something very special about the road we were on.

"We're definitely driving along a Ley Line now," I said slowly, "I'm positive." And for some reason, I felt that my eyes were glued to the narrow road that was unfolding before us until it disappeared into another patch of forest about a mile further ahead. Though it was hard to see clearly in the waning light, I had this strange feeling that the darkened sky above the forest was vibrating with an enormous energy. It

297

was almost as if it was a pressure cooker that was about to explode. Then another flash of lightening illumined the sky again and for a short moment, it seemed to me that I saw thousands of tiny particles whirling above the forest ahead of us.

I stopped the car and leaned towards the window, trying to get a better look at what I saw.

"Why'd you stop?" said Janus leaning forward too.

"Just look over there," I said, pointing at the forest, "... have you ever seen rain falling upwards?"

"Rain falling upwards?" said Jacob leaning towards the window too.

Another flash of lightening lit up the sky. This time we could all see clearly. What I'd mistaken for many thousands of rain drops whirling above the forest wasn't rain but branches and rocks and all sorts of debris that was literally being hurled up into the air.

And then we saw it!

The enormous funnel-shaped monster running down from the black storm clouds... a tornado!

And it was headed straight in our direction!

Following the old road through the forest, straight towards us!

"Oh Lord," whispered Jacob. "We really are right on top of a Ley Line..."

We sat there paralyzed.

Another blinding flash of lightening left no doubt in our minds. The huge monster was following the old road through the forest and was heading straight towards us. Now it was no more than two to three miles away, ripping up everything in its pathway. Trees, rocks, boulders, bushes—everything. Already we could feel the force of it pounding down towards us.

Clumps of earth, rocks and branches began hitting the car, and we felt the car begin to shake.

"Turn around, Starbrow!" yelled Janus, the first of us to awaken from our daze. "Turn around!"

I grabbed the wheel and frantically began to turn it.

"Stop!" said Jacob, grabbing the wheel. "It's no use! We'd never be able to out-drive that tornado. It's following this old road—and as long as we are on the road, we'll be in its way."

I let go of the wheel and took my foot off the gas. Jacob was right. That was why I'd felt such a strong tingling sensation between my eyebrows when we first started driving on this old road. It was right on top of a Ley

Line. A Ley Line, which was now being activated by a tornado!

"But what are we going to do then?" cried Janus, just about to burst. "Let's run into the forest!"

"No," said Jacob, "that would be certain death."

The three of us stared into the furious storm and knew time was running out.

"But we're finished if we don't get away!" cried Janus.

"You're forgetting that there is a Force which is stronger than all the tornadoes in the world," said Jacob. Janus and I stared at him. "Don't you remember what Kuthumi said to us in the Blue Temple? The Force is stronger than electricity, more powerful than a nuclear bomb, mightier than the sun?"

"Do you really think we have time to focus on the Force now?" I cried in disbelief.

"Got any better ideas?" said Jacob and leaned back in his seat.

Janus and I knew he was right, so we both leaned back in our seats and took a deep breath. Just before I closed my eyes, there was another flash of lightening and I saw that the funnel-shaped monster was right in front of us now, not more than a mile away from the car. Trees and branches and rocks whirled around us. In another minute or two, we would be swept away by the tornado!

"The Force is the One and Only Reality," said Jacob in a loud voice. Janus and I repeated after him. "The Force is Infinite, Eternal and Unlimited. The Force is Immortal, Invincible and Unconquerable. The Force is All-Powerful. This Mighty Force is Fully Present. Here and Now. In you and in me. I AM One with the Force. I AM THE FORCE!"

As Janus and I repeated after Jacob, I focused all my attention on the Force within me. The Pure, Unlimited Consciousness that was my True Self. The Force that was the Source of All Life, the Intelligence back of All the Universes and All the Dimensions and All the Worlds, in All their Infinite Variety... Truly the Force was stronger than even the mightiest tornado.

I heard the windshield crack as a huge branch smashed into the front window, but I paid it no heed. I heard the side mirrors and windshield wipers being torn off, but I didn't open my eyes. The car shook violently as if we were about to be lifted up in the air.

"Moncler and Telperion and Starbrow are One with the Force," said Jacob. "Wherever they are, they are totally and completely protected by the Force. The Force nourishes, sustains and takes care of them. The

Force protects them and guides them. The Force goes before Moncler and Telperion and Starbrow and makes their pathway straight..."

Janus and I repeated after Jacob. I saw in my mind's eye how the Force was making a straight and peaceful pathway before us, with no tornadoes or storms.

"We know that the Highest Good for All Concerned always happens," said Jacob. "The Force's Will be done. God's Will be done."

After I said the words—God's Will be done—an incredible feeling of Peace settled down over me. The same deep peace I had felt many hundreds of years ago, when close to Glastonbury Tor, I was surrounded by soldiers and killed by Lord Gavin. And I knew, with complete certainty, that I really was One with the Force, that I was the Force. And I also knew that the Force that I was, truly was Immortal, Invincible and Unconquerable. Even if we did not escape the tornado, even if I had to leave my body and this brief life on Earth. Even then I would still be the Force.

I opened my eyes.

The tornado was less than 500 yards away now. The force that emanated from it was enormous. Five more seconds and we would be sucked into it and hurled into oblivion. Everything suddenly seemed to move in slow motion. But I was no longer afraid. I was no longer afraid of dying. For I knew who I was. Even if I had to leave this body, leave this Earth, I would survive. I would go on. The only thing that I felt a bit sad about was that if we left now, we wouldn't fulfill our mission. That we wouldn't anchor the New Vision and give humanity that one last chance. That one last chance to become aware of exactly what I was realizing at that very moment—that we are all One with the Force.

The moment I had that thought, the mile-high tornado suddenly veered sharply to the left, almost as if it had been pulled aside by a giant invisible hand. The tornado turned off the road and plowed straight through the forest on our left side. The huge wave of energy generated by the tornado's sudden left turn was so enormous it lifted our car and all the trees and bushes in our vicinity straight up into the air and flung us into the forest on the other side of the road. I was aware of the world turning, windows smashing and Jacob tumbling over me as we were thrown over to the right side of the car. I knew we were sailing through the air—car and all. For a split second, everything went black and I was sure we were all going to die.

But we didn't die. Instead the car miraculously straightened itself out

300

so we were right side up, flying through the air. It was almost as if some invisible force had straightened out the car. And for a brief moment, I thought I saw my guardian angel Ticha in my mind's eye.

Then the car landed with a violent thud and ripped its way along the ground until it smashed into a huge mound of upturned earth. I felt myself being hurled forwards and then back into my seat as branches, rocks and earth rained down upon the car and in through the windows. For a few seconds, the violent after-wind of the tornado came pounding through the windows. Then the wind began to die down and I felt the cool rain on my face. Soft, sweet, healing rain. I was alive! My whole body was aching and I was cut and bruised, but I was alive! At the very last moment, we had been saved by the Invisible Hand of the Force.

7

A Helping Hand

I looked over at Jacob. He was lying in a heap, blood oozing from several nasty gashes on his face and hands. But his eyes were open and he was staring at the roof of the car. He had a few twigs in his hair.

He let out an agonizing moan.

"Jacob! You're alive!" I cried in a hoarse whisper.

"Just barely..." He groaned and put his hand to his bleeding cheek.

"Janus!" I whispered hoarsely, "What about you?"

There was no answer.

I tried to move, but there was broken glass, earth and branches everywhere so it was difficult. I made an effort and turned my head to look around. The back seat was empty! Janus wasn't there!

"Janus!"

That was when I realized that he hadn't been wearing a seat belt. Oh God, I thought, he must have been thrown out of the back window.

"Oh no, Janus..." I said, trying desperately to undo my seat belt.

Jacob realized something was wrong. "Where is he?" he asked, rousing himself.

"He's not here!" I whispered hoarsely.

We managed to untangle ourselves from our seat belts, but it was impossible to open the car doors because they were blocked by earth and debris. So instead, we crawled out through the broken front window.

Once out, we looked around in shock. The whole area around the car was like a huge bomb crater. It seemed as if our car had been tossed more than fifty yards into the forest—and then landed, miraculously, right side up. How that ever happened was beyond me. All around us, all the trees had been completely leveled to the ground. In the distance, we could see the tornado making its way south. It was already at least two or three miles away. But where was Janus?

302

"Janus!" we shouted, not wasting a moment brushing ourselves off. Jacob still had twigs in his hair.

We ran towards the road. My whole body was aching, especially my right arm and shoulder which had been mashed into the car door when we hit the ground. But I was alive and could still move and run. Jacob must have hurt his left foot, because he was limping as he ran.

But neither of us noticed. We were desperate to find Janus.

"Janus!" we shouted.

Suddenly I thought I heard this faint moaning sound coming from a huge heap of trees and branches some yards from the road. It was a strange looking pile of debris because it almost looked like it had been carefully stacked by invisible hands. In fact, it reminded me of one of those huge bonfires they make in Denmark on Midsummer's Eve. Jacob heard the sound too because we both started running towards the heap at exactly the same moment.

"It's got to be him!" I cried.

"Janus!" roared Jacob.

Sure enough, we could hear Janus moaning from underneath the huge pile of debris. And I even thought I caught a glimpse of a faint golden light coming from the heap... Was it Telperion's sword. But by the time we reached the pile, the light had disappeared.

I was seized by a sudden fear that Janus was dead.

"Janus!" I cried in despair, "where are you!" Jacob and I began frantically moving the branches and pieces of wood. As soon as we'd removed the top layer, we saw Janus' face was down below us. He looked badly bruised and blood was oozing from a gash on his forehead. His eyes were closed and he was moaning as if he was in terrible pain.

We continued to work frantically, removing all the wreckage and debris that was piled on top of our friend. After we'd removed quite a bit, we came upon a really massive tree trunk. It was lying right on top of our friend and it must have weighed at least a half a ton. Jacob and I staggered and struggled to lift it, but we couldn't so much as budge it.

We huffed and we puffed.

"Damn!" cried Jacob. "Telperion is the only one of us who's strong enough to lift this, and he's trapped underneath it!"

"But we have to lift it!" I cried in frustration. "I mean, what if it's crushing him to death!"

We huffed and we puffed some more.

Nothing happened.

303

"Rise up!" I cried in frustration. "Rise up!"

And then I remembered the night when I'd tried to lift the potted plant on my windowsill using the Power of Thought and had failed so miserably. I failed then because I didn't believe I could do it. But that was then. That was when I had yet to learn that the Force was in me. The same Force that Jedi Master Yoda used to lift Luke Skywalker's spaceship out of the Dagobah swamp. The same Force. And that same Force was in me.

I stared intently at the tree trunk and saw it rise up in my mind's eye. "Rise up!" I said, speaking the Word of Command while pushing the trunk with all my might. "Rise up!" I cried.

Jacob was straining so hard the veins were sticking out on his forehead. I focused my attention on the Power in every muscle of my body as I summoned the Force. The heavy tree trunk began to move ever so slightly.

"Rise up!" I spoke the Word of Command again. "Rise up!"

With a suddenness that surprised us both, the trunk suddenly rolled away from the heap, toppling us both over. We both rolled on the ground for a moment, laughing out loud.

"Not bad, Starbrow!" I heard Jacob say as we rushed back to Janus.

"For a split second there, it seemed light as a feather," I muttered, scrambling after Jacob.

"Yeah," he muttered back. "I know what you mean."

But we didn't have time to speculate because we heard Janus moaning again.

We began digging him out.

"Hold on, buddy!" cried Jacob, "we're on our way!"

We shoveled and heaved like two maniacs until we'd finally managed to dig our way clear down to Janus. We were both terrified that he'd been crushed under the heavy load, but when we dug away the last bit, we found—to our great delight and surprise—that our friend was lying on his back, safe and sound inside a strange pocket. Apparently, during the fury of the tornado, Janus had been miraculously flung into this deep ditch. Then to top it off, a bunch of young trees had fallen on top of the ditch, forming a protective layer across the ditch so when all the debris came piling down, Janus was protected by them.

Jacob and I removed the last of the young trees and climbed down to our friend.

"Janus!" I cried and grabbed his hand.

Janus opened his eyes and looked at us. "What time is it?" he croaked.

"It's a quarter to eight," laughed Jacob and gave me a look of relief. "But we don't much feel like a night on the town without you."

"A night on the town?" said Janus hoarsely and sat up with a dazed look on his face. Except for the ugly gash on his forehead and some cuts and bruises, he looked pretty OK.

"Yeah, you know, we were planning on saving humanity from total annihilation and stuff like that," I laughed.

"Then what am I doing down here?" he asked, still dazed.

"That's what we'd like to know," said Jacob as we helped him to his feet.

"How are you feeling?" I asked.

"Feeling?" groaned Janus, holding his head, "... sort of like a hangover from hell." When he saw the road and the rain of destruction all around us, he seemed to remember what had happened. "What happened to the tornado?"

"It veered away at the last moment," I said. "Then our car was sucked up and hurled into the woods—and you, apparently, went flying out the back window."

"Yeah," groaned Janus, starting to remember, "that'll teach me to wear a seat belt in the future!"

"It must have been quite a ride considering where you landed!" said Jacob, pointing down at the strange crater where Janus had been lying. "All I can say is it's a bloody miracle that you weren't crushed to death under all that stuff!"

"Somehow or other, everything seemed to have landed perfectly, so instead of killing you, all this stuff actually protected you from being crushed," I said.

"Yeah, I know," said Janus, looking thankfully up at the dark sky. "Thank you, Vildis."

"Vildis?" I said in surprise. "Why do you mention her?!"

"Well," said Janus slowly, "the moment I got thrown out of the car window, I caught a glimpse of my guardian angel Vildis... and then it was as if I saw these shining hands guide me—none too gently mind you—but guide me all the same... down into that ditch..."

"I saw the same!" I cried. "I mean, just as our car flew out of control, I was sure I saw Ticha's face."

"Strange isn't it!" said Jacob, scratching his head, "but I did too. I know I saw Lia's face—clear as day. But I presumed it was because I had

305

really crossed over into the next dimension!"

We stood still for a while, contemplating our fate and looking around at what remained of the forest. But we didn't see our guardian angels or any other sign of life in all the destruction around us.

"Well now at least I better understand why they're called guardian angels," I said.

"Yeah," said Janus, who now seemed more himself again, "but what about the car?"

We walked, or should I say limped, slowly back to the car. It was totally and completely wrecked and half covered by plowed up earth and branches and bushes.

"I don't think Avis is going to be happy about this!" said Jacob.

"No dude," said Janus, "and if we don't get a move on quick, there won't be any Avis left to be unhappy about this either!"

The car was on its side, so Jacob stooped down and checked the gas tank. "There's a hole in the tank. It's a miracle the car didn't explode when we hit the ground."

We stood for a minute in the pouring rain, looking at the remains of our car. Then Jacob checked his Ashtar Command watch. "We've got 4 hours and 5 minutes left till it's time for the Activation Meditation," said Jacob, "and we've still got at least 30 miles to Glastonbury... car or no car. I don't see how we can possibly walk 30 miles in 4 hours."

"Do we have a choice?" I asked as I pulled my backpack out of the wreckage. Jacob and Janus followed suit and then we walked back to the road. It was still raining, but raining less, as if the tornado had taken the thunderstorm with it. Things were very quiet as darkness seemed to descend on the demolished old forest. In fact it was getting so dark that we were having difficulty seeing... except for this light further down the old road... the very same road which we'd been driving down so innocently just a short while ago.

"It's a car!" cried Janus, seemingly suddenly revived. He ran out onto the road and began waving his arms. The car stopped about two hundred yards away from us, right where the first pieces of debris began to fill the road.

"Stop!" cried Janus and began to run towards the car. Jacob and I ran after him. The car was a battered blue Volkswagen van. The windshield wipers made a squeaking noise as they swished back and forth.

When we reached the car, the driver, a young woman with bright red cheeks and long curly red hair, had already rolled down her window. At

306

her side sat a little boy with short dark hair, who was staring at us with big eyes. He looked like he was around five years old. The woman was also staring at us in surprise.

"Are you really real?" she stammered, looking at us as if she'd seen a ghost.

"I'm afraid we are," I said, realizing how strange we must have looked to her, all battered and bruised as we were, "but our car has just been demolished by a tornado! And we must get to Glastonbury as fast as possible..."

"Glastonbury?" she said in surprise.

"Yes, Glastonbury or at least some place nearby. It's an emergency... Can you give us a lift...? It's important."

The woman just stared at the destruction ahead of her.

"You see the tornado..." Jacob interjected, trying to get her to understand the gravity of the situation.

"A tornado?" she repeated slowly, looking at all the destruction in front of her. "Is anyone else down there?"

"No," said Jacob. "We were the only ones on the road when the tornado struck..."

"Then grandmother was right," she said, turning to the little boy.

"Mother," cried the little boy, tugging at her arm, "you've got to give them a lift...!" For some reason, I had a feeling that the child knew we were on a mission. "Mother!" he cried again. "Don't you see it's important!"

She looked at each of us again and seemed to revive. "Hop in," she said.

We hopped into the back seat gratefully and she turned around and began driving back down the road. As soon as we started moving, the little boy turned around and started staring at the point between my eyes.

"Tornadoes in England," the woman muttered, obviously still in shock. "This never happened in England before."

Then she turned and looked back at us for a moment. "As far as I can see, the three of you look like you need to see a doctor. Don't you want me to drive you to the nearest village so someone can have a look at you?"

"It's very kind of you," I said, "but it's of the utmost importance that we get to Glastonbury as quickly as possible."

Just then, she turned off the old road and I felt an immediate lowering of the energy. I sighed in relief because I knew we were no longer driving

307

on a Ley Line.

"Well, then you're lucky, my friends," she answered, obviously perking up, "because Lance and I just happen to be on our way to Glastonbury!"

Jacob and Janus and I winked at each other and smiled. I peeked at my watch—it was eight o'clock. So we could still get to Glastonbury in time. I leaned back and sighed. And then realized just how much my body was aching. Up until that moment, I'd been too tense to even notice, but now... well, now, there still wasn't time to notice. The only thing that mattered was getting to Glastonbury in time.

"Why is it so important for you to get to Glastonbury on a night like this?" asked the woman. "... with all these weird storms and tornadoes and God knows what? It just doesn't make sense."

Her words just sort of hung in the air.

"And obviously," she continued, "you're not from Glastonbury... you're not even from England, by the sound of your accent."

It was the little boy who broke the ice. "They're elves, Mom," he said. "Can you see the star on the man's brow?"

"Yes, darling, I can," she said, patting him on the head.

"Can you?" I cried, startled at her answer.

"But of course," she said, matter-of-factly.

"That's interesting," I said slowly, "Up until now, only small children and dogs have been able to see who we really are."

She laughed softly. "Not all adults have lost the ability to see with the heart," she said in a gentle voice. "And the Sight is strong in my family."

"The Sight?" I asked, again surprised. "Are you a priestess of Avalon?"

"A priestess?" she laughed. "Well no. I wouldn't call myself a priestess, but I can read auras and from the start I noticed that the three of you were emitting a very strong and radiant light."

Little Lance was leaning over the front seat and fingering Jacob's staff. "Is it a magic staff?" he asked solemnly.

"You bet it is!" smiled Jacob.

"Are you druids or something like that?" the woman asked.

"Eh... not really," I said.

"Well what are you then?!" she said laughing. "Here you are, three beautiful young men who look like elves... One with a magic staff, one with a shining sword, and the third with a bright star on his brow. Why you look as if you've just stepped out of a fairy tale."

"Well, in a way we have," I replied, deciding it was safe to be honest with our clairvoyant driver. "We're on our way to Glastonbury to activate

308

the Power Spot on Glastonbury Tor at midnight tonight."

"Is that all?" she replied with a laugh. "I've heard that one before! Every other New Ager that visits Glastonbury Tor says they're on a mission to activate the Power Spot. But I've never seen it happen!"

Her reply didn't sit well with Janus. "But they didn't have these," he said, patting his sword, Jacob's staff, and the star on my brow.

"Yes, that's true," said the woman as she pulled the car over to the side of the road and turned around and looked at us. "But what's so special about them? I feel a great power coming from them."

"The staff, the sword and the star are interdimensional weapons or "Keys"," answered Jacob, showing them to her. "The Power Spot on Glastonbury Tor can only be activated if you are in possession of these keys."

She didn't say anything, but stared in fascination at our three interdimensional "Keys". When she was satisfied, she said, "Well then, there's no time to waste, is there!" and drove on quickly. A few moments later, we'd come to a small town called Frome. Signs of the violent storm were everywhere to been seen. Branches and debris, fallen signs, garbage cans and overturned benches were lying scattered all over town. But there weren't many people outside, except in front of the police station where a bunch of policemen were talking to a small crowd of people.

"Black April," said the woman. "The whole world seems to be in an uproar. First earthquakes and volcanoes, then storms and tornadoes. I wonder what will be next?"

No one answered. For some reason, I had the feeling it was best if we conserved our strength for Glastonbury.

Jacob leaned forward and patted the little boy on the head. "You know your son also has a very strong aura, too."

"Yes," the woman answered. "Lance is his name. Mine is Gail."

"Do you live in Glastonbury?" asked Janus.

"Sometimes," replied Gail. "My mother lives there—right at the foot of Glastonbury Tor. We're actually on our way to visit her right now. You see she called me a few hours ago and sounded totally out of it. She said that strange things were happening on Glastonbury Tor."

"But grandmother always says strange things are happening on Glastonbury Tor!" cried Lance.

"That's right, my dear, but today she really seemed out of it. As if she had seen a ghost or something. I can't explain it, but I've never heard her so upset before. And what with all these storms and tornadoes, I thought it best we went and looked in on her."

Gail was silent for a moment and then she continued, "You see the 'Sight' is very strong in my mother Rebecca. Over the years, she's seen many strange and wondrous things on Glastonbury Tor. But today her voice sounded different. As if there was more, much more to it this time. And now I've met the three of you! Three modern-day elves who just survived a tornado and who are determined to get to Glastonbury—by hook or by crook—because they say they're on a mission to activate the Power Spot! Now wouldn't you say there's a certain synchronicity here, between the three of you and my mother! What about you Lance, what do you say to all this?"

"I'd say they're on an adventure!" cried the little boy, hopping up and down on the front seat. "Three elves on an adventure!"

After Frome, the narrow country road was dark and deserted. But as I peered out the window, I could faintly make out the apple trees, which lined the narrow road. Some were even beginning to bloom. At last we were in Avalon, Appleland!

About 15 minutes later, we came to Shepton Mallet, another small, sleepy town, which Gail drove through quickly. Now, she said, we were only about 10 miles from Glastonbury. And as I gazed westward towards Glastonbury, I heard thunder rumbling in the distance and knew, in my heart of hearts, that once again we were heading into the heart of a terrible storm.

The road wound its way through an old forest. Suddenly two cars passed us going in the opposite direction—the first cars we had seen in a long time. A couple of minutes later, three more cars passed us going in the opposite direction. That was when I noticed that the road was again covered with debris and earth and rocks and branches. Then we rounded a bend and saw many lights up ahead. The cars in front of us were being instructed to turn around and drive back to Shepton Mallet by a team of policemen. Gail drove up behind the last car in the line and stopped. Up ahead we could see the reason all the cars were being sent back. Another tornado had apparently just plowed through the area, completely ripping up the next stretch of road. To our right were the remains of what once must have been a house. Now all we could see were bricks and stones lying scattered all over, like match sticks tossed by a terrible storm. About 50 yards away, in the forest, there was a truck that had obviously been thrown from the road, just as our car had been.

"Holy Mother Goddess," cried Gail in horror. As far as we could see, this tornado had been even more powerful than the one we'd just survived. Here the road was completely impassable, blocked for as far as the eye could see by enormous piles of rubble.

To our right, we saw rescue workers milling around the ruins of the house. I wondered if anyone had been in the house when the tornado hit.

Gail rolled down her window as one of the police officers came over to our car.

"The road to Glastonbury is completely blocked," he said. "You'll have to turn around and go back."

"Do you know if I can drive over to Wells and then to Glastonbury from there?" asked Gail.

"I'm afraid not," replied the police officer. "According to the reports coming in, this last tornado plowed through all five roads leading to Glastonbury. Now all of them are blocked. There's nothing to do but go back and wait until tomorrow. Once the storm passes, the civil guard will be able to clear some of the roads I'm sure," he said and motioned for us to turn around.

Jacob and Janus and I looked at each other, each thinking the same thing. All roads to Glastonbury blocked? I looked at my watch. It was 21:00. And we couldn't wait until tomorrow.

"Does that mean that we're not going to visit Grandma?" asked Lance.

"Yes, my dear," said Gail, as she turned around the car. "We'll just have to wait until tomorrow."

"What about your adventure?" the little boy asked us.

"We have to go on," said Jacob. "We can't wait until tomorrow."

"Why not?" asked Gail.

"Because we have to start our activation meditation on Glastonbury Tor exactly at midnight," I said. "In three hours from now."

Once we were out of sight of the police, we pulled over to the side of the road.

"But you heard what the officer just said," said Gail. "All the roads to Glastonbury are blocked, so how will you get there?"

"They can use their magic, Mommy!" cried Lance, pointing at Jacob's staff.

"That's right," Jacob replied as he patted the little boy on the head. "We can use our magic."

Then we thanked Gail and Lance for the lift and got out of the car. As we were saying goodbye, Gail hurriedly scribbled her address in Glastonbury on a piece of paper. "When you've activated the Power Spot,

311

why don't you stop by for a nice cup of tea!" she said.

"Thanks!" said Jacob, "we will!"

"Good luck with your mission!" Gail said solemnly.

As she pulled out, Janus cried, "The Force is with you!"

Then we watched little Lance waving madly at us as the car disappeared out of sight.

After that, we stood in silence for a while contemplating our situation and surveying the seemingly impassable belt of destruction which lay before us. We were tired, aching all over—and drenched to the bone. And we still had 10 miles to go to get to Glastonbury.

"So what do we do now?" said Janus. "Try to find a way I guess..."

Jacob sat down on a huge fallen tree trunk, with a weary look on his face. "There's 10 miles to Glastonbury," he said.

"Well," said Janus, "if we run, we can still make it."

"But even if we could make it in three hours, we don't know the way," Jacob replied, obviously feeling pretty low.

"Well what about the map?" asked Janus.

"The map only shows the roads," said Jacob. "And the roads are blocked."

"I guess we could force a path through all this wreckage," said Janus, "couldn't we?"

"Well maybe," said Jacob, thinking the matter over. "But even if we could get through all the devastation that's blocking the road here, we won't be able to tell from the map how to get through 10 miles of woods, hills and fields in total darkness. Not to mention the fact that we're in foreign country—in a place which we don't know at all—which is being ravaged at the moment by freak storms and tornadoes."

"Kind of ironic, isn't it?" said Janus gazing westward towards Glastonbury and the gathering storm. "Here we are, on a mission to save Mother Earth, and it's Mother Earth herself who's preventing us from saving Her."

"Whoa, mate!" said Jacob, obviously rallying, "let's not forget what this is all about. Our mission is to save humanity, not Mother Earth. Mother Earth will be just fine, you know that. Even if that nasty knock on the head made you forget you know as well as I do that all these storms and tornadoes are just Mother Earth's way of riding herself of all the negative thoughts of humanity that have been polluting her. Remember She's doing all of this so She can ascend into the higher dimensions. No, there's no doubt about it... Mother Earth will be just fine... it's humanity I'm worried about!"

"Then maybe we should ask humanity to give us a hand?" said Janus. "Maybe the police would help us if we told them about our mission. You know, give us an escort or fly us over to Glastonbury in a helicopter or something."

"Yeah, dream on," chuckled Jacob. "Don't you remember what those two guys back at Stonehenge told us... how the authorities reacted when they tried to tell them about the Ley Lines. Can you imagine what they'd say if we told them we were on a mission to save humanity from an axis shift... why they'd probably just laugh us right out of the nearest police station."

"Then what are we supposed to do?" cried Janus despairingly. "We're so close, so very very close... we can't just give up now!"

"Well if you'd just stop talking for a minute or two so I can think," said Jacob and buried his head in his hands, "I might be able to come up with something!"

"What do you say, Starbrow?" said Janus, turning towards me. "Maybe we should meditate..."

I didn't answer him either. All the time Janus and Jacob had been talking, I'd been sitting on a huge rock with my eyes closed, focusing my attention on my heart. *Follow your heart, for your heart alone knows the way*. As I focused on my heart, I seemed to hear a voice within me speaking. A voice I was sure I recognized... and the voice was saying... *Use the Sight, Starbrow, use the Sight*. Was it Ticha?

I opened my eyes and looked around. Everywhere I looked, there was destruction. And as I gazed into the forest, all I saw was darkness and more darkness. And the great shadows of tree upon tree, fading into the ever deepening dark of this old forest, as the howling wind made the trees creak and sway. Besides that, the only other sign of life was back at the road block where the police officers and rescue workers were trying to make sense of all this devastation.

Use the Sight, Starbrow, use the Sight. I closed my eyes again and focused my attention on the star on my brow. The moment I did that I saw a light pulsating in my mind's eye. Like a star sending out rays of light into every corner of my consciousness, making it possible for me to see. To see. Not only with my physical eyes, but on all levels of my consciousness. That was why my name was Starbrow, that was my special gift.

Then I focused my attention on my heart and asked it to tell me the

313

way to Glastonbury Tor. Immediately I felt a quickening in my heart—
and a strong pull in the direction of the dark forest to the left of me. I
opened my eyes and looked into the forest. About 50 yards from us, right
between two huge old trees that had survived the storm, stood two
luminous beings. I blinked and looked again. It was true because they
were still there. There really were two luminous beings standing between
those two mighty trees. They were tall, slender creatures, surrounded by a
golden light. They lifted their arms and motioned for us to follow them.

"Moncler! Telperion!" I cried softly and smiled. "I think we've got
ourselves two guides."

8

An Obstacle Course

Jacob and Janus looked at me in surprise. I raised my arm and pointed towards the forest, directly at the two luminous beings who were motioning us to follow them.

"What guides?" asked Jacob.

"I don't see anyone," said Janus, looking in the direction I was pointing.

"Follow me, and you will see!" I cried as I leapt forward with renewed hope.

My two friends jumped up and followed me as I led the way into the devastated forest. Everywhere there was destruction, huge potholes and fallen debris. At one point the going was so tough that I had to stop and look down to keep from stumbling. And then, when I looked up again, the two beings were gone. I looked around me in sudden despair.

"What's up?" cried Jacob, running up from behind.

"Are you sure you know what you're doing," cried Janus, close on his heels. "I don't see any guides!"

I paid my friends no heed but scanned the dark forest, looking for the light I knew I had seen. At first, all I saw was blackness.

"Don't tell me you're losing it, Starbrow!" cried Janus.

No, I wasn't losing it because there they were—about 50 yards ahead of us—the two luminous beings. Once again, they motioned for us to follow them.

"No," I cried with renewed vigor, "I'm not losing it! Follow me!" And I began running again towards the light, Janus and Jacob scrambling after me.

We hurried on into the forest, until we came to the spot where the two beings had been standing. Now we were at least 100 yards inside the forest and we could no longer see the flashing lights of the police cars

315

down by the road block. But we heard the muffled sound of a car honking in the distance. It sounded like it was coming from another world. I tried to concentrate my attention on my heart and the point between my eyebrows—at the same time. As soon as I did, I was able to see the two beings again, shining in the darkness a little further ahead. They seemed like shooting stars to me, that had descended into the darkest night. I began running again in their direction.

I kept on in this manner, with my friends following, until we were deep in the forest, surrounded on all sides by the blackest night. Everywhere we looked, the darkness seemed to deepen.

When I stopped for breath, Janus put his hand on my shoulder and said, "I sure hope you know what you're doing Starbrow! Because I can't see a thing..."

"Focus your attention on the point between your eyebrows," I said, catching my breath. "And then focus your attention on your heart." I waited a moment while he tried what I said. "Now focus on both points at the same time—the point between your eyebrows and your heart."

Jacob joined him and they both followed my instructions.

"Alright," I said, "now look straight ahead."

My friends opened their eyes and looked straight ahead. Exactly at the spot where the two luminous beings were standing.

"I can see them!" cried Janus. "I can see them!"

"It's amazing," cried Jacob, "... there really are two luminous beings out there!"

"Who are they?" said Janus in wonder.

"Tuatha De Danann, I expect. The Star Elves."

"The Star Elves?" said Janus. "Are they still here?"

"Yes," I said, "they're still here." Then I began to walk towards them. "It's time to follow them again."

The luminous beings now turned sharply to the left, directly towards the place where the tornado had plowed through the forest. The closer we got to the belt of destruction, the more difficult it became to navigate. In places, we had to climb over huge mounds of earth, rock and trees that had been churned up by the tornado. In other places, there were deep pits. But our guides lead us deftly forward and it was easier now because Janus and Jacob could also see them.

When our guides came to the heart of the devastation, they stopped and waited for us to join them. Before them towered huge mounds of tree trunks, branches, earth, rocks and bushes. It was as if the tornado had

316

decided to make a huge impenetrable wall all around Glastonbury so that nothing—neither man nor beast—could pass through.

We approached the two luminous beings who were standing silently in front of the high mounds, waiting for us. They were both tall and slender, and their lovely long hair fell down around their strong shoulders. Their faces were clear and beautiful, and their eyes shone like stars. One was a man, dressed all in gold, the other was a woman, dressed all in white.

"Greetings, my Brothers in the Light!" said the man and bowed solemnly before us. I could hear his clear voice inside my head.

"Greetings, Starbrow, Moncler and Telperion," said the woman, also bowing kindly to us.

"Greetings, Rayek and Rayel!" I said and bowed deeply before them.

"You remember well, Starbrow," said Rayel, smiling softly.

"Who could ever forget the Star Elves when first they have danced with them under the stars?" I smiled and looked into the clear eyes of the elf woman.

"We're delighted that you are still here," said Janus.

"Yes," said Rayek, "at least for a little while."

"Where are the other Star Elves?" asked Jacob.

"The others have left the Earth and have returned to the stars from which they came," said Rayek. "We are the only ones left now."

"Why did the others leave?" I asked, feeling a deep sense of loss at the thought.

"Ah..." he replied slowly. "It has been a long time coming my friend. You see humanity's wanton destruction of nature has made most of the Earth uninhabitable to my people."

"But what about the Whispering Forest?" I asked.

"The Whispering Forest was cut down many years ago by humankind," sighed Rayel. "Today there is a shopping center where our holy birch grove once grew."

"Oh," I cried, "I'm sorry to hear that. It was such a beautiful place." And I remembered the magical birch grove, which had been at the heart of the Whispering Forest.

"But why have you stayed behind?" asked Janus.

"We have been waiting for you," said Rayek. "We are the last Guardians of Avalon. For fifteen hundred years now we have guarded the Power Spot on Glastonbury Tor, waiting for the day when you would return and anchor the New Vision in the collective consciousness of humanity."

317

"But we'll need a bulldozer to get through this wasteland," cried Janus.

"Do not fear," said Rayek. "We will lead you to Glastonbury Tor. But there isn't a moment to lose. Mother Earth has had enough. Time is running out for humanity. Come my friends!"

Without further ado, Rayek and Rayel turned and began to climb the tall mound of earth that towered before us. They moved swiftly and skillfully. And even though the forest was completely destroyed, it was obvious that they were still in their right element. After a short climb, the two elves stood on the top of the first mound. "Come, friends!" cried Rayel down to us. "Avalon is waiting for the Guardians of the Earth."

We began to climb up the mound. It was difficult in the dark and took us a bit longer than the elves, especially since we almost couldn't see a thing. Rayek and Rayel reached down with slender hands and guided us up the last bit of the way.

"No doubt there's Star Elf blood in the three of you!" cried Rayel.

The elves led us carefully on, over this first huge mound of debris. We had to tread carefully because of the sudden gaps between the piles of branches. It was tricky and more than once I saw Jacob totter, almost losing his balance in all the confusion. Next to the elves, Janus was definitely the most nimble of us. He seemed to have very little trouble maneuvering through the wreckage.

When we had crossed the first mound, we began to climb down again, which was a lot easier than climbing up. But still, it required caution because one false step and a landslide of rocks and debris would come tumbling down over us.

Once down on the wet ground again, we hurried after the elves. They had gone ahead and were now leading us under two large beech trees, which had fallen down along a steep rocky ledge so a tunnel had been formed underneath them.

After the tunnel, we scurried over another mound as fast as we could. Rayek and Rayel were now moving very quickly, and it wasn't long before the three of us were panting and covered in sweat. But the elves never looked back. They just continued, certain that we were right behind them. After scaling a few more tricky mounds of destruction, the elves led us through a long, deep ditch which was now filled with rain water. At various points, the water was almost up to our knees. Finally, the elves led us up and out of the water by crawling up a long, slippery tree trunk that had fallen into the ditch.

Then, we again came to an area where the center of the tornado had passed. Immediately, I felt that strong tingling sensation between my eyebrows again. But here the feeling was so strong that it was as if my entire body was vibrating faster. I felt the earth underneath my feet pulsate with energy and power, as if I was standing on some kind of power station.

"Why is the energy so much more powerful here?" asked Jacob.

"Because we are standing on a Ley Line," said Rayel.

"Then it's true that the tornadoes move along the Ley Lines?" asked Janus.

"Yes, it's true," said Rayek. "The tornadoes are Mother Earth's way of cleansing the Light Grid of all the blockages which have accumulated in the Grid throughout the centuries because of humankind's negative and disharmonious thoughts and actions."

"Does that mean there will be more tornadoes along this Ley Line?" asked Janus.

"Not for the next couple of hours," said Rayek. "So you need not worry. For the moment, it's safe to move along this Ley Line."

Once again, Rayek and Rayel turned and began to move swiftly forward through the destruction before us. It was like an obstacle course, as we darted after our friends, weaving our way in and out of the debris as fast as our legs could carry us. So difficult was the course, that without our guides, we soon would have lost our way.

Then after another 10-15 minutes of really hard going, the obstacles seemed to lessen and there was less debris. The tingling sensation between my brows also began to subside and the pulsating feeling under my feet grew less. And then the scene changed. Instead of destruction and havoc, an ancient forest lay before us. And in the flickering light of the Star Elves' auras, I could dimly make out the dark green ivy that wound its way around the trunks of those ancient trees. Clearly, we had passed through the obstacle course laid down before us by the tornado. Now all we had to do was get to Glastonbury Tor as fast as we could.

I looked down at my Ashtar Command watch. The bottom display read 01:58:21 TO ACTIVATION MEDITATION. The top display read 25:58:21 TO AXIS SHIFT. We had less than two hours to make it to the top of Glastonbury Tor. And we still had almost ten miles to go! I looked at the darkness ahead. Rayek and Rayel were already a good way before us, running through the forest as swiftly and as gracefully as deer. Clearly they knew we didn't have much time. We began to run after them. The last lap had begun.

9

The Veils Are Lifted

The moment we left the tornado belt I had this strange feeling. On the other side of that belt of destruction, the forest was shrouded in a heavy mist. A mist, which crept along the ground and swirled up along the ivy-covered tree trunks. In fact, the mist was so dense and heavy that we couldn't see the sky or much of the forest around us. It was as if we had stepped into another realm, hemmed in on all sides by the impenetrable wall of destruction left by the tornado. And here, in this strange no-man's land of mist and fog, heaven and earth seemed to meet.

Rayek and Rayel were already quite far ahead. Fortunately for us, we could faintly make out their luminous bodies as they moved between the trees. There was a strange, brooding silence about the mist and forest, as if the storm and torrential rains had taken place somewhere else, while in here, at the center of the storm, everything was as silent and lifeless as a forgotten grave.

"Weird place, dudes," said Janus, sniffing the air suspiciously. The mist was so heavy that it muffled his voice making him sound as if he was far, far away, in some dismal and forgotten place.

"This is the weirdest fog I've ever seen," said Jacob as he peered into the mist.

"Yeah," I said, "It almost seems like it's alive or something." The fog was so thick that I was having a hard time breathing. And with each step I took, it got worse. I stopped and leaned against a tree. I felt as if the thick wispy tendrils of mist and fog were closing in around me.

"What's wrong, Starbrow?" asked Janus, stopping next to me.

"I can't... I just can't breathe," I gasped. The fog's eerie tendrils were pressing against me from all sides.

"Come on now Starbrow," cried Janus. "Get a grip! The elves are getting way ahead of us."

I took another step forward and stopped, riveted to the ground. The tendrils were holding me back! The fog was alive! "Leave me alone," I cried, frantically, "leave me alone! I haven't done anything to you!" I started swinging my arms madly back and forth, beating the fog.

Jacob and Janus looked at me in surprise.

"What's going on?" cried Jacob. "I don't see anything!"

"They're everywhere!" I screamed desperately, trying to extract myself from the clutches of the horrible tendrils that were smothering me. It was awful, horrible, as if I was being sucked into their strange world.

"Help!" I cried, "help me!" I beat the air around me with my arms. Then suddenly I heard a clear voice inside my head saying, "Leave it alone, Starbrow!" It was Rayel. "Do not focus on the fog!" she said.

I looked up and ahead to where she and Rayek were standing, looking back at me. The eyes of the two elves shone like stars; a clear white light that could easily penetrate the mist and the fog that surrounded me.

My eyes met Rayel's. "The Sight is strong in you, Starbrow," she said, "do not let it take you into the astral planes and the lower dimensions. Focus on the Force."

I closed my eyes and tried to follow her command. I focused my attention on the Force. On the Divine Presence within me, on the Divine Presence within everything and everyone. Pure Presence, Pure Life, Pure Love, Pure Light. A Light when all other Lights go out. Immediately it helped. It was as if the clutching tendrils instantly withdrew themselves because they no longer dared touch me. I was a beacon of Light in the dark. I breathed easier and could move. I took one step forward and found that nothing hindered my path. I saw the hands of my friends, of Jacob and Janus, stretching out to help me. I took their hands and together we ran on.

"Thank you friends!" I said softly as I sprang forward, feeling the hot blood running in my veins again.

The Star Elves led us onward through the forest at an amazing speed. Over stock and stone they ran, gracefully as if from another world, leaping and whirling before us, between tree and bush, over hill and dale. It took all our will power to keep up with them, so swiftly did they run. I felt my heart thudding in my breast as it pumped at maximum capacity and my legs felt like lead—and still the elves ran before us. Jacob stumbled and lost his bearing for a moment, and fell into a water hole. But Janus was there, helping him up again and urging us on. Of the three of us, Janus had the most strength and managed best—and it touched

321

and surprised me how he kept a watchful eye on Jacob and me.

At last, we emerged from the forest, but the fog followed us. Also here, out in the open, it seemed to billow and penetrate every nook and cranny. Still, there were some open patches where we could faintly make out the landscape around us. Fields and pastures I saw, and small clumps of trees here and there. In the distance, I thought there was a bit of light, as if from a lonely farmhouse. Sheep brayed somewhere, but there was no time to look. Rayek and Rayel were already far ahead in the open field before us, running over the cold, brown earth with such light elven steps that they almost seemed to float over the ground.

We had just emerged from the forest and run past a lonely clump of trees, a last outpost of the great forest, when we became aware of several dark shadowy figures off to our left. As if on command, the three of us stopped at the very same moment and stood looking at the shadowy figures. The light was dim as we stood there gasping for breath and regarding the figures curiously. That was when I realized that whoever or whatever they were, they were standing next to a burial ground with several ancient Celtic stone crosses. The crosses must have been very old because their circular tops were broken and great cracks disfigured the rune carvings that ran along the stones.

I shuddered; it all had such a cold, eerie feeling to it. The shadowy figures seemed to me to be darker than the blackest night and colder than the coldest ice. And they stood there perfectly still, not looking at us, but looking down at the graves before them. Somehow I knew these shadows were fettered, in a way I could not fathom, to this burial ground. If they had faces, I couldn't see them, but I knew in my heart that they were sad... terribly, terribly sad and quite without hope. Torn, it seemed to me, from something or someone they had loved very much.

Suddenly the eerie silence was broken by a terrible wail.

"I won't leave you!" shrieked one of the figures pitifully. Her voice sounded as if it was burdened by centuries of suffering and loss.

"I want to stay here forever!" wailed another.

"You cannot leave me!" whimpered a third. "You cannot!"

"Say you love me," begged a fourth, "say you love me and you'll never leave me!" The sound was so pitiful it pierced my heart.

"My work! My great work! Now I'll never finish it!"

And the eerie wailing continued, a dirge of pain and sorrow. And still they did not move, so enslaved were they by their own despair. It was pitiful to see and my heart went out to them, wishing there was a way I could bring an end to their sorrow and suffering.

Janus was moved to the quick and pulled his sword out of its sheath. Then he advanced slowly towards the lamenting figures. I moved to call out to him, but when I opened my mouth no words came out. Jacob raised his staff, but it fell lifelessly from his hand and landed with a clang on the cold ground. Janus had almost reached the tormented figures when I was overcome with a hideous feeling of dread. I was sure something terrible was going to happen, but I did not know how to avert it.

Janus raised his sword over the head of one of the shadowy figures and I knew in my heart that my friend wished to put an end to the poor creature's suffering.

Slowly Janus began to swing.

At that very moment Rayek's clear voice pierced the mist, "Leave them alone, Telperion! And turn your eyes to the Living Present!"

Janus' sword was already moving through the air and in just a split second his sword would cleave the shadow.

"Leave them alone, Telperion!" called Rayek again, his words echoing in our hearts. "The task is not yours!"

Janus froze in midair and struggled for a moment with the pity in his heart. Then slowly, ever so slowly, he mastered himself and turned back towards the elves.

Rayek had run swiftly back and spoke the Word of Command to Janus.

"Let them be!" said Rayek. "The task is not yours, my friend. They are Earthbound souls in thralldom to the flesh. Mother Earth is releasing them now from their long captivity. Their destiny is not yours. Leave them alone, my friend and focus now on the Force."

Janus closed his eyes and began breathing deeply. Rayek touched Janus on the forehead and quickly spoke words in a tongue we did not understand. When he was done, Janus seemed to breathe easier. He put his sword back in its sheath and began to walk after Rayek. The spell was broken. I felt the hot blood in my veins again and the young life in my heart. Jacob picked up his staff and we followed Janus.

"Remember your mission," said Rayek to the three of us. "Nothing is more important than this."

Then he began to run and we ran after him.

Rayek and Rayel led us across fields and over stone fences and through hedges and along overgrown creeks and streams. On occasion we caught glimpses of the lights from a farmhouse or an old house that seemed to

323

gleam and twinkle in the mist and fog that billowed and moved and covered the land like a living thing.

Then the elves led us down a very steep hill. At the bottom of the hill, the fog was thick and impenetrable again. It was hard to make out the shining forms of the elves ahead of us, but I tried to focus on them and forget about the fog. But with each step we took, the feeling of being surrounded on all sides by an impenetrable wall of fog and mist seemed to grow upon us. Then I became aware that it was more than just a fog surrounding us, rather it seemed as if we had entered a strange phantom world because I was sure I could hear voices whispering in the fog, speaking of things long gone and forgotten.

We stumbled forward and I knew my companions also heard the whispering voices—and then I became aware of fleeting figures moving in and out of the mist. Some were dark and heavy, while others seemed light and radiant.

Suddenly, as if by some unspoken agreement, the three of us stopped and stood perfectly still, looking around in the fog. Somewhere in the distance, church bells began to toll. Dong, dong, dong, they rang, a deep melancholy dirge it seemed, a requiem as if they were calling us to some mystical service. Jacob instinctively clutched his breast, feeling for the cross he once wore. Then, to our right, from deep in the swirling mist, we heard monks chanting an old Gregorian hymn. It made me smile because the sound of their voices was so sweet and soothing, a divine ray of light in all the darkness that surrounded us.

For a moment, the mists parted and we could dimly see the procession of monks in brown robes walking slowly through the mists. They walked with their hands clasped together in prayer and their hoods drawn down over their faces. Such a deep sense of peace and bliss emanated from them that I felt a burning desire to run to them and seek sanctuary from the storm that surrounded us.

Jacob crossed himself twice and began to walk towards the monks with a blissful expression on his face. Janus called out to our friend, but no sound came from his mouth.

Jacob walked as if transfixed.

Then a voice, a clear sweet voice, spoke clearly inside our heads. And I knew it was Rayel.

"Leave them alone, Moncler!" she said. I turned around to discover Rayel running back to us. And now she stood, in all her radiance, before us. Her eyes of love bore down upon Jacob and she said, ever so gently, "I

324

know my friend how you long for the Light... the blessed Light... but the Light is not to be found in the past. Leave them alone. Your task is to move forward to the Living Present!"

Jacob looked longingly after the monks, then he looked back at Rayel's shining face. "Leave them alone, Moncler," she said again gently and then she rose up to her full stature and spoke the Word of Command to Jacob. "Remember your mission," she said. "Nothing is more important than this."

Jacob hesitated for a moment and then turned away from the monks, away from a past he also had shared. "Yes," he said to Rayel. "You are right, we must move on."

Rayel said no more, but turned and ran back to Rayek, who stood waiting for us on top of a small hill in the distance.

We followed her as quickly as we could.

The Star Elves lead us ever onward, over hill and dale, around a high stone wall and down an ancient path lined with old apple trees.

As I sniffed the sweet scent of the apple blossoms, it dawned on me that today was the first day of April and if it had been some other lifetime, we might have had time to linger and enjoy the sweet smell of Avalon... Avalon... where we now were heading... and the thought of it, the thought of seeing Avalon again, my Avalon of the heart, the place that was once my home... somehow gave me renewed strength and I ran like the wind after the shining elves before us.

Until our way was blocked by a wide, rushing stream whose waters flowed quickly by, churning and bubbling right before our eyes. It was so foggy that it was difficult to see the other side, but we sensed that the stream was deep and wide and cold—and would be difficult to cross. The elves led us along the stream for a while, obviously looking for a way over. Finally, we came to a place where a big tree had fallen across the rushing stream. It would serve well as a bridge.

"Thank you, friend," said Rayek, patting the old tree. Then he sprang up and ran swiftly across the turbulent waters below. Rayel ran across after him. I climbed up after her and began to run across the trunk.

"Be careful!" cried Rayel. "The trunk is very slip..."

I guess watching the elves made me forget how difficult it might be for a human (or Starseed in training) to perform the same feat. Because I hadn't taken more than two or three steps when I slipped and fell backwards into the rushing stream below.

I landed with a great splash and sank like a stone. The water was icy cold and very muddy. I struggled my way up to the surface, coughing and spitting.

"Dana!" cried a woman in a clear voice. I looked around, expecting to see Rayel and Rayek, but instead I saw a white boat in the water next to me.

And I was no longer gasping for breath in a cold, muddy stream, but swimming in a crystal clear lake. Sitting in the front of the white boat was a dark-haired woman who was holding her hand out to me. The woman was incredibly beautiful, sitting there so nobly in her long white robe. The little silver knife she wore in her belt was shaped like a crescent moon and looked strangely familiar—and then I knew her. But of course, she was the Lady of the Lake—the High Priestess of Avalon!

"Morgaine!" I sputtered and reached out to grab her hand.

"Dana!" she said chidingly, as she took my hand, "How could you be so careless?"

Then, as our hands met, Morgaine's small white hand turned into Rayel's slender elven hand dragging me up the bank of the stream. The Sight of Morgaine had vanished; now all that remained was the elf woman Rayel and me, sputtering and coughing.

"Morgaine!" I cried and looked around in bewilderment. "The Lady of the Lake! Morgan Le Fay! She was here just a moment ago!"

"Starbrow! Are you okay?" shouted Jacob and Janus from the other side of the stream.

"He's alright," cried Rayek, "Come across now, but watch your step."

"Are you alright, Starbrow?" asked Rayel, removing the twigs that were stuck in my wet, tangled hair.

I shivered.

"I guess so," I said, slowly. "But I swear I just saw Morgaine. Morgan Le Fay... I knew her in a past life."

First Jacob, and then Janus, crawled slowly across the stream. "What happened?" said Janus as soon as he was over.

I just stood there shivering. "I know it sounds weird," I said, "but I just had a vision of Morgaine, Lady of the Lake and High Priestess of Avalon. I saw her as plain as day—as if I was still Dana and living in Avalon."

"The veils are lifting," said Rayek, looking around with concern. "The dimensions are opening." All around us, we could see shapes emerging and disappearing into the mist. "There is not a moment to waste, my friends," he continued. "We must hurry. If we don't reach Glastonbury

Tor before midnight, it will be impossible for you to activate the Power Spot."

"Can you go on, Starbrow?" asked Rayel.

"I must," I said. "But I'm completely soaked."

Janus was already pulling stuff out of his backpack. "Here," he said, "I brought along some extra rain gear. You take it. It's from Fashion Flash, so you ought to feel right at home in it!"

I laughed. "I never thought I'd be so happy to see anything from Fashion Flash as I am now!"

I peeled off my wet clothes in a fashion flash and put on Janus' extra gear. Then we started out again.

"It's almost eleven o'clock and we still have five more miles to go," said Rayek. "If you want to reach Glastonbury Tor before midnight, you must run as if you have winged feet."

"Then so it shall be!" cried Jacob, springing forth.

"The Force is with us!" cried Janus and I as we leapt after him.

"That's the Spirit!" cried Rayek, running before us. "Now for the last lap!"

If we thought Rayek and Rayel had run fast before, it was nothing compared to now. Right from the start, it took all the will power I possessed to keep up with them. And on and on, through mist and fog they ran, never tiring or stopping, but only slowing down occasionally when they got too far ahead of us.

As we ran through the mist and fog, I once again was overcome by the feeling that all the countryside around Glastonbury was fading—and becoming more and more dim and indistinct. Everything seemed to take on a ghostlike quality. Even the farms and houses we passed seemed ghostlike and nebulous, almost as if they existed in another dimension. And the lights in the windows became fainter and fainter, just as the shadowy bushes and trees we ran by seemed to flicker in and out of our reality. It was weird... really weird... like the whole world was receding... ebbing... fading away... and I wondered if it was only me, or us, or if perchance, the people who lived in the farms and houses also felt it.

In the distance a dog was barking, but his voice sounded strange, a mere echo of his former dog self.

At the same time as the "real" world began fading, other, unexpected things started appearing. It was as if, from time to time, a gaping hole or pocket would appear in the fog and then strange and wondrous sights could be seen. Once we passed several rings of standing stones that

327

loomed up on top of cold hills. Brooding, cold and inhospitable, and hiding I was sure some dark and terrible secret that could not bear the light of day. But there was no time and we ran on.

A little later, we passed a lake that was so big we couldn't see the other side. But even more strange, a long, sharp sword emerged from the middle of the lake just as we approached. It was set with many precious stones and runes—and glimmered coldly, reflecting the light of a full moon we could not see. We all stopped for a moment to look at it, so beautiful was its strange sheen. And then we saw that the sword was being held above the surface of the water by the delicate white hand of a woman. Janus looked longingly at the sword and I knew he was in danger. Jacob whispered something in his ear and he covered his eyes with his hands. Then he turned away from the lake and ran on.

The elves led us down a narrow pathway lined with hedges on both sides. To our left, we could hear the sound of music, flutes and violins as we ran by, playing a melody which I knew once had been merry. But now, as the tune wafted through the billowing fog, it seemed melancholy and sad. We ran on.

A little further down the pathway, the hedge opened up to our right to reveal an old house with a beautiful thatched roof. We heard the sound of sword fighting and galloping horses coming directly from the house, which seemed almost transparent. As we looked at the house, it seemed as if the dimensions or worlds intertwined and we saw knights in shining armor on horseback with lances raised charging right through the transparent house!

"Whoa, dudes," cried Janus, stopping, "can you believe this!"

"It's as if we can see two worlds at the same time," I cried, coming to a halt next to him. "Glastonbury past and Glastonbury present!"

The Star Elves called our names in their clear, melodious voices, "Remember the task at hand, Starbrow, Telperion, Moncler. Remember the task at hand! Time is running out!"

We knew they were right so we turned and ran on.

The landscape changed and opened out into a vast expanse. And still we ran on. Over hill and dale. Then suddenly, looming up on our left side, we saw a great castle, wondrous and fair. And the castle's towers shone, white and brilliant, reflecting a sun we could not see as its great banners flapped in a brisk wind we could not feel. The three of us stopped and stared at the castle in awe. What was it and where did it come from? I was seized by an overwhelming desire to run to this enchanted castle and seek shelter from the storm we were caught in. I was sure we would find a safe haven there, protected from all harm behind its massive walls. Janus smiled as he gazed at the mysterious castle and then slowly he drew his sword from its sheath.

"It's Camelot!" he cried, transfixed. "Camelot!"

"Camelot!" Jacob whispered softly, standing besides him.

"Camelot!" I cried and fell to my knees, overcome by fear and trembling.

"We must go to the castle and offer our services to the King," said Janus, slowly.

"Yes," said Jacob, as if in a trance.

Then again we heard the clear voices of the Star Elves insides our heads, speaking now the mighty Word of Command.

"Let it be!" they said. "Let it be!"

Then it was Rayek, speaking to us like a kindly elder brother, who said, "Remember the task at hand, Starbrow, Telperion, Moncler. Remember the task at hand! Time is running out!"

I stood up and turned from the castle and gazed in the direction of our two luminous guides. There they stood, a little way from us in the billowing fog. Our only fixed point in this strange, ghostlike world.

"Do not let the opening of the dimensions confuse you!" cried Rayel in her sweet melodious voice. "Every second you linger is a precious moment lost. Let it be! Let it be!"

And again, Rayek, the kindly elder brother spoke, "Only 45 minutes now remain until the midnight hour! Only 45 minutes, friends! Now is your time. Telperion, Starbrow, Moncler! Now is your time. Run my friends, run! Now is the time to run for your lives!"

His words broke the spell of the strange vision and each of us looked at our Ashtar Command watch at the very same moment. The bottom display flashed 00:45:22 TO ACTIVATION MEDITATION!

"Come!" cried Janus.

"Now is our time!" cried Jacob.

And we turned from the radiant vision of Camelot and ran after the elves. Faster and faster.

And faster and faster ran the elves.

Faster and faster.

I heard my heart thudding in my breast. And the sound of my friends panting on either side of me.

Faster and faster we ran.

329

And then Jacob stumbled and gasped, "I can't run any further!"

Janus grabbed him and steadied him.

And we heard the voices of the Star Elves speaking soft words of encouragement in our heads. And then, looking up, our friends, the Star Elves had run back and were standing before us.

"Don't give up now, friends! The end is almost in sight," cried Rayek, touching each one of us on the head, conveying some hidden strength to each of us. "Now is the time to use everything you have learned. Focus on the Force. Feel the Force working in and through you as you run! Let go and let the Force run in you."

"Come!" cried Rayel, "Now is your time!"

We started running again.

As if in a trance.

Running. Running. Running.

Faster and faster.

And faster still.

Soon I knew that without some miracle we would collapse and so, with a last effort of will, I began focusing on the Force in me as Rayek instructed. The Force running in and through me. That Invisible, All-Powerful Presence that was the Source of All Life, All Energy...

And then, little by little, I became aware of it. Aware of the Force.

"The Force is Energy, Moncler!" I cried softly, gasping for air. And then the words came, almost of themselves. "The Force is Energy! Infinite Energy and Infinite Life! With the Force, all things are possible!"

I forced myself not to think of my tired body or aching legs, but to completely focus my attention on the Force. On the Force that was running in and through me.

"The Force is running through me!" I cried again, mastering my body with my will.

"And through me!" cried Janus, great warrior that he was.

"And through me!" cried Jacob, drawing upon the strength of his wizardry.

"And the Force is stronger than electricity..." declared Janus in a loud voice.

"... and more powerful than a nuclear bomb!" cried Jacob.

"... and mightier than the sun!" I heard myself saying in a voice I'd never heard before.

And so we ran, and the more I focused on the Force, the more I felt myself to be the Force—and not the body called Starbrow that I was

330

running in.

No! It was no longer my body with so and so many muscles burning so and so many calories that was propelling me forward... No! It was the Force! The Mighty Force that was running in and through me, and the more I allowed the Force to run through me, the faster I ran. And the faster I ran, the faster we all ran. And we ran! For dear life!

Over hill and dale.

On winged feet.

Dedicated. Determined.

Faster than fast.

Swifter than swift.

Or so it seemed and we were three.

The three companions.

Running, running, faster than ever before.

And so we ran. Onward and ever onward.

Not heeding the swirling mist or fog, not heeding the murmuring voices or the shapes that loomed all around us. Neither sight or sound or sign could dismay us any longer. Because now we were transformed.

And transformed we ran. Agents of the Force, in a wild race against Time, allowing the Force to run, run like the wind, in and through us.

And then I knew, fleeting shadows that we were, as the dimensions opened, that this was the final countdown and that we were on a mission, running, racing against time, the Mighty Force running, racing against time, across the murky face of Mother Earth... and so we passed into the night... Moncler, Telperion and Starbrow.

And so the Mighty Force ran, in us and through us, without faltering... or tiring... onwards and onwards...

We were right behind the Star Elves now. And they led us forward, resolutely, towards that mighty hill that we knew was waiting for us. Unseen as yet, but not unfelt. Though our physical eyes could see naught, still we knew that the dark swirling mist and fog were emanating from that same mighty point before us where all things seemed to be coming together in the all-pervading darkness before us. And I knew, in my heart of hearts, that yes, now we were nearing Glastonbury Tor, Avalon, Heart Chakra of the Earth. And with each step we took, the Force seemed to grow, the Force emanating from the ground, the Force emanating from the air, the Force emanating from the wind and from the trees and from the Elves—and from us.

I was aware of gathering ghostlike shapes in the mist that seemed to whirl past us and through us. And then, for some reason, I could see and Janus and Jacob could see, and all became visible to our eyes. And we saw them as they stood now, row upon row, close together, in one long procession. And their souls we knew, because saints they were, and druids and knights and priests and monks and priestesses and mystics and nuns and wizards. Of all sorts they were. All on their way to one and the same place. To Glastonbury Tor, Heart Chakra of Mother Earth. All initiates they were. Initiates who had throughout the ages come to Avalon, driven by the same burning desire in their hearts for Peace and Harmony and Love and Enlightenment... driven they were... for themselves and for all beings that walked the face of this our beloved planet.

Yes, they were there.

And we saw them.

Old Joseph of Arimethea, the Christian pilgrim, who long ago planted his branch of thorns on Wearyall hill in Glastonbury where it grew into the Holy Thorn that blossoms every Christmas in the dead of winter in memory of Our Savior and his great gift to humanity. And there too was King Arthur and his pious Knights of the Table Round—Lancelot, Galahad, Percival—all kneeling humbly before a cup which shone like the sun above their heads, and we knew it to be the Holy Grail. And their blessed heads were surrounded by halos because we knew the Holy Spirit was upon them. And there, over yonder, was Merlin and Morgan Le Fay drinking from a holy well because its pure, healing waters brought new life to body and soul. And further along still, a group of men and women in early 20th century garb were seeking the wisdom buried in the ruins of old Glastonbury Abbey. And I saw, with the Sight that was given me, that their Third Eyes were open because they too were seeing clearly now through the veils.

And that was when I realized there were more, many more people. Swarms of people, people everywhere, people from other continents, from the far corners of the globe, people who were gazing at the heavens and studying the clear starry night we could not see in hope of catching glimpses of UFOs or other great celestial beings. And all of them, every one of them, every soul in the long line of pilgrims was on their own

332

sacred quest, on their own sacred pathway to Peace, Harmony, Love and Enlightenment. And all of them were searching, yearning, all of them were on their way to Glastonbury Tor. And I felt my chest expand as if the deepest longing of my heart, the innermost yearning of my soul for Love and Light and Enlightenment had now burst forth, into a mighty flame, which was urging me onward, carrying me ever forward. The longing of the Force for the Force That I AM.

And when I knew that, things became even more clear. Because I had the Sight. That was my gift. And so I saw... the long procession, the endless ranks of pilgrims, all could I see. And I knew them and I knew that the mighty Force was also working in and through them. And they raised their arms as one and stood there row after row after row with arms raised—and then I heard them, in my heart and in my mind and in my soul, cry out together in one great voice, all saying, "Run Starbrow! Run Moncler! Run Telperion! Now is Your Time! Now is Your Time! The Force is with you!"

And the earnestness of their cry ignited the Power of the Force in our hearts. And it blazed forth, a mighty flame that throbbed and pounded in our breasts, sweeping away everything in its wake. And so we sprang forth, Moncler, Telperion, Starbrow, and ran onward, from the rows of pilgrims who stood in the mist and fog, crying out our names and showering us with their prayers and their blessings. And onward still we ran, towards Glastonbury Tor, through the menacing darkness before us, straight into the heart of the terrible storm that was awaiting us. Onward and onward, until we lost all track of time and space.

10

The Staff, the Sword and the Star

And so, with the Star Elves as our guides, we came at long last to the center of the storm and the end of our journey.

"Here at last is Glastonbury Tor," cried Rayek, coming to a halt in the darkness. We stood by his side, panting and gasping for breath. He pointed ahead, into the inky blackness at the hill we could not see. But even though we could not see the Tor, shrouded as it was in mist and fog, we could feel the violent shaking and quaking of this mighty Power Spot. We were not in doubt; we were witnessing the eruption of an immense, etheric volcano.

Then Rayel spoke soft words to us. "A few yards ahead, you will find a narrow pathway which you must follow, as quickly as you can, to the top of the Tor. If you hurry, you will reach the top in time! There's still 15 minutes to the midnight hour! So go now my friends, with Godspeed!"

"But what about you?" I cried, still trying to catch my breath. "Aren't you coming with us?"

"No," said Rayel. "Our mission ends here. We, the last Guardians of Avalon, now entrust you three—with the staff, the sword and the star—to activate the Power Spot on Glastonbury Tor. We place this solemn duty of anchoring the New Vision in the collective consciousness of humanity in your hands. For the Highest Good of All." Then she stepped forward and kissed each of us on the brow.

"But where are you going?" cried Janus.

"Now that our mission on Earth is over," said Rayel, "we will follow our brothers and sisters and return to the stars we came from."

"But... that means we'll never see you again..." I stammered.

"Never is a very long time, dear Starbrow," said Rayel gently, and then she smiled at me and continued, "And you must remember, oh dearest of friends, that even as we come from the stars, so also do you. Soon your long mission on Earth will be over—as ours now is—and then we will no longer need to say goodbye to each other. But now, dearest friends, time is running out! There is not a minute to lose."

"Quickly now Brothers in the Light! The end of the world is upon us! Run like the wind!" cried Rayek, giving us each a hasty kiss on the brow as Rayel had done. "The Force is with you! Run now my friends! Run! To the top of Glastonbury Tor you go!"

I looked at my Ashtar Commando watch. The top display read 24:13:19 TO AXIS SHIFT. The bottom display read 00:13:19 TO ACTIVATION MEDITATION.

Indeed, there was not a second to lose.

We looked at our friends one last time and charged into the blackness before us. As we ran, we felt the ground quaking beneath our feet and the air itself seemed thick with a strange foulness as if here, at the Heart Chakra of Mother Earth, a cosmic heart attack was underway. In my own heart, I knew our great Mother was writhing in agony.

It was so dark that we could see nothing and after a few moments, we had lost our way. Jacob got down on his hands and knees, feeling the ground like a blind man, groping for the pathway.

"Here!" he cried and his voice sounded distant and hollow, "Here is the pathway!" I peered into the inky blackness before us and dimly discerned the dirt pathway he had discovered.

Jacob got up and we began to run silently along the path, concentrating all our attention on the winding pathway before us. First Jacob, then Janus, then me at the rear. The night was so black and the mist so thick that several times Jacob had to stop and search the ground to make sure we were still on the path. The way up was getting steeper and steeper, and in one place, the path veered so suddenly that Jacob almost tumbled down the side of the Tor.

I looked at my watch again. The bottom display read 00:07:57 TO ACTIVATION MEDITATION and we still weren't near the top.

I looked up and with the Sight that was given me, I saw how the Tor was spewing out huge etheric clouds to all sides. We really were witnessing a fully activated etheric eruption. Wave after wave of noxious fumes washed over us, pounding us furiously. Then one especially savage wave was upon us and I lifted my arms as if to avert a blow, but it was no use. The powerful etheric wave hit me like a bulldozer and I tumbled backwards, landing on the hard ground with a thud. Everything went black. I couldn't see.

335

"Moncler! Telperion! Help!" I shouted. "Where are you?"

I groped around frantically in the icy darkness that was closing in around me.

Then, off in the distance, I heard Janus crying, "Starbrow! Moncler! Where are you! I can't see!" He sounded far away as if he was trapped in some deep cavern.

The noxious etheric fumes seemed to grow worse and I thought I was going to suffocate. Then, just when I thought all life was about to leave me, I felt something touch my leg. It was a hand!

"Starbrow!" coughed a familiar voice, "Is that you?"

"Jacob??!" I cried.

"Yes..." he coughed again.

Then I felt another hand touch my head.

"Janus!" I cried, "Is that you!"

"Starbrow! Moncler!" Janus cried, "Time is running out. Focus on the Force!"

I closed my eyes. It made no difference. Everything was still black.

Then I realized the significance of Janus' words.

And of all the Masters' words.

The Force is the One and Only Reality. The Force is Omnipotent and Omnipresent. The Force is our Ally.

"I AM THE FORCE!" coughed Janus, standing up in the terrible darkness that was all around us.

His moment of supreme courage was instantly rewarded; the etheric released us momentarily and we could move again.

"I AM THE FORCE!" Jacob and I cried, getting up after our friend, the mighty Elf warrior.

And though I had opened my eyes, still I could not see. The blackness was utter and complete.

"We must get back to the path!" cried Janus, casting himself on the hard ground and crawling forward, searching frantically for the path. Jacob and I fumbled after him. I could feel the grass under my hands, but no path.

"It is nowhere to be found!" cried Jacob in despair.

We crawled back and forth, frantic to find the path leading to the top, but we were lost.

"We must have light!" I shouted.

The Earth trembled and sent another huge etheric wave of noxious fumes down over us. And once again we were overcome and fell tumbling to the ground.

"Focus on the Force," I cried to my friends as I tumbled to the ground. The Force. I AM THE FORCE.

Wave after wave of etheric discharge swept down over the hill, pounding us mercilessly.

"Light! Light!" cried Janus desperately, "We must have Light!"

A heavy silence descended upon us and the blackest despair overtook us. So great was our hopelessness, now so close to our goal, that none of us could speak.

I buried my head in my hands. "All this way," I cried out to no one in particular, "through so many lifetimes. From the stars we came, to the Earth—and now we're stuck, defeated at the end!"

"The stars," cried Jacob, "The stars, Starbrow! But of course! That's it! Why didn't I see it before. We must use them. We must use the star, the staff and the sword! Why didn't I see it before. They *ARE* Light. And We *ARE* Light! That's what we are! *WE ARE THE LIGHT!*"

Jacob stood up besides me and raised Moncler's magic staff high into the air.

"I know who I am!" he cried. "I AM MONCLER!"

The moment he spoke these words, his staff burst into Light, a blazing torch that illuminated the blackness around us. And there he stood, his True Self revealed, Moncler, mighty Wizard that he was.

"I AM MONCLER!" he proclaimed in a loud voice. And though the etheric fumes washed over him, they could not quench the light in him, because Jacob knew who he was. He was Moncler, a mighty Wizard who'd come from the distant stars to help humanity.

Janus stood besides him and cried in a loud voice, "I AM TELPERION!" And then he raised his great two-handed sword toward the sky in defiance of the darkness around us and it too burst forth, a mighty flame from hilt to tip.

"Never again," he cried, "will I forget! Never again will I forget who I am! I AM TELPERION!" And the dark clouds that swept over him like an avalanche were powerless against the Light that he was.

Telperion and Moncler turned towards me with raised sword and blazing staff.

"Yes!" I cried and opened my arms wide. "I AM STARBROW!"

And the moment I spoke those words, I felt an explosion of light in my brow. And it was as if the sun itself had taken abode in my forehead, filling my whole body, my whole being with a dazzling white light. "I

337

know who I am!" I cried joyously. "I AM STARBROW!"

Then in one perfect movement, we grabbed each other's hands and turned towards the top of the Tor. Now we knew where it was. The light which was us, illuminated the way. And we could clearly see the path and the long row of stone steps a little further on.

And we ran forward. But no longer did we need a pathway to find our way to the top of Glastonbury Tor.

"Follow your heart, for your heart alone knows the way!" I shouted and leaped forward into the darkness, Moncler and Telperion at my side.

And the darkness parted before us.

And we ran.

And the staff and the sword and the star blazed forth, a great light in the darkness. And our hearts led us forward, in the final countdown toward the heart of the heart... Glastonbury Tor.

We leapt up the stairs and ran as if possessed, and suddenly we were there. On top of that great hill. And before us, no more than 20 yards from where we stood, was the old medieval tower we were seeking.

I looked at it in wonder, for indeed it was but a faded memory of the great White Tower we had seen in Shamballa. And now it stood before us, belching out a great etheric storm. But we were neither dismayed nor deterred. We ran straight to the tower.

Janus looked at his Ashtar Command watch. "1 minute and 22 seconds until midnight," he cried.

With a mighty sense of purpose, we stepped into the tower.

Immediately we felt the enormous surge of energy that was rising up through the hard stone floor. The light we radiated lit up the inside of the old stone tower and we saw the two stone benches, one on each opposing wall.

We stood in a circle in the middle of the tower. Moncler raised up his blazing staff, Telperion held his brilliant sword high, and I spread out my arms. And in the light that shone from the star on my brow, I saw my beloved friends, Moncler and Telperion, standing before me like two giant pillars of light.

Then we cried in one mighty voice:

"WITH THE FORCE AS MY WITNESS
I NOW CLAIM
MY RIGHTFUL PLACE
AS GUARDIAN OF THE EARTH"

338

We stood for a moment in silence and felt the energy of the Power Spot surge through our beings; and then we sat down. I took the low stone bench on the right wall; Moncler and Telperion sat down on the stone bench on the left wall.

We looked at our Ashtar Command watches. The top display read **24:00:08 TO AXIS SHIFT**. The bottom display read **00:00:08 TO ACTIVATION MEDITATION**.

"Are you ready?" cried Jacob. "7-6-5-4-3-2-1-NOW!"

11

The New Vision

"IN THE BEGINNING: THE FORCE
HERE AND NOW: THE FORCE
AT THE END OF THE END: THE FORCE
HERE, THERE, EVERYWHERE: THE FORCE
FROM ALPHA TO OMEGA: THE FORCE
IN HEAVEN, UPON EARTH: THE FORCE
IN THE GREATEST, IN THE SMALLEST: THE FORCE
IN FIRE, IN WATER, IN EARTH, IN AIR: THE FORCE
IN ME, IN YOU, IN EVERYONE: THE FORCE
ABOVE ME, BELOW ME, AROUND ME: THE FORCE
IN ME, THROUGH ME, FROM ME: THE FORCE
IN MY THOUGHTS, IN MY WORDS,
IN MY ACTIONS: THE FORCE
THE FORCE IS ALL IN ALL
ALL LIFE, ALL INTELLIGENCE, ALL LOVE
THE FORCE IS THE ONE AND ONLY REALITY
AND SO IT IS!"

The sound of our voices echoed back and forth between the stone walls of the old tower. And with each word, our voices grew in power until we sounded like a mighty choir. Then, just as in our past life in the Crystal Cave, the formula of the Great White Brotherhood opened a gateway to the higher dimensions. And through the gateway flowed a multitude of strange geometric forms, fiery letters, pulsating colors and beautiful, high-pitched tones. As we chanted, the sound of our voices continued to grow in power until I felt I was completely one with the Force. And the moment I felt that Oneness, I knew the activation had begun! The geometric forms and colors suddenly became living images that were

340

crystal clear to behold. And then it was there: The New Vision!

In my mind's eye, I saw a mighty wave of Light flowing down from Heaven to Earth... sweeping across the oceans and the mountains... washing over the continents and the countries... sweeping into the cities and the towns...into the buildings and the skyscrapers and the slums... into the suburbs and the refugee camps... into the mansions and the palaces... into the hospitals and the prisons... into the government buildings and the schools... in through each and every window and door... into the heart of every man, woman and child on Earth... a Light that awakened the slumbering Force in all people... in presidents and politicians, in factory workers and farmers... in business people and movie stars, in street kids and gang members... in mothers and fathers, in sisters and brothers... in the young and old... and they arose, altogether as One... in a magical instant of no-time... and transformed sickness into health... poverty into wealth... pollution into purity... darkness into light... misery into faith, hope and love... All this I saw in my mind's eye... The New Vision... all people, all races, all nations, all religions... all united in the Force... all One with the Force... One Glorious Garden of Goodness... One Heavenly Hymn of Harmony... One Blissful Blessing of Beauty... One Law of Life and Love... One Wonderful Wealth of Wisdom... One Rainbow River of Riches... One Celestial Song of Sweetness... One Perfect and Profound Peace... One Living, Loving, Laughing Life... on Magnificent Magical Mother Earth... Our Heavenly Home in the Universe... and then I knew... Heaven is on Earth now...

And there we lingered... in a place beyond space and time... until the Hour of Truth was upon us...

I looked at my Ashtar Command watch again. The top display read **00:02:23 TO AXIS SHIFT**. Two minutes to midnight. Two minutes to the Hour of Truth. For almost 24 hours now, the three of us had repeated the Great White Brotherhood's formula and allowed the New Vision to flow through our consciousness.

Now there were only two minutes left, two minutes until the Hour of Truth when all would be revealed and we would know whether or not all the other volunteers had reached their Power Spots and performed the activation meditation as they were entrusted to do. And we knew that without the simultaneous participation of all 139 groups, it would be impossible to generate enough energy to re-establish the Light Grid.

But that was a possibility I did not choose to contemplate.

I looked over at Jacob and Janus and knew with 100% certainty that they had made the same decision. Not to contemplate the unthinkable.

And so we waited. As the Hour of Truth bore down upon us.

And then, inside my head, I heard a clear voice. It was Sananda speaking the Word of Command.

"Arise now, Guardians of the Earth!" he said, "Now is the Appointed Time—the Hour of Truth. You have come so far, through many galaxies, through many lifetimes, to arrive at this sacred moment. So arise now and go up higher! This is the Holy Instant you have been waiting for, for so long. Focus now your full attention on the formula and the New Vision. Let nothing else enter into your consciousness, nothing else. This is the critical moment. Do it NOW!"

We stood up as one and now it was us who spoke the Word of Command in one mighty voice:

"IN THE BEGINNING: THE FORCE
HERE AND NOW: THE FORCE
AT THE END OF THE END: THE FORCE
HERE, THERE, EVERYWHERE: THE FORCE
FROM ALPHA TO OMEGA: THE FORCE
IN HEAVEN, UPON EARTH: THE FORCE
IN THE GREATEST, IN THE SMALLEST: THE FORCE
IN FIRE, IN WATER, IN EARTH, IN AIR: THE FORCE
IN ME, IN YOU, IN EVERYONE: THE FORCE
ABOVE ME, BELOW ME, AROUND ME: THE FORCE
IN ME, THROUGH ME, FROM ME: THE FORCE
IN MY THOUGHTS, IN MY WORDS,
IN MY ACTIONS: THE FORCE
THE FORCE IS ALL IN ALL
ALL LIFE, ALL INTELLIGENCE, ALL LOVE
THE FORCE IS THE ONE AND ONLY REALITY
AND SO IT IS!"

342

I felt the star on my brow explode into light. And then the Light and the New Vision merged and melted into one, and in my mind's eye I saw a shimmering, shining New World, made of Light, surrounded by Light, and penetrated by Light. I felt every single cell and atom in my body also be penetrated by the Light. And there were no longer any boundaries between my body and the Light which flowed down from Heaven, no longer any division between my mind and the shining New Vision. The all-encompassing Light was in all places, at all times.

Then, with the Sight that was given me, I saw the hundreds of other Power Spots around the Earth be penetrated by this same Light as the shining New Vision flowed from each and every Power Spot and swept across the Earth. And my mind was one with the minds of all the other volunteers. And our minds were one with the minds of all the other beings on Planet Earth because in Truth there was only One Mind, One Vision, One World, One Light.

Then I clearly heard these words: "Heaven is on Earth now." And everything turned into Light.

Somewhere on the edge of my consciousness, I heard a bird singing and felt the warm rays of the sun on my face. A soft breeze was caressing me and I felt incredibly peaceful. For some reason, I thought I was in the Relaxation Forest, but then I realized it could not be so because I was lying on something hard and cold. I opened my eyes and found myself stretched out on the stone bench in the tower on top of Glastonbury Tor. Outside, the sun was shining and the darkness was gone. I sat up and looked around. The bench against the other wall was empty.

I got up and stretched and then I walked to the doorway of the tower and looked out. Jacob and Janus were standing by the edge of the Tor, surveying the view. The sun was shining and there wasn't a cloud in the sky.

We must have activated the Light Grid and established the New Vision because Mother Earth obviously had not made an axis shift and we were still alive!

I walked over to my buddies.

"Good morning, Starbrow," cried Jacob, "we were waiting for you to wake up!"

343

"Yeah," I said, "I guess I overslept!"

From where my friends were standing, it was plain to see that it was only up here on top of the Tor that the weather was fine and clear. Down below us, the rest of the countryside was still shrouded in mist and fog. The Tor where we stood was like an island surrounded by a sea of gray mist and cloud.

"What's going on?" I asked, rubbing my eyes.

"As far as we can tell, the mists seem to be receding," said Janus. "We've been out here now for about 10 minutes, and just a few minutes ago, the mists were much higher up the hill than they are now. Now you can see the tops of those trees over there. A few minutes ago, you couldn't see them at all."

We were silent for a moment, watching and waiting.

And sure enough, the mist and fog was receding. Now we could see the tops of a cluster of old oak trees still further down the hill which only seconds ago had been hidden by the mist. And the mist, the mist of Avalon, continued to recede, until soon, it was almost completely gone.

And then we found ourselves gazing at a vast beautiful landscape, bathed in a deep deep peace.

And a wonderful light... an unearthly light... a light that was more than just the ordinary light of the sun... seemed to caress everything we saw.

It was radiant to behold.

I turned to my two friends and said, "It looks like we did it! ... we prevented the axis shift!"

"Yes," said Jacob, slowly. "It seems so! Did you guys see the way the New Vision just sort of spread out over the whole Earth?"

"Yeah," I said, still smiling, "it was pretty amazing, wasn't it!"

We walked back over to the spot where the path began, the path we had come running up the night before. As we gazed out into the distance, we could see the town of Glastonbury down below, waking up to a new day. Already there were a few cars on the winding country roads down below us.

"So what do we do now, dudes?" asked Janus. "I suppose even though we just prevented an axis shift, we could still go down to town and grab a little breakfast..."

"Have you lost your mind," cried Jacob. "Or did you forget that Sananda and Ashtar said we've only got two to three years to change the whole world—and prevent a new axis shift. I mean we're talking about changing the mentality of every single human being on Earth—and

344

replacing their negative thinking with the Positive New Vision!"

"And since there are about six billion people on Earth," I added, laughing, "I doubt if we've got time for breakfast."

"You dudes really are something!" cried Janus, "and me thinking that now we'd have a little time to party on..." Then he looked down at the ground for a moment and turned thoughtful again. "But there's just one thing guys... it's not all up to us, is it?"

I turned and looked back at the old tower behind us.

"No," I said and smiled, "it's not all up to us."

Jacob and Janus turned to see why I was smiling. And then they saw it too. How the old tower glinted in the sunlight and suddenly seemed transformed into the beautiful White Tower we had seen in Shamballa. And I knew they saw him too, the young man who stood in the doorway. He had those clear blue eyes I loved so much and they sparkled and danced in the sunlight as he smiled at us. Standing next to him were the three beautiful and luminous women we knew so well, surrounded by their bright golden auras. The four of them waved to us and pointed to the sky. We looked up and saw, far above the tower, high up in the sky, the great silver starships shimmering in the sunlight. And from the greatest of the ships, a mighty beam of light shone down upon us. And the light was so bright, that I knew it could only come from... the Most Radiant One...

"You see," I smiled and said to my friends, "we are not alone!"

Then we turned and began walking down the hill.